S0-AZS-351

Angel in His Arms

"Don't run away, angel," Kincade murmured against her lips. "I won't hurt you. I just want to kiss you, to let you kiss me. Would you like to?"

It was wrong, and it would lead to trouble. She knew that as well as she knew her own name. But there was something in his gentle urgency that transferred to her, and she felt the faint sparks that he'd lit that first day she'd seen him flare into a blaze. . . .

PRAISE FOR

Touch of Heaven

The National Bestseller by
MICHELLE BRANDON

A gloriously romantic tale of love, passion—and a little celestial meddling. . . .

"A sparkling western romance with a delightful twist!"
—AMANDA QUICK,
New York Times bestselling author of *Rendezvous*

"Touches of humor and love scenes that sizzle make this a fast-paced adventure . . . A treat to read!"
—*Rendezvous*

Diamond Books by Michelle Brandon

TOUCH OF HEAVEN
HEAVEN ON EARTH

Heaven on Earth

Michelle Brandon

DIAMOND BOOKS, NEW YORK

This book is a Diamond original edition,
and has never been previously published.

HEAVEN ON EARTH

A Diamond Book / published by arrangement with
the author

PRINTING HISTORY
Diamond edition / September 1993

All rights reserved.
Copyright © 1993 by Virginia Brown.
This book may not be reproduced in whole or in part,
by mimeograph or any other means, without permission.
For information address: The Berkley Publishing Group,
200 Madison Avenue, New York, NY 10016.

ISBN: 1-55773-940-4

Diamond Books are published by The Berkley Publishing Group,
200 Madison Avenue, New York, New York 10016.
DIAMOND and the "D" design
are trademarks belonging to Charter Communications, Inc.

PRINTED IN THE UNITED STATES OF AMERICA

10 9 8 7 6 5 4 3 2 1

Dedicated to my son Michael,
who cooked the hamburgers while I wrote,
and to my son Eric, who waited
so patiently for us both.

Heaven on Earth

Prologue

"SORRY I'M late, Ian." Tabitha grabbed the ship's rail to keep her balance and peered thoughtfully at her companion. A glassed-in lantern swayed wildly from a hook overhead, splashing dim light over his face. "You look a bit green. Shouldn't, you know. We're dead. Can't get seasick."

"It's no' tha'." Ian gave a long sigh and shook his head. "I'm afraid I willna be able tae do wha' I've been sent tae do."

"Nonsense." Tabitha gave him another sharp glance, taking in his kilt, flowing shirt, and the plaid slung over one shoulder. She lifted a brow. "*I'm* here. I've quite a hand for this guardian-angel business." She preened a bit, patting the stiff cambric ruff around her neck. Her skirts, flared at the hips by a farthingale, swayed in the wind. "Had quite a bit of success last time, you see."

"So I was told." Ian sighed again, but the sound was lost in the wind and the creaking rigging of the ship. The deck rose and fell, and greenish sea froth splashed and swirled across the polished deck. Lanternlight now swayed erratically across the pair.

Ian clutched at the rail as a wave lifted the ship. "I'm afraid this is a lost cause, coming here."

"Your descendant, right?" Tabitha nodded understandingly. "Well, let's give it a look and see what can be done, Ian. No point in wailing unnecessarily." As they proceeded

1

below deck she muttered to herself, "Silly Scots. Always so blasted melancholy about things. No notion of levity at all. Pity."

The companionway below deck was musty, narrow, and dark. At the far end, a single lantern shed a fuzzy halo of light. Ian led the way while Tabitha struggled with her wide skirts in the narrow passageway, muttering vague imprecations under her breath about the ship's deficiencies. When Ian paused in front of a door and turned to give her a doleful stare, she glared at him.

"Really, Ian MacDonald, you have no faith in me at all. Or in yourself. P'raps 'tis why I was sent to help you. With me as your adviser, you cannot possibly fail."

Even in the dim light his misery was obvious. He shook his head. "Ye canna understand the situation, then. Dinna they tell you aboot it?"

"Only that I was to help you, as I have *experience* in these matters." Tabitha gave him her most confident smile and raised her plucked brows. "I even gave up a concert by Beethoven to help you, so you must know that I intend we shall take care of the problem anon."

"Anon." Ian shrugged. "As ye say, Lady Tabitha."

"Yes, as I say. Now, let us enter and see exactly what must be done to help your descendant from trouble."

The small, stuffy cabin was much darker than the companionway. No light pierced the gloom; a faint glow through a porthole made greenish by some sort of mold became slowly distinguishable from the anonymous blur of wall, floor, and ceiling. Scuffling sounds broke the thick quiet, as if someone were disrobing. Then a curse sounded, harsh and a bit hazy. Tabitha glanced at Ian in surprise.

"Some light would help here," she murmured.

A sudden shaft of moonlight shot through the thick porthole and illuminated the cabin enough to distinguish the lurching male shape stripped down to buff trousers. Light glinted on his dark hair and the sheen of bare shoulders. He was swaying dangerously with the pitching motion of the ship, muttering curses as he stumbled toward a prone figure lying in a narrow bunk. It was obvious he was attempting stealth, and just as obvious he was failing.

Tabitha shifted her gaze to the sleeping form and gasped. It was a young woman, her face and mane of pale blond hair just visible above the blankets pulled up to her neck. She looked soft, sweet, and innocent. Tabitha turned quickly to Ian.

"He doesn't belong in here. He intends to molest that girl, by God."

"It does look tha' way," Ian admitted gloomily.

Tabitha gave a sharp shake of her head and snapped, "Well, this is what you're here for. He must be stopped."

"I know."

"God's eyes," Tabitha muttered with a heavenward roll of her eyes. "I see that you are sadly unaware of your abilities. Let me give you a slight demonstration of what we're allowed to do—keeping in mind that we are not seen and heard unless we allow it, and that we can only arrange circumstances, not interfere with mortal choices." She gave a pleased smile. "Horatio would be so pleased that I have finally remembered that."

"Horatio?"

"Never mind. Watch, and learn."

With a sweep of her hand, Tabitha turned back just as the man reached the bunk and put out a hand to touch the girl. An unlit lantern dangling from the ceiling immediately parted company with the hook holding it and smashed down on the man's head. He reeled, cursed, and slumped to the cabin floor, groaning.

Tabitha turned to Ian with triumph. "There. See how easy it is? I have rescued your kinswoman quite effectively, and—"

"Nay, she isna *my* kinswoman."

Her mouth still open, Tabitha thought for a moment. "Oh? How unusual. I was under the impression that we normally assisted our descendants."

"We do."

A frown creased her brow, and Tabitha glanced back at the man on the floor who was still groaning and holding his head. By this time the woman had awakened, and she let out a piercing scream as she sat up in the bunk and stared at the man in horror. Then she screamed again; the sound was high-pitched and earsplitting.

The thunder of footsteps on the upper deck sounded, and realization began to dawn as Tabitha glanced back at Ian in dismay. He looked at her and nodded gloomily.

"Aye. My kinsman, the black sheep, the rogue of the MacDonald clan—on my mother's side, God bless 'er—this is my descendant. Kincade MacKay—scoundrel, wastrel, and now it seems, a ravisher of women." His voice betrayed a faint bitterness as he added, "I canna see the sense in helping a mon such as this one."

Tabitha turned to stare. The man on the floor grabbed at the edge of the bunk to haul himself to his feet. His tall frame seemed ridiculously large in the small cabin, and as he stood there with an expression of pain and confusion on his face, he growled at the screaming girl to shut up.

"Stupid doxy," Kincade MacKay muttered, "why'd you ask me in here if you—" He stopped, peered closely at her in the bright shaft of moonlight, then groaned loudly. "God. You're not Alice."

A loud hammering sounded on the cabin door, and the quivering girl glanced toward it with an expression of relief as well as something else. Then she looked back up at the man swaying over her.

"No," she said on a choked sob, "I'm not Alice."

"Oh God." Loud voices lifted outside the door, and it shuddered with the force of fists hitting it. Kincade gave a sigh of resignation, and his mouth twisted with wry humor as he muttered, "I think I'm in trouble."

Tabitha looked at Ian. "Oh, dear," she said distinctly. "Oh, dear me."

Chapter
1

IT WAS not, Kincade reflected as he tested the strength of the bonds holding him, going to be one of his better days. As it looked now, it might be one of his worst, if he survived it at all.

He frowned. His head hurt, his stomach rolled, and the tight ropes holding him pinioned to the side of a damp, stinking cell cut into his wrists quite painfully. No, not one of his better days.

He closed his eyes and leaned his dark head back against the wall, pondering the mistake that had cost him his freedom. Stupid. If he hadn't drunk so much good scotch whiskey with the first mate, he wouldn't be here now. Nor would he be here if he'd resisted temptation in the form of a common doxy with a lazy smile and huge breasts. His weakness. One of them, at any rate.

Kincade winced as a pain stabbed through his skull. He felt as if he'd been hit with a belaying pin. He hadn't; it had been that damned lantern, providentially falling from a hook in the ceiling and smashing his head and waking that silly chit into screaming hysterics. Perhaps if she hadn't been so rudely awakened, he might have been able to leave without her knowing he'd been there. Or at the least been able to explain his mistake. As it was, she had, and he hadn't.

Wonderful. Life held such droll twists and turns. It was

becoming quite amusing trying to figure out how to survive.

A chill racked his body, and he tried to warm himself by thinking of hot sand and tropical beaches—bloody hell. It was hard thinking of anything except that he was half-naked and tied to a wall in the hold of a stinking ship. The sailors who'd taken such obvious glee in roughly dragging him to the brig hadn't allowed him to put on his shirt. Or his boots. He glanced down at his bare feet. Damn, thieving jack-tars were probably in the fo'c'sle gambling over who got them. They were good boots, too; he'd stolen them from an aristocrat before he'd left London so hurriedly.

Kincade coughed, and winced in renewed pain. One of his ribs must be cracked. The sailors had pummeled him quite cheerfully all the way to the brig, since there was nothing a midshipman liked better than a little judicious punishment—as long as it was someone else's.

A shiver tickled his naked spine as Kincade pressed against the rough wood of the wall and wondered when—or if—someone intended to come and see about him. After all, he was a dangerous felon now, and they needed to keep him in good shape for his trial. That should be another farce. He couldn't wait to see what Miss Goody-Two-Shoes had to say about him.

She'd looked properly shocked at seeing a man in her cabin, especially a man with his pants open and a lump on his head. He must have been a charming sight indeed, sprawled on the floor like a gigged frog. Kincade spared a sigh of regret for his wasted youth. He should have learned restraint instead of the easiest way to part a pigeon from his purse.

There hadn't been too many choices during his youth, unfortunately. He supposed he could have joined the Royal Navy, but he had an aversion to being half drowned and eating maggots, even in the interest of patriotism. No, he'd avoided that avenue at all costs, having had some narrow escapes from being *persuaded* to join the navy and see the world.

Instead Kincade had opted for the life of a young man of good birth who had fallen down on his luck. The good-birth part was true enough. Back down the line there were plenty of noble ancestors. Scottish, of course, and probably all mad as loons, but supposedly noble in the interest of dying for the Cause, whatever the hell it happened to be at the moment.

Kincade had no such leanings. He was much more interested in survival, which had precipitated his decision to leave Scotland at a very young age. Scotland, with its cold mountain crags and constant wind, was a mournful place, with few redeeming features as far as he was concerned. He'd come to hate the terrain, climate, and even the food.

The thought of haggis made him shudder. Disgusting stuff in his opinion. Almost as detestable as oatmeal.

The ship heeled sharply, and Kincade slid on the floor and managed to pick up a splinter in his back. Oh yes, he thought gloomily, he was definitely having a bad day. Maybe his worst yet, in fact.

He pressed his feet against the opposite wall and pushed himself to a sitting position. Then he rested his head back against the wall. A fellow prisoner would be nice. Misery may not really love company, but it certainly appreciated a sympathetic audience.

A scuffling sound in the companionway caught Kincade's attention. A key scraped in the lock and the door swung open. A midshipman stood outlined in the doorway, peering inside with a doubtful expression.

"Come in, lad," Kincade said cheerfully. "I seem to be at loose ends for the moment. I would offer you a spot of tea, but seem to be caught out. Did you bring some with you, I hope?" He gazed at the tray in the youth's hand with aching expectation.

"Yes, sir." The boy edged closer.

Kincade frowned impatiently. "Come in. As you can

see''—he jerked his head toward his bound hands to show that he could not lower them, much less use them—''I am unable to scratch anything that may itch, not to mention actually launch an attack. And bring that tray over here. I'm starving.''

Still approaching cautiously, the boy eyed Kincade for a long moment. ''Took four o' the crew ta git you down 'ere, sir. I doan want my head bashed in laik th' second mate's.''

Kincade gave him a pleased smile. ''Did I do that? Good. Haven't lost my touch.''

The boy glanced down at the tray in his hands. ''Brung ye some food, but I doan knows as to how yer s'posed ta eat, what wi' yer hands strung up an' all.''

Kincade looked at him with a speculative gleam in his eyes, then changed his mind. ''Where would I go if I did manage to overpower you, my lad? It ain't like there's a wide range of choices. After all, we *are* in the middle of the Atlantic, a bit too far out for me to swim back.''

Still hesitating, the boy shuffled from one foot to the other, and stared at Kincade so anxiously that he wanted to throttle him. He waited as patiently as he could, though his stomach was churning and growling at the mere thought of food. Finally, as he seemed to reach some sort of decision, the boy drew near enough to set the tray on the floor near Kincade's feet.

Kincade looked up at him. ''Do I eat this with my toes? Not that I would mind, see, but it'll prove a bit awkward.''

''Here. Spoon.'' The boy picked up a utensil and held it out, then frowned when Kincade stretched his arms to the limits of the rope and still failed to reach him. ''Guess it won't work.''

''No, lad. It certainly doesn't appear that way.'' He leaned forward, sniffing suspiciously at the tray. ''What did you bring, anyway?''

''Oatmeal. Has a bit o' salt pork in it fer ye.''

Kincade sagged back against the wall and closed his eyes again. ''Take it away,'' he said tonelessly. *Oatmeal.* As far as he was concerned, it would be like eating premasticated horse fodder. No, definitely not one of his better days.

"Take it away?" There was the sound of scuffling feet on the floor, and the boy repeated slowly, "Take it away?"

Kincade opened one eye to glare at him and said, almost snarling, *"Get it out of here."*

The boy squeaked with fright and grabbed the tray, then backed from the cell and slammed the door behind him. It was dark and gloomy again, and Kincade gave a vicious kick at the opposite wall. That only succeeded in making his toe throb like the devil, and he contemplated his misery for a brief moment before deciding to sleep.

At least in sleep he would not have to think about his bruises, the cold, or his empty belly.

By the time the second mate was sent to escort him topside for his trial, Kincade was almost glad to see him. Anything was preferable to his present misery.

"You won't look so cheerful soon enough," the battered second mate said as he tied Kincade's hands behind him. The ropes were tight and chafing, growing tighter as the mate jerked Kincade above deck.

The sunlight stung his eyes, but felt warm on his bare torso. "Easy, old man," Kincade muttered when the mate half dragged him and he narrowly missed tangling his feet in a coil of rope on the deck. "Still miffed because of a few bruises? They'll heal soon, and you'll feel much better. Besides, it was all in fun, nothing to sulk about."

"We'll see how much fun you think it is to swing from a yardarm."

The mate's brutal comment caused Kincade some dismay. "Steady on, fellow. Hanging? Because of a misunderstanding? I'm not a member of the crew, you know, but a passenger."

"Not a *paying* one, the cap'n says."

"Oh." Kincade felt his dismay stir into alarm. "Found

out about that, did he? Well, I'm certain we can clear things up with a little—*oof!*''

The second mate's elbow found Kincade's stomach with a resounding thud that took away his breath. By the time he was able to breathe normally again, they were on the quarterdeck and the captain was glaring at him. Things did not look favorable.

A chill wind whipped at Kincade's bare chest. His trousers were damp and clinging to him soggily. Shivers racked his body. The second mate gave him another vicious shove that sent him staggering forward. He had a vague view of the offended female as she stood just behind the captain, but it was only a brief impression of wind-whipped skirts and sunlight gleaming on pale hair before a belaying pin hit the back of his legs with a savage *whack,* sending him to his knees.

Pain lanced through him, and he felt the harsh comfort of the deck slam into his knees. He finally managed with some effort to look up at the captain's severe face.

"You are charged with attempted rape, sir," the captain intoned. His attitude befitted that of a judge sentencing a murderer.

"I was not—"

"Shut up," the second mate said, and hit him in the lower back with the belaying pin. The pain left him breathless.

When he caught his breath Kincade half turned, flashing the mate a murderous glance. He wished his hands were free for just a moment. He'd show the damn mate a thing or two that could be done with a belaying pin and a vivid imagination.

"Oh, do stop that," an indignant feminine voice demanded. Kincade glanced from the second mate to the girl he was accused of raping. Or attempting to rape, that distinction seeming to have escaped the crew, in his opinion.

She was twisting her hands together in front of her, and her face was turned toward the captain. Though she wore a dainty dimity dress and carried a frilly parasol, and her hair was coiled in silky blond curls atop her head, there was nothing fragile and feminine in the stern look she was giving the captain.

"I see no point," she said sharply, "in beating a man who has his hands tied behind him. Besides, he looks miserable and wretched enough."

"Thank you," Kincade muttered. Miserable and wretched, was he? He'd like to see Miss Fluff look so good after a night and the better part of the morning spent in a dingy cell without a change of clothes.

Matter of fact, he might like that very well.

Captain Hanover snorted derisively. "He's a felon, miss. And if havin' his hands tied is the worst that happens to him, he'll be lucky. He'll have a lot more to worry about than a few bruises before the day is over."

"Captain Hanover," she continued without glancing at Kincade again, "I must insist that you release this man at once."

Kincade's head snapped up.

"Release him, miss?" Hanover scowled. "Why should I do that?"

"Because I retract my charges." Her brisk tone seemed to confound the captain. There was a moment of awkward silence broken only by the flapping of canvas sails and the snap of loose halyards. Then the captain shook his head.

"No. He's been accused of a serious charge—"

"I was mistaken. It was dark, and I was frightened and only half-awake. Now, in the light, I can see my error."

"Error?" Hanover's face began to turn a ripe purple. "I don't see how you can call rape an error, miss."

Her composure never cracked. "In the first place, it was not rape. This is my cousin, and he must have stumbled into the wrong cabin."

"Cousin." The captain looked doubtfully from Kincade's dark head to the girl's pale locks.

"Yes," she said, "third cousin on my mother's side,

twice removed. I haven't seen him in a long time, you see, so it was easy to mistake him in the dark.'' She fiddled with the lace on her dress cuff. Kincade watched in detached fascination.

What a facile little liar she was. He wondered why she was bothering, but she continued with hardly a break.

"We're on our way to visit relatives, and as it was so late when we boarded, I did not have a chance to visit with him very much. Due to a raging case of *mal de mer,* I have not been out of my cabin since boarding. You must excuse all the trouble. Normally I am much more organized than this.''

"Are you?'' Hanover glared at the girl, then back at Kincade, who had the good sense to keep all expression from his face. "You've stirred up a hornet's nest, miss.''

"As I said, Captain, I apologize.'' The girl gave him a cold stare that should have frozen Hanover in his boots.

The captain rubbed a hand across his mouth and looked back at Kincade. "I'm afraid that makes no difference. Even if you claim he's your bloody *mother,* he hasn't paid his passage.''

Kincade's brief flare of hope was quickly extinguished. He *would* remember that, the scurvy bastard.

"He didn't?'' Giving a regretful shake of her head, the girl glanced toward Kincade. "Silly wretch. You can never remember the most important things.''

He took his cue. "Sorry, my pet.'' Kincade wasn't certain what he was supposed to say—God, he didn't even know her name and hoped he wasn't asked for it—so he improvised the best he could. "You know how I forget things since the head injury.''

"No excuse. Let me handle all the details from now on.'' She turned to the captain and said brusquely, "Release him at once. If you will send one of your crew to my cabin, I will give you the money for my cousin's passage.''

After a hesitation, in which Kincade prayed that his luck would hold and this girl wouldn't change her mind, the captain snarled a reluctant order to release the prisoner.

Kincade sat back on his heels and gave the second mate a promising smile.

"Do untie me, old man. And don't think I'm the type to carry long grudges."

Shifting uneasily, the second mate fumbled at Kincade's ropes with a few earnest tugs. When he bent to help him to his feet, Kincade added with soft menace, "I usually take care of my debts quite quickly."

The mate dropped the belaying pin and stepped back. He eyed Kincade warily as he came to his feet and rubbed at his arms, trying to restore circulation. It hurt as the blood flowed back into starved veins and muscles, and Kincade decided to restrain any notions of justice for the time being. There was always later.

First, he had to find out just what the prissy Miss Whoever-She-Was had on her mind. He didn't doubt for a moment that she wanted something from him. In his experience, people never admitted mistakes. Or offered aid without the expectation of recompense.

"Cousin, dear," he said as she passed close by him on her way down from the quarterdeck, "do let me assist you back to your cabin."

She looked startled. "That's not necessary. I think it best if you find yours and return to it and dress. It's quite chilly in the wind."

"I agree." Kincade took her arm. "I just want to express my regret—and appreciation—properly."

"Perhaps later."

"Ah, but I have had an entire night in which to reflect on the error of my ways, and I know that you will be most entertained."

Up close, Kincade decided that she was fairly pretty. Straight little nose, wide-spaced blue eyes, delicate bones that made her look much more fragile than she behaved— not bad. Not bad at all. Skinny, with only the suggestion of any curves under her fluffy dimity, but not bad at all.

"Very well," she was saying stiffly, glancing at the captain, "come along if you must."

The wind cut into his bare chest with a vengeance, but Kincade managed to keep the shiver out of his voice. "Right-ho, sweet cousin."

Chapter 2

ELIZABETH LEE gazed speculatively at the large man standing in the middle of her tiny cabin, dwarfing the stark furnishings. She knew he was going to ask for an explanation, and she didn't have one. Neither did she have any idea why—except in the interest of fairness—she had spoken out. The man was more than likely a rogue and worse, deserving of whatever befell him.

He certainly looked like the type of man who invited trouble. In her experience handsome men always caused trouble. And this one, with his broad shoulders, lean muscles, and a face that could undoubtedly draw sighing glances and dreamy feminine smiles, was more handsome than most. It was his eyes that drew her attention, however, glittering as green as a panther's beneath thick, spiky lashes that were lowered in a sulky drift.

There was intelligence in those eyes, an intelligence that was both startling and disquieting. It was clear she couldn't dismiss him as one of those charming, senseless men who relied on good looks and larceny to line their pockets.

He looked far more dangerous.

He looked away, then back, and then she thought she must be letting her imagination run away with her, because there was only open curiosity in his eyes, not some secret ambition. He glanced meaningfully toward her bunk.

"Well, love," he said easily, "shall we have a go at it, then?"

She stared at him, then realized what he meant and what he thought, and snapped, "No!" Her cheeks burned with heated embarrassment. "I have no designs on your person at all, if that is what you think."

Those vivid green eyes focused on her, and his dark head tilted to one side as if assessing her. Elizabeth swallowed an indignant retort that would only sound forced.

His handsome face bore a host of bruises and several cuts, which probably needed attention. His bare chest—disturbingly naked and a deep, burnished gold that left her feeling faintly flushed—was ridged with black-and-blue marks that looked painful, although he didn't seem to be suffering.

"Please put your clothes on, sir," she said, and saw his mouth quirk into a grin.

"I'd be most happy to do so, but what you see here"—he swept a hand down his lean body to indicate the snug, damp trousers that amply outlined his male attributes—"is all I have at hand at the moment."

"You should have thought of that before you insisted upon accompanying me."

"I did, but this seemed more important."

Elizabeth shot him another glance and moved to the tiny closet that held her meager wardrobe. Her trunk was stashed under the bunk, much too difficult to drag out under the best of circumstances, which these were not. Drawing out her fur-lined cloak, she held it out to him.

"This will do for now."

He took it. "Ermine? A tidy little sum here. Do you mind me asking your intentions?"

Startled, Elizabeth repeated, "Intentions?"

"I want to know if they're honorable. I'm not usually the kind of man who can be bought, you know. Cheaply, anyway."

The flush heated her cheeks again. "Really. I should

think you would be a bit more grateful that I saved you from a certain flogging, and a probable hanging.''

''Oh, I am, ma'am, I assure you. I'm as grateful a dog as you'll ever find. I just wish you'd spoken out a bit sooner and saved me a night in the brig.''

Elizabeth made an irritated sound. ''It was late and dark, and I was frightened. And I didn't know at the time but what you *were* attempting—'' She halted.

''Rape?'' he supplied helpfully. ''I admit that I did have rather . . . um . . . carnal intentions, but not for you. I believe I had the wrong cabin.''

''So your charming friend told me.''

''Did she?'' He shrugged his shoulders inside the warm cloak. ''Took her long enough.''

''Perhaps your night in the brig will make you more cautious the next time.'' Really. The man was most ungrateful.

''There's always hope.'' Tilting his head to one side, he regarded her with a steady gaze that made her shift uncomfortably. ''What's your name? Since we're *cousins,* it might be best if I can identify you upon request. I'd hate for Hanover to suspect a trick. He'd still like to give me a taste of the cat, I think.''

''Cat?''

''A charming little device they use as gentle persuasion aboard ship. It can strip the hide off a man's back in very short time. I'm certain before our voyage is ended, we will have the opportunity of watching its justice at work. Hanover seems the type.''

The ship rose slightly on a swell, then dropped. Elizabeth grabbed at his arm to steady herself.

He caught her easily, his long legs spread for balance and his hands circling her upper arms.

''Hey, I like you, too,'' he murmured with a wicked grin, and before she knew what he intended, he bent his head and kissed her.

Elizabeth froze. She certainly hadn't expected anything

this forward. Not from a man who had just escaped severe punishment for almost this very thing. He must be a dangerous lunatic.

Oddly she didn't push him away at once as she should have done. He smelled of wind and salt air. His mouth, warm and gentle at first, grew harder, more urgent, and her lungs expanded with indrawn breath. This was crazy, insane, utter madness, but there was a delicious heat spreading through her body and leaving her weak in his embrace. The feel of him against her—the smooth taut curve of his bronzed muscles beneath the open cloak, the faint rasp of his beard stubble, the pressure of his lips moving against her mouth, the curve of her jaw below her ear, then her lips again—combined in a wash of confusing reaction. It was intriguing. It was foolish.

Elizabeth pulled away with an effort and managed to look up at him with what she hoped was boredom.

"Now that we have that out of the way, do you suppose you could tell me your name, sir? For the same reasons, of course."

"I asked first." His mouth twitched in cynical humor. "But since I'm a gentleman—"

"I doubt that."

"—I will be courteous enough to reply. Kincade MacKay, at your service." He swept her a bow that should have looked faintly ridiculous because he was still wearing the fur-lined cloak. Somehow he retained an air of elegant grace.

"Mr. MacKay, I would greatly appreciate it if you would confine your comments and actions to what is considered proper. I am not a tart, nor am I a meek, frail female in need of male protection. In fact, it seems to me that in this situation, it's the other way around."

"Does it?" His eyes flashed with a brief reaction that could have been anger, but was gone so quickly she couldn't tell. "I admit I have been in better circumstances."

"Yes. Well. As soon as we dock in New Orleans, I will

be most happy to allow you to go on your way and forget this deception. Until then, I would appreciate it if you would be kind enough to avoid my company as much as possible.''

He inclined his dark head gravely, his suddenly blank expression making her think of a statue. Elizabeth could detect no reaction to her words in his husky voice.

''Whatever you say, sweeting.''

She stiffened. ''My name is Elizabeth Lee, and I prefer that you call me Miss Lee when you are expected to call me anything at all.''

''Won't that seem a bit formal in public—Lizzie?''

Annoyed, she opened her mouth to say something sharp when he interrupted with, ''Ground swell.''

She stared at him blankly, then realized what he meant when the deck of the ship rose suddenly, then dropped abruptly away. It left her briefly airborne, and she went sliding toward him again. His arms went around her in a quick embrace. As she was pressed next to his body Elizabeth felt the rising press of his interest nudging against her. First startled, then embarrassed, she would have shoved him rudely away if she hadn't wanted to pretend ignorance of what was happening.

Still engulfed in his embrace, she heard him remark dryly, ''One learns to anticipate this rising—ground swells, I mean.''

Furious, and hot with humiliation, she shoved away from him and heard his soft laughter. ''You're absolutely insufferable.''

''Yes. I've been told that before.''

Elizabeth indicated the door with a jerk of her head, her body stiff. ''Please leave. And do not return. Tell everyone I am ill, or that we quarreled, or whatever you want, but do not come near me again.''

The corners of his mouth turned up in a mocking smile. ''I do hate family squabbles. I'll give you time to get over this, Cousin Liz.'' He sauntered to the door, then turned back to look at her. ''I'm certain you'll let me in on your reasons for my *rescue* when you're ready. Don't keep me in suspense too long. I hate surprises.''

As the door shut behind him Elizabeth shook her head in amazement. The man was a lunatic. And he obviously thought she had ulterior motives for doing what she considered fair and honorable—well, with a lie just to keep him from being flogged. Which he probably deserved. She'd met the fair Alice and known at once why he'd been bumping about her cabin in the dark. Idiot. Rutting male. Why on earth did he think she would want any kind of assistance from him? It was beyond imagination.

Elizabeth sank to the sparse comfort of her bunk and looked down at her hands. She tried to remember all the excellent reasons why she'd embarked on this journey. It was difficult.

She smoothed a wrinkle from her dimity skirt and frowned. There were times when life seemed determined to withhold any sort of happiness from her, even small pieces. When she tried not to think about her loneliness or the reasons for it, it seemed that the memories were stronger and sharper than ever.

Well. She'd known from the first that matters were not as they should be. And really, she had her own goals, anyway.

Yes. Perhaps she was fated to lead crusades in the cause of feminist suffrage. If she had married Martin, he would never have approved of her working for female equality. He was a stubborn man, and would have kept her from even attending meetings, much less active participation. It was probably just as well that he had married someone else. . . .

Elizabeth rose from the bunk and reached for her pamphlet on socialism, spiritualism, and women's freedom. *The Woman's Guide to Mental Stimulation, Spiritual Evolvement, and the Liberty to Pursue Social Justice.* She would read, and dismiss the extraordinary Kincade MacKay and his convoluted imaginings from her mind.

*   *   *

"Well." Tabitha and Ian exchanged glances. "Well," Ian said again. "I suppose we were no' needed tae help out wi' his problem at all."

"Don't be too certain." Tabitha nodded wisely. "I've been convinced my duty was over before, and found that disaster lurked just around the corner."

Ian glanced up and down the narrow corridor. "So wha' do we do wi' ourselves? I canna think it will be helpful just tae dangle from the shrouds or hang on the mizzenmast."

"No, I daresay not." Tabitha smoothed a friz of hair back from her forehead, frowning at the sticky sea mist. "In the past, I have found it most helpful to prowl about and learn what I could from casual conversation. Once—oh, it was very exciting—I overheard an abduction plan, and was able to foil it." She tugged at the ruff around her neck and muttered discontentedly about the damp making it wilt. "Appropriate shipboard clothing seems in order here."

Ian blinked in surprise as Tabitha suddenly wore a wide-necked shirt, loose-fitting trousers, and a straw hat perched atop her frizzy hair. Her somewhat pudgy frame did not complement the costume, but she blissfully ignored her outlandish appearance as she smoothed a hand over the loose collar of the shirt.

"Much better. Now. Where were we? Oh yes. Let us just see what is in the air. I don't trust that captain. And the mate has squinty, mean little eyes. I'll show you what to do." She curved one hand through the air, and in the next instant they were standing on the foredeck. "See how easy it is? And much more convenient than just traipsing down musty corridors."

Murmuring an indistinguishable comment, Ian smoothed the pleats of his kilt with one hand. The wind threatened to tear the bonnet from his head, and he eyed Tabitha with a look of desperation.

"I'd like tae go below, Lady Tabitha."

"Oh. Of course. P'raps we should pop in on your

diabolical descendant anyway. Seems quite a rogue, he does, though a handsomer devil I've rarely seen. Related on your mother's side, you say?''

"Yes," Ian agreed faintly, "my mother's side. Lady Tabitha, do ye know if this is why we were sent here? Tae keep him from harming tha' young lassie?''

Tabitha gave him a startled glance. "Why, I assume so. Hmm. P'raps I should inquire further. God's teeth, but I forgot to pay attention to those last things Horatio was saying. He drones on so that I—well, never mind. Let us see if the dangerous Mr. MacKay will reveal the reason.''

With another sweep of her arm, they were in Kincade's cabin.

Kincade stood in the small space, his amused expression vanished. Miss Lee's cloak was flung carelessly over his bunk, and it draped there in luxurious reminder of his circumstances. And dependency.

Though he owed her a grudging gratitude, Kincade wasn't at all pleased to be indebted to a woman. Especially a woman as icy and contained as Elizabeth Lee. He had detected her scorn when she looked at him, and that irritated him.

Women. Trouble, all of them. If a man didn't find himself sniffing after them like a devoted puppy, he found himself running away from them like a whipped hound dog.

Kincade located a purloined bottle of brandy and splashed some in a rather dingy glass. He downed it in a single swallow, then poured some more. Dammit. He was in a fine mess. As usual, it had all started with a bet, but he'd been so sure he would win, so bloody sure. Well, he hadn't. And now he was on a ship bound for America, of all the godforsaken spots to end his days.

"America." He shook his head and groaned.

After flinging his long body into his bunk and banging his head in the process, Kincade swore long and hard. Rotten luck seemed to dog him. Not that he didn't deserve some of it, because he hadn't always played by the rules, but there were times he felt as if fate had a particular desire to see him ruined.

Well, he shouldn't complain; he was still alive—and without a pretty pattern of stripes on his back—so he would make the best of it. Thirty was young to surrender to despair.

"Here's to life, liberty, and the pursuit of happiness," he said with a mocking smile; his voice sounded too loud in the quiet of his empty cabin.

He downed the last of the brandy and placed the glass on the floor, then stretched out as much as possible on the bunk. Ships weren't made for men taller than six feet, he thought idly, hanging his feet off the bed. Ships didn't seem to be made for anyone who enjoyed comfort—and Kincade was a man who enjoyed comfort—but this was the only way he knew to cross the Atlantic.

Rather gloomily he contemplated the tiny cabin and its sparse furnishings. He was damn lucky to have even this; he could have ended up sharing a cabin with one of those ugly brutes he'd seen above deck, or worse—lashed to the shrouds while the captain amused himself with various forms of retribution all in the name of justice.

He'd tasted justice in most of its forms, or what other men deemed justice. As yet he had not managed to decide if there was such a thing.

Life had never been especially kind to him, and any gift horse usually dropped dead or took colic within a very short time. Like Elizabeth Lee.

Now, there was a gift horse such as he had rarely seen. Not that she would have been the first woman to pursue him for less than honorable reasons, but he was pretty damned certain that was not her intention. Despite her kiss.

He smiled ruefully. He'd thought himself much more jaded than to respond to a simple, brief kiss. Apparently he still had enough unjaded interest to spare a little for a skinny female with big eyes and a sharp tongue.

He wondered what she wanted from him. There would be something, that much was certain. But it would have been nice, he mused rather wistfully, to have someone do him a kindness for no other reason than that they wanted him to have it.

After a while the slap of the water against the ship's sides and the rhythmic motion of the hull rising and falling made him drowsy, and Kincade wrapped himself up in the blankets on his bunk to sleep. He'd think about Miss Lee and her outrageous actions tomorrow. Or later than that, if he could. Right now all he wanted was to forget everything that had brought him to this pitching tub in the middle of the Atlantic.

Chapter 3

"YOU'RE A vile creature, Kincade MacKay." Elizabeth looked at Kincade with exasperation as he sketched her an elegant bow that would have been proper even in Queen Victoria's drawing room.

"So glad you noticed."

She glared at him; her cheeks were flushed with heat. He was mocking her, everyone else in the public dining hall was watching and listening, suddenly avidly interested in the two of them. Lowering her voice so that the others would not hear, she hissed, "Stay away from me."

"I can't. Your beauty drives me mad."

"Devil."

Lazily reaching out, he took her hand in his with all the outward appearance of an affectionate male cousin, but there was a steely glint in his green eyes that made them glitter like shards of bottle glass.

"I'm tired of waiting your pleasure, sweet Liz. Tell me what it is you want from me." He kept her hand when she tried to jerk it away, and though his voice was low, there was an unmistakable current of tension in it. "You only *think* I'm a devil now. Keep toying with me, and you'll know just how much of one I can be."

"Really." She succeeded in yanking her hand away. "Why can't you understand that I don't want *anything* from

you? Not even your casual conversation? I only want you to
stay away from me.''

He regarded her steadily for a moment, then sat down on
the bench beside her. ''It's been two weeks since you so
kindly rescued me from the clutches of our marvelous
captain—for which I do thank you, especially after witness-
ing his notion of light punishment yesterday—and I find it
hard to believe that you did it out of the goodness of your
heart. After all, it cost you more than a few clever lies.''

She waved a hand in dismissal. ''A few dollars, pounds,
whatever it was. That's all. It was of no matter.''

''To you, perhaps not. To me—I have my pride.''

Elizabeth lifted an eyebrow. ''Do you? I had not considered that.'' When Kincade's eyes flashed dangerously, she
added, ''Not that you don't, just that it had not occurred to
me. I beg your pardon.''

He sat and observed her for a long moment. The other
passengers in the dining area talked in a low hum of
conversation, and dishes clattered and flatware rattled as the
ship rolled.

''I'm beginning to think you really mean that,'' he said.
''No hidden traps here? No forgotten words for the captain
if I say or do something you don't like?'' His voice lowered.
''And no one sent you after me?''

''No. Nothing and no one.'' She looked at him curiously.
''You must have known many unsavory people in your life,
Mr. MacKay.''

''Oh, many.'' He looked at her uneasily as if not quite
certain she was being truthful. ''Well, I may not be too old
to be surprised.''

Elizabeth smiled. He was really quite handsome, with his
sleepy eyes and sulky smile, the interesting arrangement of
harsh angles and arresting planes in his face. He made her
think, oddly enough, of the scene she'd once viewed in the
Sistine Chapel, depicting the fall of Lucifer. None of the
sinners in that painting had looked particularly remorseful,

and neither did Kincade MacKay. She realized he was little more than a fast-talking swindler.

She'd heard enough from the girl Alice to know that he'd lied like a fiend to get aboard the *Tom Hopkins* and had taken, with no compunction, a berth assigned to another gentleman. That the other gentleman had neglected to pay for his berth had been Kincade's bad fortune. Elizabeth suspected he was running from trouble, but despite that, and despite his annoying insistence that she wanted something from him, she couldn't help but feel a certain warmth toward him.

Heaven help her if he discovered it. He was the type of man to use honest sympathy as an open invitation, then leave the woman crying her eyes out over an empty purse.

"Yes," she said, "I daresay you're not so far into your dotage that life may yet have a few surprises for you." The sulky line of his mouth curved upward into a genuine smile.

"Possibly, but usually they're nasty surprises. If you don't mind, I'd just as soon know what's coming."

"Such cynicism, Cousin Kincade."

He grinned, and it gave his face such a boyish appeal that Elizabeth felt a funny tightening in her chest.

"I learned in a hard school, Cousin Liz."

Since their conversation had ceased to interest casual listeners, Elizabeth leaned forward slightly and murmured, "Don't call me Liz. I've told you several times that I prefer Elizabeth. Or Miss Lee."

Kincade crossed his arms over his chest, stretched out his long legs, and leaned back against the wall, looking completely comfortable on the hard dining bench. "I daresay. Liz sounds a bit familiar, and you do strive for formality."

Elizabeth tapped a finger against the book she held as she returned his assessing gaze. "Yes, I do."

"Tell me—Elizabeth—why are you such a philanthropist?"

A faint smile curved her mouth at his obvious skepticism. "If you mean, why don't I intend to make you pay dearly for my brief generosity, that's easy enough to explain. I felt responsible."

"Responsible?" His dark brows shot up in surprise. "For my being in your cabin in the middle of the night with less than honorable intentions?"

"Yes. After all, they weren't really directed at me, and I am certain that Miss Alice was quite chagrined that you failed to arrive when promised."

Kincade laughed ruefully. "That she was, or so she claimed the next day. I imagine she's the one who told the captain I did not pay for my passage."

She traced a finger around the edge of her book before saying slowly, "It's paid for now, so you've no need to worry."

"Not about that, at any rate."

"No, not about that."

A moment of silence stretched between them, and Kincade shifted restlessly.

"What are you reading?"

She looked down at her book. An impish inspiration made her look up at him with a limpid gaze and say, "*The Women's War on Whisky,* by Frances Fuller Victor."

He seemed stunned. "What?"

"It's a volume on temperance, and how there are brave women leading a crusade to battle the evils of alcohol."

"Good God."

She smiled. "Did you know, Cousin Kincade, that the Women's Christian Temperance Union was founded to organize wives and daughters and mothers into an effective social force designed to eradicate drunkenness and pave the way for women to enter public office?"

He stared at her. "Surely you're joking."

"No. There are temperance meetings in England, you know."

"How the devil would I know that?" He scowled. "Do I look like I would attend any?"

"No, you certainly don't." Elizabeth thought her reply pointed enough, and apparently so did Kincade.

"Damn right, madam." He stood up. "Since you're reading seditious literature, I'll leave you to it."

When he stalked from the dining area, Elizabeth bit back a laugh. Too bad she'd not known earlier how easy it would be to be rid of his company. But then, she might have missed the opportunity to learn a little more about him.

Admittedly he fascinated her. He could be witty, urbane, and shockingly crude, and though his behavior had frustrated and annoyed her, she'd also recognized a certain wary resignation in him. This had made her curious because it confirmed her impression that he was intelligent.

Somehow she did not believe he was merely a sly scoundrel. His manners were too perfect for him to have been a common thief all his life.

Lord, Elizabeth thought with a wry laugh, she had truly grown bored if this is what she spent her time thinking. She'd be glad when they reached New Orleans. She was anxious to go home, though it would be rather embarrassing to return a single woman after she had left to be married.

Well, those who cared about her wouldn't ask, and those who didn't care didn't deserve a reply. It wasn't as if she didn't have anything to occupy her time. She had the crusades.

And she certainly had the time. There would be no more thoughts of marriage for her; she'd eschew that life for the more rewarding life found in Noble Causes. It had become apparent to her that she was destined for something far more worthwhile than devoting her life to a man. She would devote her life to human beings everywhere.

It was a grand cause, and her offer of help had been accepted by WCTU with great glee. She'd received her letter from them before leaving for England, and she was glad she had something other than mere grief to absorb her now. No, Martin Malone would never have understood her determination.

Soon she would be in New Orleans and from there she was going west, out where the male-dominated territories and states had more saloons than trees. That was where her destiny called, and she would answer.

Kincade stood at the rail, watching the sea grow choppy. Green-and-white waves pounded against the hull of the ship with increasing fury, growing higher and higher. He glanced up at the sky. Thick clouds scudded across the surface, seeming to meet the horizon in a curtain of grayish mist.

"Looks bad, don't it?" a sailor observed cheerfully, and Kincade slanted him a sour look.

"Like pea soup. Is there a storm brewing?"

"One helluva storm, Cap'n Hanover says. See what we're doing?" He waved a careless hand to barrels and cargo on the aft deck. "Battenin' 'em down. That's so's th' wind don' snatch 'em away, see, an'—"

"I get the idea, sailor. Thank you." Kincade felt as green as the choppy waves. He was rarely ill and couldn't recall having ever been seasick, but the notion of being tossed about on an angry sea was definitely unnerving.

He could hear the seaman laugh, but didn't find it very amusing. It wasn't that he was particularly afraid, but he had the impression that no one seemed very worried about a storm that looked potentially dangerous. He just hoped the first mate and the captain didn't get soused to the gills on this particular night. All the other nights were fine, but not this one.

"Not used to the sea, are ye', guv'nor?"

Kincade wondered wearily why the sailor did not go about his duties and leave him alone. He turned and leaned an elbow on the top rail. Sea spray wet his arm, and he gave it a thoughtful glance before looking back at the sailor.

"No, I'm not used to the sea. As a matter of fact I despise the sea."

The man grinned and went about lashing down cargo and securing hatches. "Well," he said in the same cheery tone.

"If ye get too a'feared, ye can always climb up th' davits an' hide in one o' th' lifeboats."

"I'll keep that in mind."

Kincade eyed the swinging boat with mild dismay. It was suspended high above the deck. He hoped that he was never called upon to actually get in one of those tiny boats, because it was damned sure certain he wouldn't do it. No. He had a healthy respect for terra firma under his feet, and he liked it that way.

When he turned back to the rail, Kincade stared with increasing anxiety at the churning waves and plunging hull. It didn't look good. No, it didn't look good at all. Then he glanced up at the quarterdeck and saw the captain and the first mate at the wheel. One of them was lashed to it, and for an instant he imagined it was some bizarre punishment. Then the realization of just how rough the sea was likely to be made him stand bolt upright.

"Excuse me, sir."

Kincade whirled, too absorbed to have noticed the laboring sailor trying to pass him with heavy coils of rope over his shoulders.

"What's the captain doing?" he stopped the man to ask, and the sailor flashed him an impatient glance.

"There's a blow comin', and he's tied Simpson to th' wheel to keep us on course."

"Jesus."

"Aye, and I'm thinkin' that it's a bit too bloody early for it meself, but I ain't th' cap'n." He scowled. "An' I ain't had too much rum in me like him, neither."

Kincade wanted to groan aloud. The ship had begun to pitch and roll with unearthly shrieks of strained wood and taut lines. Foam blew up over the side rail to splatter the decks. His hands gripped the rail tightly, and he decided that he'd better prepare for the worst.

With that thought in mind, he went below decks to take what few belongings he had and put them in a bag—just in case. A cold sweat broke out on him, and he wondered if he'd survived his uncle's best efforts to kill him just to drown at sea. It would be a great joke on him, he supposed, but he'd have little time to appreciate it.

By the time he reached his cabin, the bosun's pipe was a shrill echo in his ears and there was a stampede of feet above decks. Dammit. He knew they were going to sink. He tried to recall if he'd seen any land in the last few days, but couldn't. He'd not paid much attention to passing blurs on the horizon, being more intent on fleecing several gentlemen out of their purses with a bit of cardplay.

He wished he'd paid more attention. If land was anywhere close, they might make it ashore if the ship sank. If not—well, he had a good idea of how things would end if the ship didn't weather the storm.

God. Why hadn't he wed that stupid, mewling London chit as her rich papa had wanted? He should have. Then at least he'd only have died from boredom and an overabundance of in-laws instead of salt water in his lungs.

Now he had no choice.

He was in his cabin throwing his meager possessions into a bag when a knock sounded on his door. It was loud, so as to be heard over the storm, and he bellowed, "Come in!" without turning.

"Are we sinking?" a voice asked, and he straightened to look at Elizabeth.

"Dunno. I just like being prepared for all eventualities."

Elizabeth's face was pale and drawn, making her eyes look like two huge blue pools. He noted it with a sense of detachment, thinking that his expression was probably just as miserable, then turned back to his packing.

"Oh," she said. "What—where are you going?"

"Topside. If it comes down to it, I intend to be near enough to see what that crazy bastard Hanover does. I figure he's the type to shout 'Every man for himself!' about five minutes after he's safely in a lifeboat."

"Do you?"

Kincade closed his carpetbag with a snap, then looked up at her. "Do I what?"

"Think the captain would leave us to drown?"

"In a minute. But personal prejudices aside, I don't know what he'd actually do. I just don't intend to take any chances."

She watched him silently for a moment, and he felt a flash of irritation. They'd been yelling to be heard above the storm, and he saw that she'd put a hand to her throat as if it hurt. For some reason he felt a pang of pity for her.

"Hey, Lizzie, this is probably just one of those tests Fate likes to throw at us now and then. We'll be all right."

She didn't immediately correct his use of the name Lizzie, and he knew that she was pretty frightened. Since she'd corrected him every time he used it for the past two weeks, it was a fair indication of how upset she was.

"Come up on deck with me," he suggested. "We can watch the fun from there."

Her eyes widened ludicrously, absorbing the gray light coming through the porthole, so that they looked like mirrors. "Are you mad? The wind is blowing so hard we'd be swept overboard."

She had a point. He shrugged.

"All right. We can go to the dining hall. It's closer to the lifeboats."

She offered no arguments, but went with him through the narrow, crowded passageways. People were jostling one another and children cried loudly, making the storm seem a lot more immediate than it had before. Kincade smothered the urge to shove them all aside. He knew he was behaving irrationally, but he'd had this fear of the sea since he was a small boy and his parents had drowned crossing the Channel. That he had boarded a ship at all only proved to him how desperate he'd been to leave England.

"Kincade?"

He looked down at Elizabeth. Her face was contorted in

pain, and he realized he'd gripped her arm too tightly. He immediately relaxed his hold.

"Sorry."

"That's quite all right," she said. Her words were lost in the chaos, but her attempt at a smile eased him somehow.

As the day progressed, the storm worsened. Kincade and Elizabeth weren't the only passengers to seek refuge in the dining hall. The bolted-down tables, with safety rails to keep food and dinnerware from sliding to the floor, offered the only stable source on the ship. No food was served, of course, as the galley fires were extinguished to lessen the possibility of fire aboard ship. Everyone huddled in fear and misery.

Kincade's unusual spurt of sympathy for Elizabeth did not abate as the hours wore on. He began to feel a reluctant admiration for her. She did not go into hysterics at each lurch of the ship as other women did, but huddled closer to him as if for protection. Normally that would have only annoyed him. It was vaguely surprising to discover that instead of resenting her dependence on him—even for so small a thing as comfort—he rather enjoyed it.

Perhaps it was only because if they were to die, he'd like to have something nice to his credit just in case St. Peter bothered to inquire before consigning him straight to hell.

More than likely, however, it was because she felt good in his arms, where he could determine the gentle swell of womanly curves beneath her gown. He'd thought her too skinny before, but now, riding under his palm and spread fingers, he detected those delectable attributes that definitely pronounced her female. It was intriguing, and if he weren't so certain watery death waited just ahead, he would do his best to explore those feminine virtues.

No one seemed to notice his uncousinly embrace, except perhaps Elizabeth, who was too terrified to care. It was, Kincade thought wryly, a statement on his character that even staring death in the face, he could contemplate such things.

When a loud scream of wood sounded above deck and the ship plunged violently, then shuddered and listed sharply to one side, everyone panicked. In the chaos, Kincade jerked to his feet and pulled Elizabeth with him and headed for the door.

The scene that met his eyes on the top deck was from all his worst nightmares. Rigging lay like tangled spiderwebs all over the deck, and a sailor was trapped beneath a heavy mast. He looked dead. *Very* dead. Sails were ripped in places, and loose lines snapped and popped in the frenzy of the wind.

"Bloody hell," Kincade muttered, and without thinking, dragged Elizabeth with him across the deck. He didn't know where he was going or why, only that he could not just wait to die without doing something.

The wind blew fiercely, lashing waves over the deck and drenching him. He leaned against the press of wind, feeling his way along the deck housing until he found a spot that wasn't too battered. The ship lurched, someone shouted that she was heeling, and he heard a hoarse order to reef the topsails.

As the ship heeled sharply he felt himself sliding across the deck. He struggled, but it was as if a giant hand were pulling him toward the gunwale. Grabbing at a rail built around a yawning hatch, he clung to the fidley with one hand and Elizabeth's arm with the other.

"Get back below," he managed to shout at her, but the wind carried his words away and she looked up at him with frightened bewilderment. He wanted to rage at the fates that brought him there, the wind, the ship, and Hanover, but there wasn't time. There wasn't time for anything but holding on to the rain-and-sea-slick railing as the wind tore at him and the plunging motion of the ship took him ever closer to the gunwale.

Just as he managed to regain his footing and a better hold

on the railing, the wind brought the ship around in a sharp lurch. The efforts of the crew kept her prow up, and the vessel gave a heavy buck and dropped into a deep trough between waves.

Ground swell. Or near enough to it to catch him unprepared. The deck was suddenly gone from beneath him, and he fumbled for his footing. Elizabeth was torn away from him by the motion of the ship and the wind's brutal power, and slung against the upper housing with a vicious force.

Kincade had little chance to feel regret; he saw the deck slide past his feet, then the rail, and he was over the ship's side with a brief feeling of weightlessness before the water closed over his head. The icy shock numbed him, and he instinctively closed his mouth and held his breath. It was pitch-dark, and he felt a great boiling of bubbles around him, and other, unidentifiable objects that he didn't care to think about.

With a kind of anger, he thought of his wasted life, and was surprised that he had few regrets. Then he was clawing his way upward, his lungs straining and bursting for air. As he broke the surface he dragged in a deep breath, but water immediately filled his mouth and he choked. The storm still howled, and he could see the blacker outline of the ship skidding away on the pounding waves.

Kincade wondered what the date was, then knew that it didn't really matter when he'd drowned. No one would care. And no one would miss him.

"God's holy toes." Tabitha turned to Ian with wide eyes. She clung to the taffrail with both hands and strained to find Kincade in the inky sea. "I believe we've lost him."

"Probably no' the greatest loss, but I do feel rather badly," Ian said. "I've failed."

"*We've* failed, and that won't do. No, by God, we have *not* failed."

Tabitha wrenched away from the rail and made her way to the lifeboats. They swung wildly from the davits, long falls securing them. She grabbed one of the lines and gave it a sharp tug, then turned just in time to see Elizabeth Lee leaning over the rail.

"Oh, my holy garters," Tabitha said again, rather help-lessly, as the lifeboat slid down and plunged toward Elizabeth. Almost desperately Tabitha gave the falls another yank and made a move of her hand that sent the small boat sailing out past the rail of the ship. As it swept past, however, it took Elizabeth with it and both tumbled into the seas with a splash.

Ian watched, horrified. "I believe tha' we may hae lost both of them. I'm sure tha' this will no' go well with those who sent us, madam." He made no move to hold down his wildly flapping kilt, but stared numbly into the waves beyond the ship.

"Have some modesty as well as faith," Tabitha snapped, and launched herself into the air. After a moment of grave contemplation, Ian shrugged and followed.

Chapter 4

NEVER HAD she felt such icy cold. It seeped into her bones, numbed her arms and legs, and the heavy weight that was her skirt dragged her down and down and down into the depths of the black sea. Clawing for air, Elizabeth fought her way up toward the distant sheen of light. She kicked her legs, tangled them in her skirts, and tried not to sob with frustration. If she opened her mouth, she would be drowned that much sooner.

Then, to her utter amazement, something solid was thrust into her hands. She grabbed it instinctively and, within a few moments, found herself sucking in salty air and a fair amount of seawater. She choked, coughed, spit out the water, and clung tightly to the buoyant object. Upon closer inspection, she saw that it was a box of some sort. Caulked, sealed, and bobbing in the water, it had rescued her.

Elizabeth shivered. Rain pelted her, and waves rose so high she was reminded of tall buildings. It was cold, so very cold, and she thought briefly of the way the weather had grown warmer the closer they got to America, and wondered when it had changed into this chilling rain.

As the wind howled and she saw the hulking shape of the *Tom Hopkins* fade into a gray curtain of mist and greenish seawater, Elizabeth began to perceive that she was in grave danger, wooden crate or not. She couldn't hang on to it

forever, and if the crew of the *Tom Hopkins* did not look for
her . . . Just the thought made her desperate.

"Help!" she screamed. She instantly realized the futility
of screaming as water washed into her mouth and the wind
carried away her words. And worse, the weight of her heavy
skirt was dragging at her and her fingers ached from holding
on to the box.

A huge wave crashed down on her, pushing her under-
water and almost tearing the box from her grasp, then she
popped up again. She was doomed. Tears stung her eyes,
saltwater stung her nose, and her life began to pass slowly
before her blurred vision.

She thought of her parents, long dead now but very dear
to her, and thought of her cousin Annie, whom she would
never see again. Poor Annie. Would she weep when she
heard of this? Or would she march determinedly on a
crusade in the name of her poor, departed cousin?

Another wave lifted box and Elizabeth to a towering
peak, and she had a brief, paralyzing glimpse of heavy seas
and desolation before she was tossed back down. She lost
her grip on the box, gasped and swallowed more water, and
grabbed for it again. It was spinning just out of reach.

Elizabeth paddled madly and tried to hurl her body
through the waves toward the box, but failed. She felt
herself being dragged down by the weight of her skirts.
Despair made her grab at anything, and she caught a coil of
loose rope that immediately gave way. It snaked up around
her almost as if it were alive.

She fought free of the clinging line, caught a brief
glimpse of light and water and a dark shadow, then was
dragged under again. Her lungs ached; her legs throbbed; it
was hard to paddle now. Only instinct drove her on, making
her claw her way toward light and air and life.

As she broke the surface again something snagged her
hair and pulled harshly. There was no time to wonder what;
there was only the reflexive reaction to break free. But when
she jerked away, she felt the sharp pull grow even more

harsh and opened her mouth to cry out with the sudden pain. Seawater rushed in, gagging her.

Coughing and choking, Elizabeth heard over the roar of the wind and the wash of water, "Be still, damn you."

In that instant Elizabeth knew that she wasn't alone in her drowning. She managed to turn and grab at the arm reaching from out of nowhere to pull her to safety. She clutched it with all her strength and pressed her face against the taut, flexed muscles of a forearm.

"Great," she heard, "just bloody great. All full of affection now, ain't you? Give over—you'll pull me in on top of you, and then where will we be?"

Kincade. And he was in some kind of boat, because she felt its rough sides scrape against her arms and chest as he pulled her upward. The rocking motion made the small vessel dip, almost depositing her back into the ocean. Then it rose on a high swell, and with a grunt of effort from both of them, Elizabeth went up and over the side.

Kincade fell back with her atop him. She sprawled in a graceless, sodden heap over his lean frame, and there was the sharp scent of wet jute and bilge water in her nostrils.

"Hey, d'ya mind?" came the grumble from beneath her, and she felt him push her away. He rolled her to the side, and sat up with one leg bent at the knee and an arm draped over it, as if they were lazing about on a fishing outing instead of adrift in a stormy sea. "Do you happen to know anything about sailing, Cousin Liz?"

She stared at him, trying to breathe normally and see him through the tangled mess of hair in her eyes. She shook her head when she realized that he expected a reply.

"Too bad." He slanted a glance around them. "Neither do I."

The small vessel rose on another wave, then veered sharply to one side, dropping off into another trough as more water showered down on them. Seawater slid about in the bottom of the boat.

"You don't?" She sat up and sucked in a sharp breath

that hurt her aching chest. Bending over, she coughed so violently that she spit up a fair amount of ocean.

Kincade waited until she was through, then said in the same mild tone, "No, I don't. I was hoping that you did. I never learned. Hate the sea. Don't know how fish stand it."

After a moment he pushed to his knees, looked around, and seemed to make some sort of decision. He picked up two oars and held them out to her. "I think it's safe to begin with this. Or would you prefer bailing?"

She looked at him blankly, then between shivers and chattering teeth managed to say, "I'll bail."

"Excellent choice. That would be my preference."

It was hard to hear him over the wind, but his calm tone eased the worst of her fears. He must be joking of course. Most men knew how to sail a boat.

Elizabeth clawed away the wet tendrils of hair in her eyes then took up the bucket he gave her. She began sloshing seawater over the side almost as fast as it poured back in. It looked as if it would be a losing battle, but she was vaguely aware of Kincade pulling steadily at the oars with an expression of determination on his wet face, and was ashamed to stop or complain.

The small boat rocked beneath them; the wind tugged at waves and lifted them high, sent them crashing down only to lift them to another swell. Their situation didn't look very promising, she thought with dismay.

"The *Tom Hopkins* is gone," Elizabeth said after a time. "Do you think they'll come back to look for us?"

Not looking at her, Kincade leaned forward, and then back, dragging the oars through the heavy water and adjusting to keep the craft from tipping. "Doubt it. Not for a while, anyway. They probably don't even know we're gone."

While they had been struggling with the boat, the wind had begun to lessen some, though the rain still beat down and the seas were rolling mountains of froth and sour-smelling water. Kincade's dark hair was plastered to his skull. His face was wet, and there was a long scratch on one side of his cheek. Elizabeth had the thought that she probably looked just as wet and miserable.

"Do you think we can . . . can . . ."

"Survive?" he finished for her, flashing her a guarded glance. "Since neither one of us knows the first thing about what we're doing, I can only hope that God really does look out for fools." He worked the oars, pushed back into the stern of the boat, and grabbed at the madly thrashing tiller. Immediately the boat ceased some of its wild plunging, and a satisfied expression softened Kincade's face. "I suspected this had a purpose. Let's see what we can do. I may not be a sailor, but I've always been a damn good survivor, Lizzie."

"Elizabeth," she corrected, and was rewarded with a moody smile.

"Right-ho."

As darkness fell the shriek of the wind died to a soft whine and the waves seemed a great deal less menacing. Kincade had fished a few items out of the sea and dumped them into the bottom of the boat, and Elizabeth, though sore and aching, had given up the bucket for some oars.

Finally Kincade said in a weary voice, "Since we don't know where we're going, why don't we try to make ourselves more comfortable? We can always plot a course tomorrow."

Elizabeth nodded wearily then realized he couldn't see her in the dark. "That sounds fine with me."

A brief inspection revealed a case of tinned goods, a small crate of various spices easily recognized by their pungent smell, and some baling wire. "A motley assortment," Kincade muttered. "And quite useless."

"Useless? What about the tinned goods?"

"Do you have an opener with you? Neither do I. Maybe we'll be lucky enough to scoop more valuable flotsam from the ocean tomorrow. Right now I don't care."

While he'd been talking she'd felt him moving about in the craft carefully. When he reached out and took her by the arm and said "Take off your skirt," she gave a violent start.

"You must be insane."

"Don't be a bloody little fool." He sounded angry. "Do you think I'm so skirt sweet I want to fool with that when I'm wet and cold and hungry? I just thought you might be warmer if you took off your wet skirt. Besides, we can use it as a shelter if these oars and baling wire hold."

Elizabeth felt foolish. Of course. She *was* cold, and it only made sense—but when he'd suggested it, she'd remembered with sudden clarity the kiss he'd given her and the reactions it had provoked.

She struggled silently out of her wet skirt and handed it over to him. It was a crisp cotton weave, quite light, and dyed a dark blue. Her heavy petticoats clung to her legs in clammy folds, and after a moment's brief consideration, Elizabeth removed them as well.

"Here," she said. "Fold these and put them in the bottom. It's better than lying on bare planks, and since everything is wet anyway . . ."

"Right-ho," he said, sounding faintly amused in the dark. "This is getting pretty interesting. Got anything else to be donated in the name of charity and comfort?"

"No."

"Too bad. Hope you don't mind if I don't participate in this clothing drive. I've got a lot less to donate than you do."

"I don't mind at all, Mr. MacKay."

He laughed softly. "Whatever happened to Cousin Kincade? Have we gotten more distantly related all of a sudden?"

Elizabeth tried to keep her voice steady despite her shivering. "I think all of that pretense is no longer needed. We are, after all, strangers. Since our situation has thrown us into close . . . proximity, I think we should keep our relationship on a far more distant plane than before."

"Ah."

There was no sign whether he agreed or disagreed to that singular remark, and Elizabeth hesitated to pursue it. When he had done whatever it was he was doing with her skirt and petticoats, she heard his boots scuff along the bottom of the boat with a slight squelching sound.

"All right. I've prepared our little bower. Not exactly dry, but it'll do." He touched her lightly on the arm. "This way, my dear Miss Lee. I wouldn't want you to get lost and tip over our boat."

She flushed slightly, glad he couldn't see her face. Elizabeth stood up and moved awkwardly toward the stern. Kincade guided her with one hand, swore softly when she accidently trod upon his toes, then reassured her in the next breath.

"I'm used to women underfoot," he added blandly.

"No doubt you are, but pray, do not think that I am one of them."

"I wouldn't dream of it. Besides—you're not my type."

"Thank heaven. I don't consort with—" Her sharp retort went unfinished as she stumbled over a seat, half fell, and was caught under her arm by his strong hand.

"Watch your step, sweeting," he murmured, and there was a faint edge to his voice that kept her silent.

Elizabeth lay stiffly on the wet pile of clothing on the bottom of the boat, and began to wonder why Kincade had bothered to erect a shelter over them. The thin cloth would do little to keep out rain or wind. It flapped loudly, and sounded almost like a sail popping.

The familiar motion and noise slowly made her drowsy despite her anxiety and the strange sensation of a man pressed close to her back. She heard Kincade's even breathing, felt his warmth scorch her even with their wet clothes and the slap of the bilge water around them. Didn't he feel it? Was he as immune to her closeness as he claimed?

He wasn't.

Kincade silently damned Elizabeth for being so testy, even as he damned himself more harshly for being exactly what she thought him. Stupid male urges. Always ready, it seemed, even when common sense dictated otherwise. Why did his body always have to respond to the scent and feel of a warm female? It was a curse. He should be responding more readily to the cold wind, wet clothes, and empty belly.

A fool, that's what he was. He'd always been a fool. No sense in remaining one, he'd told himself time and again, but still, he frequently found that he reacted exactly the opposite from what he knew he should do. It must be his mad Scottish heritage. Rash, impulsive ancestors had passed on a surplus of impetuosity and a dearth of restraint.

It occurred to Kincade that this wasn't the first time he had found himself drawn to a woman who rejected him. Resistance seemed to whet his appetite, and he couldn't understand that, either.

Kincade shifted uncomfortably and stared up at the taut fabric of the shelter he'd erected, wondering what they would do when the food and water ran out and they still hadn't found land. He had little hope of the *Tom Hopkins* returning for them. It would be nice, of course, but in a storm, ships got blown off course and small boats rarely survived. Hanover hadn't seemed the type of captain who'd turn around and look for two passengers, one of whom had annoyed him excessively.

He stretched out, heard Miss Elizabeth Lee give a soft moan in her exhausted sleep, and scooted close enough to feel more of her delicious warmth. It seeped into him, that special female heat, spreading through his body in a slow wave of anticipation that he knew would go unfulfilled. Never mind. He could at least get warm. Or warmer. He'd explain it to her tomorrow if she protested.

Right now he would surrender to the heady feeling of a woman in his arms again, and the tantalizing scrub of his groin against her soft, welcoming buttocks. Her pantalets were thin, and he marveled that she didn't wake up as he nudged close. She had to feel his heat; bloody hell, he felt it as if he was ablaze.

When she didn't wake up, Kincade put one arm around her waist, his hand splaying over the fine linen of her blouse. Her clothes were quality. He wondered for a moment who she was, and why she was traveling alone.

In the past two weeks he'd only been able to discover for certain that Elizabeth—*not* Lizzie—had some sort of militant antipathy against alcohol—God only knew why—and was an enthusiastic proponent of women doing things like voting and taking public office, and probably ending up smoking cigars and wearing pants. He had no objection to the latter. It would make life very interesting indeed if women took to showing off their legs in snug-fitting trousers.

A dreamy smile curved his mouth at the thought. His eyes half closed; he envisioned Miss Lee wearing thin trousers that showed her long legs. Of course, he had only his imagination to go on, so he had to guess at the shape of her thighs and calves.

That took several minutes, and by the time he had visualized not only her legs but her firm, curved buttocks and small, plump breasts, he had advanced almost to the point of fiery need. Ridiculous.

The boat tossed, a wave sloshed over the side, and he gave a long sigh. This could evolve into a dangerous situation if he let it—or maybe it had possibilities. After all, if it appeared that they were doomed, Miss Elizabeth Lee might loosen up. And if they weren't rescued at all—who'd know or care what they did?

That gloomy thought dampened his growing ardor enough that he began to grow sleepy. He would think about Miss Lee's seduction tomorrow. Tomorrow would be soon enough.

"What a rascal."

Tabitha sounded disapproving, and Ian nodded gloomily.

"Aye, tha' he is. I wouldna ha' been surprised if he ha' no' rescued the lass."

"Not rescued her?" Tabitha turned in surprise. "But why wouldn't he?"

"Lady Tabitha—ha' no one told ye aboot the braw caitiff?"

"Obviously not." A peevish pitch edged her words. "I suppose Horatio thought it not necessary." There was a short silence, then she asked, "What *is* a braw caitiff?"

"Knave. Blackguard, good-looking—and tha' he is, tae gi' the devil his due—villain."

"Never have understood how you Scots roll your words as you do." Tabitha shifted position on the wooden crate they rode. "I quite agree, however. He is very good-looking, if you like men with hair as black as sin and eyes that are prettier than a woman's. But he's also a wickedly larcenous rascal. I noticed when he won that Portsmouth merchant's money at whist yesterday. Appalling."

"Aye."

"But, Ian, he's your kinsman and we have saved his life for the moment. You must recall that every person has a certain amount of goodness in them. It may not always show, or perhaps they do not realize they possess it, but it's there. I finally perceived that we cannot always judge others unless we know their hearts. Even the most wicked can be kind to his mother, or animals."

"Och, tha's no' so comforting."

"Oh, don't sound so gloomy. I believe your kinsman has the potential to rise above his past behavior. He's not always been dishonest and unchivalrous, has he?"

"No, he hae no' always been such a bloody bounder. I hae heard there was a time he showed promise." Ian rolled his *R* on the final word, shaking his head regretfully.

"There. You see?" Tabitha splashed her feet idly in the water. She gazed at the makeshift shelter and the two sleeping occupants. "Who knows what will happen? Circumstances may change our Master MacKay."

"Aye, but tha' dinna mean it will be for the better."

"I knew you'd look on the bright side of things." Her tone changed from dry to thoughtful. "Perhaps you should endeavor to allow your descendant to actually work at honest toil for a time, and thus learn to be unselfish. That might give him some ideas."

"Aye, tha' it might. The last time he worked at honest toil, he altered the ledgers in the steward's accounts so tha' he wa' gi'en thrice the amount of money needed tae go into the city and purchase goods. He used tha' money tae gamble wi' at one of those London clubs gentlemen favor, and before it wa' all over wi', he lost it on a turn of the card and had tae flee a step ahead of the Bow Street Runners." He shook his head, gloom settling on his features. "I dinna think he will hae any ideas tha' we will like, Lady Tabitha."

"That remains to be seen," she said after a moment, though her voice was less certain this time. "There's always a first time, Ian. And besides—didn't I tell you? I was a complete success with my last assignment. I see no reason why Kincade MacKay cannot learn a great deal about himself."

"I've a notion it'll take more patience than I've got."

"That is probably why they sent me to you." Tabitha nodded with wise satisfaction. "If *I* can learn patience, anyone can. Now pay attention. We shall give Kincade something to think about in the days to come."

Chapter
5

"WOULD IT be possible for you to stop swearing like that?"

Kincade turned his head and squinted at Elizabeth in the blinding sun. "Swearing like what?"

"Like a drunken sailor—fluently."

He gave an irritated grunt, sat up, and readjusted the petticoat turban atop his head. "How do you want me to swear, may I ask?"

"Not at all, really. But if you feel you must swear, use less offensive words."

"Then what's the point in swearing?" Narrowing his thick, lush lashes over eyes that seemed to reflect the green sea and throw it back in splinters, Kincade shifted to a more relaxed position in the bow of the small boat. His action set the craft to rocking wildly, and he stared with moody concentration over the wide expanse of sun-chipped waves.

Elizabeth drew in a quick breath. Their logic differed so vastly that they could never hope to come within shouting distance of compromise. In the four—no, five—days they'd been bobbing about in the Atlantic, not once had they agreed on anything other than the most necessary choices for survival.

They'd dined on raw fish and pungent spices, caught rain in the bailing bucket, and managed to squabble about almost everything. Kincade had no idea where they were, except somewhere close to America, but he resented her suggestions as to direction.

"West is where the sun sets," he said with a glance at her, "and that's where I intend to steer us."

"But we might miss the eastern coast entirely that way. I think we should—"

"You, madam, are not in charge here."

His terse remark immediately raised her hackles. "And you are? By whose vote?"

"This is not exactly a democracy." His green eyes flashed sullenly. "Right by might. Besides—women aren't allowed to vote."

"Oh! How absolutely, insufferably—*male*—you are."

"Born that way." He propped a bare foot against the opposite side of the boat to counteract her sudden motion. "You're going to upset us. Stop floundering about like a mackerel."

Primed to a fury by his careless assumption that she had no right to protest, Elizabeth deliberately rocked the boat. Kincade glared at her.

"You'd prefer anarchy, I suppose? That ought to work out real well, Lizzie. You just carry out your little revolution down there under the canopy, and I'll sit out here in the sun wearing your bloody petticoats on my head and fishing for our supper. Nothing will get done then. We both need to work at survival, or we'll be at the bottom of this godforsaken ocean of seaweed and fish piss. Then will you be happy?"

"Much happier than sitting in this boat with you."

It was a stupid reply, and even she realized it. Elizabeth sucked in a deep breath and curled her hands into fists. He looked at her with a sardonic expression that told her he knew she'd let her temper get the best of her, and she felt another mortifying flush heat her cheeks.

"Very well. So I wouldn't be happy being at the bottom of the ocean. But that doesn't mean you have the right to command just because you're a man."

"I see." The corners of his mouth turned down in a wry grimace. "You want to vote, I perceive. All right—vote. I vote for me, you vote for you—a tie. Who do we get to cast the deciding ballot? Anarchy. See, Lizzie? Why bother? Just bait your hook and help me catch some fish. We can have our bloody revolution later."

"First of all, my name is Elizabeth. Secondly, 'later' is no solution." Her voice was grim. "Yesterday—or was it the day before?—you said we'd worry about fixing the tiller *later*. Now the tiller's gone, and you don't have to worry about it anymore."

"How did I know the damned thing would break off in the night?" He gave his fishing pole an irritable snap, and the baling wire coiled around the end of the oar, so that he had to draw it in and untangle it. "Not that it matters if we have it or don't. There's been no sign of land in five days and I don't know where the hell we are. Neither do you." He muttered another oath as the clumsy hook caught in the bend of his index finger, extracted it carefully, then smoothed out the wire and cast the hook and line back over the side.

Elizabeth was close to tears. He had no sympathy at all. No sense of the disaster looming over them. He just went on fishing and doing the small tasks that kept them afloat. It was as if he had no conception of the distant future. There was only *now* for Kincade. And of course, later. Later was for unpleasant things. Now was for—now.

She cleared her throat and asked, "What do you intend to do?"

He looked at her, his brow crowding his eyes in a frown. "Fish. Then row some more. What do you have in mind?"

Elizabeth cupped her forehead in her palm and mumbled an indistinct reply that she was glad he couldn't hear after her recent lecture on swearing. Then she straightened, inhaled deeply, and picked up her clumsy fishing oar again. The strain was making her irritable. Kincade was making her irritable. Worse, her monthly cycle had come on her that morning, and Kincade had been so matter-of-fact about it that she'd not even been allowed the luxury of modesty.

"It's a fact of life, you know," he'd said, looking at her with an expression she couldn't decipher as he tore a swath of her petticoats into strips. "Don't be such a prude. D'ya think I haven't heard of those things?"

"Knowing you," she'd said in an agony of embarrassment, "I am quite certain you know much more about the female body than I do."

"Yes," he agreed imperturbably, "I probably do."

She'd not spoken to him for hours, but huddled in misery beneath the shady canopy he'd erected in the stern before finally rejoining him to help fish.

As the sun began to set, its brilliant rays mirrored on the glassy sea almost hurting her eyes, Elizabeth asked softly, "Kincade? Do you really think we'll end up . . ."

She couldn't finish the sentence, and he looked at her with a guarded expression. "No. Don't ever think that way. Once you give up, it's all over. We'll make it. We've made it this long, haven't we? And survived a storm that would have drowned a fish, to boot."

After swallowing the lump in her throat, Elizabeth said, "You're right. I'm sorry I said those nasty things to you. I was right, but it was rude of me to say them."

"You're so bloody polite, Lizzie. I can see that you were brought up well."

There was a tinge of bitter irony in his voice that made her look at him closely, but the sun was behind him and his face was in shadow. Only the taut line of his broad shoulders and the curve of his naked chest was visible, glowing a burnished bronze in the molten sheen of sunset.

"Elizabeth," she said mechanically. "I'm sure you're making one of your double entendres again, but you *are* right. I was brought up to be a perfect, polite little lady."

Kincade turned back to his fishing. He shifted position on the narrow seat of the boat and propped one bare foot up on the side.

"So what happened to change you?"

Elizabeth couldn't help a soft laugh. "I grew up and found out that being polite isn't always the best thing. For me, anyway. And—I found a cause."

"Cause. I suppose you mean that bloody nonsense about pouring good whiskey into the mud."

"Partially. There are other things important to me." She tucked her feet under her and swished her line through the water in a way that she hoped was enticing to fish. The tiny bits of raw fish on the hook might—just might—draw a *big* fish.

Kincade gave her a moody stare. "I know I'll hate myself for asking, but what other things?"

She smiled. "Women's rights. We have some, you know."

"So you keep telling me—hey!" Kincade's oar dipped sharply, and his line went taut. "I think it's a big one."

In the excitement of catching the fish, her irritation with him was forgotten. Kincade had grown quite skillful at cleaning fish with a knife he called a *sgian dhu*, or dirk. He'd pulled it from his boot top, and now wielded it with swift efficiency.

By the time the fish—Elizabeth thought it might be a sturgeon—was gutted, she'd carefully poured spices into a bowl fashioned from a sea turtle's shell. The hapless creature had been snared their first day in the net Kincade had made from part of her petticoats. Elizabeth had choked and gagged at first, and glared at Kincade for not seeming to care, but she devoured it anyway.

In the past few days she'd grown a great deal less finicky about what she ate.

Kincade carefully sparked a fire in one of the empty spice tins and positioned it beneath the turtle shell as Elizabeth slowly added water. He kept an eye on the fire to make certain it didn't burn a hole in the boat, while she hastily boiled the fish in spicy salt water. It was the best system they could manage, and more than once Elizabeth had thanked providence for the well-protected, dry matches found in oiled pouches in the small boat's supplies. Providence had done well in stocking the lifeboat.

"This shell won't last much longer," she said when they had almost finished eating, and he nodded.

"I know. Maybe we'll catch another turtle."

"Maybe we'll find land."

"Right-ho." He settled back against the side and hooked a long leg over the rail. "Since we're wishing, might as well make it a good one."

The boat rocked, and the last, dying rays of the sun bathed Kincade's face in a rosy glow. He was really much too beautiful, she couldn't help thinking. He shouldn't be. No man should be allowed to be that beautiful.

Her mind shifted to the first night adrift, when he'd held her close in his arms and she'd felt his desire against her back. She'd known what it meant; she might still be a virgin, but she wasn't ignorant. She'd read quite a bit and knew how reproduction worked. In theory, at any rate. She'd never felt the sensual tug that would make her want to allow a man that intimacy, even with Martin. It had been definitely unsettling when Kincade had touched her and aroused such instant response.

Uneasy at the memory, she tilted back her head and stared up at the purple and rose sky. Something wheeled in lazy circles above, and a faint, plaintive cry drifted down on the wind. A sea gull. She smiled. How free it looked, how absolutely—

"Kincade." She sat up with a jerk. "Look."

"What?" His dark head tilted back. "A gull? You're excited about—" The implications struck him then, and he sat upright. "Bloody hell. We must be—"

"Near land," she finished in an excited burble. "At least a day or two away. Don't you think?"

"I'm afraid to think." His voice was calm, and she felt a surge of disappointment when he said, "It doesn't necessarily mean what you think. Sea gulls can fly for long distances. Or it might have been pushed this far by a storm."

"It doesn't look very tired," she pointed out, "doing all those lazy circles in the air. It looks like it's fishing, to me."

"Maybe it is." Kincade straightened slowly. There was an odd note in his voice. "Maybe it is."

By the next morning—neither of them slept at all—they could see the faint, hazy line on the horizon that might mean land. Elizabeth closed her eyes in gratitude. She'd been so afraid they might drift in the wrong direction during the night and never see that smudge on the horizon.

It took them almost the entire day to row close, and by the time they were within shouting distance, the tide was crashing in huge breakers over sandy spits and high rocks.

"Too dangerous," Kincade commented, ignoring Elizabeth's cry of disappointment. "We might end up on the rocks or coral."

"What do you suggest—that we paddle around until dawn?"

He gave her a mild glance. "No. The tide will probably go out then. We'd be caught in a cross tow."

"How do you know so much?"

"I don't. It's all conjecture, Lizzie love. Now help me keep this clumsy boat out here for a while, at least until the tide is high enough above the rocks."

"Elizabeth," she muttered, but he ignored her.

It was an agony, waiting. But at last he said in a curt tone, "Let's give it a try."

Without a rudder to steer, it was difficult. Kincade put Elizabeth to two oars and positioned himself in the stern, using one oar at a time to weave the small boat through the turquoise waters. Silky white foam laced the sandy beach, and here and there an outcropping of bright rock glistened wetly. Kingfishers picked in the water, feathers shining in the late sun, darting forward with their catch and ignoring the approaching boat. There was no sign of civilization on the dot of land before them, only a sweep of white sand and tightly packed palm trees.

Despite their apprehension, the landing was easy. The small boat glided over the water at a swift pace, lifted on a swell, and hurtled forward. It missed the last of the jagged rocks guarding the entrance to the cove, then bumped against the sandy floor.

Elizabeth was jolted slightly forward, lost an oar, and bit her tongue. She ignored the pain in her eagerness to scramble from the boat.

"Wait a minute." Kincade caught her by one arm. "Do you suppose you would find it too taxing to help me?"

"Oh. Sorry. What do you want me to do?" She looked up at him with a faint twinge of guilt.

"For one thing you could help drag this bloody boat up a little farther. I'd rather not lose it to the tide. Better than that, you can help carry ashore our few prized possessions. If it's not too much trouble, Cousin Liz?"

She glared at him. "My name is Elizabeth, as you know very well. I am not your cousin, and you don't have to be so sarcastic. I guess you're going to pretend you aren't glad to find land?"

"No, not at all. I'm just wondering how much different it's going to be here than afloat."

"What a gloomy fellow you are."

"Experience, sweeting, has taught me that rarely is anything easy. This is only a tiny dot of land, and if there isn't any fresh water or food, we're in just as bad a shape as we were in the middle of the Atlantic."

Elizabeth didn't bother to reply as she took the crate he handed her, set it on one of the thwarts, then accepted his assistance as he lowered her over the side of the boat into the water. She allowed herself to feel a delicious anticipation as the cool, clear water tickled her feet, calves, and thighs. When it was around her waist, she felt the sand beneath her and smiled gleefully.

"I'm touching land."

In the next instant a wave knocked her off her feet. She came up spluttering and coughing, her hair streaming down into her eyes. Kincade was unkind enough to laugh, and she glared up at him through the wet ropes of her hair as he looked down at her.

"I forgot to mention the incoming waves and the fact that it will take some adjustment to solid land again," he said, leaning over the side and smiling down at her with an innocence that made her want to choke him. "Are you all right?"

"I'm fine," she said through clenched teeth.

"Great. Take the crate. I'm right behind you."

Elizabeth flashed him an exasperated glance as she took the small crate and stumbled ashore. Kincade, she noticed wryly, leaped nimbly from the boat, grabbed up the line tied to the bow, and leaned into it, dragging the craft slowly up onto the beach.

When she tried to help, he gave her a sardonic look and told her to get out of the way.

"As much as I like the idea of help, I can't think you'd be much of one. Besides, you'd probably get hurt and I don't intend to play doctor."

Since he wore no shirt, she'd already noticed his taut and bulging muscles. Elizabeth realized that he was right, despite his rudeness. She stood back while he fought the boat up onto the beach as far as he could.

Sand crusted his bare feet and legs, and he dug in deep as he strained. Sunlight glinted on his burnished skin, and his hard, lithe body was a study in strength and purity of line. Despite what she should be thinking, Elizabeth found herself admiring him. For such an unprincipled rogue, the man epitomized male beauty. A sun-gilded Apollo and David and Ulysses all rolled into one. He took her breath away, and she found it disturbing.

Finally the boat was mostly out of the water, and Kincade dropped to his knees in the sand and spread his hands on his thighs. He was panting, but muttered, "That might be far enough.'' Then he bent his dark head and dragged in a few deep breaths.

Elizabeth watched silently. She sat on the crate she'd brought ashore and waited for him to recover his breath. When he looked up at her, his green eyes resembled pieces of jade, hard and glittering.

"So, Lizzie, here we are, stranded on a deserted island in the middle of nowhere. I'm having fun. How about you?"

She laughed. "You're quite mad, but you do have a unique way of putting things, Kincade."

"So I've been told."

He rose to his feet in a graceful motion like a restless cat, then grabbed up the end of the rope and tied it to a nearby palm. The tree was only a sapling, but it was the only one near enough to use as anchor for the boat. Without saying anything, Kincade clambered back into the vessel. He stripped it efficiently, handing some supplies over to Elizabeth and bringing the rest with him.

By the time they had the boat unloaded, it was dark. A breeze washed the shoreline and curled the surf into waves of lacy froth. Moonlight showered down, and in the thick foliage behind them, night creatures called and rustled as if completely unworried about the new species now inhabiting their island.

Kincade's voice drifted to where she sat with her back against a rain-pocked boulder. "Maybe it won't be hard finding something edible here after all. Plenty of birds anyway."

Weary and vaguely frightened despite her relief, Elizabeth turned her head to stare at his moon-silvered profile. He was leaning back against a palm tree, one leg drawn up and his forearm draped over his knee. He was bare-chested as usual, his skin the sheen of muted gold coins.

"Maybe now we can open those tins in the crate," she said, keeping her voice steady with an effort.

He shifted against the palm, and its fronds rustled slightly overhead. "Right-ho. I'll just whip out my sword and hack away."

"I had in mind," Elizabeth said crossly, "using a sharp rock or your dagger."

"No, you had in mind *me* using a sharp rock or my dirk."

"Well . . . yes."

He gave a discouraging grunt. "I'm not enamored of the notion, love. Sharp rocks have a way of inflicting very painful gashes, and I won't dull the blade of my dirk."

Elizabeth sat up with a jerk and snapped, "You avoid any kind of work at all, don't you?"

He stared at her coolly, his eyes cold and glittering in the pale light. "If I can. Any objection? I don't hear you prattling about what *you* intend to do." When she didn't reply, he added, "Ah, I forgot. Equal rights do not necessarily mean equal division of work. A man's work is a man's work, right?"

"No, that's not right."

"Can't tell it by your actions, Lizzie. You seem to be awfully good at delegating, and pretty bad at taking up your share of the load."

"Look, Kincade MacKay, if you think for one moment that I won't do what I am capable of doing, you're absolutely wrong."

"Who stacked the crates? Who took down the canopy and brought ashore the baling wire and oars? Who anchored that damn boat so it wouldn't float away on the next tide? And who," he almost snarled, "wandered around the beach picking up pretty shells and pieces of driftwood?"

She flushed. "I was looking for shells suitable for use as dishes. And the driftwood is for a fire." She pulled her knees up under her chin and felt her pantalets tighten around her thighs and hips. They were still damp and uncomfortable, with sand scraping against her skin adding to her misery.

Kincade leaned back against the tree and looked away from her. After a moment he said, "I don't think we're getting off to a very good start. Why don't we begin again? Let's call a cease-fire of hostilities. If we don't, it's going to be damned unpleasant around here.''

She was faintly surprised by his remarks and after a short silence passed, nodded. "Sounds good to me."

"Excellent. Right now the beach is good enough for the night. Tomorrow we'll scout around and see what we can find. Who knows? Maybe on the other side of this lobster pot in the Atlantic, there's a thriving little town."

"That's too much to hope for."

"You're right. I'll settle for fresh water and a crate of rum."

"You would."

He laughed softly and leaned forward to stare at her in the dusky gloom. "Cheer up, Lizzie. This could be the Garden of Eden. Maybe we've found paradise and don't know it. Now, isn't that an interesting supposition? What if we are really dead, and this is heaven?"

Tabitha looked at Ian with an uplifted brow. She plucked a piece of fruit from a tree and looked at it dubiously, then wandered back to Ian and shook her head.

"You may be right. Your kinsman is a complete bounder. Well, maybe not a *complete* bounder. He certainly does have a novel way of regarding things, though, doesn't he?"

"Aye." Ian looked sourly at the couple drowsing on the beach and shook his head. Moonlight made his fair hair shine and emphasized his frown. He kicked his heels against the boulder he sat on and said, "It's hard for me tae like him."

"I can tell." Tabitha turned her attention from the piece of unfamiliar fruit to Ian. "I have a feeling he's not as hard-shelled as he pretends to be, though. P'raps that's the only way he's been able to survive. It should prove interesting to see how he behaves now that they're on an island alone together and he has no one to answer to but himself. And Elizabeth. She depends on him, I think, though she won't admit it.''

Ian gave a soft hoot of laughter and adjusted the bonnet atop his pale blond hair. ''She micht do better learning tae depend on herself. Kincade MacKay hae never gi'en a thought tae helping any mon but himself.''

''If that's true, don't you think it's time he changed?'' Tabitha smoothed the white cotton of her loose sailor's trousers with one hand and peered closely at her companion. Finally Ian sighed.

''Aye, it's more than time he changed. But tha' doesna mean he will.''

''That's up to both of you,'' Tabitha replied so mildly that the Scotsman scowled. ''Remember, you are allowed to arrange circumstances like we did with the fish and tinned goods—by the way, we forgot the tin opener—but must never change the direction of his thoughts or reactions. A cardinal rule, I'm told. I admit it a rather annoying one, when it would be so easy to just wave a stick and make a person behave correctly, but rarely is anything learned that way. Horatio taught me that. Took a while, but that's another story.''

Rather glumly Ian said, ''I thought when I died, all this wa'd come tae an end.''

''Oh, so did I. Dying is only the beginning of learning. Or so they say. But you'll find out. After all, you've only been dead—what?—a hundred years. I died over three centuries ago. Was murdered, actually, but as I said—''

''Tha's another story,'' Ian finished. The ghost of a smile curved his mouth. He smoothed one hand over the soft wool of his kilt. ''Well, I s'pose I'd best put on my thinking cap if I'm tae help this bloody fool of a Scot. He thinks he doesna need anyone else in his life, but he'll find out like I did tha's no' necessarily right.''

''Good.'' Tabitha beamed. ''It's an important lesson.

And I think he must be willing to learn, because he's already offered Elizabeth a gesture of peace.''

"I just hope it's for the right reasons.''

"Oh.'' Tabitha seemed faintly startled. "Yes, that would be good, I suppose. . . .''

Chapter 6

ONE OF Kincade's first efforts was to build a signal fire. He chose a high, limestone butte almost free of foliage and spent several hours hauling driftwood and other flammable substances to the site. Then he primed it, lit it, and stood back.

Elizabeth watched in silence. "Don't you think we should have built a shelter first?" she finally ventured to say, and blinked when he turned on her.

"I'd much prefer being rescued to burrowing cozily into the sand for the rest of my life."

His retort made her chin tilt defiantly, and she lapsed into a stiff silence that was a reproach. Kincade took special pains to ignore this. He looked away from her toward the sea, where sunlight burned on the waves and reflected back in glittering shards of light that hurt his eyes. It was vast and empty, and he could only hope that they hadn't drifted too far from the usual shipping routes to this uninhabited island where nothing lived but exotic plants and creatures.

When he glanced back at Elizabeth, he saw the strained anxiety in her eyes and felt slightly ashamed. After all, it was hard on her, too. And she'd not complained very much. She supervised more than she should, but she seemed to be a naturally bossy female and he supposed he shouldn't hold that against her.

"Come on, Lizzie. I'll build your bloody shelter, then. Do you want four bedrooms? A turret or two? Perhaps a water closet—"

"A roof and four walls will do nicely, thank you."

"Of course. Where I get the materials—or tools—is not your problem, I imagine."

"No, it isn't. It's ours."

He felt a flash of surprise. "You intend to help?"

"Of course. I'm not exactly too weak and fragile to do certain things, though I admit I don't have your strength."

"How diplomatic of you."

"Oh, Kincade, do you have to be so sarcastic all the time?"

"Yes. It's one of my best character traits. Irritation used to be, but I found that sarcasm has a much better flow to it."

His hand flashed out to catch her by the elbow when she glanced up at him and didn't see the rock in front of her. "Watch your step, Lizzie. I wouldn't want that pretty white skin of yours to have bruises."

She looked at him strangely and withdrew her arm from his grasp. "It's not white anymore. I'm burned the color of a boiled lobster."

"Only in certain places. It's very enticing."

Her cheeks grew pinker, and he noted with interest that the flush colored her neck and that intriguing area he saw just below the collar of her blouse. He'd tried not to look too hard at her curves in the past days, mainly because she took obvious pains to avoid that, and partially because he wasn't certain what he'd wanted to do about it. But the thin pantalets molded her slender body too closely at times, and the rather tattered blouse revealed that far from a lack of curves, she had nice, firm breasts. He remembered the feel of them beside his palm that first night adrift, then wished he hadn't.

"So what shall we build our palace from, Lizzie? Oak? Pine? Stone?"

Her stare was withering. "I refuse to play your game any longer. You know very well my name is Elizabeth."

"Ah yes, so you keep reminding me."

"Palm fronds and driftwood."

"What?"

"The hut. And we can use baling wire to hold it together."

"How ingenious." He didn't bother to tell her that he'd already conceived plans for their shelter. He'd wait until he saw if it worked out. Thank God, the island seemed to possess a natural abundance of fresh water as well as game. Mostly birds as far as he could tell, but the thought of something other than fish set his mouth to watering.

When they reached the bench again, he glanced down at her, almost smiling at the self-conscious manner in which she tucked a strand of pale blond hair behind one ear.

"How about dividing duties, Cousin Liz? I realize that I can't do anything so audacious as make suggestions of my own, so you decide who does what."

She considered his half-mocking suggestion seriously. "All right. I'll cook, only because you don't seem to have the least notion of what's edible and what's not. You can start on the shelter."

"Was your decision based on my adventurous desire to eat strange plants for breakfast this morning?"

"Somewhat. Regurgitation is not my favorite pasttime."

"Mine either. It was just an experiment, and now we know not to try eating that particular plant again."

She shuddered. "Yes. Now we know."

Kincade dragged a booted foot through the sand, looked down at his footwear, and decided that he'd better wear them as little as possible. When they wore out, he wouldn't have any more.

"All right," he said, "you boil up some seaweed, and I

will look for oak planks—all neatly sawed, jointed, and so forth.''

Without glancing at her again, he moved toward the line of trees up on the sandy ridge. He'd seen a spot in his earlier explorations that looked like a good place. If he built a hut there, they could still watch the sea for ships and be able to reach the signal fire quickly. In his opinion the fire was crucial. He intended to nurse it along and hope that a passing ship would see the smoke and come to investigate. After all, this island didn't look to be inhabited.

He thought, in the distance, he saw faint smudges of land. When they were more rested, well fed, and ready, he intended to head for one of the hazy streaks and see if it was an inhabited island. Not now, though. Now he had to concentrate on survival here.

By the time dusk deepened the brilliant blue waters of the cove and sent long shadows across the beach, Kincade had managed to erect a tidy brush shelter and Elizabeth had succeeded in opening some of the tins with a sharp rock.

Both felt rather pleased with themselves.

It had taken Kincade a couple of hours to find and drag back enough fallen logs to use as corner posts, and then he'd had to use a baling-wire-and-oar saw to hack through long stalks of a bamboolike plant. These he had woven into the framework made of sturdy logs and convenient saplings until a basketlike structure began to emerge. He had used huge palm leaves for a roof, though it would only be a temporary one, and left openings for two doors. It was his habit to leave alternate escape routes.

Elizabeth glanced up from where she was stirring something over a low fire and smiled at him when he approached.

"I got the tins open," she said in a voice that vibrated with triumph. "And so far the turtle shell is still intact as a cooking pot, though I can't keep the fire too high."

Kincade flopped down on the remnants of her skirt that

she obviously intended to use as a table of sorts. "What was in the tins?"

She flashed him a mischievous smile. "It's a surprise. The best part is—it's not fish."

"No?" He allowed one corner of his mouth to edge up in a smile. Breaking off a stalk of grass, he stuck it between his teeth and watched silently as she took great pains with whatever it was she was cooking. He rolled to one side and leaned on his elbow to observe her.

She reminded him of a pixie, with her cloud of soft blond hair streaked white in places by the sun. Her profile was delicate, reminiscent of Botticelli's *Venus Rising from the Sea*. The body he had once thought of as skinny, he now regarded as alluring. His revised thinking could become inconvenient, considering their situation. Or it could prove to be quite satisfactory.

Elizabeth peered into the turtle pot, gave a satisfied nod, and using one of the empty spice tins, began to spoon out the contents into seashell bowls. There was a faintly familiar smell to the dish, but it didn't occur to him what it could be until she brought him the meal. He looked down at the contents with a mixture of disgust and dismay.

"Oatmeal?"

"Isn't it wonderful?" she said happily. "It was a bit damp and musty, being in those tins and all, but it's a perfect food. I can make bread with it, maybe, or—"

He shoved the seashell bowl away with an abrupt motion that startled her. "Keep the bloody stuff."

"What do you mean?"

Kincade turned away from her bewildered disappointment. "I hate oatmeal," he finally said.

"Well, I wasn't too crazy about half-raw turtle, but I ate it anyway." Her tone was faintly accusing. "I put lots of spices in this. There's cinnamon, and I think the other is ginger. . . ."

Groaning, he rolled to his back and bent an arm over his eyes. "Lizzie, you don't understand."

"You're right. I don't understand."

He shifted his forearm to glare at her. "Well, try hard. I hate oatmeal in any form. It's a dislike I acquired in early childhood, and I've no intention of forming an attachment for it now. Horses eat oats. I don't."

"Horses eat grass," she pointed out, "and you weren't too picky to try that."

"That's different."

"Is it? I don't see the difference."

He sat up with an abrupt motion that made her scoot backward on the bench. "Dammit, I ate oatmeal morning, noon, and night for thirteen years. It was shoved down my throat whether I wanted it or not, and when I left Scotland, I swore I'd never eat another bite of it. I haven't. I don't intend to."

"Very well." She scooted back a bit more. "It seems that you aren't hungry enough then."

He grimaced. "Don't throw my own words back in my face, please."

"Why not? That's what you said when I wouldn't eat any raw turtle."

"Half-raw." He kicked at a fold of the cotton material spread over humps of sand. Several minutes of uncomfortable silence passed before he said suddenly, "All right, dammit, give me the bloody stuff."

An expression of surprise flickered briefly over her face, and he smiled grimly. "Didn't expect it to be this easy, I take it. It occurred to me that I cannot expect you to follow my advice when I don't." He held out his hand. "My oatmeal, please."

Elizabeth placed the seashell in his palm and watched with silent attention as he regarded the steaming oatmeal. She cleared her throat.

"It has lots of cinnamon. Maybe that will disguise the taste."

Her hopeful words made him smile. "Maybe it will."

It didn't, but Kincade had to admit it was a vast

improvement over the grass he'd eaten that morning. And it was better than nothing, which was the other alternative at the moment. But still, it was oatmeal, which he associated with his unhappy childhood.

If he closed his eyes, he could still see the dank, gray stones of the castle, hear the terrified scurrying of the servants through the long halls and dark corridors. And he saw himself, just as frightened but trying not to show it, cold and hungry and alone, fed the barest amount to keep him alive and starved of any love or affection. It was a mystery to him why he even thought of the bloody place anymore, or why there were moments when he wanted to return. In triumph, of course, as the conquering hero come home to accept his just due. What a bloody stupid dream. . . .

"Kincade?"

He looked up at Elizabeth, and something must have shown in his face, for she bit her lower lip and sat back on her heels in the warm sand.

"It tastes much better than I thought," he lied. "Thank you."

It was an effort to speak normally, and it was obvious Elizabeth noticed. He felt like hitting something, or doing something outrageous just to dispel the feeling that crept over him.

Instead he looked at Elizabeth's anxious expression. "What did you expect from me? I told you I hate oatmeal."

She looked down at her hands. "It's not that I'm fishing for compliments, Kincade. I just . . . you looked so miserable for a moment, that I thought—"

"Don't think. Not about me, anyway. And I'm not miserable. Aw, Christ. Are you going to cry?"

Her head snapped up. "No. I don't care if you like the blasted oatmeal or not." She rose gracefully to her feet and moved back to the cooking pot, where the smell of spiced oatmeal mingled with the stench of charred turtle shell. He watched her silently, half admiring the way she moved so

daintily and managed to look like a lady even wearing
nothing but cotton pantalets and a ragged blouse.

"You can tell me that the shelter I built is unsuitable if it
will make you feel better," he offered, and she gave him a
wry smile.

"Slap for slap?"

"Tit for tat, something like that." He smiled at the faint
flush staining her cheeks. "For a modern woman, Miss
Elizabeth Lee, you sure do embarrass easily."

"I'm working on that. It's a holdover from the days when
I was supposed to be shy and retiring."

"Shy and retiring? You?" He scoffed loudly, scooped up
the last of his oatmeal with his fingers, then set down the
seashell bowl. "Not a chance, Miss Lee. Not a chance."

"You didn't know me then."

He returned to sprawling lazily on the cotton spread. "I
don't know you now." He lowered his voice to a husky
drawl. "But I'd like to."

Safe territory. This was familiar, the land of double
entendres and hidden meanings. He felt safe with this kind
of conversation.

Elizabeth was looking at him without speaking, her wild
mane of blond hair tumbling around her shoulders like raw
silk. It almost hid her face from him. He wondered what she
thought, then told himself he didn't care. Not really. She
liked him enough, he supposed, though he knew he could
aggravate her with a careless word or suggestive glance. He
also knew she thought of him at times in a much more
intimate manner than she would admit. Probably even to
herself.

He'd noticed her sidelong glances, the deliberate look
from beneath her lashes at his bare chest and muscles. In the
enforced intimacy of the small boat, it would have been
impossible to avoid an occasional glimpse of forbidden
territory. He'd thought it added a certain piquancy to the
days, an excitement that kept him from leaping overboard in
boredom.

Now there were plenty of bushes and hidden spots to conduct private functions, and while there was a certain relief in that, he couldn't help a feeling of disappointment. He'd liked her morning toilette, when she attempted to clean herself with a scrap of her petticoat and a liberal amount of salt water, and while he'd had to keep his back turned, he'd often closed his eyes and imagined the uncovered areas she was washing.

"So," he said, more to keep his mind from that dangerous direction than any real desire to show off, "come up and see the house that Kincade built."

Elizabeth turned toward him without smiling. "On rock or sand?"

"Rock, of course. I've built enough houses on sand in my lifetime, Lizzie."

"Elizabeth," she corrected, though rather absently. "Let me eat first. I may need to see this on a full stomach."

"More than likely." He swung to a sitting position and, with his legs crossed at the ankles, waited patiently for her to eat. When she was through, he rose to his feet and held out a hand. "Leave the dishes for later, my charming little scullery maid. Come along, and be sure to make all the proper comments or you'll hurt my feelings."

"Oh, that would be a disaster, I'm certain."

"That it would, sweeting."

In spite of himself he was really curious about what she'd think of his efforts.

"It's not finished, of course," he said when she stared silently at the small structure. "And I forgot the turrets. Maybe later . . ."

She flashed him a humorous glance. "Later. Of course. And the water closet, too."

"Naturally." He tried to look indifferent to her opinion of the hut, but when she turned back to him with a smile, he stifled the foolish impulse to break into a grin.

"It's wonderful, Kincade. I don't know how you did it." She glanced from him to the hut and walked slowly to it. "I would never have thought you could do so much in one afternoon.''

"Neither would I. Fortunately there's an abundance of bamboo, or whatever that stuff is.''

"Yes. Bamboo.'' She ran her hand over the woven bend of a wall. The walls only went halfway up, and there were only openings instead of real doors, but the bottom of the hut was covered with a thick layer of packed-down sand, and the roof would keep out the sun. A brisk breeze blew through the open top half.

Elizabeth turned back to peer at him from beneath the portal of what would be a door. "I think it's wonderful. I'm astonished at your creativity and your resourcefulness.''

"I'm not finished.'' He shifted restlessly, feeling a bit ashamed of his reaction to her efforts earlier. She made him feel young and foolish. He looked away, then back, and tried to think of something noncommittal to say. "I think I'm through with the easy part. I have to figure out a roof that will keep out the winter rain, and how to make door hinges, but other than that—a piece of cake.''

Her lashes lowered over suddenly troubled eyes that made him think of lapis lazuli, all shimmery and blue and deep. "Do you think we'll be here very long, Kincade?''

"A week is a long time to me.'' He shrugged, realized she wasn't looking at him, and said, "Maybe not. We might be on a main shipping route. If we're lucky.''

Elizabeth skimmed her fingertips over the smooth green bend of the leafy bamboo walls. "I've never been very lucky.''

"I am.''

She looked up at that, an expression of incredulity on her face.

He grinned. "Lucky enough to stay alive more times than I can count, sweeting. By all rights I should have drowned this last time, but here I am, not only alive and kicking, but marooned on a tropical isle with a beautiful woman. Now how could I get any luckier?''

"Not having been marooned at all would be a start."

"Or having two beautiful women—hey. What'd I say?"

She'd started to cry, and cursing under his breath and feeling very awkward, Kincade moved toward her. He put a clumsy arm around her shoulders, not at all accustomed to offering comfort to anyone and not knowing how it should be done. He also felt a fair amount of irritation, because he had no idea why she was weeping into her shirttail. God. It was *his* shirttail she was weeping into. He recognized it now, and wondered when she'd filched it.

"Just don't blow your nose in my shirt, if you please," he said when she finally subsided into faint hiccups. "And if you don't mind telling me—why are you wearing it?"

With her face pressed against his side, so that he felt the dampness of her tears, Elizabeth laughed softly. "I washed mine. I had to have something to wear, and as you didn't seem to need yours, I borrowed it."

She stepped away from him and his arms fell to his sides. He looked down into the brilliant, gemmed blue of eyes awash with tears. She should look all red and weepy, but crying seemed to agree with her. Her eyes looked soft and warm, though damp, and her nose wasn't at all red.

He felt something shift inside him, some small tearing like the crumbling of a stone wall, and had the desperate thought that this girl was going to end up mattering to him.

"I'd like my shirt back, please," he said.

She looked startled. "Back?"

"Yes. Insects are beginning to bite, and—may I have it back *now*?"

Comprehension dawned in her eyes, and she bit back a laugh. "You really are a devil, you know. You may have your shirt back when mine is dry, and not before. No free peep shows for you, Kincade MacKay."

"You're a hard woman, Elizabeth Lee."

She glanced back at that and paused several feet away. He

felt her wide-eyed assessment more than saw it, sensed a response to him that should have shamed him but did not.

"Not nearly as hard as I should be, I'm afraid."

Kincade watched her walk back down to the beach and he was afraid to follow her. He might do something stupid, like kiss her again. Not now. It wasn't the right time. He knew that. Hadn't he always been able to sense the right time for these things? Well—maybe not *always,* but often enough to stay out of too much trouble.

It was a good thing he had his wits about him. Otherwise he might do something stupid and irrevocable.

A storm blew up that night, tearing the flimsy roof from the hut and drenching the occupants. Elizabeth and Kincade huddled under the shelter of a thick clump of palms and shivered as lightning cracked and thunder boomed.

"Sounds like two frigates pounding away at one another," Kincade observed, and Elizabeth looked up at him.

"Really?"

"Don't sound so hopeful." He brushed impatiently at a stream of rain pouring from a broad, fan-shaped leaf onto his head and added, "It was a simile."

"Oh." She slumped back against him.

"Besides, who's going to fight a sea battle here? Not the Turks, certainly, who are quite happily fighting the Russians, who have diversified their talents in Romania."

She thought for a moment, then said seriously, "Just a few small countries on the African continent are still actively at war, I think."

"Ah, let's not forget the Bulgarians who were massacred by the Turks. Or the Serbs, who have joined everyone else in the civilized world to declare war on Turkey. Those feisty Turks—can't seem to keep their greedy little hands to themselves."

"Why do I get the impression you don't really care? Do you?"

"No, not particularly at the moment. Right now I'm more

worried about this damn waterfall running down my neck. I wonder if the wind is going to blow down our house.''

They peered at it through the sheets of rain. ''I don't think so,'' Elizabeth said after a moment. ''It looks sturdy. All it needs now is a better roof.''

Kincade sounded faintly peevish. ''If you will recall, I did tell you that.''

Still shivering from the cold rain, Elizabeth looked up at him, outlined against the darker shadows. An occasional flash of lightning revealed his face, and she felt a moment's sympathy. He looked wet and unhappy, probably a mirror image of herself.

''Yes, I recall,'' she said. ''And it wasn't a criticism. Just an observation.''

When he shifted position slightly, Kincade's rock-hard arm pressed close to her breast. It was unnerving. He didn't seem aware of it, and she remained stiff and silent. Even if she said something, he would turn her words around so that she'd look foolish, or make one of those caustic comments that could sound innocent until one looked beneath the surface or listened to his tone of voice.

Earlier that day when he'd been talking about eating oatmeal for thirteen years, he'd looked abjectly miserable. She had sensed much more than a simple aversion to oats. It had eased the sting of his reaction.

Then she'd thought that she must be reading things into words. ''Borrowing trouble always ends badly,'' Annie had always said, and she'd found that her cousin was usually right about those things.

Another shiver racked her body, and her muscles contracted. To her surprise, Kincade put out an arm and drew her close to him.

''Body heat,'' he said shortly. ''Better than nothing.''

She didn't argue. Nor did she argue when he pulled her against him and lay down with her on the mat of tamped-down grasses beneath the clump of palm. It looked as if the storm would last all night. . . .

*   *   *

When she woke the next morning, Kincade was gone.
There was only the bruised grass to show where he'd been.
She sat up and yawned, blinking at the bright sunlight
filtering through the thick canopy of leaves overhead.
Everything looked crisp and sparkling, fresh from the
storm.

Elizabeth rose and went in search of Kincade.

She found him down on the beach, energetically wading
out into the surf. She watched for a moment, surprised. He
did nothing with energy, only a lazy kind of efficiency. It
amazed her that he accomplished anything at all, as he
moved with such indolent grace and carelessness.

But now he had dragged up on the sand a variety of
objects, some of which looked rather macabre from a
distance. She approached slowly, growing slightly queasy at
the sight of a body sprawled on the sand.

Kincade looked up and saw her staring. "Dead as a
doornail," he said flatly. "Drowned, I guess."

Elizabeth cleared her throat. "Who is he?"

"How the devil should I know? He just washed up, like
these crates here."

He indicated a pile of rubbish with a wave of his arm, and
Elizabeth recognized ship's stores among the wreckage.
"What's in them?"

"Probably more oatmeal, but if we're lucky, a few other
things, too."

She glanced dubiously at the dead sailor. "Then I
suppose we really did hear two ships firing on one another
last night."

"Don't be stupid." Kincade used a long metal bar he'd
found to open up a crate. "Just one ship, and it was
probably breaking up on the rocks. Or at the least washing
things overboard—what-ho!"

She looked at him with interest. "What did you find?"

He grinned wickedly. "Nectar of the gods. Ambrosia.

Bracing libations. Intoxicants, blue ruin, demon rum—the very best of spirits, my dear.''

When he held up a bottle with a cork in the top, Elizabeth stared at him in disbelief. *"Alcohol?"*

"Actually a few bottles of cheap rum mixed in with a decent supply of brandy." Kincade gave a nod of obvious satisfaction. "The Lord giveth, and the Lord taketh away. I like it best when He giveth.''

"You're not going to *drink* that.''

He glanced up at her. "Not all at once, of course. That would be wasteful.''

She stiffened. "You know how I feel about spirits.''

"I believe we are both aware of the other's opinion. If you want to give a temperance lecture, feel free. But give it to our friend over there. He could bear it better than I can.''

Elizabeth couldn't look at the poor drowned man. "I do feel—''

"Why don't we thrash this out later?" Kincade cut in. "There's stuff we can use here, and I'd like to bury this gentleman before he becomes damned unpleasant to have around.''

Unnerved, Elizabeth spun on her heel and waded into the surf to begin pulling out whatever she could manage. Some of the wreckage floated tantalizingly out of reach.

"We could take the boat and get it," Elizabeth suggested when she paused to rest, and Kincade shot her a frowning glance.

"We could if it was here.''

She whirled around at once and saw that their boat was gone from its mooring. Her face must have reflected her panic, because Kincade stopped what he was doing and rose from his knees to come to her.

"Listen, Lizzie, don't go all to pieces. I doubt we could have used the bloody boat anyway, not for a long voyage. And we must be in a fairly well-traveled shipping lane, because that vessel was a merchantman. There will be another ship soon, and we'll signal them with a fire.''

His fingers dug into her upper arms when she choked on a half sob, and Elizabeth was proud of herself for not yielding to tears like a thwarted child. She nodded.

"You're right, of course. It was just that I felt less helpless with a boat."

"Helpless? I'd like to see the day you felt that way."

Kincade released her arms and stepped back. He peered at her closely, obviously satisfied that she wasn't going to annoy him with hysterics, and went back to the crate he was prying apart.

"Tools in here, I think. Probably not the ones we need. Those would be at the bottom of the—well, do look here."

Elizabeth stepped close and looked over his shoulder. It was a castaway's dream. Rows of labeled tin goods lined the wooden crate. Canned fruits, vegetables, and salted meat lay in neat rows. An opener lay nestled among them.

Kincade was shaking his head. "Providence must like one of us, sweeting. I can't imagine any other reason for this divinely good fortune."

"Certainly not your sterling behavior."

He looked up at her. "My behavior?"

She indicated the crate of rum and brandy. One of the bottles was open. "Imbibing for no good reason, while—"

"Let's get this straight." His eyes narrowed and his voice was dangerously soft. "You are not my keeper, nor are you my conscience. I got rid of one long ago, and the other I've never had. Do you understand?"

"I'm certain I don't care." She looked away. Then she noticed the drowned sailor no longer lay on the beach. She looked back at Kincade.

There was a white, pinched look around his nostrils, and she realized that he must have buried the dead man while she was scooping up yards of rope and pieces of wood from the surf. Of course. She supposed under those circumstances he must have needed liquid fortification. It was gratifying to know that he had not wanted her to have to help him, or watch while he took care of it.

"You're absolutely right," she surprised both of them by saying. "I apologize for interfering where I had no right."

Still slightly wary, Kincade gave a short nod and went back to his scavenging.

It wasn't, Elizabeth thought with a sigh, the most auspicious of beginnings, but their second day on the island could have been worse. Much worse.

Chapter
7

A CHEERY blaze burned in the shallow pit in front of their hut, casting leaping shadows on the dangling fronds that thatched the roof. Elizabeth stretched out her hands to the blaze, watching as Kincade finished the last of his crab-and-mussel gumbo.

He lowered the wooden bowl and managed a weary grin. "Not bad, Lizzie. As a matter of fact, pretty damn good."

She smiled slightly. "I thought so, but such lavish praise isn't necessary."

"Isn't it?" He laughed and set the empty wooden bowl on a small hump of sand. "I have to admit, you do very well with what we've been able to scrounge around here in the past week. And I think you're smart to save the tinned food for lean times."

"Thank you." She swept him a mocking curtsy from her kneeling position in front of the fire. Driftwood burned with a bright flame, illuminating the hut. "I think you're just glad it's not oatmeal, however."

He grimaced. "That did cross my mind, I admit."

"Hmm. Never fear. The bounty of the sea shall keep us alive, while you—our stalwart buffer against the elements—will keep us safe from harm."

"What execrable literature you must read."

"On occasion." She leaned over and swept a crude log bench free of sand, then sat down on it and crossed her legs

81

at the ankle. "But you've already seen an example of my more uplifting reading material."

"Ah yes, the—what was it?—*War Waged by Wanton Women on Whisky*, or something like that?"

"*The Women's War on Whisky,* by Frances Fuller Victor. I believe you referred to it as seditious literature."

"And right I was." He locked his hands behind his head and stretched luxuriously. "That kind of nonsense is likely to start a riot in most quarters."

Elizabeth smoothed her sand-crusted pantalets free of the tiny, irritating particles and said demurely, "That is exactly what is intended. As a matter of fact, my cousin Annie— whom I am on the way to join as soon as we are rescued—wages a quite energetic battle against alcohol. She once collected more than a thousand abstinence signatures in a single week."

Kincade eyed her warily. "Not many from men, I would imagine."

"On that score you are wrong. Many men sign. Men of good sense, breeding, and—"

"And with a pitchfork at their back, I'll bet." Kincade abandoned his relaxed pose. "This isn't a crusade to dispose of my brandy, is it?"

She turned innocent eyes on him. "Why, Kincade MacKay. What a suspicious creature you are."

"With good reason. I've observed your methods at close range, Miss Lee. They smack of pawky tactics."

"Pawky?"

"Excuse me. A holdover from my Scottish heritage. It means sly. Clandestine. Covert."

"I'm devastated by your low opinion of me."

He snorted rudely. "The devil you are. You enjoy this sort of conversation, don't you?"

Firelight warmed her face, and she couldn't help a smile. "I admit that I do. Shameful, isn't it? You're such a worthwhile adversary at times."

"Only at times?"

Kincade moved to stretch out in front of the fire; he looked lithe and relaxed, and dangerous, a contradiction that would have amazed her if it were anyone else. Not with Kincade. She had discovered in the week they had been marooned on the tiny island that he possessed a multifaceted character that she hadn't begun to understand. Just when she thought he was as arrogant and wicked as she'd named him, he did something nice. And did it so naturally that she knew he had no ulterior motives. He was a mystery.

"So you intend to join up with a militant relative and cleanse the world of demon rum, do you?" Kincade mused aloud. He scooped up a handful of sand and let it trickle slowly from his palm. "I would think that your opponents would be as numerous as this fistful of sand, m'dear. Think twice."

"I've considered it for a long time." She propped her elbow on one knee and cupped her chin in her palm. "I believe in the cause. And I believe that women should have a certain amount of equality."

"Certain amount? Why not march for mastery? Why stop at a little oppression?"

"Really, Kincade." She looked at him with growing irritation. "Women have to begin somewhere. You wouldn't believe the injustices that are done."

He shot her a quick glance. "Oh, wouldn't I? What makes you think women have cornered the market on injustice? And what makes you think a group of chanting females can wipe it out?"

"There are enlightened men who agree with us, you know. In 1851, Wendell Phillips said in a speech for women's rights, 'Every step of progress the world has made has been from scaffold to scaffold and from stake to stake.' Does that suggest anything to you?"

"Right-ho. That dear Wendell was highly intoxicated when he spoke on behalf of militant females. Not that I don't agree with his sentiments."

"But only as they pertain to men, right?"

Kincade stretched like a lazy tomcat and said, "Right. I shudder at the mere thought of women loose in politics. Haven't we men managed to mess them up enough for you? Must you compound the misery for the world?"

"Must you assume we're inept?"

He laughed, and sat up in a graceful swing of his long legs and rested his arms atop his bent knees. "Oh, I think women are quiet 'ept' in some areas."

"I can imagine which areas you mean," Elizabeth said dryly. "Does everything always come down to sex with you, Kincade?" The moment the words were out, she wished she could bring them back. Saying that word so casually to Kincade was a mistake. She saw it at once in the quick narrowing of his eyes, the transfer of his gaze from her face to her body, the rapid appraisal and hot gleam that leaped in the jade depths.

"Eventually," he said in a flat tone that betrayed none of what she saw in his eyes. "I think that's the way it was intended, you know."

"What, for men to go about trying to repopulate the world without regard to common sense or gentler feelings?" A surge of anger made her add hotly, "And to indiscriminately pursue one woman, then leap on the first available female just because the other is momentarily unavailable is the most unforgivable, iniquitous—" She faltered to a halt, seeing his steady gaze fix on her.

Kincade leaned close. "Why do I get the feeling that you aren't talking about your cause anymore?"

Embarrassed, she looked away from him and murmured, "I am, it's just that . . . that I know women who have endured such things."

"You mean been thrown over for another woman?"

She whipped around to glare at him. "No. I mean—I mean that—blast you. Yes. That's exactly what I mean, if you must know."

"Your husband?" he asked softly.

She shook her head and stared past him into the shadowy

world of tall palms and rustling grasses. Night birds made small murmurs in the trees, and an occasional owl screeched loudly as it made a kill. She shuddered.

"Betrothed?"

Her gaze shifted back to his face. Firelight flickered over his features in a shimmery glow, reflecting in his eyes, but she saw no trace of laughter or mockery. She took a deep breath.

"Yes. Martin. I met him in New Orleans last year, and he proposed. I accepted. He had to return to England to make all the necessary arrangements with his family, and I was to follow. But when I arrived . . ." She couldn't continue.

"Merry old Marty was already married?"

Elizabeth looked down at her entwined fingers for a long moment. She didn't cry, but she could feel the hot humiliation flushing her entire body. It made her stomach churn, and she took another deep breath.

"He married not long after his return to England. He claimed he sent me a letter explaining, but I suppose it crossed in the mail packet at the same time I was on my way over. His family had a certain disregard for Americans, you see, and I believe there was a bit of a row about the entire thing. And then, too, there was a young English lady of good family whom he knew a bit too intimately, I guess you could say."

"Ah," Kincade murmured, and Elizabeth was vaguely grateful that she didn't need to elaborate.

"At any rate," she continued, "I discovered that I wasn't that enamored of Martin after all, and my cousin Annie had written telling me I was needed in the WCTU. I knew I could come back to that, and that my destiny—"

"Wait. WCTU? What's that?"

"Women's Christian Temperance Union. Don't you recall my telling you about it?"

He waved a vague hand. "I try not to remember things like that. So that's what you were doing aboard the *Tom Hopkins*."

"Yes. Going home. Or to New Orleans, anyway. Home is in Natchez."

"Where the deuce is Natchez?"

"Mississippi." Elizabeth looked at him curiously. "Where were you going, may I ask? You don't seem to know much about America for someone planning an extended stay."

"I don't." He leaned forward and fed the fire a fresh stick of dry wood. "I've never been there."

"Are you on an adventure?"

He grimaced. "So it seems. I certainly never meant to end up here."

Elizabeth laughed at the pained expression on his face. "Neither did I. But what I meant was, do you have some business in America?"

He turned to look at the fire, and the flames made his eyes gleam as green and dangerous as a panther's. "One can only hope."

She paused in reflection. "Kincade, are you running away from someone or something?"

"Absolutely. Always have been. My uncle used to say it was from life, but I'm more of the belief it was from death. An unaccountable difference of opinion, I'm afraid."

Though Kincade's tone was light and mocking as usual, Elizabeth detected the bitter irony in his words. His thick lashes lowered to hide the smoky green of his eyes from her, as if she could read the truth there. She sat silently for a time; it didn't seem the right moment to ask more questions.

A piece of burning driftwood collapsed in a shower of sparks that spiraled upward, and the sound of ocean waves hitting the beach made a rhythmic thunder that was comforting and intimidating at the same time. Kincade seemed fascinated with the fire, and for a while she thought he must have forgotten the topic of conversation.

Then he said, so softly she almost missed the thread of intensity in his voice, "It's not a pleasant thing to know your own kin wants you dead, you know."

"Your uncle?"

"Yes." A faint smile touched the corners of his mouth. "I suppose it would be fair to say he just wants me out of his way, and doesn't care if I survive or not. If I was locked away forever, he'd be just as content, I believe."

"What an odious man."

"Oh yes, quite. And delights in it. I could tell you things—" He paused, swung to a sitting position, his tone light. "But I won't."

She caught her breath, having had a brief glimpse into his innermost thoughts. "You can tell me whatever you like, you know."

"I know. It just never pays." He rose to his feet in an abrupt motion and came to her, laying his hand atop her head. He lifted a strand of her hair in his palm, watching as it slithered through his fingers. She'd washed it earlier in a clear pool not far away, and it was still damp. She shivered at his touch.

"Cold, sweeting?"

"No. How could I be cold with the weather so balmy?" Another shiver made a liar out of her, and she managed a faint smile as she looked up at him. The words she'd been about to utter died on her lips.

Kincade was gazing down at her with lazy intensity, and there was a slight smile on the erotic curve of his mouth that reminded her of a hungry tomcat, predatory and waiting. She swallowed the sudden lump in her throat.

"Kincade?"

His hand shifted to cup her chin, holding it in his warm palm, his fingers lightly caressing her cheek and jaw. "You're very lovely, you know. Eyes like the turquoise sea, hair like sunlight—do you know what you do to me when you watch me, angel? It makes me burn all over when I catch you at it, and you try to pretend you weren't when I know you were."

Elizabeth squirmed, and felt the hot blood beat a fiery path to her cheeks and spread through her body. He knew.

It was humiliating that he'd noticed the way she looked at him when she couldn't help herself.

"No," she started to say in denial, "I don't—"

"Yes, you do. Why do you think it takes me so long to do the simplest things sometimes? I can feel you watching me when I'm working, or even shaving with that poor excuse for a razor."

She pulled away and said stiffly, "I just thought you were slow."

His laugh was soft, rich, a throaty purr that made her heart beat faster. "I can be, sweeting. Sometimes being slow is preferable. Want me to show you what I mean?"

She would have shaken her head no, but there wasn't time before he'd knelt in front of her and taken her face between his palms. She was acutely aware of his touch and heavy-lashed eyes, the sensual shape of his mouth, and the dark beard stubble over his jaw. He radiated male power and rampant sexuality, and she found herself leaning toward him as if she were in a dream.

Even his kiss had a dreamlike quality to it—slow, burning across her mouth in a light, fluttery caress that was hot and arousing. He seemed to be aware of her reaction. When she drew back slightly, he followed.

"Don't run away, angel," he murmured against her lips. "I won't hurt you. I just want to kiss you, to let you kiss me. Would you like to?"

It was wrong, and it would lead to trouble. She knew that as well as she knew her own name. But there was something in his gentle urgency that moved her, and she felt the faint sparks he'd lit that first day she'd seen him flare into a blaze. Maybe she'd been waiting for him to kiss her again; some nights she'd thought of it, and remembered the way he'd touched her intimately in the boat. She'd been expecting it, waiting for it, and he must have known.

Stupid, stupid, stupid, she told herself when he folded her into his embrace. She was only trying to assuage the raw hurt and humiliation Martin had dealt her. It would end badly.

But then a small voice argued inside that he wouldn't really care why she yielded to his kisses, would he? He'd not said he loved her, and maybe this was what she needed to cure the pain inside. Maybe love, even physical, would ease that hurt.

Elizabeth breathed deeply, inhaling the musky male scent of him and the salty tang of the sea air, and lifted her arms and put them around Kincade's neck.

Chapter 8

"HE NEEDS tae be stopped."

Ian's growled comment seemed to shake Tabitha from her wide-eyed daze. "What? Oh. Yes. Yes, he certainly does." When Ian made a movement of one arm, she put out a hand to halt him. "But maybe not now."

"No' now? When? After the bairn comes screamin' into the world?"

"Of course not." Tabitha gave him an impatient glance. "It hadn't progressed nearly that far. This is just a kiss. And I think what they're about to discover will help them both."

"Riddles, madam. Ye're talking in riddles."

"Not really, Ian. You see, I noticed the last time I had to help someone, that a certain degree of intimacy follows companionship between a man and a woman, and it somehow seems to bind them closer together. Do you understand?"

"I understand tha' he's about tae make a mistake wi' the lassie."

"Think for a moment. During the past week Kincade has actually made great progress. He's worked hard to build a shelter that she will like, and deferred to her several times in an argument. Isn't that a bit out of character for him?"

"Aye, an' I'm thinking he'll get wha' he wants an' go right back tae being a blackguard."

90

"Possibly. Men do tend to think that way. Unless they're in love, however."

"In love?" Ian's incredulous gaze shifted from Tabitha to the embracing couple, then back. "I hae seen no sign tha' he's in love, madam."

"Most men never see the signs." Tabitha nodded thoughtfully. "My opinion is that we should let them make this decision without our interference. He is, of course, your kinsman, so you have the final word."

Tabitha's unusual deference to his judgment gave Ian pause, and he said grudgingly, "Aye, then, we'll no' interfere wi' him now. But I dinna think we will like th' consequences."

"P'raps not. Why don't you come with me for now? After all, you did so well at spotting that wrecked ship and getting its supplies washed ashore here that perhaps you can spot a rescue vessel for them. Then, with a bit of ingenuity you can send it sailing this way and remove *both* of them from temptation, don't you think?"

"*I* think, madam," Ian said with a sigh, "tha' ye're a mistress of manipulation, tha's wha' I think."

"Oh no," Tabitha said with a laugh. "But thank you for the compliment. I merely *arrange* matters, as you will learn to do. Remember—there are times it's better to let them get burned a little as a warning than to have them consumed by an inferno later."

"Saints preserve us all," Ian muttered as he followed Tabitha into the surf. They rode the crest of a wave and disappeared into the mist.

When Elizabeth put her arms around his neck, Kincade almost pulled away. This was too easy. He shouldn't give in to the urges that had been prodding him so hard for the past week and a half. He knew better. What could come of it but trouble? After all, they were on this island alone, and it wasn't as if he could walk away afterward. Where would he

go when she began to pout and cling and want more of him
than he was willing to give?

But it was hard to wrestle with logic and reason when
there was a fire blazing inside him that threatened to turn
him to bonemeal and ash. He'd been riding this particular
fence for far too long, and his need for Elizabeth was almost
out of control.

The long days spent watching her do the most mundane,
domestic tasks in her thin pantalets and the shirt tied just
beneath her small, firm breasts had taken their toll. He'd
memorized every inch of her he could see, and imagined the
rest of her so many times it had become a consuming need
to discover the truth.

Kincade lifted her from her knees and dragged her close
to him, his palms on each side of her face as his mouth
lowered to crush her lips. He kissed her with an urgency that
did nothing to quench his fire.

The hunger made him harsher than he intended; his
fingers closed with involuntary cruelty in the wealth of her
silky, pale hair, clutching it as if he were drowning. For a
moment he felt as if he were, as if waves of water were
closing over his head and sucking him under. He couldn't
breathe. He could only feel. There was only this, the satin
press of her skin against his bare chest, the warm, female
smell of her in his nostrils, and he lost all sense of time and
place and reason.

Ridiculous, really, he told himself in a brief moment of
clarity, that he should be so skirt-smitten. Especially when
the object of his desire wasn't wearing skirts, but an
appealing bit of cloth that only made him flinch every time
he looked in her direction.

"No," he said against her mouth when she tried to pull
away, the word hoarse and sounding like a growl, "don't
move away from me. I won't . . . hurt . . . you."

He didn't mean to hurt her. He only wanted to savor the
sweetness of her lips, caress the smooth fabric of skin and
muscle that lay temptingly beneath his open palms. And oh

God, he wanted to put himself inside her and show her how wonderful it was to touch the clouds.

"Kincade . . ." Her voice was soft, sounding drugged with response, and it made his body tighten with the fierce desire to possess her fully.

He dragged her up against his body, cupping her buttocks in his palms to crush her against the solid length of him. She shuddered, and murmured soft, indistinct words in his ear. He tried to hold to the last vestige of restraint, but when she moved against him, her hips rubbing across him in innocent eroticism, he groaned aloud.

She was awkward and inexperienced, and instead of cooling his desire, it only inflamed his need for her. He wanted to share that need with her, make her want him, too. He unfastened her blouse, his fingers swift and efficient at the knot under her breasts, his hand sliding between the folds of material.

When he cupped her breast in his palm, he drew in a ragged breath and buried his face in her hair. His other arm curved behind her, supporting her as she sagged against him.

"Kincade . . ."

She couldn't say anything else, it seemed, just his name in a husky litany that drove him even closer to the edge of control.

"Angel," he muttered, and kissed the arch of her throat and her mouth, then slid downward to the tempting valley between her high, upthrust breasts. She was a marvel of color and texture, of creamy skin and rose-tipped breasts, of golden peach where the sun had tinted exposed areas. She felt soft, inviting, a sensual feast for a starving man.

He bent her backward, sliding one hand up to capture a taut nipple between his thumb and finger, hearing her sudden gasp as he rolled it in a leisurely, erotic motion. He kissed her again, and when she opened her lips slightly, he met her tongue with his. Her body shivered with reaction;

she moaned softly as he continued to tease the taut nub with his fingers.

Slowly he moved his head back down, until he was only a few inches from the tight, tempting peak of her other breast. When his lips closed around it and his tongue flicked across the bud in lightning-quick darts, she arched up into him and wound her hands in his hair, holding his head still.

"Kincade . . . please . . . please . . ."

He moved with her toward the cloth-covered grass mats in front of the fire, slowly knelt without releasing her, taking her with him. Her arms were still around his neck, her breasts flattened against his chest, so that he could feel the tight buds of her nipples rubbing against his bare skin enticingly.

Still kissing her, he laid her gently back and smoothed one hand over the slender span of rib cage and under the waistband of her drawers. She was warm, so warm, heated silk and exquisite velvet . . . his hand slid down to her flat little belly, caressing and exploring. When his fingers touched the nest of silky curls at the juncture of her thighs, she jumped slightly, and he lifted his head to gaze down into her eyes.

She looked up at him, long lashes curling over chips of azure sea, trust and some other emotion he didn't want to recognize shining in her gaze. For a moment he paused. She trusted him. He saw it in her eyes. *Oh dear God, what a time to discover I have a conscience after all. . . .*

"I can't," he said thickly, half groaning, half panting. "You don't know what's happening to you."

Elizabeth took his face between her palms, and her small pink tongue came out to lick her lips before she whispered, "Yes, I do. I'm a bit inexperienced, not ignorant."

"Lizzie . . ."

"*Elizabeth.*"

"Angel . . . God." He leaned over her, his weight braced on one hand spread on the mat below her, head hanging down as he struggled for control. "You don't know what you're saying." He lifted his head, looked back into her eyes with a tortured groan. "I didn't mean for you to—you're supposed to stop me, dammit."

She lifted slightly and curled her arms around his neck again and drew him slowly down to meet her parted lips. In a soft, almost pleading voice, she said against his mouth, "I don't want to stop you, Kincade. I want you to teach me. Teach me what you know."

"Jeezus!" The word exploded from him almost violently, and he closed his eyes against the soft desire he saw burning in her face. He couldn't do it. In spite of the touch of her damp skin under his palm, that moist crevice beneath his exploring fingers. She didn't seem to know how to move, what to do, but clutched at him with wild, awkward motions. *Inexperienced.* Innocent. He couldn't hurt this innocence. It was a sin to tarnish sweet trust with what he wanted to do to her. Unless . . .

His lashes lifted. He heard his own voice sound tight and rough, almost desperate when he asked, "Have you ever been with a man, angel?"

She shook her head, a cascade of wanton gold curls in the firelight. "No. Not like this. Kisses, yes."

An entire string of lurid words formed in his mind, and he spared a wish that it was different. He looked down at her in the soft fire glow, at her lovely breasts, soft skin, the rosy flush that invited his lips to explore, and sat back on his heels. He moved his hand and covered her exposed curves with her shirt.

"This is insane. I can't do it." He raked a spread hand through his hair, frustration welling in him so high and hard that he wanted to slam his fist into the sand to release the tension. His groin hurt, and he shifted to ease the pressure. She was looking at him, confusion plainly written on her lovely features. He laughed harshly.

"Well you might stare at me. It isn't every day you see a fool by choice, sweetheart. Close your shirt. *Close your shirt, curse you!"* She complied hastily, her cheeks flushing a bright pink that made her eyes look even bluer. He buried his face in his palm.

He felt her move, heard the rustle of her clothing, the whisk of sand shifting. The fire popped, and somewhere in the trees a bird called out, muted and soft, as if afraid.

Elizabeth cleared her throat. "I suppose you're right." He looked up at her warily. She was shaking as if chilled, and her chin was tilted upward in a defiant gesture that almost made him smile. "It would be terribly awkward if we were to become . . . intimate . . . here. There would be no place for you to escape me, would there?"

Her words so closely imitated his earlier thoughts that he jerked in surprise. A faint, wry smile curled her lips at his reaction.

"Yes, I thought that might have something to do with it. After all—where could you go to avoid me?"

He shrugged, made his voice light. "It would be difficult."

Firelight gleamed on her pale hair as she nodded and said, "I suppose I should thank you, but somehow I don't feel very grateful at the moment."

Kincade just watched her, and felt a wash of shame when she rose to her feet and walked into the shadows beyond the firelight and hut. He couldn't recall ever having felt so bad about the way he'd treated a woman. And the irony of it was, this time he had tried to be noble.

Still shaking, Elizabeth went to sit by the small pool of fresh water she'd found their first day on the island. It was ringed by outcroppings of rock and exotic flowers, and Kincade had hacked a path to it with a sharp knife he called a machete that he'd found in one of the crates washed ashore.

She tucked her knees up under her chin and wrapped her arms around her legs. Why had he stopped? And even more disturbing—why hadn't she *insisted* that he stop? Instead she had been angry and hurt because he had. Not very logical, she admitted to herself wryly.

She rocked back slightly and curled her fingers under her sand-crusted toes and stretched. He'd been right when he said she watched him. She did. She couldn't help it. He was so well made, an Apollo in tattered breeches and bare feet. His physical form took her breath away, made her feel all hot and funny inside. There was a grace and masculine beauty to Kincade MacKay that she considered almost indecent, and certainly tempting. She rather thought the devil would look like him, packaged in an enticing frame with unholy beauty gracing his features.

Yet it was more than his appearance that drew her.

Almost helplessly Elizabeth wondered when she had begun to look forward to their verbal sparring matches. She liked making him angry, irritating him, then making him laugh. Even correcting his improper usage of her name had a certain enjoyment. It was a triumph of sorts, she supposed, that she could affect him at all. He certainly affected her, with every word, every glance, every lazy movement of his efficient, hard-muscled body.

She swallowed a surge of chagrin and embarrassment, and tilted back her head to look up at the sky. Moonlight filtered through the thick canopy of leaves, and she could smell the faint fragrance of night-blooming flowers. They grew wild, with a heady, sweet scent that was intoxicating. She'd seen birds with brilliant plumage decorating the trees like scarlet, green, and yellow ornaments.

If she had to be stranded somewhere, she supposed that it could have been worse. Not that this island only had the beautiful creations of nature, however, as she had glimpsed the dangerous ones, too. Wild pigs thrashed about in the thick underbrush, and she'd glimpsed a huge snake as thick as Kincade's forearm draped in a banyan tree. It had slithered with silent efficiency toward her, and if Kincade hadn't moved quickly with his sharp knife, she might have been devoured and digested by now.

Pelicans, herons, cranes, and flamingos decorated the island with colorful beauty and graceful flight, and she rarely returned from a fishing foray without an exquisitely beautiful new seashell to add to her collection. Black-and-white wood ibises nested high in the tops of knobby-trunked cypress trees and wild tamarinds, filling the air with raucous cries that cut into the night.

Pale blue and lime-green water glittered under the hot sun, remarkably clear in places. Sometimes as she waded in the shallows, she peered through the water to the waving forests of sea fans and coral. Tiny crabs and other crustaceans lived in the serene cove. It had been easy to form a trap of baling wire and tightly woven vines, and she'd managed to catch crabs to fill their cooking pot.

It was a tropical paradise, as Kincade had so mockingly pointed out, but it wasn't enough. Survival wasn't enough. She wanted to go home, to live in civilization. There was a restless yearning inside her that needed to be filled, a sense that her life was meaningful.

There had to be more to life than just surviving, though that could be difficult enough. The days stretched endlessly ahead of her without meaning. There were the daily tasks to be done, of course, the gathering of food or mending their shelter, but Kincade took care of most of that.

He kept the signal fire lit, and added to their hut. He set her to weaving grass mats with the harsh-bladed grasses on the island, and showed her how to cover them with what was left of her skirt. They made fairly comfortable beds on the floor of the hut. Kincade had even managed to fashion crude furniture from saplings, reeds, and some kind of cane.

They both should have been too exhausted from focusing on survival to think of—other things.

Elizabeth rested her forehead on her drawn-up knees. He was right. She didn't know what was happening to her. She only knew that he could ease that ache inside her somehow, that insistent throbbing that had not ceased simply because he'd removed his hand. She knew enough about the mating process to know that Kincade could assuage that ache; she also knew that it would change her forever, just as he knew it.

Restless, she shifted position on the rock, then stood up. She should go back to the hut. There was no point in delaying her return because there was no escaping him. There was no escaping herself.

Chapter 9

"WHAT ARE those?"

Kincade glanced up from the small pasteboard rectangles he held in one hand. "Devil's Bible. History of the Four Kings. A Child's Best Guide to the Gallows—playing cards, m'dear. Found 'em in one of those crates, along with a pair of dice—children in the wood, my uncle used to call 'em. Care to try your luck?"

"I believe you've already informed me that *you're* the lucky one." Elizabeth shifted on the bark bench. It was early afternoon, and hot. To escape the heat they had retreated to the shade of the hut beneath spreading fan palms and banyan trees.

Kincade flipped a hand through the cards, and she watched in fascination as they riffled through his palms. They looked flimsy, and a little worn. The backs of the cards had pictures of small dogs in various poses.

"Luck is usually made, sweeting, not inherited." He smiled slightly. "It takes a certain amount of concentration and a good memory. For instance, if I were to deal you some cards, could you foresee which ones you would get?"

"Of course not."

"I can."

She scooted closer and frowned at him. "How?"

"Ah, that's a secret." He shuffled the cards again; his lean fingers were quick and graceful, and the cards flowed from one palm to the other smoothly. "I tell you what—if I can tell you which cards you chose, I win."

"Win what?"

He shrugged. "Whatever you want. Name the bet."

"There's a trick to this, isn't there?"

"No trick. I either name the cards correctly or I don't." A faint smile curled one corner of his mouth. "What have you got to lose, angel?"

She laughed. "All right. I'll put up two of my favorite seashells."

"Seashells." Kincade looked pained. "With all the shells lying around on the sand and in the water, that seems a bit shabby, my sweet."

"Sorry, I seem to have left my ten-pound notes aboard the *Tom Hopkins*."

"Not very foresighted of you. All right. Seashells it is. My choice?"

She nodded solemnly. "Your choice."

Elizabeth knew he would cheat, but she was ready for something to interrupt the boredom of the day. She'd already gathered oysters and a few crabs, and it was too hot and sticky to nap. Card tricks were a much better option.

"My father used to play cards," she said, and he flicked her a glance from beneath his heavy lashes.

"So did mine. I hope your father had more sense as to the stakes." Before she could ask a question, he spread the cards on the grass mat between them and said, "Choose."

"How many?"

"Three, four, however many you like."

She hesitated, then slid three cards from the fanned pack. "All right. I have them."

He nodded. A shaft of sunlight glittered in his black hair as he leaned back. "Now look at 'em, remember 'em, then put 'em back."

She did as he said, and leaned her elbows on her crossed knees, resting her chin atop her clasped hands as she watched him shuffle them again. "Tell me what I chose," she said, anticipating that he would do it.

"Five of clubs, three of diamonds, queen of spades."

"Wrong." She laughed with delight. "Almost right— two out of three."

He shook his head regretfully. "Guess I'll have to work on that trick some more. Here. Let's try it again. Choose four cards this time."

She did, and again he missed one. "You now owe me four seashells," she reminded him, and he flashed her a crooked smile.

"I don't have any shells. It'll take me all day just to find four that will suit you. Tell you what—give me one more chance to break even. Double or nothing this time."

"Double or nothing. Do you mean—"

"If you win, I owe you twelve seashells. If I win—aw, I hate seashells. If I win . . ." His voice trailed off, and he thought for a moment before he looked back up at her. "If I win, you owe me a kiss."

"A kiss . . ."

"What have you got to lose, angel? You can choose as many cards as you want for me to try and guess."

"Somehow I think I shouldn't do this," she retorted, but she smiled. After a short silence she said, "All right. Twelve seashells to a kiss that you can't name all the cards I choose."

"Done."

As he shuffled the cards he gave her a lazy smile, and his eyes glinted softly beneath the brush of his lashes. For some reason she felt a slight qualm. Silly. It was only a game. And he didn't seem to be very good at it.

When he'd spread them on the mat again, Elizabeth chose carefully, singling out cards from between others in case he'd memorized the order of them. She pulled out six, and held them cupped in her hand as she spread them to study. After a moment of concentration she slid them back into the deck and put her hand over them.

"Let me shuffle."

He looked amused. "By all means. Help yourself."

Rather clumsily, and with none of Kincade's practiced skill, she shuffled the cards, turned them over to satisfy herself that the ones she'd chosen were not somehow arranged in a secret order, then put them down. She looked up at him with a gleam of triumph in her eyes.

"What did I pull out?"

"The six of clubs, knave of hearts, ten of diamonds, two of diamonds . . . um . . . king of clubs, and three of spades."

Elizabeth stared at him. He stared back, his black brow lifted inquiringly. She met his guileless gaze and gave a helpless shrug.

"That . . . that's right. How did you do that?"

"Concentration, angel." Leaning forward, he put his elbow on his bent knee and gazed into her eyes. "Now, there is a little matter of payment?"

"Payment?"

"You know—seashells and kisses."

"Oh." She flushed. This was dangerous ground. Neither of them had mentioned the other night, not daring to invite trouble. Yet here he was, near enough to start her pulses racing and do queer things to her insides, demanding his kiss. His voice was soft, husky, tempting.

"Not going to renege, are you? Extremely bad form. In some circles, that would cause talk. Maybe a duel." His slow, lazy smile was sensuously wicked. "I won't challenge you, though."

"My heartfelt gratitude." She tilted her head to one side, regarding him with grave attention. "I never renege, Mr. MacKay."

"Mr. MacKay? How formal we're being. Is this your demeanor every time you lose a bet?"

"No, only when I lose bets to gamesters."

"Gamester? Me? Why, Miss Lee, I'm shocked that you even know about such scoundrels."

She gave him her sweetest smile and said, "I've been living on this island with one for two weeks now."

"Hussy," he said with a laugh. "But you're right. So, are you going to pay up, or do I have to call in the Bow Street Runners?"

"Oh no, I'll pay my debt." She leaned forward and gave him a quick peck on the cheek, then sat back on her heels.

His gaze was faintly reproachful. "If you had won, I wouldn't have cheated you with half your seashells."

"Meaning?"

"That wasn't even half a kiss."

Somewhere in the treetops a bird called out, its voice loud and lilting; breakers crashed on the sandy shore, and the wind rustled palm fronds with a slight noise. Elizabeth inhaled softly. She knew better; if she allowed him even this one small liberty, she was inviting disaster. Kincade was watching her with a faint half-mocking smile that dared her to refuse him, mocked her if she did not. She took another deep breath and decided to take the chance that he would behave honorably again.

"Close your eyes." Though he lifted a brow, he did as she said. Elizabeth studied him a moment, the rugged angles and planes of his face, the beard stubble that always seemed to grow back too quickly no matter how often he shaved, and the thick brush of his lashes lying like silken fibers against his cheeks. A small scar touched one side of his face, a thin white line pale against the dark teak of his skin.

Elizabeth scooted closer to him across the grass mat, and reached out and took his face lightly in her palms. She bent forward and brushed her lips across his in a fleeting caress, then touched the tip of her tongue to his mouth. He stiffened, and she felt his chest rise and fall with ragged rhythm. His lips parted slightly, and she teased them with her tongue until her own breathing was too fast.

He tasted of salt, and brandy, too, she thought, though she wasn't certain. There was a clean masculine scent to him, arousing and faintly drugging at the same time, making her want to lean closer and breathe more deeply of him. Her eyes closed, and she slanted her lips over his and slid her tongue into his open mouth.

That simple yet complicated move unleashed the invisible chain that seemed to be holding Kincade still; his arms came around her with a sudden force that pushed the breath from her lungs in a *whoosh*. He inhaled it, one hand spreading over the back of her head as he moved his lips over hers, and she knew then she'd lost any control she had over the situation.

Kincade dragged the hard flat of his palm over her back and down to her buttocks, curving her against his body as he rose to his knees. She felt the heat of his arousal even through his pants, burning against her as he held her close to him. An odd throbbing began deep inside her, aching and spreading upward, shortening her breath and turning her insides to a hot, quivery stew.

It felt as if he were touching her everywhere, when the only parts of their bodies to touch was from breast to hip. Elizabeth shivered when his free hand moved to push aside the edge of her blouse. Her hands were trapped between them in small fists, and his move released them. Instinctively she spread her palms against his bare chest to hold him away.

The soft round of her palms encountered the thunder of his heartbeat beneath them, his quickened breathing, and the tight curve of his muscle as he resisted her effort.

"No, angel," he muttered, "don't push me away."

Push him away? She could barely breathe, much less exert enough pressure to push him away. Her head fell back as he kissed her cheek, brushed over her lips in a caress as light as a butterfly's wings, then husked over her fevered skin to the arch of her throat. His mouth pressed hotly, nipping lightly then kissing the tiny bites he inflicted before she could protest.

Kincade rearranged her in his embrace so that the hard, hot detail of his body fit into the notch of her thighs, a steady pressure that made her writhe with uncertainty. She wanted something; she didn't know what. It eluded her, that answer to the aching inside.

His hand on her breast moved to cup the firm flesh in a tender caress, his fingers teasing the taut peak until she moaned. He lifted his head and gazed down at her, his hard jade eyes glittering with triumph.

Elizabeth closed her eyes. She couldn't look at him and know that he was aware of her reaction, aware of the hot, melting center that ached so sweetly. It was maddening to have these reactions and have him know it. . . .

The sound of the surf grew louder and louder in her ears until she thought it would overwhelm her. Kincade bent his head to kiss her again, dragging her into him with soft caresses and tortured breaths. She was on fire with it, on fire with the need to touch him as he was touching her.

When he released her abruptly and held her at arm's length to gaze at her from under his lashes, she felt as if she'd been tossed into the sea to bob aimlessly. She could barely breathe; her lungs worked with strangled gasps.

Kincade's erotic mouth curved into a faint smile. "Paid in full, sweetheart."

His words rambled about in her brain for a moment while she tried to make sense of them. "Oh," she said finally. "I suppose so."

Why had he stopped? She didn't understand. He was as unsettled as she was. Didn't he want her? She flushed and looked away, and he laughed softly.

"See what you do to me?"

She glanced back, saw the steady gleam of hunger in his eyes and the obvious arousal of his body. She struggled to sound as nonchalant.

"You do the same thing to me, you know. Perhaps we should have stuck with the seashells."

"Probably."

Kincade rocked back on his heels, then rose to his feet and stared down at her for a long, long moment. Nothing was said. In the silence, a wood ibis gave a shrill cry that could be heard above the pounding surf. She shivered and shut her eyes. This was madness. She would go insane if she had to stay here alone with him much longer. All her common sense seemed to flee when he touched her, and the mental vision she had of throwing herself at his feet and begging him to take her was horrifying.

When she opened her eyes, Kincade was looking beyond her to the curl of surf and blinding white curve of beach. Blue-green waters caught the sunlight and threw it back in glittering chips; a soft breeze rustled the broad fronds of palm trees and dark strands of his hair. He turned to her again, his expression remote and somehow angry.

Kincade took a step back, his bare feet sinking into the warm sand beyond the grass mat. "What do you want from me, angel?" He spread his hands. "I can't give you anything. Not like what you need. I don't have it to give."

Her flush deepened. "I don't want anything from you."

"The hell you don't." His growling reply made her look at him quickly, and he bent to take her hands into his. "If you didn't want anything, sweetheart, you wouldn't look at me like you do. And you wouldn't kiss me like you do. Even if you won't admit it, you want this. . . ." His hand moved over her body in a skillful caress that made her gasp. "And this, too . . ."

She knocked his hand away. "Stop it."

"Why? We both want the same thing. Only, I'm not too hypocritical to say that I do. You're hiding behind female protests just like women have always done, while crying out the other side of your mouth that you want equality. Well, equality means taking the bad with the good. You want to be like a man? Fine. Don't be so bloody coy about sex. Men aren't. Find me a man who *won't* tell a woman he wants to bed her when he does, however he sugarcoats it."

She surged to her feet, glaring at him. "I'm certain that the men you know are so blunt and crude, but most of the men I've met are gentlemen."

The curve of his mouth tightened. ''Don't complain to me about it. God knows, I've tried to make up for 'em.''

''Curse you, Kincade.''

His eyes narrowed. ''You're too late on that score, angel. I've been cursed for more years that you've been on earth.''

Tension crackled between them; Elizabeth felt like breaking into wild sobs. Without saying another word, she turned and fled into the trees behind the hut.

Kincade refused to follow her. He knew he should, but he threw himself down on the grass mat just outside the hut and crossed his arms behind his head. He stared up at the trees and pieces of sky overhead.

What had possessed him to tease them both that way? He knew how tight a line she walked, saw it in her glances and every movement she made. He walked the same tightrope, but the major difference was he knew there was no safety net underneath. Elizabeth had no idea why she felt as she did, nor what was involved in easing that restless ache.

''God,'' he muttered, and closed his eyes. If he had any sense at all, he would move to the other side of this island and put as much distance between them as possible. It was a losing proposition any way he looked at it. If he made love to her—his body responded at the mere thought of it—it would certainly ease the tension between them.

But the consequences to Elizabeth could be disastrous. Not even considering the possibility that he might lose himself enough to put a baby in her, he knew that though she claimed to be a modern woman, she would expect him to love her once he'd taken her virginity. That would be fine as long as they were stuck on this scrap of sand and trees in the middle of the Atlantic. The thing was, it was only a matter of time before a ship came along and found them.

And Kincade knew that Elizabeth Lee would expect him to love her off this island as well as on. He wasn't at all certain he could do that. He'd spent his entire life avoiding

emotional entanglements, and he didn't intend to let his
male urges catapult him into a mess now.

That was his intention.

A mocking smile curved his mouth. What was it about the
road to hell being paved with good intentions?

He closed his eyes to block out the sight of blue sky and
brilliant green foliage. A vision of Elizabeth, her blouse
open and her small, perfect breasts bared to his touch and
mouth clouded his mind, and he groaned. He thought of her
too often this way, with her hair in a sultry tumble around
her shoulders and her lips parted and moist and tempting,
blue eyes shaded by silky dark lashes and half-closed
with desire . . . *Christ*. It was a wonder he wasn't insane
from it.

Half the time he thought he should go ahead and take her
and damn the consequences; the other half of the time he
told himself he may be a bastard, but he wasn't *that* big of
a bastard. It should, he thought wryly, be interesting to see
which half of him won the battle.

Normally it would have been an easy decision. But with
Elizabeth it wasn't. Despite his reservations, his resistance,
and the certain knowledge that it was dangerous, he'd
grown to like Elizabeth Lee. Sometimes he was tempted to
tell her that, but he didn't want to make a fool of himself.
Not again. He'd done that far too often in his life.

He grimaced with wry humor and sat up to retrieve the
bottle of brandy he'd hidden in the knobby shadows of a
cypress tree. The roots provided perfect hiding places from
nosy female teetotalers. Elizabeth was so ingenuous, though
she tried hard to be worldly and modern, chattering about
her ridiculous cause as if it were the quest for the Holy Grail
instead of liquor.

Kincade took a healthy sip of brandy then recorked it.
Quests usually ended the same; the only result was the loss
of life or dignity or both. Nothing mattered in the end. There
were damned few Holy Grails, and he certainly didn't think
temperance was a good cause.

Not that his opinion mattered in the least to Elizabeth Lee, because she obviously believed in it. She would defend her bloody cause with all due dignity and enthusiasm, despite anything he might say to the contrary. That was another trait he liked about her, her tenacity.

Plague take her.

Kincade replaced the brandy in its hiding place between webbed roots, then lay back to watch the sun rise higher and higher before it began the downward descent on the western side of the island. As it trailed fire and crimson-tinged shadows behind he began to worry about Elizabeth.

She hadn't returned. Not that there was a great deal to worry about, but there were alligators on their little island paradise that just might decide Elizabeth would do nicely for an afternoon snack.

"Bloody hell," he muttered finally, and sat up to rake a hand through his hair. "Inconvenient bit of female."

After a moment he decided he'd best go look for her and endure his punishment, whatever it was. He ambled down the path he'd hacked through the foliage and tangled vines, admiring his handiwork. If necessity was the mother of invention, survival was the father. It was strange what survival would force a man to do. Manual labor or exertion in any form had never been one of his favorite pastimes, a fact that had frequently driven his former tutors into paroxysms of frustration.

Now, against all likelihood, he found himself a carpenter, blacksmith, architect, and general handyman. It was a good joke on him, he supposed. Fate must be snickering up its sleeve.

Kincade found Elizabeth asleep on a sun-washed rock above the small, wooded pool of fresh water. It was the only fresh water on the island, beginning somewhere in the middle of the limestone rocks and wending its way through thick trees and over a jumble of low, flat boulders to splash into a moss- and flower-ringed crevasse.

Finding her was a shock. By tacit consent, neither of them

visited the pool when the other was there, as it was a washing and bathing facility as well as source of fresh water.

He shouldn't have come, he told himself, not this close anyway. Not without shouting a warning first. His throat tightened.

Elizabeth was asleep on the rock, her bare body soaking up warm, filtered sunshine like a sponge. She looked like a golden goddess lying there, her cloud of sun-streaked hair swirling around her and framing the impudent thrust of her breasts.

Kincade leaned back against a tree and stared. He'd seen her body before, of course, but there was something so subtly arousing about her lying there in innocent, naked sleep that he had to hold to the trunk of the tree to keep from falling to his knees. He was only a few yards from her, almost close enough to reach out and lift a silky fall of hair or caress the swell of her tempting belly.

A shudder ran through him. The noise of the waterfall grew too loud for him to bear, thundering down in tinkling harmony with the blood beating through his body. He had to leave, now, before she woke or he did something foolish.

He must have made some sound, or maybe Elizabeth sensed he was there. She stirred and sat up, and her gaze fell at once on him as she shook the hair from her eyes. She had a dazed, sleep-drugged expression on her face.

''Kincade?''

Her voice was soft, languorous, almost drowned out by the sound of the falling water and heated pulse of blood in his ears. To Kincade, it was a sultry siren's song, a soft beckoning.

Without stopping to consider the consequences, he moved toward her.

Chapter 10

IT SEEMED to take her several seconds to realize that she was unclothed; by the time her brain absorbed the message, Kincade had reached her side. He didn't give her time to protest, didn't give himself time to think.

He pushed away the hands she lifted to cover herself with the scrap of her damp blouse, and said against her throat, "It's too late for that, angel. I've already seen every inch of your beautiful body."

Her head fell back; he kissed her throat, her mouth, the line of her jaw, and her closed eyelids, using the weight of his body as leverage against her feeble struggle. When she murmured something inaudible, he dragged her into his embrace, lifted her from the flat, warm surface of the rock, and carried her to the springy moss cushion beneath a tree.

She was shaking. He covered her body with his, threading his fingers through hers and pushing her bare arms back into the moss with gentle pressure.

"I won't hurt you," he said against the satiny curve of her cheek, and knew he lied. "God . . . I want to hold you close like this. . . ." His mouth covered her half-parted lips, smothered the faint sound she made, then drifted down to lavish attention on the tiny pulse throbbing in the hollow of her throat. His breathing was a harsh rasp.

"Kincade . . . I want . . . you to love me," she whispered into the heated air between them, and he heard the doubt in her voice. A warning sounded somewhere in the back of his mind, and he lifted his head to gaze down at her with a faint frown. He pushed a damp tendril of white-gold hair from her eyes.

"Angel—are you sure?" he managed to get out thickly.

"I'm sure." She looked wide-eyed and breathless, as guileless as an infant and just as vulnerable. A twinge of guilt shot through him, and he pulled slightly away. But then she shifted under him, rubbing her breasts across his bare chest in a way that made tiny sparks shoot through every nerve ending he had.

Kincade resisted the surge of unfamiliar guilt. It wasn't as if she didn't want him, as if he hadn't wanted her for much longer than he cared to think about. And it wasn't as if he could help himself.

He lowered his head again to kiss her, releasing one of her hands as he smoothed his palm down from the sweet curve of her throat to the swell of her breast, cupping it. She moaned again, an arousing, throaty sound, and his kiss grew deeper, drowning out any lingering reservations he had. There was only this, her sun-warmed skin and the delicious tang of her female fragrance, the scent of cool water and some sort of flower. His kisses whispered over her forehead, temples, lips, until he shifted so that his mouth was grazing her breast. She arched into his embrace with closed eyes, a dreamy smile curving her lips and igniting a tender fire inside him.

Aphrodite. Venus. A hundred goddesses rolled into this one delectable creature in his arms. He felt helpless against the softer emotions she provoked, the way she was giving herself to him so freely.

Kincade blew his breath softly over her breast and felt her shiver. He grasped her hand, pulled her fingers down the curve of his chest, pressed her palm against the flat ridges of his belly. He shook with reaction to her touch.

When her lashes lifted and she stared into his face with a

questioning gaze, he murmured, "See how easy it is to affect me, angel?"

A faint smile curved her mouth; doubt clouded her eyes for a moment, turning brilliant sapphire to a smoky blue. She slid her hand slowly over the taut skin of his bare stomach, and he closed his eyes and shuddered.

Elizabeth curled her hand around his hard length, touching lightly at first, her fingers shaping him and caressing him through his pants. Her hand stopped, and she looked up at him with wide eyes.

"Kincade? Are you certain that—" She paused, swallowed, and began again. "I mean, I know how it's done in theory, but you seem so . . . overlarge."

He smothered a laugh, knowing it would offend her. "I'm gratified to hear that, angel, but I assure you that I am only normal. Though it may seem unlikely to you now, your body will adjust quite nicely."

"Oh." She didn't seem convinced, and gave him a skeptical glance before her hand began to move hesitantly over him. He tensed, gritting his teeth as her inexperienced explorations took him ever closer to the edge. Finally he pushed her hand aside and reached down to unbutton his trousers.

Excitement made him clumsy, and her hand brushed him in agonizing caresses as she tried to help. He wanted to crush her to him, to pull her against him and put himself inside her. God, he wanted her with a savage ferocity that was frightening.

"You're killing me," he muttered when his trousers were undone and her hand closed around him. She didn't seem to hear. She was absorbed in her curious explorations, and he closed his eyes and tried to think of something except what she was doing. It didn't help. He groaned at the whisper-light touch of her fingers on him.

"Kincade?"

His hand closed over hers; sweat beaded his brow. "Don't do that for a minute, angel. Lord . . . don't."

"What. This?"

His eyes flew open and focused on her face as her fingers tightened around him. "Yes, *that,* you heartless little hussy. If you don't stop, I'll be the only one to have any fun."

"Hmm." Her hand grew still, but didn't move away. "You usually get all the fun, don't you."

"If I can." He swallowed another groan as her hand slid up in a teasing stroke, then grabbed her wrist and held it firmly. "Maybe I should show you how it feels to be teased unmercifully."

Her eyes widened when he sat back, spreading his thighs between her legs. He held her that way a moment, staring down at her in mute appreciation. How had he ever thought her too skinny? He must have been insane. The creamy, sun-touched skin of her thighs flowed into slender hips and a small waist before curving up to the high, firm thrust of her breasts. They were small, rounded, dazzling temptation with pink-tipped, impudent nipples.

He stared at her in helpless admiration, feeling as if he balanced on the edge of some deep, yawning chasm that could swallow him up without a trace if he yielded to that temptation. As if in a dream, he saw his hands reach out to touch her, to caress that satiny skin with light, teasing explorations that made her shiver.

Then he drew back, afraid to keep touching her or he'd lose what little hold he had on his control. She was staring at him with wide eyes, and he managed a shaky smile that was supposed to be reassuring.

"You're beautiful, angel. Jesus, I don't know how I've kept my hands off you so long. I think I deserve some sort of medal, or at the least a commendation."

His teasing words made her smile, and there was a look of relief in her eyes that he understood. The tension was far too great between them. He touched the tip of her nose with his finger.

"Want me to tell you what I like best about you?" When she bit her lower lip and nodded silently, he swept her with

a long, slow look of appraisal. "Let's see—I'll start with
your hair. It's like a silk cloud. All soft and looking as if it
was spun from gold. Your skin is the softest, though, like
the finest satin. I don't think I've ever seen eyes as blue as
yours, like pieces of summer sky. The Irish would say
they'd been put in with a sooty finger, because your lashes
are so long and thick and dark. And your mouth—Jesus,
sometimes I think I like your mouth best. Your lips are soft
and full, and your upper lip is just long enough that it makes
you look as if you're always pouting about something."

"No one looks as sulky as you do," she said with a small
catch in her voice that made him lift his brow.

"Is that so? Remind me to introduce you around some-
time."

He leaned forward, unable to resist tracing a path down
her sides, bumping over the ridges of her ribs, curving
around to come up beneath the plump swell of her breasts.
With his eyes half-closed, he slid his hands around them, his
thumbs touching in the middle, his fingers dark against her
much paler skin.

"Kincade . . ."

Her voice was soft, heated, hazy with desire. He recognized that female response to his touch and his words, and
looked up at her face. He wondered if she could tell how
near he was to losing control. She had to. It must be evident
even to the most untrained eye that his blood had turned to
steam and he was clinging to restraint with every fiber of his
being.

When she moved, her hands fluttering up to lock behind
his neck and draw his head down, his control shattered into
a thousand tiny pieces. With a husky groan that sounded as
if it came from someone else, he relinquished any claim at
all to restraint.

Elizabeth felt the change in him, the swift alteration from
gentle teasing to fierce ardor. His breathing quickened as he
spread his palms under her thighs and pulled her closer. His

kiss was hard, consuming, stealing the air from her lungs to leave her weak and breathless.

It took all her resolve not to cry out when his hands moved between her legs, thumbing through the silky curls in a slow, sensual slide that made her gasp and arch upward. Hot sparks ignited at his touch; lightning bolts seemed to crackle beneath his fingers. She whimpered, a faint sound that made him look up with a slow smile and a lazy, heated lift of his inky lashes.

"If you want to touch the stars, angel," he said in a husky rasp, "I can show you how."

"I don't . . . know."

"I'll show you."

She didn't know what he meant until he pressed the pad of his thumb against the aching focus of sensation, stroking her in a sweet eroticism that sent splinters of heat through her entire body. It was magic, hot magic. She was on fire everywhere, not just where he was touching. She breathed fire, exhaled it, was faintly astonished to see that the woods were not ablaze. The strange, aching inferno spread all through her, and she felt as if she were melting, a liquid fire closing around his hand.

When Kincade bent, and his mouth fastened on the peak of her breast in a damp kiss that made her arch toward him with a gasp, she cried out softly. He drew her nipple into his mouth gently, and the blaze grew higher and hotter.

Elizabeth didn't know what to do with her hands, what to do with anything. Something inside her seemed on the verge of collapse, or flight, or some formless reaction. The rapid movements of his hand, the damp, hot searing of his mouth on her breast, launched her into a restless yearning that seemed to have no end.

She wanted more of him. All of him. She couldn't get close enough to him. A wild urgency filled her, and she was vaguely aware of him spreading her thighs further apart. He slid a finger into the hot, damp crevice between her legs and, when she murmured a protest, claimed her lips in a lingering kiss. His tongue slid into her mouth, moving in the same rhythmic motion as his hand, and she felt a helpless response. It coiled deep inside, growing tighter and tighter until she felt as if she would explode from the tension.

When the explosion came, she shuddered with the force of it. It rolled over her, left her weak and shaking and drained, and she was only vaguely aware of Kincade muttering soft words in her ear as he held her.

"There's more stars where those came from, angel," he whispered thickly.

She focused on him slowly, on his passion-sharp features and the way his hair was wet and black against his head, his face misted as if he'd stood in the rain. A crooked smile curled his mouth.

"I knew you'd be this sweet," he said softly. "I just didn't know that you'd make me so crazy."

She had no time to dissect and examine that last cryptic remark before he was kissing her again, his mouth soft against lips that felt bruised and swollen. He slid across her body, keeping his legs between her thighs. He still wore his unbuttoned trousers. He tucked his arms under her thighs and pulled her legs over his so that his arousal slid against her in a sweet, heady stroke that took away her breath.

When he leaned away, he looked up at her from beneath the dark bristle of his lashes, his eyes hard and green. She felt his thigh muscles contract as he rocked his hips in a slow, erotic glide.

Elizabeth felt the slow spiral of flame begin again, and when his tempo increased and he moved back a little, she gave an experimental twist of her hips. Kincade muttered something indistinct, tilted back his head, and closed his eyes as he paused.

"This isn't going to work," he said more distinctly a moment later, his voice regretful as he shifted backward. He released her legs and stood up in a graceful motion, then stripped away his pants.

Curiosity battled briefly with modesty and won, and she

stared at him as he turned back to her. There was all the rampant arrogance of a young Apollo in him, in the sleek, muscled body and hot jade eyes. Her throat constricted. He could have modeled for Michelangelo. She felt suddenly shy and self-conscious, and looked away.

"Ah no, love. Too late for that," he said easily, and came back to her, drawing her close to him. "You have to look. It's required."

"I can't." Her voice was muffled against his bare chest, and she felt his laughter. He nudged her chin up with a bent finger until she was looking at him.

"It's only me, wicked old Kincade. We've gone too far to stop now, don't you think?"

"I didn't say I was going to stop."

"Then kiss me."

She turned her face up to his, and his hand cupped her chin and he kissed her gently, sweetly, with little of the fire of earlier. Slowly, with the reassurance of his warm touch and drugging kisses, she began to respond. His tongue rasped into the open flame of her mouth, touching, teasing, drawing her into him again.

Slowly he built up the fires to a heat that made her breathe in shallow pants and clutch at him desperately. "Kincade . . . Kincade . . ."

"I know, sweeting. Kiss me . . . like that. Trust me. I'll show you more stars, up where the sun was born and angels glide."

He leaned over her; his weight spread her thighs, searing into the tender flesh with his body. She felt him at her entrance, that damp, hot place that ached with empty yearning. She arched closer, and he slid inside in a slow, searing thrust that wrung an involuntary cry from her.

"Shh," he muttered against her mouth. "It will only hurt this once, only for a moment . . ."

It seemed doubtful he was right. She felt shattered, pinioned to the soft moss beneath her, unable to move. He was still, bracing his weight on one arm, his face fiercely intent. The sharp pain had eased almost immediately, but there was a dull, throbbing ache where there had so recently been pleasure, and she was disappointed.

"Don't move," he said with a groan when she pushed at him with her palms against his chest. "Don't . . . move."

"You're hurting me."

His lashes lifted, green eyes smoky with heat and some other emotion she couldn't define. "I'm sorry, love. It's unavoidable and it won't hurt long."

Disgruntled, she swallowed a skeptical reply. He didn't seem to be able to judge the limits of her pain. She felt the foolish urge to cry. What had been beautiful and romantic was now painful and, well—disappointing. That was the only word that came to mind.

Kincade must have sensed some of what she was thinking, because he gave her a wry smile and said, "I know you don't believe me right now, but I'm right. Or so I've been told by those who know."

She looked away, not wanting to explore the basis for his reasoning. Then he began to move again, slowly at first while she tensed for more pain, then with stronger strokes that were surprisingly easier. The tension grew again, coiling tighter until she arched to meet his thrusts in an instinctive movement that made him mutter encouragement.

When he finally stiffened and made a rough sound in the back of his throat, she tightened her embrace without knowing quite why. Then he pulled free, groaning as he grabbed her and held her close. A hard, racking throb pulsed between them, and she felt something warm and wet.

Kincade's face was pressed into the curve of her shoulder and cheek, and he seemed almost vulnerable. Elizabeth felt the inexplicable need to comfort him. He lay still for several moments, and she felt his muscles slowly relax.

He lifted his head to gaze down at her with a lazy smile. "I hope you don't mind trying for the stars again later."

"Well . . . I did see some stars. I think I liked it better at first, though. You know—your hand."

"Yes, well, I can imagine." He kissed the tip of her nose and tucked a strand of blond hair behind her ear. "I can only say in self-defense that I've never been any woman's first time before."

She didn't know whether to be pleased or insulted by his reference to other women.

"I'm glad you were mine," she said softly, and he shot her a quick, surprised glance.

"Me, too, angel," he said at last, and there was a queer, husky note in his voice that she'd not heard before. "God—me, too."

Chapter 11

"YOU CHEATED?"

"Look." Kincade held out the cards. "And pay attention. If you ever play cards with anyone, God forbid, you need to know what to look for." He ignored her furious stare. "See these dogs on the back? Some of them are wearing collars and some are not. And the striped balls—see how some have two stripes, some three, and so forth? You have to look close, because it's not immediately apparent."

"And the purpose of this?" Elizabeth's mouth tightened. "Besides your penchant for bragging, of course."

He looked amused. "I told you. So you won't be cheated. By anyone but me, I mean."

"Marked cards. I should have known."

"Yes," he agreed, "you should have. It was obvious to me. It should have been obvious to you. Remember this: If you know how to cheat, you won't be cheated. Another word of advice. Don't sit down at the gaming table with anyone you can't read."

"Oh, I'll remember that the next time I'm out to fleece a quail."

"Pigeon." Kincade's smile was wry. "I suppose I should not have told you about it. Now you're angry."

Elizabeth leaned back against the rough bark bench. "Don't I have a right to be?"

"No. But that's my opinion, and I've noticed that we

rarely agree on much.'' His lashes lowered slightly. ''Even the important things.''

She knew what he meant. She still had trouble accepting the change in their relationship. It was odd, since all the warnings she'd listened to since girlhood had not deterred her in the least from becoming intimate with him; after all, she'd had her cousin Annie's side of the issue as well. Times were changing drastically, the old traditions being cast off in favor of the new. Women were more modern, shaken out of the old-fashioned ruts that kept them as mere chattel. Nowadays, women did what they pleased, regardless.

Yet there was a small part of her that hadn't been able to throw off her early training. Even while telling herself that it was just as acceptable for her to have intimacy without marriage as it was for a man, she realized that the more puritanical side of her nature wasn't comfortable with her actions. Unless, of course, she was in love.

Was she?

Elizabeth didn't even want to consider that possibility at this point. Everything was still so strange and new to her. Kincade, as he had promised, had shown her more stars. He also knew how to keep her from getting pregnant, a fact that irritated her more than it relieved her, with all its inherent innuendos.

When she had naively asked why he pulled out of her so abruptly every time they made love, he'd smiled with mocking amusement that made her feel awkward.

''Haven't you ever heard of coitus interruptus?'' he'd asked lightly, and she'd had to admit she had not. His technical explanation was as enlightening as it was embarrassing.

''What?'' He'd lifted his brow at her. ''You never read the old Romans?''

''Of course I did. But I don't recall perusing that topic in my studies.''

''Ah, you should have read thoroughly. Of course, the

method is not foolproof, but there are no safe practices. Except abstinence, of course, a highly disagreeable method. There are other ways to prevent conception, my sweet; but as we have no sponges or vinegar, and—''

Her sharp exclamation had finally stopped his wicked lecture, and only his quick, fierce kisses kept her from getting too angry. That seemed to be his favorite method of ending any argument between them. She had to admit it usually worked.

Elizabeth glanced at him. She stretched out in a patch of shade and lifted a handful of sand, letting it drift from her palm in a powdery stream. She could feel Kincade's gaze on her, wondered what he was thinking. He rarely shared his thoughts with her; a few memories, maybe, those light and amusing. She rolled to a sitting position again.

''Tell me about your childhood,'' she said. His dark brow lifted.

''I cannot imagine a duller subject. Shall I confess some past crime to while away the time? Perhaps you'd like to hear how I tricked you out of the last crab the other day, or—''

She shook her head. ''No.''

He frowned and looked away from her, idly shuffling the marked deck of cards.

''I don't care to discuss it, really.''

''Why not?'' Resting her chin on the arm across her knee, she stared at him. ''Confession is good for the soul.''

He gave a derisive snort. ''Not bloody likely, m'dear. And besides, children have few confessions that make for lively entertainment, which, I perceive, is what you're after.''

''Not at all.'' She paused. ''I have childhood sins.''

''The devil you say.'' His erotic mouth curled slightly. ''I don't doubt that, come to think of it. You seem to have a singular affinity for taking on guilt you shouldn't.''

''Meaning?''

"Meaning, don't go out looking for troubles. There's plenty to go around as it is."

"That's what Annie always says."

"Annie?"

"My cousin, Annie Lee. You remember—"

"Ah yes, the militant dragon on demon run. How could I forget?"

Elizabeth settled comfortably into the sand and grass and observed, "Of course, Annie looks for trouble every chance she gets. She says that's her mission."

"Destroying liquor and lives?"

"No, just liquor. It's the liquor that destroys lives."

Kincade crossed his long legs at the ankles and leaned back against the side of the hut. Palm fronds danced overhead, throwing patches of light and shadow over his face.

"Fancy that," he said. "Those bottles seem so innocent, too. I'll bet the men who buy them have no idea how dangerous they are."

Irritated, Elizabeth said sharply, "It's not the liquor itself, of course, but the people who buy it. Some people just cannot drink. It controls them."

"So you're going to save them from themselves? How noble. Have you and Cousin Annie considered what you'll do if they don't want to be saved?"

She pushed at a strand of hair in her eyes. "Yes. Since the poor wretches have little self-control, we intend to see that all temptation is placed out of reach."

"Going to pour it in the sea, are you. How annoying. And I don't wish you joy of it."

"If you will think a moment, you will recall what began *your* troubles on board the *Tom Hopkins*."

His dark brow lifted. "Going into the wrong cabin."

"And just why did you go into the wrong cabin?"

"Dammit, because it was late, dark, and all the bloody doors looked alike."

"No, because you were drunk. Mr. Bellows told me. You and the first mate had sat up half the night drinking."

His mocking smile did not reach his eyes. "So we did. You are well informed."

"Well, then—"

"Elizabeth," he said softly, but she did not miss the underlying menace in his tone, "I find this subject boring. If you persist in discussing it, I think I will go and check the signal fires."

"Coward."

"At every opportunity. That's why I'm still alive, and most heroes are dead and buried." He rose in a fluid motion that made her turn to look up at him. "Please excuse me. I hear duty calling."

Ian MacDonald looked closely at the odd fruit Tabitha had handed him. "Wha' is this?"

"I'm not at all certain. A mango, I think. Or maybe it's just an orange."

"Looks small for an orange."

"Doesn't it? Well, I daresay we'll find out what it is sooner or later."

"Faith, madam!" Ian exploded. "D'ye think we can stay here tha' much longer? How can we condone wha' happened when our backs were turned?" He put a hand over his eyes and moaned.

"Yes. That's a shame. Matters progressed much more swiftly than I anticipated. Though she seems madly in love with him." Tabitha sighed and shook her head. "No, I wasn't quite expecting that yet. It must have taken longer than I realized to find the—Ian, don't carry on so. If you weren't already dead, I'd swear you were about to pop off in a fit of some kind."

Between incoherent sputters, Ian choked out, "Madam, ye canna think tha' this is less serious than it is."

"Don't be a nodcock. Of course I don't. I simply have learned to accept the unexpected and unpleasant, while you want to rail like a madman at those around you instead of doing something about it. This must be why you were sent to me. I take it you never learned to progress from idea to action when you were alive? Don't glare at me like that. I only mean to help.'' She shook her head. ''All right. Do we weep and wail, or do we think of what should be done next?''

Ian stared at her. A slight breeze ruffled his pale hair and tugged at the hem of his plaid. Finally he shook his head and said with a sigh, ''Ye're a most surprising woman at times. D'ye ha' any notion of wha' can be done?''

''None at all,'' she said cheerfully. ''But that doesn't mean that I won't soon, ye great addlepated ox. Listen to me for a change, if ye please.'' Tabitha drew in a deep breath. ''Now, you know that you were sent to help Kincade MacKay from some grave trouble. I do not believe that the trouble is Miss Lee, truly I don't. Unfortunately Horatio was not available when I asked, and I must try to reach him again.'' She shook her head with a frown. ''Off somewhere in Louisiana, I think, wherever that is, instructing someone who's less adept at this sort of thing than I am. Poor wretch. Well, when he is available, we will find out just what it is that you're supposed to do here. I can't imagine that you are to follow this rogue around the world for the rest of his days. That would smack too much of purgatory instead of paradise, and it's just not Horatio's style.''

Somewhat mollified, Ian drew in a deep breath. ''Verra well, madam, I will be patient. But if we canna find out just wha' it is tha' I am tae do, I willna wait. I will ask Horatio's superior for instructions.''

Tabitha stared at him in horror. ''Nay, 'twould not do at all. Think how it would look if I were to be thought derelict in my duty—oh God's eyes, Ian—just be a bit more patient.''

''As long as something happens soon,'' he said. ''The ship will be here before long, and I want tha' blackguard on it.''

"He will be." Tabitha nodded quickly. "He will be. Just remember that they both have free will about their lives."

"I canna forget, it seems," Ian said grimly. "But tha' doesna mean tha' I won't think of a way tae keep tha' bloody rogue from ruining the lass any more than he has already done, madam."

"You roll your *R*s so well," Tabitha said with a glance of admiration. "However, you might keep in mind that she wants to be with him more than she wants what is good for her. That much is obvious."

"Whose side are ye on?"

Tabitha gave him an uncertain stare. "I vow, I'm not that sure at times, Ian. I just pray that the ship we've managed to steer this way hurries. It won't do to allow them *too* much time together, that much is certain. Undesirable events seem to occur. But just remember—"

"Aye," Ian growled. "I know wha' ye're aboot tae say. We canna change their thoughts or actions, only the bloody circumstances around them. I think we should fetch the blasted ship before the night is past."

Tabitha frowned. "I've run into trouble in the past when I've become too hasty and don't consider all possibilities, Ian. We must be certain that we won't cause any undue complications by bringing the ship here. But I will tell you that I think Kincade MacKay is in some sort of grave danger from someone. Horatio said something most puzzling when I spoke with him. P'raps I should have listened more closely, but I was in such a hurry—never mind. We'll figure it out. Shall we go now?"

"Aye, but 'tis my opinion tha' our bonny lad is only in his usual female trouble." Ian shook his head. "He seems tae ha' a penchant for trouble."

Kincade had snared one of the small pigs that roamed the island, and it was roasting over a spit on the beach. A hot, sizzling aroma spiced the air, and Elizabeth's mouth watered as she helped turn the handle of the spit.

"Roast pig," she murmured dreamily. "Heaven on a stick."

Amusement curled Kincade's mouth. "You're easy to please."

She slanted him a glance and laughed. "Not really. It's just that I've been dreaming of civilization. You know, hot baked bread fresh from the oven, steaming platters of goose and chicken—this pig is a blessing."

"I take it you've grown tired of our meager supply of tinned food?"

"If I remember correctly, I was threatened with dire consequences should I try to feed you oatmeal when there was anything remotely suitable within reach." She scraped a thin stream of sizzling juices with an expert flick of her wrist and shallow spoon, dropping them into a seashell cup.

Kincade looked up from where he knelt beside the stone-ringed fire. "There's more to those bloody tinned goods than the oatmeal."

"I know. I just enjoy teasing you with it. Ouch!" She dropped the spoon into the bowl and stuck her burned finger into her mouth. Kincade sat back on his heels.

"Careful. The fire might be hot."

She laughed. "Not the fire—the grease. And it is."

"Put your hand in cool water. That'll help." He watched as she stepped to the small bucket of water nearby and plunged her hand into it. "Not the drinking water," he said with a shake of his head. "I meant—"

"It's not like we can't get some more, and this was close." Elizabeth turned in her half crouch to look at him. Firelight mixed with fading sunlight to make his face an interesting collage of shadows. The trick of light and shadow gave him the appearance of an exasperated Lucifer, she thought, with a wicked slant to his eyebrows, and a hot, jade glitter in his sleepy-lidded eyes.

He returned her stare. "Have I got soot on my face?"

"No." She turned back to the bucket, gave her hand a final swish, then took it out and dried it on a clean scrap of her petticoat. "Thank heavens for so many petticoats," she remarked. "Though I thought they might drown me when I first fell overboard."

"They almost did. I don't know why women persist in wearing all those ridiculous clothes. It's bound to be deuced uncomfortable, and it's certainly inconvenient."

"For men to remove them, you mean?"

His eyes glittered with laughter. "Precisely."

"What do you favor for women's haute couture, may I ask?"

"Certainly you may." Kincade half closed his eyes, and a slight smile mocked his lips as he murmured, "Something light and breezy, filmy, diaphanous, barely there. Like the ancient Greeks used to wear. A chiton, maybe. Or even better than that—bare-breasted, as the Cretans preferred to go with their tight waist bindings, long aprons, and enticing bodice frames that left the breasts bare and lifted up . . ." His lashes lifted at her exclamation, and he grinned. "I do dream, don't I?"

"I would call it a nightmare. I can see that it wouldn't do at all to allow you loose in public with those dreams, Kincade MacKay."

"Why not? Might be surprised at how many other men share 'em with me."

"I doubt it." She came back to the fire and sat down. "I think our dinner is ready."

Expert with his dirk, Kincade leaned forward and sliced huge chunks of meat that Elizabeth put on a woven platter. Juicy and tender on the inside, hot and crispy on the outside, it tasted better than anything they'd eaten since leaving England.

"You're so clever to have trapped our dinner," Elizabeth said when they'd eaten and were lying in replete languor on a woven mat near the fire. Flames popped and wood crackled as it burned. The delicious fragrance of their meal spiced the air. "I was getting tired of the same old thing."

"So was I." Kincade shifted, propping his broad shoulders on the rough comfort of a rock. "I was afraid you were casting eyes toward the oatmeal again. Desperation will drive a man to great lengths."

She rolled to one side, propped her head in her palm, and regarded him thoughtfully. "Why do you hate oatmeal so much?"

A muscle leaped in his jaw, but his shrug was light and careless. "I told you, I had to—"

"I know. Eat it for thirteen years. But that can't be all of it. I mean, it did keep you alive, didn't it?"

Kincade turned his head to stare moodily into the flames. "I suppose. If you want to call it living." He briefly closed his eyes. When he opened them again, a bitter smile touched his lips. "For a small boy, just being alive wasn't always enough. Oatmeal may have fed my body, but it didn't feed my soul."

"Feed your soul . . ." When shadows darkened his eyes, she tried to visualize a young, miserable Kincade. "How old are you?" she asked when the silence stretched too long and taut and threatened to drown out the feelings of companionship.

"Taking a census, ma'am?"

She ignored his mocking expression. "No, just curious, I suppose. I'm twenty-three. An old maid."

"Old maid." He nodded. "I suppose you are. Most girls are married by the time they reach your age."

"And have you never been tempted to marry?"

Kincade drew an idle pattern on the ground with the point of a stick, sliding her a half-amused, half-annoyed glance. "Once."

She wasn't prepared for the sting that short reply gave her, and was silent for a moment before asking, "Did you love her very much?"

"Love?" He gave a bark of laughter. "Not her, ma'am, not by far. No, it was her father's money I loved, I'm afraid. Don't look so shocked. You must know by now how my character is irretrievably tarnished. And her father had a deuced lot of money, money to burn.'' His eyelashes drifted lower.

"If you don't mind me asking," Elizabeth said after a moment, "why was he so anxious for you to marry his daughter?"

He grinned. "She wasn't in the family way, if that's what you're thinking. God, no. I was dreading the wedding night more than having Sir Percival as my father-in-law." A light shrug lifted his shoulders. "Sir Percival is only a knight, not really a member of the English peerage. He has a burning desire to see his line continue in a motley assortment of nobility, even if it has to be Scottish. He also has the money to buy it. I, on the other hand, have no money and a paltry title.''

"A title . . ."

"Yes, sweeting, a title. Doesn't do me a bit of good, and has probably gotten me in more trouble than it has good graces, but there you have it. I am known in some circles as the Lord of Glencairn, along with a string of other titles that don't mean rubbish. I could be a bonnet laird for all it means outside the Highlands. Does no good at putting bread on the table, I'll tell you tha'.''

His accent had drifted from a decided English clip to a faint brogue, and Elizabeth stared at him. It was the first indication he'd given of having grown up in Scotland, the first crack in his disguise as a bored English gentleman of dubious heritage.

"A lord," she said at last. "Somehow I'd always thought that lords—''

"Would have money?" he finished for her. "A charming but inaccurate fantasy at times. Of course, it would be most pleasant, and at one time Glencairn was as wealthy as any other Scottish holding. But back down the line over a hundred years ago, one of my noble ancestors fought for the wrong side. Against the English crown, you see, and after Culloden and the Jacobite defeat, times grew desperate. One of my ill-fated ancestors had the bloody bad judgment to fight for Bonnie Prince Charlie, and the clearances in the Highlands left precious little to the MacDonalds and MacKays.''

A faintly bitter smile touched the corners of his mouth. ''Some of the Highland clans disappeared altogether. We were left with little more than a crumbling stone castle from the time of the Bruce, and a portion of land that supports a few *clachans* that are as poor as the proverbial church mice. As if that weren't bad enough, my father took what little was left and tried to increase it by gambling on worthless stocks in a miserable shipping enterprise. It failed, of course. I remember that I papered one wall of the niche I used as a hideaway with the useless certificates he gave me after the barrister brought the bad news from Edinburgh.'' Kincade paused, and the silence was thick when he added softly, ''Then he and my mother were drowned returning from a holiday, and my uncle began the fine tradition of thievery that was to be the main source of MacKay income.''

''Thievery?''

''Nothing petty, I assure you.''

Elizabeth hesitated. Kincade looked utterly miserable despite his obvious effort to seem nonchalant. But he was at last answering her questions, and she couldn't resist the temptation to learn more about him.

''I assume you don't mean chickens and cows,'' she said, and Kincade laughed softly.

''Hardly, my sweet. I cannot imagine dear Uncle Dougal with a hen under one arm and a milk cow trotting docilely at his heels. It boggles the mind to try.''

''Then what? Jewels? Money?''

Kincade shifted restlessly and looked away. His mouth turned down in a moody line. ''No. Nothing so trivial.'' He flicked her a quick glance, then said softly, ''He steals souls, sweeting.''

''Oh Kincade,'' she said crossly, ''I thought you were serious.''

''I am.''

She stared at him in exasperation, but he didn't look away, and he didn't try to tease. A disquieting tremor shook her. "What do you mean?"

"My uncle," he said, his brogue growing so thick it took her a moment to understand him, "is a bloody trustee in th' Presbyterian Church of Scotland. He's an elder of the kirk and sits in the Grand Assembly of the Scottish Church. In short, he passes judgment on those poor souls who ha' been accused of crimes. He declared me a heretic, among other things. Using false charges, he has confiscated MacKay lands for the use of the church. If I go back, he means tae ha' me hung."

Elizabeth stared at him. "But . . . but that's archaic. No one has that much power anymore."

"Is it naow?" Kincade sucked in a deep breath, and his brogue lessened. "Aye, not many anymore, I'll grant you. But Dougal MacKay has a lot of influence in the Highlands near Glencairn, and I canna say that the church knows the truth of it."

"But why would he do that?"

Kincade shot her another bitter smile. "It's the only way he can take away Glencairn. I inherited it, you see, and he wants it. Though he won't get much more than a few simple crofters out of it."

"But Kincade—"

"As a child," he said softly, looking away with a strange, distant light in his eyes, "I suspected him of murdering my father to get Glencairn. I wasn't with my parents when the ship went down. Dougal was surprised at the time, I recall. He'd thought we all went on a family holiday. The barrister came from Edinburgh and spelled out the details of my father's will. As only son, I inherited not only the castle and that small spit of land, but the worthless bundle of shipping stock to boot. Dougal was named my guardian." A bitter smile mocked his lips. "Dougal stayed for the funerals, then went back to Edinburgh with the barrister, leaving me behind in 'good' hands. He didn't seem too worried about the future. I suppose he never thought a small boy would survive cold stone walls and a diet of oatmeal and water for long without sickening and dying. But I did. I lived to become a young man who wanted his inheritance. When I reached my majority, Dougal MacKay began to get worried. By all rights, he should have inherited long ago. But I've managed to outwit him every time, sometimes barely, but I've done it.''

A chill shuddered down Elizabeth's spine. She suddenly realized why Kincade had such a jaded outlook on life. She didn't say anything—*couldn't* say anything—and after a moment he shrugged.

''Murder charges were levied against me.''

''Murder . . . oh, Kincade. Did—'' She jerked to a halt.

His mouth twisted. ''Did I do it? No. It's a long tale, and not very edifying, so I won't bore you with the details. Suffice it to say that I left Scotland at the first opportunity and went to England. Not long ago Dougal began to actively pursue getting me out of his way. I suppose he's grown tired of waiting for me to kill myself off, and has decided to help.''

''Now I know why you asked if anyone had sent me after you. You thought I'd been hired to . . . to—'' She couldn't finish, and he smiled faintly.

''Yes. Kill me. You wouldn't be the first female assassin to have tried. Dougal is quite innovative at times.''

''Then why did you consider marrying the English girl?''

''For money, of course. I told you. At the time I had the silly notion that Dougal might be satisfied with a mere fortune.''

''He doesn't want money?''

Kincade looked grim. ''No, lass, he doesn't want money. He wants Glencairn, every bloody stone of it and all that goes with it, little though it is. He won't rest until it's his.''

''You said you hate Scotland, so give it to him.''

''No. It's mine by right and birth, and the bastard will have to kill me to get it, by God.'' His expression changed abruptly. "And maybe I lied. Maybe I don't hate Scotland at all, but only said that since I can't have what's mine."

Elizabeth looked away from his suddenly fierce expression and blindly lifted another palm of sand. She focused on it, watching the grains drift back to the beach for a moment as she struggled to understand. Then she heard him mutter something in a wry tone and looked up. His face was as she was used to seeing it—bored, amused, with a devil-may-care smile tugging at the erotic line of his mouth, a smile that she now knew covered up a host of emotions. It made her ache inside, and her voice was husky.

"I'm sorry if I intruded where I shouldn't. I only wanted to understand why . . . why you do some of the things you do."

"You mean why I'm such a bastard most of the time? Don't be shy. You can say it. I know how I am. If you will recall, I'm the one who warned you about me."

She managed a faint smile. "Yes, I recall that."

"Good." He sat up, tossed aside the stick he'd used to doodle in the sand, and gave her a blinding smile that didn't fool her at all this time. "Since we're exposing our souls, sweeting, tell me about you. None of that ridiculous tripe about your mission in life and intention to rule the world one day, either. I want to hear the real stuff. You know, how many toys you managed to accumulate in your childhood, and what you got for Christmas when you were eleven. Things like that."

"Would you settle for the high points?"

"Decidedly. Wise choice."

"I was born in Natchez, Mississippi, lived on a farm until I was seven, and then the War Between the States broke out and my father sent my mother and me to his home in Boston."

"Boston. That's pretty far from Mississippi—God, where do you Americans get these names?"

She laughed and nodded. "Yes, it's quite far. And Mississippi is an Indian word, by the way. But Boston was safer than Mississippi at the time. After the war we returned, but things had changed a great deal. My father had money, but couldn't find enough people to work the land for him. My mother didn't want to leave home again, so we bought a house in town and stayed. Then—'' She paused to take a deep breath. ''There was an epidemic a few years ago, and both my parents took the fever and died. I was in Atlanta visiting my cousins. So I'm all alone now. No brothers or sister, my only close family my cousin Annie.''

''The crusader.''

Elizabeth smiled. ''Yes. I suppose I should mention that Annie and I went to school together, a rather radical institution in that it promoted equality between the sexes.''

''That's not radical, angel, that's suicidal. How many men do you think prefer women who bash good bottles of liquor to those women who kiss behind trees?''

''Kissing isn't everything, Kincade.''

''No?'' His eyes took on a familiar gleam. ''I'd like to show you how wrong you are about that, angel.''

When he rose in a graceful curl of his long body, Elizabeth gave a delighted squeal and scrambled to her feet, all thoughts of causes banished for the moment. She raced across the beach, warm sand flying from beneath her feet, the sound of the surf drowning out the noise of Kincade's pursuit. When she reached the edge of the woods, she didn't pause, but dashed down the narrow path toward the pool.

Dark shadows enveloped her; it was much cooler in the dense trees, and birds chattered incessantly above. The roar of the surf grew faint as she raced down the path, leaping over knobby roots and fallen limbs.

Now she could hear him behind her, and when she glanced around, she saw that he was leisurely following her. She jerked to a halt.

''Oh,'' she said between gasps for breath, ''you aren't even trying. . . .''

''Don't have to.'' He caught her to him with a swing of one arm. ''You can't run that fast. Besides, how far can you go?'' He nuzzled the damp hair at the curve of her neck and inhaled deeply. "You smell good, angel. Like pig. Umm. Like a female. I think I like that better . . . here. Don't wiggle. I only want to compare pig taste to female taste, and I'll take small bites.''

Elizabeth twisted in his embrace, laughing as she put her arms up around his neck and pressed her face against his chest. She could feel his arousal pushing against her, and it sparked an immediate response.

He tilted up her face and kissed her, and when he released her mouth, she sighed softly.

"You taste like pig, too. Sticky. Sweet. Kinda charred in places.''

"Thank you. Why don't we bathe?''

Startled, she leaned back to look up at him. "Do you mean—together?''

"Certainly. Together has a rather nice ring to it, doesn't it? Besides, it's not like I haven't seen you without these rags that barely cover you anyway. Come on. You can scrub my back.''

"With what?'' She followed him, excitement surging and making her insides jumpy. "We don't have any soap.''

"You complain more than any woman I've ever known. We'll make some from pig fat. Later. Now we'll just improvise. Come along. Be adventurous. One day you can tell your grandchildren that you bathed with a Scottish laird. That ought to make 'em sit up and take notice of Grandma.''

He didn't give her the opportunity to offer more protests, but took her with him down the shadowed path. With the sun almost down, dark shadows made it difficult to see, and Elizabeth kept close to him, trusting him to find the way in the gloom.

The sound of the waterfall grew louder; damp air seeped through her clothes to her skin, and she shivered.

"Cold, sweeting?'' Kincade murmured. He put an arm around her shoulders and drew her up into his embrace.

"No, just . . .'' Her voice trailed into silence, and he

paused and turned to peer down at her. His eyes gleamed softly in the shadows.

"What is it, honey?" His hands were warm on her arms, his fingers gentle when he lightly touched her face. She stepped even closer to him, and slid her arms around his lean waist.

"I don't want this to end," she said, her words muffled against his bare chest. She felt the even rhythm of his breathing, could feel the thud of his heartbeat. He smelled of salt and fresh air. His skin was faintly damp beneath her cheek.

"What do you mean—end?"

He sounded surprised, and Elizabeth thought with a pinch of chagrin that she would hardly be able to explain it to him when she didn't quite understand her meaning herself.

"This. You know." She waved a helpless hand at the trees and sky. A thin sliver of early moonlight speared the thick canopy of leaves overhead, and backlit Kincade's dark hair with a silvery mist. "Us. Together. Without anyone else to see or—judge."

"Judge." Kincade's hand tightened briefly in her hair. "I guess you mean the kind of people who always think the worst of a situation, no matter the circumstances. Ah Christ, sweetheart, those people don't matter. This—what you and I do together—is only between us. It doesn't matter what others may say or think."

She murmured against the smooth, taut fabric of warm skin and muscle. "I know it shouldn't, but it does. Oh, not because I think we're wrong, but because *they* will."

Kincade untangled his hand from the bright weave of her hair and pushed her slightly away from him with a gentle pressure. He gazed down at her upturned face. There was a faint question in his eyes when he said, "You're only anxious because of gossip, not because of right or wrong. How enlightening as to your character. And reassuring."

"Don't be mean. You know very well what I meant by that. Once we're rescued, things will change."

"That they will. Not that we have much to worry about
there, as I haven't seen a ghost of a ship since our
providential supplies washed ashore. Why borrow trouble,
angel? Worry about it when it gets here, because it sure as
the Lord will."

Because she wanted so badly to believe that, and to
believe in him, Elizabeth allowed him to smooth away her
fears. She wanted it to last forever; being with him was all
that mattered. And so she decided to believe in it.

When they reached the waterfall and Kincade stripped off
his clothes, she did, too. They laughed and cavorted under
the cold, falling cascade of water like two children. It was a
perfect moment, a moment to be remembered and held and
treasured forever.

Moonlight silvered the pool and made the falling water
glitter like diamond drops, and the air was soft and warm,
rocks still heated from the afternoon sun. Tropical flowers
scented the air with rich, delicious fragrance, and birds
provided a musical serenade.

"Heaven," Kincade murmured against her lips when he
held her to him and kissed her, and Elizabeth knew it had to
be true. Nothing earthly could be this perfect and last, and
both of them knew it.

Chapter 12

"YOU'RE BEAUTIFUL, you know."

Kincade tilted his head to look down at Elizabeth's face. Afternoon sunlight warmed them. "What did you say?"

She made a half-embarrassed gesture with one hand. "I said, you're beautiful. You remind me of a god, one of those Greek or Roman gods depicted in ancient mythology."

"Beautiful. Me." He was suddenly quite still, and his voice was so odd that she twisted to look up at his face. "You don't mean that, angel."

"Yes, I do. You are beautiful, with your wicked face and perfect body, and you know you are. You've got to know it. No one can look like you do and not know it." She gave a shaky laugh when he just stared at her from beneath the silky brush of his lashes. "You're only fishing for compliments, I think."

"God save us," Kincade said in a soft, bemused tone. "I think you've gone 'round the bend, angel."

"No," she persisted, "it's true. And you're not just beautiful, but you're clever, too. I don't mean with cards or dice, or sneaky tricks—though you do very well with those, I'm sorry to say—I mean that you think of things I would never imagine. Like the hut, and how you built it with hardly any tools. Most men would not know what to do, but you did. And you've made dishes, and woven mats for us to sleep on—see what I mean?"

"Angel—" He made a funny, helpless sound.

"Well, it's true." She ran a finger along the muscled curve of his forearm and shifted slightly in his embrace. They were lying on the lush cushion of deer fern, the tiny, springy fronds forming a tightly packed, fragrant mattress. She twisted to look up at him and noted the ironic twist of his mouth. Looking away, she said, "Of course, I believe that nature intended for the male to be the most physically appealing of the species, in order for propagation to be—uh . . ."

"Propagated?" Kincade said wickedly. "I take that mangled idea to be an excuse for when you females actively pursue males, when it's usually the other way around, right?"

"Well . . . yes."

He buried his nose in the curve of her neck and shoulder. "I like it when a woman makes calf eyes at me and walks with a sway that would tempt a stone statue."

"Are you insinuating that I did that?"

"No, angel, you *do* that, all the time. What's a poor man supposed to do?"

All traces of indignation faded from her voice, and she laughed. "Exactly what you do, Kincade MacKay. Follow me, of course."

"Of course. See? I knew it all the time. All this tripe about me being beautiful and noble is a crock, and we both know it. It's justification for enjoying it when I do this to you . . . and this. . . ."

She shuddered under his touch and closed her eyes, arching up into his hand. The afternoon sunlight graced the air with heated whispers that made their nudity imperative. She rather enjoyed playing Eve to Kincade's Adam. Eden. That is what their tropical isle had truly become to them, long heated days and soft, balmy nights, with the days spent splashing like puppies in the surf or shaded pool.

And this . . . the sharing of their bodies with mutual joy and exquisite pleasure, seemed as natural as breathing.

Kincade dragged his callused palm over her breasts to her belly, slipping his fingers between her thighs to graze in lush caresses that made her shiver. He kissed her until they were both breathing in short, rapid gasps.

"Kincade . . ." Her voice was urgent in his ear, and he lifted his head from the lavish attention he was giving the tip of her breast to gaze at her with passion-rich eyes.

"Yes, love?"

Her hips lifted against him in a slow, sensual slide of fevered skin and erotic suggestion. He smiled.

"Ready, are you? So am I, sweeting, so am I."

He sat up and straddled her body, his knees on each side of her legs, his sex sliding in fiery sparks over the core of her need as he pulled her to him. For several moments he caressed her with his hard body, until she was making soft little noises in the back of her throat and thrusting urgently at him with her hips.

"You always want to rush it," he muttered, though his eyes were hard and glittering with the strain he was under at keeping control. "All right. Here . . . no, Jesus, don't do that unless you want it over with before we get started."

Breathless, panting, Elizabeth reached up and brought his head down for a kiss, and as her arms went around his neck Kincade put himself inside her in a smooth movement that wrung a groan of ecstasy from her.

"Yes, that's right, sweetheart," he said against her parted lips. "It feels so damned good . . . so right. God, I don't think . . . I don't think I can stop. . . ."

His body shuddered—braced on palms pressing down into the fragrant moss and with his head thrown back, his throat corded with the effort to restrain himself. His shoulders and body glistened in the hazy, leaf-dappled light sifting through the trees.

He was, Elizabeth thought dazedly, magnificent. Pure, masculine beauty, aggressive and tender and loving all at the same time. Her throat ached from wanting to tell him how she felt. That she loved him.

"Kincade . . ." His name was a gasp on her lips. She arched upward, freeing her response as it ripped through her like the tide, crashing in roaring breakers that drowned out everything but her need and this . . . this almost painful release to pure pleasure. Her hands clutched at the slippery skin of his shoulders; her legs lifted to clamp around his waist; and her body took him as deeply as she could.

When he thrust strongly, burying himself in her so deeply she felt the shattering of her soul, Elizabeth cried out against his ear, "I love you, oh, I love you. . . ."

There was no sign he'd heard her, or that it had even registered with him as he held her tightly and drove into her welcoming body with a fierce urgency. His breath was harsh sobs in her ear, low throaty sounds that increased in tempo with his body, until finally they both exploded in a frenzy of motion and culmination.

At that moment, when he would have pulled away from her as he always did, Elizabeth instinctively clutched him more tightly. Though he sucked in a huge breath and tried to draw back, her undulating movements under him catapulted him over the edge of control. Shuddering, swearing softly, he couldn't hold back his release.

It left him drained, spent, hardly able to hold up his own weight on his arms. Sagging across her, Kincade buried his face in the damp wealth of her hair and took a deep, unsteady breath. He shifted slightly to distribute his weight more evenly, and curled his fingers into her hair.

"You shouldn't have done that," he said after a long moment drifted past. She kissed his earlobe, his temple, the sharp slope of his cheek.

"Done what?"

"Don't play the innocent with me, Miss Likely-Mother-to-Be." He tried to keep his voice from being too sharp, but she turned under him and studied his face.

"You're angry."

"Yes. Well, a little. As much as I enjoyed that, I'm afraid that it may *propagate* something we don't need. Especially here, on this godforsaken island.'' He lifted his head to frown down into her eyes. ''Why else do you think I've all but turned myself inside out to keep from doing that these past weeks? It certainly isn't because I enjoy frustration, I can tell you that.''

Her eyes closed; her voice shook slightly. ''But I love you. I wouldn't mind having your child. . . .''

''Christ.'' The word came out in a baffled snarl. ''Who do you suppose will midwife you, may I ask? In spite of my newfound talents, I can assure you that delivering babies isn't one of them.''

There was a long, telling silence, and Kincade gave a frustrated groan. ''Sorry, angel. I don't mean to be cruel, but it's the bloody truth.''

Elizabeth's lashes lifted, gilt-sprinkled tips shading a slight glaze of tears. He looked away from her, and felt a helpless shift of emotions churn inside. *No.* He couldn't allow her to love him. He had nothing to give, no way to ease it for her, and he'd never be able to forgive himself for hurting her. He knew that much already. In the six weeks or so they'd been on this blasted island, he'd discovered that he was vulnerable to this skinny, big-eyed girl with a potful of revolutionary notions. It wasn't a character flaw he was likely to cultivate with much enthusiasm.

''You don't want to love me?'' she asked into the charged silence. He swallowed the urge to shout *No!*

''I didn't say that.'' He twined his fingers through hers and lifted her hand. ''I don't want a baby. That should be simple enough to understand.''

Elizabeth watched him kiss her fingers; she didn't cry, and he was grateful for that.

''I see. Well, I certainly understand that. I just had the notion that when two people loved one another, they had children.''

''Two *married* people, angel. You forgot an important ingredient.''

''Oh, that's nothing. I'm certain we'll be married as soon

as we're rescued. After all, it's a little difficult to find a preacher when one is stranded on a—what are you doing?''

Kincade released her hand and rolled to his feet in a smooth motion. ''Married. Jesus.'' He raked a hand through his hair and wondered if his desperation was as obvious to her as it was to him.

A look of understanding dawned on Elizabeth's face as she rose to prop herself on her elbows. Her lower lip began to quiver slightly, and he closed his eyes in resignation. ''I see,'' she said softly, and this time it sounded as if she really did. ''You don't want to marry me. You haven't said you love me, either.''

He opened his eyes. Shaking his head, Kincade knelt beside her, the bands of muscle on his stomach contracting as if he'd been kicked in the belly. ''Angel, it's not that I don't love you—I don't know what love is. Terminal respectability holds no attraction for me. God, I don't know. Maybe I'm just a coward. Please try to understand. Marriage to me wouldn't be some wonderful scene where we'd spend our days and nights making love in straw huts. I can't support you, dammit, and I won't be supported by you.''

''You were going to marry Sir Reginald's or Percival's—or whoever he was—daughter for money. What's the matter with mine?''

''I know this will sound stupid, because it does to me, too, but I didn't care anything about his daughter. It makes a big difference.''

She sat up and wrapped her arms around her body as if chilled. ''Oh, it's all right to marry someone you don't love, but not someone you do. It sounds like a crock to me, Kincade MacKay.''

He smiled faintly at hearing one of his own expressions tossed back at him. ''Yes, I agree that it does. Maybe it is. After all, I did tell you—''

''That you're a bastard. I remember. And I think I agree with you now.''

''Then that should save you a lot of pain.''

She met his gaze, and there was such a wealth of scorn and pain in her azure eyes that Kincade wanted to hide his face in shame.

"Yes, it certainly should," she said softly. "But we both know it won't."

He didn't say anything when she rose and put on her clothes and left him sitting by the waterfall. He still knelt with one knee in the moss, watching her walk with slow dignity down the path.

Regret mingled with a dull ache in his chest, and he wished, suddenly, that a ship would hurry up and come before he did the unforgivable and promised to marry her. God. He was weak. Something about Elizabeth Lee made him want to do whatever it took to make her happy, and he had no idea why.

Silly female, with her dumb ideas and high-minded prattle about temperance and women's rights. Didn't she realize that she was a walking contradiction? No. Of course she didn't, and she'd be damn mad if he pointed it out to her.

Kincade buried his face in his palm and wished again, aloud this time. "God, please send a ship to get us off this bloody island."

"Well." The gaze Tabitha turned on Ian was significant. "I think he's tormented by his cruelty to her."

"*I* think," Ian said moodily, "tha' he's more tormented by the fact tha' the lass wants tae get wed tae him."

"We'll see who's right soon enough," Tabitha predicted. Her gaze shifted from the woodland pool to where the surf broke on the sand. Ian followed her gaze.

"Aye, tha' we will, because the *Merry Widow* isna a half day's sail from here."

"Yes, so I understand. I suppose that it will stop and pick them up?"

"I canna think of a better idea. It seems tha' the ship is

short of fresh water, and this island is the closest place tae get some more.''

Tabitha looked pleased. ''Ian, you really do surprise me with your ingenuity. I'm quite proud of you. What happened to their fresh water?''

He met her gaze with an uplifted brow. ''It fell overboard.''

She clapped her hands with delight. ''Splendid. You are beginning to form an aptitude for this, I believe.''

''Aye, if only I had the strong stomach tae go wi' it. It isna easy to watch, ye know.''

''Come, come, he's not that bad.''

''I dinna agree. If it'd been up tae me, Kincade MacKay would ha' been left tae drown in the Atlantic.''

''But he's your kinsman. And from what I heard, his uncle is the bigger rogue.''

Ian frowned. ''D'ye think he's telling the lass the truth aboot tha'? I'd no' put it past him tae lie tae gain her sympathy, y'know.''

''Think. What do you know about your family after you were . . . uh . . . dead?''

''I dinna just up and die, madam,'' Ian said indignantly. ''I was killed in battle, like Highland Scots should die.''

She gave him a skeptical glance. ''Really? Dying has the same end result, you know. I shouldn't be too proud of how you popped off, if I were you.''

''Nay, 'tis no' the same at all,'' Ian growled. ''No' tae a proud Highlander, by God.''

''All right, all right. Let's not quibble about the best way to die. It's rather grim, and serves no purpose. Besides, *I* was murdered, so I believe that my death was much more tragic.''

''Tragic?'' Ian's eyes bulged. ''Wi' all the flower of Scotland lyin' on the bloody field of Culloden in the name of the bonnie prince? Nay, 'tis a sad ending tha' it cost so much tae lose so much.''

''Ah, Culloden.'' Tabitha was immediately diverted.

"Did I not hear Kincade mention that was the beginning of the fall of the family fortunes?"

"Culloden Moor ruined most of the Highlands, madam. No' many Highlanders kept their homes or land after, I can tell ye tha' much. Why, the pipes were banned after, and the wearin' o' the filabeg and plaid."

"Filabeg? You mean those short skirts Scots wear?"

Ian glared at her. "'Tis no' a *skirt*. In ancient Gaelic 'twas called a *feileadhbeag*. Some Highland Scots still call it a filabeg and plaid."

"Plaid is the design."

"Nay, plaid is the blanket tha' a mon wraps about his body and o'er his shoulder, and holds wi' a pin or brooch. Tartan is the design o' the plaid."

"Then what in heaven's name is a kilt?" Tabitha asked crossly. "I'm certain I heard someone refer to that garment as a kilt."

"'Tis a word tha' the Sassenachs first used tae refer tae the filabeg, madam."

"Sassenachs. You mean me. English."

"Aye."

The word was a low growl, and Tabitha studied Ian in silence for a moment. "I see," she finally said. "Well, filabeg it is, then. Now, back to the problem at hand. It is obvious to me that Kincade must be necessary to Some Greater Plan. His demise would probably throw the entire thing out of kilter."

"I canna see tha'. Seems tae me one less rogue in the world would be better."

"We aren't always fully informed, I suppose. It's part of our growth to find the reason behind things, to look beyond the surface." She eyed Ian for a moment. "Which, if you don't mind me saying it, is probably why you are here with me now. You see only the obvious, only the surface. If you had researched your Bonnie Prince Charlie more carefully, you might have had enough sense to stay at home instead of trotting off to Culloden Moor."

Ian stared at her with his mouth slightly open in amazed silence. When Tabitha strode up the beach a few yards, he followed mutely.

"I wonder what well-dressed women are wearing in America these days?" she mused aloud. "I rather fancy a costume I wore in Texas, but I don't think buckskin and feathers will be quite the thing in a city like New Orleans."

The *Merry Widow* sailed away from the nameless island that was a part of the Florida Keys with two new passengers. Cousins, they told the captain, though he was overheard voicing his private doubts as to the veracity of that particular claim. He didn't seem to care one way or the other, and wedged them into cabins already occupied, using a flurry of soothing cajolery that somewhat mollified the current occupants.

Kincade found himself quartered with a rather ebullient Creole gentleman from Louisiana who was partial to playing cards—badly, it turned out—and so he set himself to earning a few pounds for the future. He caught sight of his cousin Liz on occasion and was always the perfect gentleman, asking after her health and saying she seemed to be recovering well from their ordeal.

If there was anything she wanted to say, she didn't. Her manner was perfectly polite, if distant.

By the time they docked in New Orleans, Elizabeth could talk to Kincade without wanting to cry. It wasn't as hard as she'd thought it would be, though she had momentary lapses on occasion.

"Yes, I've sent my cousin Annie a wire," she told him once they were in New Orleans. "She is delighted to learn that I am still alive. I leave in the morning to join her."

Kincade looked down at her, his gaze briefly reflecting some reaction she couldn't interpret before he looked away.

"Wonderful, Cousin Liz. I wish you great success, though not in any part of the country I'm in at the moment, of course. I happen to enjoy a spot of brandy now and then.''

Her smile was dry. "I noticed that you brought what was left with you.''

Kincade grinned, and his eyes sparked with old mischief when he said, "I couldn't leave it behind, could I? It might have fallen into the hands of temperance termagants.''

"And well it should.'' She paused, then blurted out, "You might be relieved to know that I am not in imminent danger of . . . propagating, by the way.''

"No?'' His gaze sharpened suddenly, raking her with a swift glance before he shrugged. "I'm certain you are most relieved.''

"Most.'' She stuck out her hand, saw his faint look of surprise, then his wry smile as he took it. "Farewell, Kincade MacKay. I wish you a good life.''

Still holding her hand, he hesitated, then swore under his breath and bent to kiss her. That brief meeting of their lips almost made Elizabeth lose her self-control, but then Kincade was straightening and saying calmly, "I wish you all the happiness in the world, Cousin Liz.''

She thought later that if she hadn't had the presence of mind to walk away, she would have thrown herself into his arms and begged him not to leave her behind. It was not one of her most memorable moments.

Interlude

HOT SUNSHINE poured down, and bright blooms draped over lacy ironwork, lining the banquettes of New Orleans. A humid breeze stirred the flowers and tugged at flowing skirts of the women in the French Market. The sharp smell of river and produce mingled in an unlikely aroma.

"Delightful, isn't it?" Tabitha observed, and Ian gave her a withering glance.

"If ye're fond o' the stink o' fish, aye."

"Oh, rubbish. Must you always see only the worst? Try and see something in color for a change, instead of the gloom of gray all the time. Look—flowers. Boiled shrimp. Flaky pastries. Bright cottons, silks, and satins. See? No gray at all."

"Wait a spell and the clouds will dump rain on ye quick enough. It rains every day here."

"And then the sun comes out again." Tabitha gazed at him in exasperation. "You are the gloomiest individual I've ever met. If someone gave you a sack of silver, you'd be moaning because the sack was made of wool instead of silk."

"A silk sack canna hold much silver," Ian pointed out. "It's no' sturdy enough."

Tabitha glared at him, then gave a shake of her head. "Never mind. As I was saying earlier, you must listen to reason about our purpose for being here at all. I realize I

152

don't know exactly what we're to do for your kinsman, but I shall find out. My fault, I suppose, since I was in too big a hurry to listen closely to Horatio.''

Ian muttered something indistinct, and Tabitha's eyes narrowed slightly.

"Did I hear you say something about *Sassenachs*?" she demanded. "Don't be odious. If you still harbor grudges against the crown, I'm not the proper person to blame for what happened so long ago. Go talk to King Henry. And take a fan with you, because that old blighter is in a very warm area, unless I miss my guess."

Tabitha's tart tone wrung a faint smile from Ian. "'Twas no' King Henry I blame, but George, may the fiends take him and the Duke of Cumberland both. The duke was a bloody butcher, make no mistake aboot tha'. Murthered half the Highlands, he did."

"Is that so. How interesting. I must have been having tea elsewhere when that happened. You know how it is, and if that offends you, too, I apologize. It's history now, you see, and therefore not quite the main topic of conversation except in certain circles."

Ian looked startled. "It occurs tae me, madam," he said thoughtfully, "tha' one's own history is most important only tae him. At one time Culloden Moor was on the lips of all. Now 'tis but a footnote in English history books."

"Oh, but you're missing a very important point, Ian. I think you've forgotten that there will always be those who are interested in their ancestors, and the sacrifices made by them. Not every person, true, but enough so that in the years ahead someone will smile and nod appreciation for what was given or lost." She put a hand on his arm, her voice very earnest. "Look at what you lost on Culloden Moor with all the brave men of your time, in the hopes that there would be a better world ahead of those who followed you. I don't think the nature of the sacrifice makes as much difference to time as the nature of the sacrificed."

"I dinna follow your reasoning, madam."

"Think—you lost your life in battle for a cause you believed in, is that not true? And you've wandered like a lost soul in the Hereafter because your original cause failed. Now you have another chance to succeed with a cause everyone considers lost—Kincade MacKay. He's your kinsman, Ian. Help him succeed."

"But the rogue only wants tae succeed at thievery, madam. D'ye suggest tha' I help him wi' tha'?"

"Don't be idiotic. Help him live up to his promise, to become the considerate human being he should be. Fight for his soul just as hard as you fought for Bonnie Prince Charlie."

A sudden light gleamed in Ian's blue eyes, and a faint smile curved his mouth. "Aye, madam, I believe I see wha' ye mean. Maybe Kincade can be helped after all."

She nodded with satisfaction. "Good. Then you won't mind at all watching over him alone while I seek out Horatio and see what can be done about this murderous uncle. Dougal, I think? He sounds like a bad sort of chap, for all that he pretends to be so good and pure. I'm not at all certain of the protocol involved in interfering with a man of the cloth. After my time, you see. In the old days, he would have lost his head, as was proper. Which explains why I've seen a few people wandering about with strangely cockeyed heads, but that's another matter. I must be off. I do believe that we can end this quite satisfactorily, p'raps even in time for the opera by Bizet. He is new—have you heard him?"

"Nay, madam, I ha' no' heard him. Does he play the pipes?"

"Pipes? Oh, you mean those pig bladders. No. He composes operas. *Carmen* is quite nice, I think."

Ian's frosty glare didn't disturb Tabitha in the least. She smiled and patted her hair into what she seemed to consider a more pleasing arrangement.

"Do watch over MacKay while I'm gone, Ian. He seems to have a rather reckless nature. Keep him alive until I return. It will be the saving of both of you, I think."

Ian opened his mouth, but Tabitha gave a quick flip of

one arm and was gone, leaving him standing in the French Market while life went on around him. He stood for a moment, then shrugged and snapped his fingers. Nothing happened. He tried again, and vanished.

Chapter
13

Tucson, Arizona—May 1878

"ARE YOU accusing me of cheating?" Kincade stared at the cowboy across the table from him. An idle smile played at the corners of his mouth.

"Not yet," the man replied. "That'll come after I see what you got up your damn sleeve."

"My arm, and only my arm." Kincade gestured to the pile of money in the middle of the table. "You just don't like a man who plays a better game of poker, old boy."

Kincade leaned over the pasteboard cards fanned on the table, reaching for the glitter of coins. There was the quick rasp of a chair being pushed back and the man was on his feet, a revolver in one hand. Just as quickly the other players abandoned the table in favor of the bar across the saloon.

As Kincade's gaze came to rest on the pistol only a few feet from him, he heard the man growl, "Don't touch th' goddamn money until I see what you got up yore sleeve, you damned Englishman."

Kincade stared warily at the black eye of the heavy pistol. "Scotsman," he corrected mildly. "Do put that thing away. It might go off."

"Damn right it might go off. It'll go off mighty quick if you don't show me what you got up your shirt sleeves, mister."

After briefly considering his options, Kincade decided that things did not look favorable. Not that he'd even needed to cheat. This man was a bloody poor player, overbluffing and betting wildly. Lord, why had he ever decided to come west? He should have stayed in New Orleans, where at least the men were partially civilized.

The Americans of his acquaintance seemed to be a rather impetuous lot, and while normally he didn't mind, it seemed that the farther west he went, the more belligerent they became. Kincade decided to try tact one more time.

"If you shoot me, sir, the authorities will be quick to hang you. Do consider that."

The man spat a stream of tobacco juice onto the sawdust on the saloon floor. "Not for killin' a card cheat, they won't. Nobody likes a card cheat."

"Nobody likes a jackass, either, but that doesn't seem to matter—hey!"

Alarmed when the man thumbed back the hammer of his pistol, Kincade came to his feet. He was rapidly seeing the foolishness in trying to divert Colby with small talk.

"You prissy-talkin' bastard," Colby was saying, glaring at him over the long barrel of the pistol, "I ought to plug you so full o' holes they could use you as a tea strainer."

Kincade's mind worked rapidly. The man was drunk, and his aim might be off. On the other hand, he was so close he'd have to be a really bad shot to miss. He calculated his chances of kicking the gun from his hand before he could pull the trigger, and took a wary step back with his hands spread wide. He'd have to catch him off guard, no matter what he tried to do.

"I'm not armed, you know," Kincade said conversationally, hoping that the man would be distracted. A second, that was all he needed—a second's inattention.

All conversation in the Sweetwater saloon had stopped; attention was riveted on Kincade and his antagonist. No one seemed inclined to halt the confrontation, however. Kincade registered that fact at almost the same time as he registered the distant noise of singing coming from outside.

Hymns? He wondered if his mind had been affected by

the strain, then knew it had not. The singing was growing louder by the moment. Wonderful. He hoped it got louder. Anything to divert this brute's attention from the pistol just long enough . . .

The saloon doors burst open and a portly female bellowed, "Den of iniquity! Hall of shame! Save them, sisters, *save* our poor, deluded brothers!"

As Colby half turned in surprise Kincade's right foot came up and connected with his wrist. The pistol went flying into the sawdust and the cowboy gave a howl of rage that went unnoticed in the immediate chaos of hymn-singing, ax-handle-swinging women.

Kincade made an agile swipe, scooped up as much of his winnings as he could, and was out the doors before the cowboy could do more than sway and yell.

Dodging swarming females, Kincade barreled across the wooden boardwalk toward the street, hell-bent on flight to the next town. He had no intention of hanging around to meet up with that angry cowboy again, nor did he wish to be lectured on the evils of alcohol by a bunch of chanting women.

Behind him he heard a loud crack, and turned to see if someone was shooting at him. Another crack sounded, and he recognized the distinctive sound of glass shattering. Howls of rage cut into the air.

Kincade grinned and turned back around. He immediately ran into someone and put out a hand to catch them. Then he heard a familiar voice say in shocked tones, "Kincade MacKay."

The world reeled, then righted again, and he was staring down into the sea-blue eyes of Elizabeth Lee. He should have known.

"Angel," he said faintly, and gave a helpless shrug. "It's been a long time."

"Almost eight months," she said, staring up at him as if he was the first man she'd seen in that long.

Kincade realized suddenly that he'd missed her. And that he was damned glad to see her. He grinned.

"You with those fire-eating females inside the saloon?"

"Yes. Tucson is the site of a temperance meeting this week, and I fear that my cousin has been seized with an overabundance of righteous zeal."

"Ah, righteous zeal. That can be a bloody nuisance at times."

"To some people, yes."

A smile trembled on her lips, and his gaze came to rest on her mouth with a fleeting wistfulness that he knew he shouldn't indulge.

"I suppose you've been vastly inconvenienced by our visitation upon your saloon?" Elizabeth said, dragging his attention away from her mouth and back to the present.

"Actually, angel, you may have saved my life. These Westerners are a volatile lot, which I do think the guide-books should have mentioned. However, I believe I upset a certain gentleman to the point where he was about to—I think he said, 'fill you so full of holes you can be a tea strainer,' or something like that. Pithy and to the point, anyway."

"Kincade?" She clutched at him with genuine concern, then seemed to catch herself and stepped back. "Are you hurt?"

He considered saying yes to see if she would offer to nurse him back to health, then remembered the furious cowboy and gave a regretful shake of his head.

"No. It has become necessary for me to leave town, I believe. I hate to say this, but standing here in the middle of the street with you won't ensure me a long life."

She nodded, but her eyes—those pieces of blue heaven—held his gaze. "You were cheating, I presume?"

"Why must you assume I'm not a good enough player to win honestly? I can, you know, little though you may credit it. Look—I have to go." He took a step away, felt an odd lurch in his chest, and paused. "Unless you want to hide me somewhere for a while," he added, then wondered irritably why he'd suggested it.

"Hide you?" She seemed startled by the notion, but nodded slowly. "Very well. I'm sure that Annie won't mind terribly. If you don't stay long and I tell her who you are, that is."

"I wouldn't count on that."

His dry tone made her flush, and she said quickly, "No, I never told her *every*thing."

"Very wise of you. I shouldn't like to have—by the by, was she the leader of that group?" When Elizabeth gave a laughing nod, he groaned. "I thought so. Lord save us. She looks like a bear in skirts."

"Annie is very kind, and she's also a wonderful person. You wouldn't say things like that if—"

"Angel. I hate to bring this up, but it ain't healthy for me out here right now. Do you suppose we could finish this conversation elsewhere?"

After several seconds of thought Elizabeth said, "Yes. Come with me."

Ian gave Tabitha a sour glance. "'Tis aboot time ye got here. 'Twas you who managed tha' they meet again, am I right?"

"Yes." She didn't look at him as she smoothed wrinkles from her short skirt and billowing bloomers with one hand. Dust blew down the street, and she waved it around her with a quick flip of her hand. "I do admit it seems to have worked out better that the ladies went into Sweetwater Saloon to sing instead of standing outside. And Kincade did look happy to see her, didn't he?"

"Madam," Ian growled, "at tha' moment the rogue most probably would ha' looked glad to see the de'il hisself show up tae rescue him from a well-deserved bullet."

"I daresay that's possible. Well, you've allowed him to waste over half a year wandering around alone without any change at all, I see. I simply thought he should be allowed one more opportunity to improve."

Ian made a choked sound that drew Tabitha's interested gaze. Finally he gasped out, "Ye ha' no' been here tae see wha' I ha' been through wi' tha' mon. Kinsman or no', I can tell ye tha' I ha' been tempted more than once tae let him kill hisself by wha'ever means presented itself next, I can tell ye tha'."

"Calm down, Ian. I realize it must have taken longer than I realized to return, but I was . . . distracted. Yes, I had trouble locating Horatio, and then—well, never mind that. But I was certain you could handle whatever came up."

"Aye, so I did." His eyes narrowed on her. "Ye stopped tae listen tae a concert, dinna ye? Och, don't bother tae deny it. Guilt is on yer face plain as dirt."

"Well, who knows when Bizet will put on another opera, for heaven's sake? I just forgot that time is different there than here, that's all. It didn't seem like so very long . . . but don't glare at me so. I did manage to find out some interesting things about Dougal MacKay."

"Sich as?"

"*Sich as,*" she mimicked, "he is definitely behind the attempts on Kincade's life. It seems that the charming Scot did not lie to Elizabeth about that, at least."

"But Dougal's a thousand miles awa' or more. And he's a churchman."

"Not a very sincere one, it seems. Really, Ian, don't be so naive. You must stop judging people on their appearances. Dougal hired some men to find Kincade and kill him. Of course, after he was reported to have drowned in that storm off the Florida coast, the search was suspended."

Ian brightened. "Ye don't say. Then there is no danger naow."

"I didn't say that." Tabitha sighed. A burst of noise from one of the saloons drew her interest for a moment, then she looked back at Ian. "There was an article in the *New*

Orleans Picayune, or some ridiculous name like that, reporting the news about MacKay and Miss Lee's rescue from the island. Horatio directed my attention to a barrister in Edinburgh, and I left a copy of the paper on his desk. Yes, I know, interference. But unless this matter is resolved, Kincade can never come to terms with his past. Unfinished business can haunt a man, you know.''

Ian stared at her, aghast. '''Tis no bloody wonder I've been so busy trying tae keep him alive. If ye ha' any notion of how it's been—''

"Do not fret so. I realize you've taxed your resources to the limit, and I've come to help you.''

"Taxed my—I'll ha' ye know, madam, tha' countless times, I've had tae think of a distraction so he dinna get hisself shot by a mon he's won from at cards or dice, and naow he's here and someone else wants tae put a hole in his head. I tell ye, I'm about tae let the daft lad get wha' he well deserves.''

"So you've given up? I didn't know Scots did that. I seem to recall that even when outnumbered on Culloden Moor, you fought to almost the last man.'' When Ian sputtered an incoherent reply, Tabitha continued calmly, "Well, I suppose you know best.''

Ian hooked his thumbs in the wide leather belt at his waist and rocked back on his heels, ignoring the team of horses bearing down on them as they stood in the middle of the road. The wagon passed within inches, and when the dust had settled, he said calmly, "I ha' no' given up, madam. I was merely expressing my doubts.''

"My pardon. By the way, your skirt is hiked up a bit too far for modesty. Oh, don't say it—your kilt.''

Ian made a strangled sound, which Tabitha ignored. She turned to look up, then down, the street and turned back. "I believe they have gone to her hotel room. That could have most interesting consequences, don't you think? P'raps she can help us look after him until we discover just who it is that Dougal MacKay has sent to kill Kincade this time.''

''He'll ha' tae be a bloody swift villain tae kill Kincade MacKay afore the mon can do't hisself, ye know,'' Ian said between clenched teeth.

''Well, that's our task, then, to keep him alive until we find a way to save him, isn't it?'' Tabitha smiled at Ian's muttered comment. ''Don't be profane. Let's see what the handsome Lord of Glencairn is about now, shall we? If I recall his predilections, he's romancing Miss Lee out of her garters by this time. . . .''

Elizabeth tried not to stare at Kincade, and she tried not to let him see how her hands were shaking. *Kincade*. And here, in her hotel room, where he had no business being and where she was trying to appear composed and not at all affected by seeing him again. She felt vulnerable, much too vulnerable, and hoped he didn't notice.

He ranged the spacious room like a caged lion, picking up fliers and pamphlets, then putting them down again with muttered comments that she was just as glad not to hear. A predatory beast in a black frock coat and starched white shirt—did he have to be so dangerously beautiful?

What on earth would Annie say? And whatever had possessed her even to speak to him, much less invite him to come to her hotel room? If the proprietor found out, they would be asked to leave immediately. Mr. Simmons wasn't too happy about his guests' avocation anyway. He said it looked bad for his establishment. Only Annie's forceful personality had brought him to agree to let them stay this long.

Elizabeth walked to a small desk and tried to look busy. She forced herself to concentrate on a sheaf of signed petitions instead of Kincade, but it was an effort. The shock of seeing him again after so long had rendered her almost mute for the moment, and their conversation had faded quickly.

After the amenities there didn't seem to be too much to say to one another. It could have been the memories, the still-sharp pain that could cut her when she let herself think about all they had shared. And his rejection.

Kincade turned, a lazy smile curving the erotic line of his mouth, his eyes half-lidded and carefully remote. He didn't seem in any hurry to renew their former intimacy, and she didn't know whether she was glad or disappointed.

"What are those?" Kincade asked, gesturing to the sheaf of papers she held.

"Signed petitions to prohibit alcohol in public establishments."

"All these people signed up to outlaw liquor?" An expression of stunned disbelief replaced his reserve.

Elizabeth nodded and said with a wry smile, "It wasn't easy. We've been crusading for some time now, and our membership is slowly increasing."

"Really. I find it fascinating that so many people are willing to perjure themselves." He flicked her a saturnine glance, and for a moment her breath caught.

Just a look, a glance from beneath the tangled brush of his lashes, and she felt the old fires flare high before she could tamp them back down. It occurred to her that he had the right idea in staying across the room from her. Heaven help her if they accidentally touched one another.

She stood awkwardly; it was only the unexpectedness of this meeting that left her reeling, she told herself. That was all.

"So," she said in a cool tone that made his brow lift, "you're still cheating at cards."

His mouth curved into a moody smile. "Your faith in me is touching. I suppose I would cheat if it was necessary, but it ain't. Not with the men I've met out here." He leaned back against a table, his hands behind him and propping up his lean frame. Elizabeth could have sworn she felt his heat, even six feet away. His smile was mocking. "You're still carrying on with noble causes, I see."

"Yes." She looked back down at the sheaf of papers in

her hands. "What are you doing in Arizona?" She looked up to see his casual shrug.

"Same thing I've been doing for the past months. Looking over America and seeing if it really is the land of freedom and opportunity."

Elizabeth tilted her head to one side. "You sound different. Your accent, I mean. It's—it's changed."

"My close association with riffraff has probably done a great deal toward that end, I'm afraid." He sounded only faintly regretful.

"And have you made up your mind about America?"

"Not really. There's so much variety here that it's hard to decide anything." A slow smile curled his mouth. "I do admit, however, that a man could do whatever he pleased without much trouble."

"If there are so many options, why are you still gambling, may I ask?"

He shrugged again. "It's quick, easy, and what I know best."

"I find that difficult to believe. The last part, at any rate. You have been educated, you know."

"Yes, but it's deuced difficult to make a living by quoting Socrates or reciting important dates in history. I haven't found a single person interested in paying to learn when the Magna Carta was signed. Or even learn its purpose. I could tutor in agriculture, I suppose, but the methods I would employ would be unsuitable here. Difference in climate, I suspect."

Elizabeth arranged the petitions in an orderly stack and put a small paperweight atop them. She could feel his gaze on her, those green eyes that still haunted her dreams at night, hot and smoky and much too appealing.

"Well," she said, "I'm certain you could find honest employment if you looked hard enough."

"I'm certain I could too." Amusement threaded his voice. "Unfortunately the only honest employment I've been able to find has involved scraping vegetable marrows or mucking out stalls. I have an aversion to both those stellar occupations.''

''But, Kincade, they're *honest* jobs, even if hard.''

''Yes. Perhaps that's one of the detractions. I seem to have a natural bent for the effortless.''

Exasperated, she snapped, ''Always the easy way out for you. You just don't want to try.''

''No,'' he agreed, ''I suppose I don't. I'm perfectly satisfied with what I do. Except when some blighter waves a loaded pistol in my face.'' A frown clouded his eyes. ''I think I'm going to invest in my own weapon. That's happened one too many times for me to be comfortable without one.''

''Oh, wonderful. Now you'll be shot twice as quickly. If a man sees that you're armed, he's much more likely to assume that you'll shoot him.''

''Sweetheart,'' Kincade said dryly, ''when a man out west sees that I'm *un*armed, he seems to find it much easier to draw. It's called having an edge, I believe.''

''So. This man who's angry with you—how do you plan on avoiding him?''

''By leaving town as soon as possible. Stage, horse, it doesn't matter how, just so it's quick.''

Elizabeth smoothed her blue polished cotton skirt with one hand and glanced toward the window. The sun was shining and a soft wind belled out the curtains.

''You could work for us if you like, Kincade.''

He seemed startled, his lean frame straightening from his languid position against the table. ''Work for you? As what—bait? A bad example? A 'this is what you'll become if you don't stop drinking' sort of thing?''

A faint smile touched her lips. ''Not quite. Annie and I were discussing the need for a gentleman employee just the other day. Sometimes it's difficult for us to manage the baggage alone.''

''I see.'' Kincade laughed softly. ''Angel, I don't think

you could pay me enough to toddle after your bloody trunks full of petticoats.''

She flushed. "Not just that. Some of the organizational details—never mind. You're not interested. And I don't know why I even mentioned it, really. I just thought you might appreciate some help at a difficult time."

She didn't dare examine her motives any more closely than that, especially not with Kincade looking at her with a hot, familiar gleam in his eyes.

"Much as I appreciate the offer," he drawled, "I'd as soon go along as I am, thank you. I will keep it in mind for the future, just in case I find myself incapable of functioning as anything but a lady's maid."

Elizabeth hadn't really expected him to agree, but she was disappointed nonetheless. He was watching her, an inscrutable expression on his face that made her retreat into idle chatter to hide her disappointment.

"Our cause is really growing, you know, with more new members every day. Temperance and reform have become a national topic now. Of course, with all this attention, we are required to move on continuously. Annie is paid very well to give public speeches, and several ministers have stepped forward to espouse our cause."

"How handy. To have God on your side, I mean." Kincade smiled when she made a soft exclamation. "I never doubted it, of course. You were so emphatic about women's rights in Eden."

"Eden." A wistful pang struck her. "I had forgotten you called it that."

He shrugged and said, "And you forgot about the serpent in Eden, didn't you. Good thing I reminded you."

Elizabeth's heart lurched. "You needn't remind me of that."

"No, I suppose not. Maybe I was only reminding me." He glanced out the window and shifted restlessly. When he glanced back at her, Elizabeth saw a fleeting sadness in his eyes, and barely heard his husky, "It was a wonderful time, wasn't it, angel?"

She opened her mouth to reply, to tell him that she'd never forget the island or him, no matter what he thought, but a loud noise outside the window distracted them both. Kincade stepped to the window and pushed aside the curtain, then laughed.

"Hullo. I think I hear our tender feminists approaching now. And they don't sound like they're singing lullabies."

It was Elizabeth's cousin Annie, and she was shouting and leading a stirring prayer against the evils of alcohol. This prayer meeting appeared to be attended by most of Tucson's law-enforcement officers, none of whom looked happy.

"Oh dear," she murmured as she leaned farther out the window, "I do hope Annie doesn't get arrested again."

"Again?" Kincade gave a short laugh. "My, my, you do wax enthusiastic about this stuff, don't you? Being arrested adds a piquant touch of excitement, I'll say that for you."

She turned to glare at him. "Kincade MacKay, I would appreciate it if you would not mock our work. Being arrested is all part of this, I have learned."

"No. Don't tell me that you are an escaped felon. Dear Lord, and here I was thinking you a well-reared female. You've changed, m'dear."

"Too bad I can't say the same thing for you. You're the same reckless card cheat you always were."

"Have I claimed different?" He shrugged. "Well, as I hear your illustrious battle-ax Annie coming much too near, I find that I'd rather face a loaded pistol instead of her enthusiasm. My gratitude for shelter in my time of need, angel."

Elizabeth made an inarticulate sound, and he paused. An odd expression flickered on his face, then he gave a light shrug.

"I wish you well, angel. I really do. I hope you're happy."

Her throat closed and she couldn't say anything. It would be too dangerous. It had started all over again, that aching emptiness inside her. It was as sharp and painful as it had been in the first weeks after he'd left her in New Orleans.

"Good-bye, Kincade," she whispered, and to her dismay he stepped forward and lifted her chin.

His head lowered, and his mouth brushed lightly over her parted lips. She closed her eyes. He kissed her with a soft gentleness, his fingers moving in whispery caresses against her cheek.

He'd meant it to be a light, sweet kiss, but just the taste of her sparked something in him that surprised and chagrined him. He didn't want it to end. He wanted to strip her layers of clothes away from her firm, compact little body and lay her on the bed in the next room and do all the things to her that he'd done in his imagination every night since Eden.

Eden. Christ. He was getting maudlin in his old age. Thirty—or was it thirty-one now? He couldn't remember. Whichever, he was too damned old to be dreaming impossible dreams. About impossible women. And Elizabeth Lee was an impossible woman, with her irritating quest. Temperance *and* female equality. Jesus. Why hadn't she taken up fencing? Or lion taming? Something likely to be more rewarding and less dangerous.

Well, he hadn't gotten this far along by being too stupid, and he knew better than to get himself tangled up with her again. It had taken a deuced long time to go for more than an hour without thinking of her since New Orleans, and he damned sure didn't need to be distracted again. It was a miserable feeling to live with.

Kincade wrenched his mouth from hers and stared down at her. Bloody hell. He'd missed her. Elizabeth, with her pale, star-frost hair and sapphire eyes, the sensuous curve of her lips and even more sensuous curves of her body—oh yes, he knew well the havoc she could wreak on him if he allowed it. And he intended to run as far and fast as he could before both of them were very sorry.

"Bye, angel," he murmured, rubbing his thumb over her top lip in a soothing caress.

When she opened her eyes, she blinked at him hazily. He could see the rapid rise and fall of her breasts as she worked for air, and forced his attention to retreat.

"Kincade . . ."

That almost undid him, her throaty murmur of his name as if they were in bed, as if he were inside her again—he dropped his arms away from her and backed away. He couldn't listen to the siren song of his name on her lips. God no, he couldn't listen.

It was too dangerous for her, and he wasn't that much of a scoundrel.

But leaving her again was the hardest thing he'd done in longer than he could remember.

Chapter 14

Dodge City, Kansas

STEAM BILLOWED from the engine as the train pulled into the station with a loud screech of metal on metal. Elizabeth stood up, smoothing her skirts with a gloved hand as she held on to the seat in front of her with the other.

"You look as if you've eaten a persimmon," Annie said in a dry, flat tone.

Elizabeth's head jerked around. "I beg pardon?" She stared at her cousin's broad face, framed by a soft cloud of short brown hair. Annie was tall, dwarfing Elizabeth and most of the men on the train, and she made no effort to appear any smaller than she was.

"I said, you look as if you've eaten a persimmon. Have you forgotten how to smile again?"

"No. No, of course not. It's just that—"

"It's just that ever since we left Tucson, you stare out the window and don't hear anything I say. It reminds me of how you acted when you first came back from England." Annie pushed back a strand of her hair and gave Elizabeth a close look that seemed to see clear inside her soul.

Elizabeth flushed, and ducked to pick up her wicker basket from the seat, stuffing her book, *The Story of My Life As a Victim of Man's Depredations* by Charlotte Pickering Spencer inside the basket before closing it. Annie was too perceptive. She should have known she couldn't fool her for long, but she'd hoped to avoid a lecture on "Men Who Fool

171

Around with Gullible Women.'' She'd heard it times without number, and Annie always added spicier advice each time.

"That man,'' Annie said, hefting her wicker hamper with one hand and a heavy canvas bag of pamphlets with the other, ''the man I saw leaving our hotel last week—did you know him?''

"Really, Annie, I'm not at all certain who you mean. I am sure there are a great many men who leave hotels, and I don't think—''

"Rubbish.'' Annie gave her a sharp glance, her bulky frame blocking the aisle as she looked down at Elizabeth. "You know perfectly well which man I mean. I saw you looking at him from the upstairs window. Besides. I know his type.''

"His type?''

"Yes. Handsome. With that wicked air about him that makes a woman want to tempt the devil at times.'' Annie nodded wisely. "Oh yes, don't think I haven't been tempted a time or two in my life. But I had sense enough to avoid falling *hopelessly* in love.''

Elizabeth stared at Annie. Well aware of her cousin's views on men, love, and the pitfalls of marriage—legalized prostitution, she called it in her more mellow moments— Elizabeth turned to look out the window of the rapidly emptying train and asked, "What did you say this town is called?''

Annie snorted. "Dodge City. I think it is probably going to be one of our toughest nuts to crack so far. Alcohol has an absolute stranglehold on the men here.''

Elizabeth hoped so. She would welcome a diversion. Even heated insults from enraged males cornered in the bastions of masculinity they called saloons would help. . . .

She held fast to that thought during the next months as she accompanied Annie to towns called Wichita, Topeka, and Lawrence.

Finally in Lawrence she met up with Kincade MacKay again, almost a year to the day after she'd first met him aboard the *Tom Hopkins*. This time he wasn't running from an enraged cowboy, but stood facing a man in the middle of the wide, dusty street.

Her heart skipped a beat, then two, as she saw that the two men were poised for deadly combat. This was a Kincade she'd never seen before, looking rather like a natty desperado in a black derby, starched white shirt, string tie, black frock coat, slim-legged trousers, and a lethal pistol strapped low to his right thigh. He looked cool and efficient, his gaze never wavering from the man who faced him.

"MacKay," the man growled, "I say you're a damned cheat and a coward."

Kincade gave an almost imperceptible shrug. "I heard you."

"Then draw, dammit."

"You're the one who's miffed, Colby. You draw if that's what you're sure you want."

Elizabeth clutched blindly at a hitching rail in front of the rickety boardwalk stretched along the street. Kincade looked different, sounded different, his voice bearing only a faint trace of the cultured English accents she was used to hearing. God, how had he changed so drastically in only a year?

The man called Colby shifted backward a step, keeping his eyes on Kincade. A crowd of interested spectators peeked out of doorways and windows and from behind scattered barriers as the two men stood in the heat and searing sun. A gunfight in Lawrence was a rarity, indeed, and had gathered an immediate crowd.

For Elizabeth, her world had narrowed with alarming clarity to this one rutted track in the middle of a wide expanse of dust and early-autumn heat. What on earth was Kincade doing? Could he even shoot that pistol low on his hip, or was this another bluff?

A shudder racked her, and she closed her eyes. Then she

felt Annie's hand on her shoulder and heard her gravelly voice in her ear.

"Steady, Elizabeth. Maybe we should go back inside where it's safe."

"No. I—I have to stay."

Annie gave her a piercing stare. "Ah."

The one word contained a wealth of understanding, but fear made Elizabeth oblivious to everything but the scene in the street. She felt more than saw the blur of motion as first Colby, then Kincade went for their guns, heard the rippling explosion of gunfire, and smelled the hot, sharp scent of sulfur and gunpowder. Colby fell, spun backward by the force of a bullet. Elizabeth felt ashamed of her sweep of relief.

Then to her horror, she saw Kincade go to his knees in the street in a slow, unhurried motion, like the crumpling of a rag doll.

"Ian," Tabitha said in a strained voice. "God's blood, he's been shot!"

"Aye, madam, well I know tha'." Ian sounded grim. "'Twas all I could think tha' would keep the lad out o' trouble for a spell."

"Yes, dying *is* a cure for mischief making, I'll grant you," Tabitha snapped, "but don't you find it a bit extreme? Couldn't you have considered another option?"

Ian glared at her. The crowd jostled around them, and men ran toward the two fallen men still lying in the street. "How else d'ye think I can keep tha' bloody fool from bein' shot in the back? And he's no' dead. Yet. He's just a wee bit blooded, is all. He'll be fine wi' a bit o' nursin'."

Tabitha shot a glance toward Elizabeth Lee, coughed at the dust stirred up by racing spectators, and nodded slowly. "Maybe you're right this time. He needs a rest, and if a little wound or two is required, it's better than being—what was it that horrid man in Tucson said?—being shot full of as many holes as a tea strainer?"

"Aye, tha' sounds close enough. This has become serious of late, y'know. No' all of these men are jus' bad losers, I think. Some of them seek him out a'purpose, and I believe they are hired assassins."

"Assassins. Yes. No doubt that would be Dougal's way of ridding himself of a bothersome nephew who happens to hold a title and lands." Tabitha frowned. "We need to counteract all these attempts, Ian. While Miss Lee nurses him back to health—what?"

Ian choked, then managed to wheeze, "Nay. I dinna plan on her bein' here when this came aboot. . . ."

"Oh, don't be an old tabby. As you can see, he won't have the strength to do much of anything now, will he?" Tabitha smiled when Ian turned to stare at his kinsman. Kincade had managed to sit up, but was pale and wobbly, reeling as he tried to get to his knees. "See what I mean?" Tabitha pointed out. "She's safe enough for now."

"God save us," Ian muttered, watching as Elizabeth broke free of Annie's grasp and ran to kneel beside Kincade. "I dinna think I should listen tae ye, madam, but I canna think of another solution, either."

"There you go." Tabitha smiled. "And if you like, I'll see that he has no energy for some time." She gave a wave of one hand, then began walking toward the crowd in the street.

Elizabeth's breath caught on a sob. "Kincade, oh Kincade, are you badly hurt?"

He was deathly pale, and held one hand to his left shoulder. It took him a moment to drag his attention to her, and there was a faint spark of surprise in his eyes before he managed a familiar, cocky grin.

"You always seem to turn up at the worst times in my life, angel. How do you do it?"

She stared at him as he wheezed, "Did I kill the bloody bastard?"

There was no need for her to reply; as his words faded so

did Kincade. With a peculiar, faintly puzzled expression on his face, he keeled over in the dust.

"Here," Annie said behind her as Elizabeth gave a cry and tried to turn him over, "let me help. A doctor will be here in a moment."

"Yes, of course." Elizabeth moved dazedly, barely aware of Colby being carted away by the undertaker, fully aware of Kincade's every unconscious moan. Three men hefted him between them at the doctor's instructions.

"Where to, doc?" one of them asked.

The physician, a portly man with iron-gray hair and a beard, shook his head. "I've no room in my office. Three other idiots are already there."

"Bring him to the hotel," Annie put in before Elizabeth could speak. "He can stay in our room."

One of the men gave her a guarded look. "Your room? Do you think—"

"I think it's not your place to question me, sir." Annie drew herself up in righteous indignation. "We happen to know this gentleman, and he is to be put in our room at once."

Still hesitating, the man peered at her. "Ain't you one of those abstinence ladies? I heard about you wimmin and how you go 'round sayin' all kinds of crazy stuff. You ain't gonna do nothin' crazy, are ya?"

"Lord save us from stupid men." Annie glared at him, and Elizabeth began to recover from her shock as she saw the militant gleam in her cousin's eyes.

"Sir," she said quickly, "this man is our cousin. We have been looking for him. Please be so kind as to put him in our hotel room. Miss Lee and I will care for him, if that's what you're worried about."

The man spat on the ground. "Ain't worried about that none. More worried about what th' sheriff might wanna say to him when he gets back."

"The sheriff is welcome to do or say whatever he likes when he returns," Annie said sharply. "Feel free to inform him. Now, it would be best if you make up your mind what to do, because if you don't hurry, he's likely to bleed to death here in the middle of the street.''

It looked to be true. Blood dripped steadily from Kincade's shoulder to form odd crimson splotches in the dust. He made a distressed sound in the back of his throat as he was hefted for a better grip, and with a resigned mutter of acceptance, the man motioned for the others to help carry Kincade to the hotel.

Elizabeth shot Annie a look of gratitude. She hadn't been able to think as swiftly. Thank heavens Annie had sized up the situation and said what was needed to be said.

When the man deposited Kincade on the bed in her room, Elizabeth fluttered about anxiously. The clean bed linens were immediately splotched with blood and dust, and as Annie gave instructions Dr. Whitney subjected Kincade to a thorough examination.

Though it was suggested that she leave, Elizabeth would not budge. She waited near the door, catching occasional glimpses of Kincade as the doctor worked on him, listening to his frequent mutters of pain as he thrashed between consciousness and unconsciousness. Her throat closed with a welling of helpless frustration.

"Hold him," the doctor said briskly, and one of the men grasped Kincade by both arms.

"Sheeit!" he exclaimed an instant later when Kincade jerked free and managed to almost knock him down. "Help me, Dolan."

The man named Dolan leaned forward, and with both men catching and gripping Kincade tightly, they were able to push his shoulders back against the mattress for the doctor to continue his examination. Kincade groaned, bucking and heaving, and another man had to come and help hold him as the doctor probed for the bullet in his torn shoulder with a long, thin instrument.

Elizabeth squeezed her eyes shut and inhaled deeply, but it was the rusty scent of fresh blood and sweat. A wave of weakness washed over her when she heard Kincade's guttural groans, and she was glad he was unconscious. She felt faint. She couldn't stand it, knowing they were hurting him and there was nothing she could do. At least he wasn't conscious.

"Got it," the doctor finally said with a sort of strangled gasp, and Elizabeth opened her eyes in time to see him lift a bloody chunk of something in the needle-thin forceps. "Ain't nothing tears a man up more than a forty-four slug," he muttered wearily. He glanced at Elizabeth standing weakly by the door. "Your cousin made it through this, but that doesn't mean he'll make it. That slug did a lot of damage, but missed vital organs. If he doesn't die from a fever, he might live."

The terse words did nothing to reassure her, but she managed a nod. "We . . . we'll nurse him."

"That's up to you, young lady." Straightening, the doctor slid Kincade a speculative look and signaled for the three men to release him. "He's out. Go on home, boys." He began wrapping up his bloody instruments in a towel, and glanced at Elizabeth. "You may be just nursing him for the hangman's noose, you know."

A wave of panic made her voice quaver. "Hangman?"

"Yep. Colby is dead. Your cousin shoots straighter." The doctor frowned slightly. "Though I could have sworn that Pete Phillips told me Colby had MacKay dead to rights. Colby was known to be a dead shot, and this young man's just a beginner, from what I hear. Don't know how Colby missed. Well, it was his last mistake, I reckon."

"Colby didn't miss," Elizabeth pointed out. "Mr. MacKay is wounded."

"Yeah, but not bad enough to make a difference to the outcome. Our local sheriff doesn't care too much for folks shooting each other."

"But they were both shooting at each other. Won't the sheriff realize that?"

"I don't rightly know. I'm just the local sawbones, not a

lawyer, miss. If I were you, by the way, I'd get him one. If he recovers—well, you can worry about it then, I guess.''

With that cryptic advice, the physician gathered up his bloodstained instruments and left. Annie bustled around the bed, removing the remnants of Kincade's shirt that had been thrown to the floor, supervising the replacement of fresh linens under him. When the hotel maid had gone at last, she looked at Elizabeth.

''I suppose we should take off the rest of his clothes and bathe him as best we can for the time being. He might as well rest in comfort.''

Elizabeth stared dubiously at Kincade. He looked so big and pale and strange lying in the bed. Long lashes shadowed his cheeks, and lines of pain were etched around his mouth. She looked back up at her cousin's smooth, capable face and felt a wave of relief wash over her.

''Thank you, Annie. I suppose I'm absolutely useless in an emergency.''

Annie smiled and said kindly, ''Nonsense. You're just too involved, that's all. It's much easier for someone who's not emotionally attached. Of course, it will be you who sits beside him until he either recovers or—until he recovers. I have work to do.''

''Yes, I know. I'm sorry. This is all such a wretched inconvenience to you. . . .''

''I won't listen to that. This straight-shooting rogue obviously means something to you. Therefore he does to me, too.'' Annie's voice softened. ''Honey, this is him, isn't it, the man you were shipwrecked with.''

''Yes. Kincade MacKay.'' Emotion made her voice quaver, and to hide the depth of her feelings, Elizabeth added in a light tone, ''He's nothing more than a rogue, of course, as you said. I knew that all along.''

''Of course you did. But he's a human being, and I approve of your generosity of spirit.''

Annie's acceptance made Elizabeth feel less foolish and more humanitarian. She thought about that when her cousin helped her bathe him; she blushed in faint embarrassment at the removal of Kincade's clothes.

"Well," Annie said, gazing down at him with unabashed admiration and attention, "well. He's certainly a well-made devil, for all that he's no more than a rogue."

Elizabeth couldn't answer. She was remembering Kincade's body next to hers, the taut, smooth feel of his skin under her clutching hands. It was enough to drive her crazy if she thought about it too long, and she hurried through his bath and covered him with a clean sheet that looked stark white against his dark skin.

He tossed and turned fitfully, occasionally throwing off the sheet. Annie left her alone with him and went to her temperance meeting. When it was quiet in the hotel room and afternoon shadows cooled the interior, Elizabeth finally relaxed enough to recline on a chaise she dragged near the bed.

She didn't realize she'd fallen asleep until she heard Kincade say in a thick, raspy voice, "Angel? Is it really you?"

She sat up, peered through the shadows, and saw him try to lever himself to a sitting position.

"Yes, it's me. Don't try to sit up, Kincade." Sliding from the chaise, she was at his side in an instant, pressing her palm against his forehead and holding him down with a slight pressure. The fact that he allowed it, and that he didn't seem to have the strength to resist, alarmed her. "Please," she said softly, "try not to move. You may hurt yourself."

A hoarse laugh whispered from him. "Colby had first chance at tha'—" He coughed, moaned at the pain that must have involved, and coughed again. "Ah Jesus, angel, I feel as if I've been kicked in the chest by a two-ton mule."

Fear for him made her voice sharp. "It's no more than you deserve, standing out there in the street like a fool and shooting at someone. What did you expect? That he'd sing you lullabies instead of shoot back?"

"Such sympathy," Kincade muttered. "Where am I?"

"You're in my hotel room. If you don't quiet down, I'll put you back in the street."

"Your room?" A strangled breath exhaled. "Damn, angel. Ye should know better than tae do this."

"I do. But you're hurt, and this is better than a cell in the local jail, isn't it? Besides, Annie suggested it."

"Th' dragon lady? Och, will wonders ne'er cease, lass."

Elizabeth lit a lamp to dispel the gloom and turned to look at him. His thickening brogue alerted her to the fact that he hovered close to delirium, and she ducked her head and made briskly efficient motions that she hoped would help. Kincade looked terrible; dark shadows marked his face, and his eyes were feverish and glazed. His skin was hot and dry to the touch.

"I'll get you a cool, wet cloth," she said, and plumped his pillow. "Be still. You don't need sympathy right now, you need rest."

And laudanum, she thought as she searched for the small brown bottle Dr. Whitney had left for him. Annie had left it on a table in the sitting room, and by the time she returned with it, Kincade was sitting up in bed with his bare legs swung over the side.

"You idiot," she gasped out. "What do you think you're doing?"

His voice came out all wrong, shaky and breathless and tinged with obvious pain. "Gettin' out o' here, angel. I canna make things . . . hard for ye . . . again."

She wanted to weep. His brogue was thick and raspy, and he felt so hot to the touch.

"Kincade MacKay, if you don't lie back down, things will be more than hard for me." She placed the bottle on the bedside table and tried to push him back to the mattress without hurting him, noting the small red stain that had flowered on the white linen bandage. "Oh, you've started your wound bleeding again. Lie down . . . no, don't push my hands away. *Lie down.*"

Kincade blinked fuzzily and collapsed back onto the bed with a frustrated groan. "Weak as . . . a bloody . . . new kitten, dammit. Silly angel. Don' ye know tha' people . . . will talk aboot . . . ye for this?"

"Probably. I've learned a great deal about how people talk in the past twelve months. I can't imagine why I ever let it bother me. Or why I worried about it after we were rescued. I've endured—stop that and lie still—much more than just gossip about being alone on an island with you."

His long lashes lifted slightly, and he gave her a hazy look from beneath them. "Strong," he mumbled. "Good lass."

His faint praise brought Elizabeth a warm feeling as she bustled about tucking sheets around him and scolding him for opening his wound. By the time she had a spoon filled with laudanum and held it over his head, he was looking at her with wry, pained amusement.

"Gone domestic on me, ha' ye? Must be the . . . sight . . . o' a helpless mon tha' . . . stirs ye."

"Helpless? In a pig's eye. Open your mouth. That's right," she said in the same tone she could have used on a small, recalcitrant boy. "Swallow it all and pretty soon the pain will ease."

Later, after he'd slipped back into an uneasy sleep, she thought of her reply and smiled wryly. She'd meant it. The first wave of gossip that had shamed her upon arriving back in New Orleans had paled in light of the things that were said about militant female suffragettes. Open animosity was common. Insults were common. Anything that could be said about Kincade recovering in her hotel room was minor compared with what she'd already heard in packed meeting rooms all over the country.

In a lot of cases, men did not like to be told that their womenfolk had thoughts of their own, rights of their own. The fact that no bill had been passed in Congress amending the Constitution and giving women enfranchisement was a sore spot. Touring with Annie had been an enlightening situation and, surprisingly, made her more sure than ever that she was doing the right thing.

Now it had led her to Kincade.

With only the lamp lit, Elizabeth felt free to examine his face. He looked much the same; a little harder, maybe, around the edges. He was thinner, and despite his gray pallor, he was darker, more sun-browned than he'd been on the sands of Eden. Underlying his pain-twisted features, the new hardness wasn't exactly reassuring.

She kept remembering how he'd looked out there in the middle of the street, his lean body in a half crouch, the pistol appearing in his hand as magically as if he were performing another one of his blasted card tricks for her. She hadn't taken him seriously when he'd said he intended to buy himself a weapon and learn to use it.

Elizabeth closed her eyes. She should have. Apparently he'd done just that, and taught himself to use it as well as any gunman. Why? she wondered with a sense of despair, why didn't he just choose an honest, law-abiding profession and stick to it? Did he have to always walk on the edge?

Rather glumly Elizabeth had the thought that she would no doubt see his likeness on a wanted poster one day soon, if it wasn't on one already. She'd prayed that Kincade would change and he had. Unfortunately it wasn't for the better.

It was a discouraging thought.

"Don't treat me like a child." Kincade slanted Annie a hot glance from beneath his lashes. Stubble darkened his jawline, and he had the peevishness of a convalescing invalid.

"Don't behave like a child if you don't want to be treated like one," Annie replied. "If you aren't having a good time, Mr. MacKay, think about us. We have to listen to your damned nonsense."

"*My* nonsense? *My* nonsense?" Kincade gave her a withering stare. "What about this tripe you featherbrained females spout day and night? Equality. Women's rights. Abstinence." He snorted. "Stupid, stupid, stupid. I don't know why you don't just wear pants and tell everyone you're a man, because you bloody well act like one."

"Do I?" Annie looked pleased. "Good. Then I ought to be able to meet men on their own ground. It's a start."

"Start?" Kincade wadded up a fistful of sheet. "I tell you what's a start, Battle-ax Annie, and that's—"

"Wait a minute." Elizabeth glared at both of them, her fists planted on her hips. "I'm getting tired of listening to you two bickering. Is that all you can do? Can't you be nice to one another for a change?"

Annie looked startled, Kincade amused.

"Nice?" he muttered with a wry twist of his lips. "This *is* nice, angel. You should have heard us yesterday."

Annie put in with a smile, "Yes, I told this lop-eared, no-good excuse for a man exactly what happens to men who complain too much."

Kincade grinned. "And I reminded her what happened to men who don't."

"Which is?" Elizabeth snapped with growing impatience.

"Why," said Kincade, "they end up joining ladies' temperance unions."

"Fat chance, Kincade," Annie jeered. "Why, we wouldn't take you if you begged."

"Madam, somehow I cannot imagine any man pleading to be within fifty miles of you strident, sexless females—"

"Enough!" Elizabeth shouted in exasperation. "My patience is gone. You two should be married to each other, the way you carry on."

Kincade laughed aloud, and even Elizabeth had to smile at the thought. Annie, buxom, ofttimes profane Annie, would sooner stand toe to toe in a shouting match with a man than she would be polite to one. It was part of her success, the complete indifference in which she held them;

her lack of deference drove some males into a complete frenzy at times.

"I would much prefer to hear a man insult me than listen to sweet blandishments that mean less than it takes for them to air," Annie had announced more times than Elizabeth could count. "Besides—insults are at least honest reactions, while sweet-talking only catches flies."

Elizabeth tried to remember that. Especially when Kincade began to recover from his wound and watched her with a waiting, predatory gaze that unnerved her. It was bad enough that she was with him most of the day; seeing the assessing lights in his eyes as he grew stronger made her remember things best forgotten.

"What did the sheriff have to say?" she asked to change the subject.

Kincade shrugged and winced at the pain. "Nothing intelligent. He told me to leave town as soon as I could sit a horse. It doesn't seem to matter that I can prove self-defense. Colby braced me, as they say, not the other way around. He also said that as your *cousin,* I was walking a thin line between being ridden out of town on a rail, and being tarred and feathered and ridden out of town on a rail."

"I don't believe that."

"It's true, angel. Trust me."

Elizabeth shot him a quick, fierce glance. "Why is it, Kincade MacKay, that when you say 'Trust me,' you sound like a snake? *'Trussst me'*—I'd sooner trust a rattler."

He grinned, completely unmoved by her insult. "I always knew you'd grow up to be smart one day. Don't ever trust anyone, angel. It's bad business."

She fell silent, thinking of the strange incidents that had occurred lately. Twice Kincade had been nearly killed, each of the incidents made to look like accidents. She didn't believe that. The laudanum had been perfectly fine when she'd given it to him the night before; someone had put a deadly poison in it, and if not for the fact that she'd accidentally spilled some and it had eaten a hole in the sheet, she would not have known before giving him a dose. Of course, no one knew anything about it. Or about the loose ceiling fixture that had almost crashed down on his head, and it was found that the cord had been sawed almost in two.

There had been no logical explanation for either episode. Kincade had shrugged them off, giving her a sardonic gaze when she'd said they just *had* to be accidents.

"Right-ho, angel," he'd drawled. "I can name a lot of other accidents, too, that can't be explained."

"You suspect your uncle."

"It does have the taint of Dougal's fine hand, I must admit. Once, in London, I was served a gooseberry tart filled with enough poison to kill half the East Row. If the maid had not dropped the serving tray and one of Sir Percival's bloody dogs grabbed the tart, I would be playing whist with my ancestors now instead of lying in your bed."

Elizabeth remembered that and glanced at Kincade to see if his thoughts were running along the same line. They must have been, because he put out a hand and murmured, "I hate to see you lose your illusions, angel. Not everyone is nice, are they?"

"No." She took his hand under the guise of checking his pulse, and then released it. "You of all people should know that I've been made most aware of that recently," she said before pausing to think about the implications of her comment. Kincade's pained grimace flustered her, and to cover her sudden confusion, she walked to the table on the other side of the room and began rearranging the notes for Annie's speech later that afternoon.

A hot flush stained her cheeks, and she heard Annie clear her throat and say something about going to the lobby for a glass of iced lemonade. Elizabeth stood dismally silent.

It was Kincade's careless comments that had made her reveal that he'd hurt her. She wished she could think of a likely excuse to flee, one that he would believe and not consider as flight. She didn't want him to know how badly he'd hurt her, or that he even had the power to hurt her.

"Angel?"

"Don't call me that." She whirled around, emotion almost choking her. "I'm not your angel. I'm not an angel at all. I'm a woman, and I don't know why I ever bothered to pull you out of the street. Ever since you've begun recuperating, you've done your best to . . . to . . . I don't know how to put it. You've tried to make me crazy again, that's all I know."

Kincade was frowning. His eyes glittered like green lamps beneath the thick fringe of his lashes.

"Have I touched you? Made any forward suggestions? No. I haven't. Why are you so angry with me, Lizzie?"

"Elizabeth. My name is Elizabeth. Can't you just call me by the proper name?"

He sat up and flung the sheets back and started to rise. When Elizabeth gave a small squeal, he smiled grimly. "Don't worry. I've got my pants on. I wouldn't want to shock you, now that you're a feminist instead of a female. I was under the impression, however, that feminists were proponents of free love. . . ."

She glared at him. "You know exactly what I meant, Kincade MacKay. Don't pretend to misunderstand me."

"Elizabeth." He sounded faintly puzzled. "Is it the strain of caring for me that has you so upset? Is that why you're being so—irrational?"

"Irrational?" She drew in a sharp breath. Somewhere deep inside she knew he was right. She was reacting with an irrational intensity that was only a natural result of being so close to him and remembering how she'd loved him so much—until he'd left her in New Orleans and not even looked back. Not once. Not until the day she'd seen him in Tucson, and then he'd had the audacity to leave her behind again. Oh yes, she knew well the foolishness of being in love with him, yet it had not made a penny's worth of difference to her foolish, foolish heart.

"Excuse me," she managed to say politely. "I believe I *am* overwrought. Don't worry. I'll be fine. And please—don't get up. It's taken you a week to sleep without waking us all up. I'll just go downstairs for a while."

She left quickly, not looking at him again, not wanting to see the steady regard in his eyes that would tell her he knew what was the matter.

"I believe I have found the source of our troubles," Tabitha said, and beckoned to Ian. "Come along. While Kincade sulks, we can figure out a plan."

"A plan," Ian said gloomily. "I dinna know how much more o' this I can bear."

"You'll be surprised at your resources." Tabitha gave a swift wave of her arm, and they were standing in the hotel lobby. Several suffragettes were there, talking with Elizabeth. Tabitha eyed them. "Do you think my costume appropriate? I rather fancy that outfit there, with the bloomers and short skirt with matching piping along the hem and cuffs."

"Madam, I dinna see the point in caring, as no one ha' seen us yet."

Tabitha's glance was reproving. "Good thing, as that skirt of yours would give them a fit of the giggles. Or the vapors. Anyway, I like looking my best. One never knows when one might be called upon to appear suddenly. These bloomers are so comfortable, I rather wish that we'd worn them in my day. Much more sensible, as long skirts hamper movement so. Don't you think?"

Ian muttered an indistinct reply.

"Do you know who created these?" Tabitha asked, ignoring his sour expression. "Amelia Bloomer. Fascinating woman. Gives wonderful speeches. As does Elizabeth Cady Stanton and Susan B. Anthony. So many talented, interesting women nowadays. Not that there weren't in my day. Look at the queen. And—"

"Madam, if we intend tae form a plan, it willna involve

female suffragettes. 'Tis a lot o' silly nonsense, if ye ask me.''

Tabitha glared at him. "I didn't ask you. Silly nonsense? No, I hardly think so, Ian MacDonald. Women should have the vote. Former slaves have been given the vote—as well they should—but they also hold more rights than women of any race, women who rock the cradles of the world and feed the pompous men who run it, I might add. Run it into the ground, if you ask me, which I know you didn't. You're too cowardly to listen to the truth, just like the other men. God's eyeballs. Dead or alive, you're all just the same. When will men admit that women are equals?''

"Equals? Don't be spoutin' tae me about female rights, Lady Tabitha. I've noticed tha' we're all equal once we're dead.''

"But why wait until then? Why can't men admit it while we're still alive?''

Ian threw up his hands in exasperation. "Dinna ask me sich questions. Do I look as if I know the bloody answer? I canna even figure out how tae keep my lunatic descendant from bein' murthered, and ye're after me aboot women votin' on issues they canna understand or care aboot.''

"Yes, that's true.'' Tabitha fell silent, surprising Ian into staring at her suspiciously. "About Kincade, I mean,'' she said after a moment. "We need to figure out a plan to keep him alive until he can circumvent his uncle's devious plot.''

"Wha' plot?''

"Oh, didn't I tell you?''

"Nay, ye dinna tell me,'' Ian said shortly. "Wha' plot?''

"Come along, and I'll explain as we go.''

Chapter
15

THE QUIET room seemed stifling without Elizabeth moving about, her presence quiet and serene and comforting. Kincade grimaced. He was getting soft in the head. He must be. Why else would he even think about things like comfort and serenity? God knew, there had been little enough of that in his life.

He shifted position and winced at the dull throb in his shoulder, then gave it an experimental move. Good thing it was his left shoulder. He'd be in trouble if it was his right arm and shoulder. Speed and accuracy were major pluses in using a pistol, he'd discovered. A stiff arm would certainly hamper speed, accuracy, and probably his very existence. The thought of being without a pistol for his protection left him cold. He didn't relish the thought of being at other men's mercy again.

Being at the mercy of women was bad enough.

Kincade grinned suddenly. Actually, being at the mercy of these particular women was rather comfortable. He looked forward to his lively debates with the formidable Annie, and, as always, just liked watching Elizabeth.

He closed his eyes. Elizabeth. Sun-cloud hair, sky-blue eyes—a veritable angel. And she avoided him as if he had a noxious disease. Maybe he did. He was certainly suffering from something besides a mere bullet wound.

Kincade sighed and opened his eyes. He lay there a

moment longer, then rose from the bed. He'd wasted enough time convalescing. He'd wasted enough time mooning over the lovely Elizabeth. What he needed to do now—and quickly—was run as if all the hounds of hell were after him.

"Damn," he muttered as a wave of dizziness swept over him. He caught at the edge of a table and held it tightly, waiting for the dizziness to pass. Loss of blood, Dr. Whitney had said.

Loss of blood, and Elizabeth had practically turned herself inside out bringing him things like liver and some sort of oxtail soup someone had told her would give him more strength. Maybe she did like him, after all. Or she was trying to finish what Colby's bullet had begun by filling him with her damn horrible soup.

Kincade crossed slowly to the window and drew back the curtain. Wagons rolled down the street, and in the distance he could hear the sounds of the national temperance meeting going on at the site of a former beer garden. He grinned. Annie loved irony.

"Bloody teetotalers," he said affectionately, and let the curtain fall back over the window as he stepped back.

The hot, angry buzz of something passed his cheek, and he recoiled so quickly the pain from his shoulder sent him slamming to his knees. It took him an instant to realize that someone had fired at him, and that the buzz had been a bullet. He resisted the urge to look out the window. They'd be gone by now anyway.

Kincade spread his hands on his thighs and sat with his feet under him, weakly contemplating the wisdom of rising. His heart was thudding crazily, and he felt light-headed. What a time to be so weak, he thought angrily, when it seemed as if every corner held an assassin. He needed to get out of town, but there was really nowhere he could go that he wouldn't be found eventually.

The futility of his situation frustrated him. He had to

recover, and quickly, or he'd be murdered before the month was out.

"Dougal must be getting fidgety," he muttered, sweat popping out on his forehead as he managed to lurch to his feet. He swayed briefly, and reached for the leather holster and pistol on a nearby table. He needed to practice. It had taken him too long to become even slightly efficient with the unfamiliar pistol—not at all as gentlemanly and civilized as a well-balanced sword—and he didn't intend to lose what little speed and accuracy he had now by not practicing.

Elizabeth had coiled up the weapon with a look of distaste at it, and put it on a table beneath the window. It lay next to his derby. He slung it around his hips and buckled it, shoving the holster down low on his thigh. Odd, how different he felt wearing it. Who would ever have thought that Kincade MacDonald Ewen MacKay—Lord of Glencairn, Viscount Dunmors—would end up in America wearing a .45 caliber pistol on his hip and wandering aimlessly? Certainly not Kincade.

On impulse, he reached for his derby. It still bore a hole in the rounded crown where some assailant had tried for him and missed. He fingered it idly. But all rights that bullet should have killed him, yet it had not. The shot had only knocked the felt hat from his head and sent him to the floor. He sighed and tossed the hat back to the table.

There were times, he reflected, when he wondered why on earth he was still alive. It defied his imagination. He should have died several times, yet he hadn't. Something had always happened to keep him alive.

"If there's a purpose for that," he muttered aloud as he swept a hand down to draw his pistol and aim it at his reflection in the cheval glass, "I've yet to figure it out."

"Figure out what?" a soft voice asked behind him, and he turned in a swift, startled crouch. Elizabeth sucked in a sharp breath and held up her hands. "Please—I'm harmless."

Kincade glanced down at the pistol in his hand. "Not

bloody likely you are," he said irritably, and shoved it back into the holster on his hip. "Don't sneak up on me like that."

"I take it you consider yourself well enough to try to die again?" Elizabeth, white-faced and visibly shaken, moved across the room. "How inconvenient. What if you fail again? Do you expect me to nurse you forever?"

He scowled. "I don't expect a damned thing, Lizzie. I don't recall asking you to nurse me this time."

She looked past him, toward the blowing curtains over the window. "If you won't even call me by the right name, I suppose I shouldn't have expected you to be grateful."

"No," he said bluntly, "you shouldn't. But I am. I know I didn't—don't—deserve your kindness."

"That's true," she said just as bluntly. "You don't." Her gaze was ice blue, her shoulders stiff and straight. She took a step back, and her glance paused at the smoking bullet hole in the wall. Charred edges puckered in the wallpaper and still smoldered. Her horrified gaze shifted back to Kincade. He shrugged.

"Wild shot, I guess."

"Good God. Someone tried to kill you again."

"Looks that way, doesn't it?"

"Kincade—what happened?"

"I really can't say, angel. I chanced to look out the window, and when I drew back—I thought it was a hornet at first." He grimaced. "A rather deadly hornet, I'd say."

Elizabeth sank to a cane-back chair and stared at him. He returned her stare coolly, more unnerved than he wanted to admit even to himself. Elizabeth's eyes looked like two huge pools.

"Kincade, this has to stop."

"You're talking to the wrong person about that, angel. I would be perfectly willing for it to stop, thank you. I've grown accustomed to days with only a minor amount of pain in them."

"Don't be flippant. This is serious."

"Believe me, beneath the flippancy I'm dead serious."

She closed her eyes, and he saw that her hands were knotted in tight fists in her lap. Her face had paled to a paper white; he felt a pang of guilt at being indirectly responsible at the same time as he felt a bigger pang of irritation at being involved in someone else's misery. He hadn't wanted emotional entanglements, yet here he was—in a tangle that he couldn't seem to escape. The horrible thing was, there were times he didn't *want* to escape, and that in itself was unnerving enough.

If he allowed Elizabeth Lee to matter too much—worse, if he allowed her to care too much about him—future anguish was guaranteed. It would be kinder to end it now, to walk away when she wasn't looking and not glance back. Wasn't that what he'd done in New Orleans? And if not for fate, time would have eased the pain for both of them. Now here they were, trapped like weasels in a sticky morass of sentimentality and hopeless emotion. He hated it, and he knew it had to end swiftly. If anything happened to him, as it was certain to do fairly soon, it seemed, there was no point in her being nearby to agonize over it.

"I'll be moving on soon, you know," he said, and saw her eyes open and focus on him. He kept his tone light, his gaze cool. "If I linger too long in one place, I may end up spending eternity in one of these godforsaken towns of dust and boredom."

"You could do worse," she said.

"Could I?" He shrugged, ignoring the twinge of pain in his shoulder. "I don't see how. I may not have much, but I do have a certain amount of pride."

"I'll have that put on your headstone."

"Do that." He glared at her. "I'd rather be dead than follow you like a whipped puppy. Is that what you want? A man who takes orders from women?"

"Is that any worse than shooting people? And cheating them at cards?" Her voice rose, quavered on the last word, then ended in a gasp. "I don't understand you, Kincade

MacKay,'' she said when he just stared at her. "Why won't you do something with your life?''

"I am. You just don't like what I've chosen.''

"And you do? Is that why you look so contented?''

"I look,'' he grated between clenched teeth, "like a man who has been shot. Am I supposed to be ecstatic about it?''

"No. You're not supposed to get shot at all.'' She was facing him like a furious kitten, and for an instant he was reminded of their battles on the island. This Elizabeth he knew. This one he could deal with. The saintly Elizabeth he'd seen since ending up in her hotel room was quickly vanishing under his stubborn refusal to agree with her. It gave him a feeling of satisfaction.

"I'm not supposed to do a lot of things, Lizzie. That doesn't mean I won't,'' he said calmly, and saw the fury rise in her lovely blue eyes.

"Idiot. Stupid, donkey-headed idiot. You're going to be killed, and you don't even care.''

"I care.'' He shrugged. "Just not enough that I'll hide in a dark hole the rest of my life. That's no kind of existence for a man.''

"And cheating people is?'' Elizabeth took several angry steps toward him. "I think you're afraid, Kincade. I think you're afraid you might be good at being honest.''

She thought he was no more than a card cheat; though he'd been tempted times without number, it was true, he was good enough that he didn't have to cheat. Her low opinion of him stung.

"Aye.'' The word was an angry growl. "And a devil of a lot of good it does when he's hungry. Or cold. Or has rain beating down on his head. What d'ya think? That I *like* being reduced to little more than a destitute card player? I don't. Unless I wanted to join Her Majesty's Royal Navy and sail the seven seas, or buy a commission in the army and stand in front of loaded cannons waving a bloody sword and daring the Turks or Ottomans or whoever England has a grudge against at the moment to shoot me, I had little choice in the matter. Employment for Scottish lords with only a pile of rubble for a home and no experience whatsoever is rather slim, I'm afraid.''

Elizabeth stared at him in the smoky light of lamp and late-afternoon sunshine. ''But you could have done something more—suitable.''

''Like what, angel? Ah, no answer. That's what I came up with, too. Marriage, as I told you, occurred to me, but I found that I had little stomach for wedding a simpering bride who would expect me to love, honor, and all that rot for the rest of my life.'' He raked a hand through his hair and managed a careless shrug. ''I probably would have made a deuced poor husband anyway, and made the chit more miserable than even she had a right to be.''

Elizabeth chewed her bottom lip for a moment. ''But if you really are a Scottish lord, and you have a title and lands, couldn't you—''

''Couldn't I use my position to do something worthwhile? I don't think you were listening. Uncle Dougal has seen to it that if I set foot back in Scotland, the militia will be more than happy to arrest me on trumped-up charges, and I will quietly, conveniently, disappear. Then he has Glencairn and I'm warming my toes in hell. Ah no, my options are rather limited, it seems.''

''It's difficult for me to understand how a man in the church has so much power. This isn't medieval England and the far-reaching influence of the pope, after all.'' Her lovely brow was furrowed, and Kincade shook his head.

''It's difficult for me to understand, too, and if I had not lived through it—barely, I might add—I would have found it most unbelievable. The fact remains that when I neared my majority and Dougal saw that I wasn't going to waste away in that great pile of cold stones, he set about arranging accidents. He doesn't dare kill me outright, you see, and cause any suspicion, but a daring fellow like me is ripe for any mishap.''

"But if Dougal is in the church, how does he use your land and money to his advantage?"

Amused by her naïveté, Kincade smiled. "It's not hard, angel. This isn't the Catholic Church, where a priest does not own land. Scotland is Presbyterian since the great Reformation. Even Dougal saw to it that I was educated, as that is one of the founding principles of the church. Not a formal teacher or a Dominie, you understand, because that would have drained away funds and he couldn't stomach that, but I was fortunate. I had a stickit minister who truly enjoyed his avocation and thought I was worth his time."

"A stickit minister?" Elizabeth echoed in confusion.

Kincade explained, "A stickit minister was one who had not been able to complete his theological studies for whatever reason—usually lack of money—but who had a rudimentary knowledge of the classics and logic and whatever else he'd been able to learn before his funds ran out at the university. I learned Greek, Latin, logic, and moral philosophy, mathematics, and even rhetoric and history. Master Cullen was my only link with the outside world for a long time, but he was finally dismissed when Dougal thought his duty as my guardian fulfilled enough to satisfy those who might question his wardship."

Elizabeth sat down abruptly. "I don't understand any of this."

Kincade waved a hand. "Don't try. It boils down to a struggle between the Evangelist Moderate factor in the Scottish Church, and is quite boring, I assure you. My uncle adheres to the belief that man is meant to acquire property, and is fond of quoting Lord Kames's *Sketches of the History of Man,* in which Kames insists that 'without private property, there would be no industry, and without industry, men would remain savages forever.' End quote."

"But stealing from his nephew can hardly be considered something a man high in the church should do."

"Ah, but stealing from a heretic would not be at all disapproved, angel. Locking that heretic up to be brought 'round to his senses would be the next logical step, and if God should see fit to take the poor deluded fellow to his reward or punishment before he was ever allowed to see light again—well, so much the better and 'tis only what a heretic deserves.''

"So you fled Scotland."

"As I said. It seemed prudent at the time, as I was young and did not know how to fight back. I still don't. I only know how to survive."

"Why not go back and face your uncle? Confront him with what you know."

Kincade stared at her in disbelief. "You've not been paying attention, angel. He has power behind him, and the ears of too many magistrates. I wouldn't last a half hour."

"You don't have enough faith in yourself."

"Maybe not, but I've got a lot of faith that Dougal MacKay can do exactly as he's threatened. He's tried often enough to send me to hell with his blessings. God only knows why I'm not already dead."

"There must be a reason for it." Elizabeth gazed at him with such an earnest expression that he almost smiled when she said, "I think there's some grander scheme and that you're important to it."

"Well, as you pointed out one time, I make a wonderful bad example."

"What do you want from life, Kincade?" she surprised him by asking.

The soft question struck deep inside him and made him feel suddenly queer and strange to himself. What did he want? Damn. He didn't know. All he knew was how to go from one day to the next, to somehow get through the hours without being killed. He'd been doing it so long, he'd forgotten any other way of life.

Angry at the emotions that question stirred in him, Kincade said savagely, "To survive. Period. Nothing else matters. Not you, not some high-minded bloody cause— nothing. And all this ridiculous posturing you do, spouting off noble words about honor and honesty and other ideals that don't mean a friggin' thing to anyone who has to deal with harsh reality, makes people want to throttle you. Stop trying to save me, angel. I ain't worth it.''

Her face was white, her eyes burning blue pools of fire beneath the delicate wing of her brows. "I believe you. You aren't worth it if you don't want to be. Maybe you're only a mask hiding all kinds of things I never believed existed until I met you."

"Don't give me that rubbish." Kincade strode across the room and grabbed her shoulders, his fingers digging into the soft flesh tightly. "You'd met disillusionment a long time before we ran into one another on the *Tom Hopkins*. Remember your precious Martin? I do. Don't try to make me feel guilty. I'm not the bastard who introduced you to betrayal."

Elizabeth said in a husky, breathless voice, "No, you are just the one who made it matter."

Kincade stared at her. A sharp pain stabbed his middle. Curse her idealism. Why should he even care what she thought? Or care that he'd hurt her? It galled him that it did matter. He didn't need this, not the vulnerability that came with caring what someone else thought about him.

"Curse you," he muttered hoarsely. "Curse you for a perceptive little witch."

Despite his anger and pain and best intentions, he kissed her, almost painfully, his lips grinding into hers with the fierceness born of desperation. And something else he didn't care to name.

"I need you, angel," he heard himself say when he finally lifted his head, and was amazed at his weakness.

Elizabeth melted into him, accepting his punishing kisses with a heated response that only made his blood run faster and his heart pound more furiously. She said against his open mouth, "Kincade, I need you, too."

"Then we're both lunatics."

His voice rasped. His mouth had moved down to find the

tiny pulse fluttering in the hollow of her throat, and his fingers toyed with the buttons of her gown. Her head fell back, and he loosened the knot of hair at the nape of her neck to let it drape in a glorious fall of wild gold around her shoulders.

Kincade buried his face in the curve of her neck and shoulder and felt the stinging silk of her hair against his cheek. He inhaled the arousing fragrance of a flowery powder and female, and it sent a surge of pure lust raging through him. Bending lower, he nipped at the tight bud of her hard little nipple through the cotton gown she wore, and heard her moan softly.

A shudder racked her, and her body arched against him in a silent offering. Kincade wanted to refuse; he knew he should, for her if not for his own sanity. But he couldn't, and he knew that, too. Damn. He'd counted on her cool resistance. Now she'd cast all the barriers away and he couldn't keep from touching her.

Somehow he had the row of tiny buttons undone and the edges of her bodice parted. Luxurious, satiny skin, heated velvet, rose petals, warm honey, and all the things that made life worth living were represented in this one lovely female.

"Elizabeth," he muttered thickly, "angel—don't let me do this. . . ."

It was his gift to her, this chance to push him away before he hurt her more.

She didn't.

Her arms lifted to curl around his neck, and she was shivering as she whispered, "But I want you to love me, Kincade."

He was lost.

Desire and desperation coalesced into a driving urgency that had him pushing her back against the sturdy edge of the table piled high with signed petitions. Kincade lifted her skirts and unbuttoned his pants. He was past common sense, past anything remotely resembling restraint. All he could think, could *feel*, was the raging desire to push himself inside her and make her his again, feel her body contract around him and take him back to Eden.

Elizabeth, his golden temptress, his sweet, maddening angel, and she wanted him. She helped guide him into her body, lifted her legs, and wrapped them around his waist, her eyes half-closed and her lips parted, her skin flushed with the same heat that engulfed him.

With one hand braced against the table, his other arm lifted her onto him, held her pressed against the flat surface of the table for leverage.

Feverishly, almost savagely, he immersed himself in her damp heat with a groan that was torn from his soul. Her hands touched the bare skin of his shoulder, rubbed down the slick flesh of his ribs then up again, careful not to touch the bandaged area. Soft little cries came from her, fluttering little noises that made him pant as he surged against her, in her, time and again until he poised on the brink of release.

Flames soared hot and sweet, and when he pushed into her with a hard thrust that tore another groan from him, he felt the small, tight contractions inside her push him over the edge. Panting, he stiffened, lost in his own ecstatic convulsions as she moaned and half sobbed her pleasure into the damp skin of his throat.

Still panting, he sagged against the support of the table with a feeling of sharp relief mixed with regret. His shoulder throbbed like the devil. Elizabeth held him tightly to her, and he could feel her nipples rub against his bare chest.

She shifted, her thighs closing around his hips as she tried to keep her balance. Kincade couldn't look at her. He felt a vague sense of shame that he'd taken her like this. But God, he'd needed this . . . needed her. Only Elizabeth, with her sweet fragility that masked a strength that was almost intimidating, could make him feel this special surge of love and tenderness.

Love.

Kincade winced. An inadequate word, at best. At worst, a meaningless emotion. What good would love do when she was hungry? When she had no place to sleep because he'd lost all their money in a poker game? It was fine for him, but not for her. He could never subject her to that, and he couldn't offer her more.

With his face buried in the sweet curve of her neck, he closed his eyes. It was hopeless. He was hopeless. He should never have given in to that longing for her, the need to see her, watch her from afar. He should have known he couldn't keep his distance. Now she'd expect something from him, something he should be able to give her but couldn't.

"Angel," he muttered thickly. She shifted beneath his weight, and he realized that he must be hurting her. He pulled away, but her arms tightened around his neck. "Are you all right, angel?"

Eyes as blue and shiny as pieces of sky glowed up at him, and he felt a wave of nausea at his own fraudulence.

"I'm fine," she said softly. "Wonderful."

"Good." He moved one hand, and a shower of loose paper fluttered with a dry, whispery sound, then drifted to the floor. "I think we're doing unmentionable things atop your signed petitions," he said.

"Blast," she said, "the petitions." Her luscious mouth curved into a smile. "We'll get more."

"Angel." He pulled her arms from around his neck and slowly withdrew from her body. Madness. He was still hard with desire for her. She knew it, and smiled at him as she slid her feet back to the floor.

Almost desperate for some semblance of normality, Kincade said lightly, "Annie won't agree with you, I'm afraid. She seems partial to those petitions."

Elizabeth gave a soft laugh. "You don't really care about those signatures, do you?"

"Well, I must admit—angel." The last word came out on a breath of frustration. "Angel," he began again when she tilted back her head and looked up at him, and he couldn't go on, couldn't say what he should, what he bloody well should have said before he'd done this to her again. He gave a small sound of surrender and took her face between his palms and kissed her hard.

"Umm," Elizabeth said when he lifted his head.

He was breathing in harsh gusts through his teeth, as if he'd run a mile. He couldn't do this. He was a coward. He couldn't hurt her again, especially after all her brave words and her fear for him so ready and apparent. Not now. He'd gather his courage again, and the next time he left her behind, he wouldn't look back. It'd be best for both of them even if it would be the hardest thing he'd ever done.

Elizabeth smiled dreamily and ran the tips of her fingers over his bare chest, exploring the bands of muscle with a light touch that made him suck in a sharp breath. He caught her hand, and kissed her palm.

"Wanton," he muttered, then stepped back, releasing her. He rebuttoned his pants as she smoothed her skirts back over her legs, then glanced up ruefully. "We could have used the bed, I suppose. I don't think I've ever made love to you in a bed."

"No," she agreed, "you haven't. But your ingenuity and imagination are usually quite stimulating."

His brow lifted. "Against a table?"

"Ah, but not just any table. A table bearing two thousand signatures promoting the prohibition of liquor. I think there must be a poetic justice in that for you somewhere."

He reached out and caught her to him. "Angel, there's a poetic justice in my life by just knowing you."

Chapter 16

Two weeks passed before Kincade was recovered enough to leave town. The morning Elizabeth had been dreading finally dawned, bright, crisp, and clear. Annie had gone on to the next stop on the tour, leaving them alone in the hotel.

"I'm certain the proprietor will be most delighted that we sinners have moved on," Kincade observed as he tucked a clean shirt into his saddlebag. He glanced at Elizabeth, and she managed a faint smile.

"Yes. He doesn't seem to believe that we're cousins. I wonder why."

"The happy smile on my face every morning, no doubt." Kincade buckled the saddlebag and slung it to the floor, then straightened.

Elizabeth's heart lurched. Morning sunlight caught in his hair, giving the false impression of a halo as he stood silhouetted against the window. Angelic was not a term one would apply to Kincade MacKay; a sulky fallen angel, perhaps, but never angelic. He was too irreverent, too profane to qualify for any term resembling virtue.

Yet he was so dear to her, and he was leaving. She'd known he would, suspected that he'd never stay long, yet the reality of it was killing her.

"How's your shoulder?" she asked when the silence spun out too long.

"Hardly sore at all. Almost as if I'd never stopped that devilishly painful piece of hot lead."

She smiled. "You go from sounding English to sounding like a Texan. Most disconcerting at times."

"Is it? How distressing. But then, maybe I can use that to my advantage in certain situations."

"You only sound Scottish when you're upset or delirious. Why is that?"

"Part of my education. Sounding Scottish is not exactly the thing in England, you understand, and if one wants to go along without a hitch, one must conform."

"I see."

"Do you? I never did as a child. It seemed a bloody bother at the time, having my knuckles cracked or my arse caned for slipping into the dialect. It wasn't until I got to England that I fully understood the situation. By then, of course, I was cured of it. I can sound as aristocratic as any Englishman I've ever met."

"And as cold." The words slipped out without planning, and Elizabeth sat in appalled silence as Kincade studied her for a moment. She hadn't wanted him to know that his leaving would hurt; she didn't want him to stay with her out of guilt.

"Cold," he said finally. "Yes, I suppose I do. I don't mean it sometimes."

"But sometimes you do." She stood up and smoothed her skirts. "Not that it matters."

"Doesn't it matter to you, angel?" He caught her hand when she started past him, and turned her. "I think you're lying."

She pulled away and glared up at him. His eyes were green frost, his mouth bracketed by fine white lines. His complexion was still pale from his injury and the days spent inside. She tossed back her hair from her eyes and shrugged casually.

"You shouldn't be so quick to call another liar when you wear that cloak too often yourself, Kincade."

"I know that. Angel, I never wanted to hurt you. You do realize we can't stay together, don't you?"

"Do I?"

"Curse you, don't answer a question with a question."

"What do you want me to say?"

"That's another question, plague take you."

She smiled. "Curses and plagues—are you annoyed with me, Kincade?"

"Extremely." He gazed at her with obvious frustration. "I can never make up my mind whether to kiss you at times like these or ignore you."

"How vexing for you."

He laughed, and cupped her chin in his warm palm. His fingers were smooth, his skin soft. The calluses from his days on Eden had faded in the past months; a relief, he'd told her once, as callused hands did not help a professional card player. Nor did they help a man who depended on a quick draw with a gun to keep him alive.

When his head bent and he kissed her, Elizabeth kept her arms stiffly at her sides. After a moment his head lifted, and a faint smile curved his mouth. He still held her chin in his palm, and his thumb dragged over her bottom lip in a light caress.

"It's time I go," he said softly, and she nodded.

"Yes. It certainly is. I wish you well, and I wish you safe. Godspeed." She pulled away from his hand and stepped back, ignoring the shaft of pain that knifed through her. It was hard saying good-bye, harder than she'd envisioned. Her heart ached and burned, seeming to fill her throat as she watched him reach for his hat on a nearby table. He moved easily now, with no trace of his injury.

He tugged his black felt derby over his hair, then bent for his saddlebags. As he slung the leather bags carelessly over one shoulder, he turned back to her. It was the old Kincade gazing at her, remote, cool, cynically amused.

"Try not to pour out *all* the liquor, angel. One never

knows when it will be needed for the next wounded man you might help.''

"I think I've done my share of nursing. The next wounded man will have to help himself.''

"Not very charitable of you, Lizzie.''

"I'm getting out of the charity business from this point forward. Surely you understand.''

His gaze was mocking, and her cheeks grew hot as she realized how much he truly understood. It was all she could do not to descend into a babble of explanation and denial that would only make things worse.

"I'll drink to your health at the next saloon I come to, angel,'' he said as he opened the door. He paused for a brief moment, then added softly, "Take care of yourself, Elizabeth.''

When the door closed behind him, she collapsed into a chair and stared at the faded carpet on the floor. Her vision was blurred with unshed tears that she refused to let fall, and she sat there so long she grew stiff.

Sunlight slanted sharply through the window before she rose and finished her packing. The afternoon train would be there soon, and she would leave Kansas and her memories of Kincade behind.

Denver was beautiful. High above the clouds, with snow-tipped mountains everywhere, it should have been a pleasant distraction. But not for Elizabeth.

"Maybe you should go home,'' Annie said briskly one day as autumn leaves fell. "Before it begins to snow and you can't get a train out.''

"Home?'' She stared at her cousin. "I have no home.''

"No?'' Annie's head tilted to one side like a bright, fluffy bird. "You have a house in Natchez, if I recall. And a tidy inheritance in a bank in New Orleans. You could do anything you want. When you've recovered from your malaise of spirit, you may return to me if you wish. You'll always be welcomed and needed.''

Malaise of spirit. That was an excellent diagnosis, Elizabeth thought. That's what she had. She suffered, not outwardly where a physician might have been able to offer some sort of assistance, but inside her soul, where no one could reach and heal.

"Thank you, Annie," she said. "I'll think about it. Not now, but later. If I left now, and had nothing to fill my days . . ."

Her words drifted into silence, and Annie nodded. "You are right, of course. Keeping busy will keep you from too much introspection. So. We're leaving Denver, and I want you to make arrangements for us."

"Of course. Where are you speaking next?"

"Virginia City, Nevada. Have you heard of it? It's a mining town, filled with men and wealth and plenty of liquor. I think we're needed there."

Elizabeth gathered up an armful of pamphlets. "Who invited us to speak there? A church?"

"The oddest thing . . . a very strange lady visited me after my lecture last night. She spoke in an old-fashioned, almost archaic manner at times, and more—oh, Elizabeth, you should have seen the garments she was wearing." Annie gave a wheeze of laughter. "Plaid bloomers, a short, striped skirt, and a blouse that looked like a sailor's shirt. Quite a sight, I assure you. But she was very nice, if a bit eccentric, and told me all about the horrendous situation in Virginia City, which I was made to understand she had recently visited. The local ministers are begging for temperance, and the speaker who was to come lecture was unavoidably detained. Thus she thought I might be able to replace her."

"How convenient that our next engagement canceled just this morning," Elizabeth murmured.

"Yes, isn't it? This sounds much more challenging, at any rate. Silver was discovered there, and in the past years Virginia City has increased in size and fortunes. They have opera houses, mansions, and a saloon on every corner."

"It sounds as if you will have a most difficult time convincing miners to give up their drink," Elizabeth said wryly.

"Probably. But anything that comes too easily is not worth having, I believe. One never truly values those things which are given lightly."

Elizabeth thought about that casual remark while she packed their belongings and exchanged railroad tickets. It was so true. Would Kincade value her less since she had so freely given herself and her love? It seemed likely. He'd not had to labor for her love, but only kiss her and whisper in her ear, and she'd fallen like an overripe plum into his arms.

Shame flooded her. If ever she saw him again, he would not find it so easy to make her yield. Indeed, if she ever saw him again, she would not allow him within fifty feet of her. She couldn't. One more farewell would destroy her.

Ian gazed critically at Tabitha. She ignored him, smoothing her short striped skirt with one hand and plucking at the plaid material of her bloomers with the other. She finally looked directly at him, her expression defiant.

"Well, I had to do *some*thing to get them together again. They're both miserable, and both too stubborn to say what should be said."

"Faith, ye're one for warning aboot going beyond the limits, madam. I seem tae recall bein' told I canna arrange emotions, only circumstances."

"Yes, that's true. And I haven't tampered with their silly, infantile emotions. Though if I could—"

"You canna do't, madam."

"I know that, Ian. Who's guiding who here?"

"I ha' begun tae wonder tha' lately. Ye were almost arrested at tha' bloody temperance meeting, and I wa' most undecided aboot how tae help ye."

"I wasn't arrested, though."

"Nay, no' because ye dinna deserve it, I vow. 'Twas

because I blew out the lanterns so tha' the militia couldna see in the dark, tha' ye got awa' as ye did.''

"I know. Thank you." Tabitha frowned. "Who would have thought those men would get so upset when I merely said that men should stay at home with the children and let the women run things for a while? It seems a simple solution to me."

"Ye should no' tamper wi' the way o' things, madam. I see tha' I will ha' tae keep a closer eye on ye."

Tabitha arched a plucked brow, not at all chastened. "I think that may be what Horatio had in mind. Your taking charge, I mean. After all, I am only here to guide you, not make all the decisions like I have been doing. And God's blood, but you have been a trial at times, Ian."

He took a step back. "Me? *Me?*"

"Aye, you. I mean, I made suggestions and you ignored them. Now look—Kincade MacKay is miserable and alone, Elizabeth Lee is miserable and virtually alone, and neither of them has learned much at all, except how to distrust each other. Does that sound like success to you?"

"I dinna think we are here tae interfere in his love life," Ian said after a short, angry silence. "We are here tae keep him from being killed by his uncle for his lands. It would be a grave injustice if a man of the church were tae succeed in killing Kincade tae get his hands on the title, ye ken, and tha' is wha' we must concentrate on. No' on love, but on life. D'ye understand tha', madam, or must I complain tae someone else aboot this?"

Aghast, Tabitha stared at him. Finally she said in a faint voice, "I believe I understand."

"Saints be praised. Then ye'll no' argue wi' me when I say we must allow them tae make up their own minds aboot each other?"

"Oh no, no argument at all." Tabitha met his quickly narrowed gaze with a smile. "But you do realize that Kincade is already in Virginia City, and now Elizabeth will be there. So whatever happens—happens. True?"

"Wi'out yer help," Ian growled.

"Oh aye, without my help. Now, let's see—I think I should wear something more suitable to where we are going. Baggy pants, boots, a flannel shirt—oh yes, and a helmet. Don't want to be banged in the head with falling rock in those mines, you know."

"Faith, but I think it's tae late for tha'," Ian said sharply. "Only a falling rock could ha' made ye so daft."

Tabitha ignored him. With a grandiose sweep of one arm, she was garbed in trousers, shirt, boots, and a miner's helmet. She gave a satisfied nod of her head.

"I'm ready."

"God save us, I dinna know if I am," Ian grumbled. He glared at her. "Ye canna interfere wi' them, madam, d'ye ken?"

"Ken? Yes, I understand, if that's what you mean. And I won't. Put them together and all the rest will fall right into place, I'm quite certain."

"Aye, tha's wha' I fear most. Dougal MacKay ha' set a trap for our bonny lad tha' is like tae succeed this time. When I saw Kincade a short time ago, he wa' engaged in a card game wi' some most evil-looking men. . . ."

"Good God. And you left him?" Tabitha swung around in a swift move and disappeared, leaving Ian staring after her in surprise. Then he gave a startled oath and vanished. The resulting breeze whipped at the curtains in the empty room.

Chapter
17

Virginia City, Nevada—October 1878

IT WAS dark and musty in the mine. Inky blackness hid even the faint spot of light at the end of the shaft, and a steady drip of water sounded loud in the eerie gloom.

Kincade dragged an arm across his face to scrape the beads of sweat from his eyes, wondering again why he had even bothered to look at this mine. Only a fool would ante up a productive mine in a poker game, and the man who'd lost it to him—and four queens—had not looked especially stupid. Hardy had been drunk, perhaps, but not stupid.

A silver mine. Jesus. What would he do with one even if it *was* productive? Besides, he had no idea what to look for. Silver did not just fall out of the rock walls upon command. He'd observed the dirty faces and weary postures of the miners often enough to know it was hard work. It would be like coal mining, a dirty, messy business with little to show for it, no doubt. Especially for a man alone.

So why was he here? Kincade sighed, and kicked at a loose rock. He held his torch higher to peer down at the rocks under his feet. Nothing. Just rocks, and some sort of black powdery stuff. Quartz glittered faintly in the flare of torchlight. No silver here, he was certain. If there was, one of the kings of the Comstock would have a hand in it by now. Those men seemed to have cornered the market on silver ore in Virginia City. Fewer claims were being filed.

There seemed to be only one option, and that was to let

it be known that this mine was for sale. Someone might be fool enough to buy it. He certainly didn't want it.

The torch flickered and sputtered, and Kincade started toward the entrance. He had a horror of being alone in the dark in the bowels of the earth; a rather premature burial did not appeal to him at all.

Once outside, Kincade drew in a deep breath of fresh air and sighed with relief. Safety. How gratifying.

He stuck the sputtering torch into an empty bucket near the mine's entrance and started toward his horse. A shot rang out and a loud *ping* struck the rock over his head. He hit the ground in a dive and a roll, sending out a spray of loose rock and dirt. Somehow his pistol was in his hand, and he ended up behind a clump of sagebrush. Dust and grit coated his mouth, and he inhaled the sharp bite of sage.

Another shot rang out, missing him by a mile, striking the wall of rock behind him and showering him with sharp splinters. He swore, squinted at the telltale puff of smoke that revealed his assailant's position, and squeezed off a shot as soon as he saw a movement. An immediate startled oath followed, and he felt a grim satisfaction.

"Hope that scared you as badly as you scared me, you daft bugger," he muttered to himself. He brought up one knee, curled his body into a loose crouch, and waited. Nothing broke the silence but his horse's nervous whinny and the shifting of hooves against rock.

Low, rolling hills slid up into high jagged peaks behind him and clawed at the sky, but from where he was situated he had the advantage of height. He could see anything that moved below and wondered if his attacker had thought of that before trying to kill him.

Dougal's men again, he supposed wearily. Would his uncle never give up? Probably not until he was dead. There were times when he thought Elizabeth had been right; he should go back to Scotland and confront the bastard, end everything one way or the other. This constant watching

over his shoulder made a man too skittish. He didn't know
who to trust, and consequently he trusted no one.

He shifted position in the rocks and heard the dry
scrabble of loose pebbles rolling down the slope. It occurred
to him that winning the mine from Jim Hardy might be part
of a plot, but he wasn't certain. If he recalled Hardy's
expression when he'd lost the mine, he doubted it.

Hardy had looked stunned, and slightly desperate. His
hands had begun to shake, and the dazed stare of shock he'd
turned on Kincade had been genuine. It was obvious that he
had been certain of winning; Hardy would have won, if not
for a stroke of pure luck that had amazed Kincade as well.
When he'd flipped over the last card and seen the fourth
queen, his mouth had gone dry. He could have sworn that
there were no more queens left in that game, but the proof
had been in front of him.

Maybe this mine was worth something after all, Kincade
mused. He slanted a glance toward the dark, gaping hole cut
into the side of the rocky hill. Maybe he shouldn't be so
quick to sell it. He'd never worked a mine before, but if this
one was worth anything, he could be a rich man, like
George Hearst who had the Ophir. Or maybe even like John
Mackay, James Fair, William Alloys, and James Flood, the
kings of the Comstock.

A noise turned his attention back to where his assailant
had been hiding, and he saw a blur of movement. His gaze
focused on a man lurching toward a horse behind a clump of
cedars; he saw him step up into the saddle and spur the
animal into a fast gallop. The man sat the horse awkwardly,
as if he'd been wounded, and Kincade smiled. Maybe his
shot hadn't been so wild after all. That should give the
bastard something to think about before he tried to ambush
him again, by God.

Kincade stretched out and holstered his pistol, then
folded his arms behind his head and stared up at the blue sky
overhead. Clouds floated in fat, puffy drifts like balls of
cotton, and the sun was warm beating down on him. Nights

were cold, and the wind blew icy chills, but the days had been warm and temperate. Of course, it wasn't winter yet.

Yes, maybe he'd linger awhile and see what the mine had to offer. It wasn't as if he was in any more danger here than anywhere else. And one of these days he'd have to stop running and face his nemesis. Maybe his luck was about to change. After all, it couldn't get much worse.

Winter would be cold here, Elizabeth thought as she propped her chin on her hands and gazed out the window of the boardinghouse where she and Annie were lodged. It was still autumn, and a howling wind blew from the north. There had been no sign of snow yet, though some said it had already dusted the passes; it always snowed there first. Now the sky was a blue so bright and polished it hurt her eyes to look up.

In the distance sunshine bathed the raw peaks of Sun Mountain. Cedars dotted the slopes; the wind blew hard at times, rattling roofs, blowing dirt and grit and even rocks. She'd gone out that morning to purchase a birthday gift for her cousin, and had lost a good hat to a gust of wild wind. It had been worth the loss of a hat, however, as she'd found just what she wanted for Annie.

A faint smile curved her mouth as she thought with a twinge of mischief how her cousin would react. Despite Annie's often mannish demeanor, rough language, and her frequently masculine humor, there was a part of her cousin that cherished feminine things. Elizabeth had chosen a lace scarf with small, delicate ribbons twined through the edges and dangling daintily. There were other gifts, a jar of Mrs. Morton's peach preserves, a pamphlet signed by Susan B. Anthony, a hand-copied lecture by Sara Winnemucca—the Paiute woman who had successfully campaigned against the federal government for fair treatment of her people—and a personal note from Elizabeth Cady Stanton, another famous proponent of women's rights.

When Annie returned from her meeting late that afternoon, she eyed Elizabeth speculatively. "You're wasting away to nothing. No meat on your bones. You look like a stewed rabbit."

"Thank you." Elizabeth smiled wryly. "I'm flattered you noticed."

Annie snorted rudely. "Noticed? Of course I noticed. Do I look blind as well as obtuse?"

"Obtuse? Why do you say that?"

Annie flung her comfortable body into a chaise and gave Elizabeth a long, hard look. "Because if I weren't obtuse, I would have seen what that man meant to you and done something about it."

Elizabeth turned away from her searching gaze. "He has a name, you know. You don't always have to refer to him as *that man*."

"I should refer to him as that bastard, really, but you might defend him, and then I would have to break into tears of chagrin."

The notion of her cousin weeping made Elizabeth smile. "I wouldn't defend him. Heaven knows, he referred to himself that way often enough. I should have believed him."

"Yes. You should have. When a man tries to tell you he's no good, darlin', he's usually telling you the only truth you're liable to hear from him. Keep that in mind the next time you fall in love."

Elizabeth shut her book and stared moodily into the low fire. "There won't be a next time."

"Perhaps not. There wasn't for me."

Resting her cheek in the cup of her palm, Elizabeth said softly, "Tell me about him, Annie. The man who made you hate all men."

"Hate them?" Annie shook her head. "No, I don't hate men. I like them. I haven't sworn off apples just because I've found a worm in one or two." She stretched her feet toward the cheery blaze in the grate. A faintly dreamy expression softened the lines of her face, making her almost pretty in repose. "He was Irish, big and brawny and as full of life as any man you'd ever want to see. Oh, a regular bruiser, he was, and as handsome as Lucifer. Blue eyes— *blue* eyes, so blue as to hurt you when you looked too close. And blond hair, almost the color of yours, with a touch of fire to it." She chuckled. "He had fire inside, too, honey, make no mistake about that."

"Did you love him?" Elizabeth asked when Annie lapsed into a lengthy silence.

"Love him? I still do. Always will. Just can't live with him. Drinks, you know. Drinks until the saloons are dry and then staggers home all belligerent and ready to fight or love or whatever notion strikes him. Most often as not, it was fighting he chose. Ah, but when he was in a loving mood, I thought I was in heaven."

"I can see why you didn't marry him."

"Didn't—bless me, child. I did marry him."

Elizabeth sat up with a jerk and gaped at her. "You did? But you've always said marriage was only a form of legalized prostitution, and that—"

"And I haven't changed my mind about that part of it. For a great many women it is. Not those who won't tolerate such treatment, however, which is one reason I travel all over this country lecturing. Haven't you been listening?"

Elizabeth flushed and murmured, "Of course. Perhaps I did not interpret you correctly. Why didn't anyone tell me you were married? I mean, all these years I thought—"

"You thought I was a proponent of free love, which I am to an extent. Yes, I married Michael Murphy and rued the day I tied myself to him. He went through every penny I had and then demanded more. Drank it up in three hellish years of one battle after another, he did. Well, I left him and told him I'd never be back. I haven't. I don't know where he is. Guess wherever he is, he's still drinking like a fish."

"No one in the family told me."

Annie laughed. "Are you surprised? After all, it's not exactly acceptable for a married woman—or any woman, for that matter—to be running around the country giving speeches about women's rights and the prohibition of alcoholic beverages. Our family has apparently decided to ignore the fact that I'm married, deeming it less respectable to have a divorced woman in the family than to have one who speaks out against abuse.''

Elizabeth leaned back in her chair. ''So that's what started you on your crusades.''

''Basically. That, and an intense dislike of watching human beings waste their lives, however they may choose to do it.''

''Is there a hidden message in that for me?''

''If you find one—yes.''

Elizabeth shot Annie a quick glance, but her cousin had leaned back against the high cushions of the chaise with her eyes closed. She felt a stirring of unease. She didn't want to hear any more. It was easier for her this way, much easier than coming to grips with life. Annie had done well in recovering, but she was tougher. There was a gritty core to her that Elizabeth lacked; she knew she did. How else could she explain her reluctance to cope?

The fire popped and hissed, shedding light in the cozy little sitting room they shared. Two bedrooms and a sitting room cost a pretty penny, and Elizabeth wondered idly if it was worth her share to espouse a cause she'd lost interest in.

''Apathy,'' Annie said suddenly, her voice loud in the still of the room. ''You need something to spark your interest again.''

Elizabeth gave a start of surprise at how closely their thoughts matched. ''Apathy?''

''Yes. You know—lack of interest in things generally found exciting. Indifference.''

''I know the definition,'' Elizabeth said dryly. ''I was just wondering why you were applying it to me.''

''Because you've lost interest in life.''

''No, not really in life, just . . . just things.''

''Rubbish.'' Annie made a steeple of her hands and

pressed her fingertips to her chin. "Now, let me see—what can I think of to spark your interest? I know. The miners."

"The miners?" Elizabeth stared at Annie. "Why the miners?"

"There was an article in the *Territorial Enterprise* relating the hardships of the miners. They're sent down in the tunnels for long, backbreaking hours, and given very little in recompense. The dangers are great, even with new innovations. Would you like to join the staff of the local paper this winter?"

"Good lord. Why should I want to do that? And anyway, what man in this town would allow it? They all seem to me to be singularly unimpressed with females as anything but house drudges."

"Ah, but I met a most fascinating gentleman in Hartford a few years ago, and he told me he started out as a reporter for the *Enterprise*. Of course, he now writes novels, but everyone must begin somewhere. He seemed to think that this paper was innovative, and the staff receptive to new ideas. I know that if Mr. Clemens thought so—you've heard of him, perhaps? He writes as Mark Twain."

"Mark Twain lived in Virginia City?" Elizabeth was surprised. "I cannot imagine why."

"According to him, he'd lost interest in other things and sought to rejuvenate his spirit." Annie gave her a keen stare. "He did recover, by the way, and this was the beginning for him. Wouldn't you like to do something other than watch the fire and think about what might have been?"

She flushed and looked away from Annie's knowing gaze. "I'm not doing that. Very much, at any rate."

"Five minutes is too long in my opinion. This is the only chance you may have to actually live, child. Don't toss it away. Youth and energy are gone all too quickly."

"All right." Elizabeth threw up her hands in mock surrender. "I give up. I'll interview miners, or even put on a helmet and boots and go down into the mine shaft with them, anything to make you happy."

"Good." Annie smiled. "And it will make you much happier than it will me."

"I just hope you don't intend to stay in Virginia City too long, because I've not seen one miner that I find even a remotely sympathetic figure. They're rowdy, dirty, and they drink too much."

"Perhaps the *Enterprise* can think of an idea to generate your sympathy," Annie said with a laugh. "I'll introduce you to the staff there tomorrow, and we'll see."

"It's called the Monarch Mine," Jeremy Lowery told Elizabeth with a smile. "The owner has only a few miners in his employ, but it should serve your purposes well enough."

Elizabeth forced an expression of polite attention. "This is really my cousin's notion, you see, so I know very little about the mining business."

Lowery shrugged. The newspaper office bustled with activity; the overpowering smell of ink and raw paper filled the air, and the hum of male voices proclaimed it a primarily masculine business. Several men glanced disapprovingly at Elizabeth, but Jeremy Lowery's gaze was frankly admiring.

He was fairly handsome, she supposed, with light brown hair, an engaging smile, and a tall, slender frame clad in a neat frock coat and pipe-stem trousers.

"Your cousin is a very—forceful—woman," he said with a grin. "I was threatened with vague promises of female retribution if I did not allow a woman to join my staff as a contributing reporter. I had no idea it would be someone as lovely as you." He cleared his throat and hesitated, then said bluntly, "Are you certain you wish to do this, Miss Lee? Most of these miners are rough and uncouth, and I fear your feminine sensibilities will be offended."

"I'm certain I can contain my repugnance long enough to write an article for your paper," Elizabeth said firmly. She gave him a serene smile, not about to allow anyone to intimidate her. "If you will be so good as to give me

directions to this Monarch Mine you mentioned, I will
interview the owner and his employees."

"Yes, well—I do wish some of the big owners had
agreed to allow an interview, but none of them would. This
is only a small operation, you understand, but if your
interest is in how the work affects the men, then it should
help you."

"I'm certain it shall. The directions, please?"

Lowery reached for his long wool coat. "I'll have to take
you there. A woman alone might encounter, ah, unforeseen
obstacles."

Elizabeth understood what he meant, and while she
resented it, she wasn't foolish enough to refuse protection.
A woman alone would be subject to unpleasant harassment
that would certainly prohibit any success.

"If you like," she said. "I appreciate your offer, though
I want to assure you that I am quite capable of taking care
of myself."

Lowery grimaced as he opened the front door for her. A
bell jangled loudly as the wind jerked the door from his
grasp. He managed to catch it before it hit Elizabeth. When
he held it open, he smiled at her indulgently.

"Modern females. You're a prickly lot, but I suppose
you've got good points about some things. Watch your step,
Miss Lee—the boardwalk gives way here once in a while."

Elizabeth didn't object to the arm he put around her back,
but she stepped from under his half embrace as soon as they
reached her hired buggy. Mr. Lowery had better learn
quickly that she would allow no familiarity. Not even a
helping hand, if the arm went with it.

It seemed to take forever to reach the Monarch Mine; it
had been dug into a rise that overlooked Virginia City.
Endless expanses of sagebrush, stunted grass, and cedar
trees rolled on each side of the rutted track they traveled; by
the time they reached the mine, she was dusty and thirsty
and cold.

Lowery halted the buggy a good distance away and said

when Elizabeth gave him an inquiring glance, "It doesn't do to come up on a man's claim without warning. Some owners get testy about it and shoot before asking questions."

"Shoot?" Elizabeth's eyes widened, and she gave an anxious glance at the seemingly quiet mine. She allowed him to help her down from the buggy and stood stiffly on the uneven ground. As he set the brake she plucked at the rich brocade of her skirts with an idle, nervous motion. Perhaps she should have tried harder to interview the miners in a larger mine, such as the Ophir owned by George Hearst. She had thought that since this mine was smaller and independently owned, it would be more interesting.

Now it seemed more ominous than intriguing, and she wished she hadn't come.

A shot rang out, making that wish a necessity as the bullet sizzled over their heads.

"Don't worry," Lowery said when Elizabeth shrieked in alarm and turned blindly toward the buggy. "That was just a warning shot meant to remind us not to come too close." His hand touched her arm reassuringly.

"No fear of that," she gasped out as she tried to readjust her bonnet. It had been knocked askew in her quick leap of fright. The wide satin ribbon had slipped behind her ear on one side, and the brim dipped forward. Her gloved hands trembled as she tugged at the knot in the blue bow.

"Hardy!" Lowery called out, cupping his hands around his mouth. "It's Jeremy Lowery from the *Enterprise*. I just want to talk to you for a minute."

Several seconds passed without a reply, then a few rocks bounced down the slope and hit the buggy wheels as a man came into view behind a boulder. Elizabeth's bonnet was tilted over her eyes, the ostrich feather dangling in a fuzzy purplish haze as she tried to push it aside to see. She finally righted it and looked up, and the breath caught in her throat.

Kincade. And he seemed just as surprised to see her. He was dressed like a miner, in wool pants and a thick flannel shirt. A breeze lifted strands of his dark hair, and she felt his gaze like a blow. Then a faint smile twisted his mouth in familiar mockery, and he came out from behind the rock.

He was limping, and he carried a rifle slung over one arm, ready at an instant's provocation to aim and fire. Her gaze flicked from the weapon to his face, and she saw his faintly sardonic smile soften.

"Angel. What a surprise."

"Yes," she managed to say, "it is."

Lowery looked from one to the other. "You two know each other?"

"We've met before," Elizabeth said coolly when Kincade shrugged. She eyed him for a moment and tried to make the mental adjustment needed at seeing him again. "I would never have guessed you worked at a mine," she said finally, and saw the mocking grin flash in his beard-stubbled face.

"No?"

"No. You aren't the type to dabble in hard labor. You prefer things to come easily to you."

"Not always." He gestured to his leg, and she noticed the crude splint fashioned from tree limbs and strips of cloth wound around his shin. He wore a knee-high boot on only one foot; the other was clad in a white woolen sock. "Rock broke my leg, I think. That should have been a dead giveaway that you weren't far away. You always show up at the worst times in my life."

"Thank you," she said tartly, ignoring Lowery's curious gaze. "I suppose there's no point in interviewing you. Unless there are a number of employees working here."

"If that's what you're looking for, you're right." Kincade took another limping step forward, his gaze flicking over Lowery. "I don't know you."

"I'm Jeremy Lowery, associate editor of the *Territorial Enterprise,* Virginia City's local paper. And you?"

"Kincade MacKay, owner of the Fourth Queen, Nevada's most worthless mine.'' He gestured toward the mine behind him, ignoring Elizabeth's gasp of surprise.

"What happened to Hardy?'' Lowery asked with a frown. "He owns this mine.''

"I won it from him in a poker game week before last. He had a straight. I drew four queens.'' He shrugged, and for a moment the gaze he turned toward Elizabeth held a familiar gleam of mockery. "I think he cheated me, though. The bloody mine has more water in the bottom than anything else.''

Lowery laughed softly. "I take it you don't know much about mining.''

"You take it correctly. I had the notion that one needed only a shovel and pick to get silver from rock. Obviously I was misled.''

"Obviously.''

Elizabeth couldn't stop staring at him. He looked the same at first glance, but there was a difference in him. This was not the same Kincade she'd last seen. The obvious difference was the change in clothes. The other was less obvious, more subtle. He was—harder. Even with the splint on his leg and lines of pain etched in his face, there was a toughness about him that was much different from the familiar indolence.

"Who does the work?'' she blurted, and Kincade's brow lifted in amusement.

"It's just me here working my claim.''

"Alone? *Working?*'' Disbelief threaded her voice, and his eyes narrowed in irritation.

"Why is that so hard to believe?''

"I shouldn't think you'd have to ask.''

He shrugged, annoyance darkening his features and chilling his eyes. He shifted position, relaxed his grip on the rifle, and flinched when his weight rested briefly on his left leg.

"Your confidence in me is most rewarding, Miss Lee.'' He looked at Lowery, who was listening to them with a slight frown. "Mr. Lowery, do you suppose you could take a list to Howell's General Store for me? I know him, and he'll send me out some supplies."

"No problem, MacKay." Lowery hesitated, then turned to Elizabeth and said, "Since there is only this one man here to interview, I assume that you would prefer seeking out another mine, is that correct?"

"Quite correct." Elizabeth felt Kincade gazing at her with cynical amusement and couldn't stop the hot flush that heated her cheeks. She was flustered by this unexpected meeting, and had no idea what to do or say, or how to feel. It was too shocking, too unnerving, and she wanted only to flee the area and his mocking gaze, and seek peace and quiet to sort out her confused reactions.

Lowery was looking at her inquiringly, and she knew he was curious about the tension between her and Kincade. She managed a smile.

"I'll wait in the buggy while Mr. MacKay gives you his list, if you don't mind." With a cool nod in Kincade's general direction and a murmured farewell, Elizabeth turned.

Kincade's soft brogue stopped her.

"It wa' good seeing you again, lass."

She turned to face him, and wished she hadn't. An odd, faintly wistful smile touched the corners of his mouth, and all traces of mockery were gone. Her heart lurched, and she noted the white lines of strain in his face and the shadows under his eyes. He was hurt. As usual, his sarcastic tongue had hidden the extent of his suffering from prying eyes.

"When did you hurt your leg?" she asked before she could stop herself.

His shrug was careless. "About a week ago. It's almost well now."

"Is it? I suppose that's why you can't put any weight on it."

"I don't want to rush my complete recovery. I've found that being in a hurry can ruin many a promising situation."

His eyelashes lifted, and the force of his gaze hit her. "It can be almost as disastrous as hesitating too long."

She stared at him uncertainly. There was something in the way he rolled his *R*s that made her wonder what lay behind his words. She took an impulsive step toward him, a hand lifting.

"Kincade—"

"Miss Lee," Jeremy Lowery said at the same time, and his voice jerked her back to the realization that she'd been about to make another mistake. Her hand dropped, and she inhaled sharply to steady her leaping pulses.

"Yes, Mr. Lowery?"

"Excuse me. I was merely going to say that I'll help you into the buggy and then help Mr. MacKay up the hill to fetch his list."

Elizabeth saw Kincade stiffen and his eyes narrow, and before she could say anything, he growled, "I don't need your bloody help up the hill, Lowery." He turned away and limped up the slope, slow and painfully, making Elizabeth think of the clumsy scuttle of a crab.

"I didn't mean to insult him," Lowery said softly, and she managed a smile.

"I know you didn't. I'm certain he's only ill-tempered because of his injury. Some people don't accept help graciously."

By the time she was settled into the buggy, Kincade was coming down the slope with his list. Jeremy Lowery went to meet him atop the small rise, and they spoke in low baritones that she couldn't hear. She folded her hands in her lap and looked away, unable to bear watching Kincade.

She could feel his presence as if he had his hand on her. Her throat grew tight, and her hands were shaking. She clenched them tightly in her lap.

A bird flew overhead, wings flapping as loudly as a ship's sails in the quiet, and she was suddenly reminded of sunny days in another clime, of soft balmy nights and pounding surf, of a small, thatched hut and a crystal-clear pool and waterfall. She shivered, looked toward them, and found Kincade's gaze fixed on her.

Lowery was striding back toward the buggy, his lanky frame loose-limbed and awkward compared with Kincade's easy grace even with an injury. Behind him, Kincade was staring at her with a strange expression.

She couldn't decide what it was, except that it seemed to hit her in the very core of her being; her breath came in oddly short pants.

Kincade looked—lost. She didn't know why that particular image came to mind, except that as he stood there favoring one leg, the wind ruffling his dark hair and tugging at the open front of his flannel shirt, he reminded her of how she'd felt since leaving their island: adrift, with no sense of direction or purpose, floating aimlessly on an unfriendly sea.

Then Jeremy Lowery climbed into the buggy and released the brake and slapped the reins against the horse's rump; the buggy jerked forward. Elizabeth did not allow herself to look back, but she was very aware of the way Kincade's gaze followed them as the buggy turned around in a wide arc and started back down the rutted track leading to town.

When they had almost reached Virginia City, Jeremy halted the buggy. Surprised, Elizabeth looked at him when he turned to her, his face slightly red.

"Miss Lee, I don't usually—that is, this is none of my business, but I feel I must tell you that I've heard of Kincade MacKay before today. He's said to be a thorough rogue. I just thought I'd tell you that."

"May I ask why?"

His flush deepened, and he looked away. His jaw clenched and a muscle flexed in his cheek. "I realize that you may already know all this, and I don't want to seem too bold, but I felt that if there was something—I just don't want you to be involved with a man of his ilk and not be aware of his reputation, that's all."

"I see. Thank you for confiding in me. And you are right. I do know all of this, so your warning is not necessary."

He looked at her, pale eyes speculative. "You sound angry. I don't mean to interfere, but perhaps you don't realize that MacKay is thought to be one of the outlaws who robbed a mine payroll of six thousand in silver last week. Two guards were killed. Sheriff Wallace has been doing the investigating, and thinks that Max Griffin's gang is behind it. He also suspects Kincade MacKay as being a member of that gang."

"If that's true, why hasn't he arrested him?"

"Probably because he doesn't know where he is."

"Ah. I have the feeling that he will soon." Elizabeth saw Lowery's flush deepen to an ugly crimson. His lips thinned.

"Do you object to justice being done?"

Elizabeth thought of Kincade's views on justice and smiled. When Jeremy glared at her, she shook her head.

"No, I have no objections to justice being done. What I object to is misguided justice. Indiscriminate justice causes more harm than good."

"Indiscriminate? And you think informing the sheriff of MacKay's whereabouts would be wrong?"

"Not necessarily. As long as the sheriff isn't the type of man who shoots first and asks questions later."

Lowery shifted, and the buggy rocked slightly with his movement. "I'm not a troublemaker, Miss Lee. I wouldn't want an innocent man's death on my conscience. Nor would I want to think I let a guilty man escape justice."

"Then you have quite a decision to make, don't you, Mr. Lowery?"

After a short silence Lowery turned and started the horse forward with a sharp slap of the reins. He didn't speak until he set Elizabeth down in front of her boardinghouse, and then he took her hand.

"Perhaps I should investigate more before I say anything to the sheriff, Miss Lee. I wouldn't want to be too hasty."

"I think that's wise. With his leg in a splint, I doubt that Mr. MacKay is going anywhere very quickly anyway."

She gave him a cool nod and was relieved when she was safely inside. She sagged weakly against the closed door and shut her eyes for a moment. Why should she even care if Kincade was arrested? For all she knew he had been part of the outlaw gang. He may even have a bullet in his leg instead of a broken bone. She was a fool, a silly fool to have let that fleeting expression on his face affect her at all.

Annie was less than surprised to hear that Kincade was the new owner of the Monarch Mine, renamed the Fourth Queen.

"Is he? And he won it in a poker game." She shook her head and laughed. "I don't think anything that man does will surprise me. What surprises me is how, with all this vast territory out here, we keep running into the man. It's sort of like divine intervention, don't you think?"

"More like divine retribution, I'd say." Elizabeth flung herself into a chair and closed her eyes. She'd tossed her new bonnet across the room, and she opened her eyes when Annie placed it in her lap.

"Shredded your feathers, it seems. Or is that ruffled your feathers?"

"Don't be coy. Say what you mean." Elizabeth glared up at her and shoved the hat to the floor again.

"I mean, you're always testy when you get around that man. And you're testy when you're not around him."

"Am I too foul-tempered for you to stand?" she snapped.

"Not all the time." Annie laughed at Elizabeth's indignant glance. "Oh heavens, don't be so serious. And don't get so upset about Kincade. You may not want to hear this, but I think you should confront him. Get him out of your life and out of your heart, or resign yourself to the fact that you love him."

"Love him—"

"It can't be hate that makes you brood over him all the time." Annie met her irate gaze without flinching. "Fantasy is always more appealing than reality, you know. After all, the imagination doesn't have to deal with things like dirty clothes and muddy boots lying about. Reality does, and if you think you love him, spend a month picking up his clothes off the floor and see if you still feel the same way. Chances are you won't.''

"I spent six weeks on a deserted island with him, for heaven's sake."

"Hardly the same. From what little you've told me, you didn't wear too many clothes, and it was more like an island paradise than real life. It makes a huge difference."

Elizabeth jerked to her feet and began to pace the floor, pausing at intervals to glare at Annie. "It's a silly idea, you know."

"Hmm."

"Well," Elizabeth said hotly, "it is. And anyway, if you will only recall, he hasn't exactly made himself available to me. He didn't stay in Kansas when I wanted him to, did he?"

"Did you tell him you wanted him to stay?"

"Of course not. That wouldn't have been fair. I wanted him to think of it."

"Men never think of things like that. It's bred into them at the moment of conception to run at the very mention of respectability, I think. Must be, or so many of them wouldn't bolt when a woman starts thinking of home and a family." Annie sank back into a chair and reached for a book on the table beside her. She opened it and began riffling the pages, then glanced up at Elizabeth. "Don't look so miserable. Do you intend to let life happen to you, or do you intend to at least put up a decent struggle to get what you want?"

Elizabeth stared at her. "How do I know if what I want is right for me?"

"You'll figure it out. You're a bright girl." Annie's smile was soft and encouraging. "My father used to have a saying. 'Don't give a hungry man a fish—teach him how to fish.' Try it with Kincade."

"Excuse me, I'm having trouble following the moral of this story."

"Oh, for heaven's sake—don't just love the man blindly, Elizabeth. Teach him how to love back."

"How am I supposed to do that?"

"I have a feeling he'll show you."

"Wonderful. I just hope you're around to pick up what's left of me when he's through," Elizabeth muttered grimly.

Chapter 18

A LOW fire smoldered in a shallow pot. Smoke curled up and filled the small canvas tent with eye-biting shrouds that made Kincade cough. Damn. The wind again, always shifting direction in this bloody country. The Washoe zephyrs, they were called, blowing down off the high ridges of the Sierra Nevada to rip through town so hard and fast that roofs ended up in the street. The wind was so fierce it pelted the tent with rocks—not sand and pebbles, but fist-sized rocks. It was enough to make him want to cut bait and run, as the American saying went. Why had he ever thought he could make something of himself with a bloody mine?

And why, he wondered, had Elizabeth Lee turned up in his life again?

It was maddening. Just when he thought he was shed of her—the reality, not the fantasy he carried in his mind like some bloody trophy—she appeared in his life again and threw him into turmoil. He stared moodily into the flames, then stuck in another stick of dry wood.

Elizabeth. He shut his eyes, and her vision appeared in haunting clarity. Silky blond hair, blue eyes so deep a man could forget his sorrows just staring into them, and the sweet, delicate perfection of features so fine and fragile it was as if they'd been personally sculpted by God. If he remembered that his first impression of her was as a skinny female who was rather plain and definitely too outspoken, it made him laugh at himself. How could he ever have thought that of her? Ludicrous in retrospect.

Kincade stretched out as much as he could in the narrow space of his tent and folded his arms behind his head to stare up at the low canvas ceiling. The tent was shaking from the force of the wind; he wondered idly if he'd wake to find it down the side of the hill again. It wouldn't be the first time it had happened, but he deemed it a bloody nuisance to have to fetch his home in the mornings before he could work his claim.

Another one of life's little irritations.

When he shifted, his leg ached, and he muttered a curse. He didn't think it was really broken, but it certainly hampered movement. The splint was a precaution. A handy precaution as it had worked out, because it seemed to have gathered a rush of sympathy from Elizabeth.

He closed his eyes and smiled blandly. He'd seen the quick flare of concern that she hadn't been able to hide. It had been quite gratifying, and very reassuring. She still cared about him a small bit, anyway.

If he had any sense, he'd saddle his horse as soon as he was able to ride into Virginia City and find her, tell her . . . tell her what? That he was a bloody fool and not worth a shilling, but that he wanted her to stay with him? That would be the height of madness. She'd probably say he was quite insane and to go away, and he didn't think he could bear it if she did. Besides that, the truth had never been exactly complimentary to him, or very welcome.

No, he had to stay where he was and keep on working his claim. If it paid off before he died from the struggle, then he could go to her and offer her more than a cot in a tent and what was in his pockets. That was about all he had now, and it would never be enough for Elizabeth.

Honest work, she'd said—why couldn't he work an honest job?

It had sounded simple in theory, and had made him mad enough to buy shovels and picks and take the opportunity the mine afforded to do something legal. But he hadn't considered the reality would be so bloody hard, so backbreaking and exhausting. He worked long hours day and night to hack chunks of rock from tunnels deep in the bowels of the earth in the slim hope that he'd find silver, and so far all he'd found was enough water to float a midsize ship, and enough rock to sink it again.

There was always the taste of grit in his mouth, and black dirt crusted his eyelids and filled his nose, and when he coughed, it felt as if his lungs were full of dust. But it was *honest work* according to Elizabeth, and therefore acceptable. He thought of the miners he'd seen with red-rimmed eyes and a mortal cough, and disagreed with her definition.

Elizabeth thought a saloon filled with music, laughter, drink, and a chance to win good money was dishonest, but slowly killing men below ground for a mere pittance was honest. He failed to make the proper connection that seemed expected of him. When the wind blew cold around him and rain poured down from the sky to fill his tent and boots, he found it impossible to equate mining with honest work.

"Curse her," he muttered, and jabbed viciously at the low fire in the metal pot. "Curse the bloody wench."

Tabitha frowned. "Perhaps his winning the mine wasn't the best idea."

"'Tis a fine time tae think o' tha' naow," Ian said sourly. "And 'tis a bloody stroke o' good fortune tha' no one challenged tha' fifth queen ye put in the deck."

"I'd forgotten they'd all been played. Good thing no one noticed, I suppose," Tabitha said with a shrug of dismissal. The wind tugged at her clothes and hair, and she looked up at the dark sky with exasperation.

"Ye suppose?" Ian shook his head. He held to his bonnet

with one hand when the wind blew harder. "I dinna know how ye justify wha' ye did, madam."

"It's quite simple. Four of a kind beats a straight. I had to do something, and that seemed the best thing. Those other men were getting disturbed, but if Kincade won the hand, there was nothing they could say."

"Aye, they could ha' said plenty if they'd thought aboot tha' fifth queen," Ian remarked. "'Tis in his favor tha' the mon who lost was so distraught he didna offer a challenge."

"Yes, yes, that's so. Don't dwell on the card game. It's over. Kincade has a chance at honest employment—which you must admit should simplify matters—and Elizabeth is close by."

"So are a number of assassins," Ian growled. "Ha' ye forgot aboot tha'?"

"This is getting much too complicated. Can't you do something, Ian?"

Perched atop a jagged boulder, Ian drummed his heels against the granite side for a moment. The wind tugged at his hair and clothes, lifting corners of the plaid to flap with a slight, popping sound. He briefly touched the gold-headed pin holding the plaid to one shoulder, then glanced at Tabitha with a sigh of resignation.

"Aye, but ye canna argle-bargle aboot wha' I decide."

"Heh?"

"Ye canna be pigheaded, madam, and tell me tha' I should ha' done this or tha' instead. D'ye ken wha' I mean?"

"When you speak the queen's English, I *ken* well enough," she grumbled.

"Ye threap o'er wha' I say as if ye ha' a personal risk in this."

Tabitha stiffened. "I do. My reputation is at risk if you botch this."

"Botch—"

"What does threap mean, anyway?"

"The same as argle-bargle—disagree, argue, be contentious, which ye bloody well are tha', madam." Ian drew in a deep breath. "All personal feelings aside, we baith should put our heads together and think of a way tae resolve this afore Dougal MacDonald manages tae see the lad murthered."

"He's on his way here, I understand."

"Aye," Ian growled, and spat into the wind. "The bloody knave took the bait quick enough, he did."

Tabitha gave a fretful toss of her head, and an impatient wave of one arm that diverted the wind around her. "I certainly never intended it to go that far. Do you think it wise for him to actually confront Kincade? One is likely to kill the other, you know."

"Aye, tha' I do, madam. 'Tis why I arranged for Dougal MacKay tae come tae America tae seize his inheritance himself. Kincade must ha' the chance tae fight back. Call me dour if ye like—I canna change yer mind and wouldna if I could. 'Tis the only way it can work."

Tabitha closed her eyes in irritation. "I think you should have consulted me before you arranged for Dougal MacKay to come to America, is what I think. I'm supposed to be giving you advice."

"Ha' more faith in me, madam. Ha' ye no' told me how I am tae trust my own instincts?"

Tabitha turned to look at him, and her eyes widened. "Why yes, I have."

"Then believe in me naow."

She nodded slowly. Then, before Ian could speak again, Tabitha gave a quick wave of one arm and was gone. He stared at the empty rock where she'd been sitting, cast a quick glance down at the rain-battered canvas tent, then vanished.

Elizabeth Lee dismounted from the buggy with a graceful lift of her long skirts and turned, slanting Kincade a wary glance. She looked uncertain, and he felt his insides churn.

"Good afternoon, Mr. MacKay," she began, but his short, sardonic laugh stopped her.

"A bit formal, ain't you, angel? It seems rather absurd after all we've been through together." He was rewarded with a bright flush on her cheeks. "Yes, you should blush, my lovely little hypocrite. I seem to recall a certain informality in our former relationship."

"The key word in that sentiment is *former*," she said tartly, and he saw by the defiant lift of her chin and the blazing blue eyes that he'd managed to rouse her temper.

"So true. Where's your charming Mr. Lowery today?"

"He's not mine, he's not charming, and I have no idea." She turned, reached into the buggy, and brought out a heavy wicker basket. "Your supplies from Howell's General Store. Mr. Howell asked if you would like for him to ride out and check on you in a few days."

"Did he? How kind. No, that won't be necessary. I feel much better."

"Wonderful." She walked close and dropped the basket in the dust at his feet. It landed with a resounding thud that stirred up a cloud of dust and made him take a step back. She smiled sweetly. "Hope your eggs didn't break."

"Vicious little pet, aren't you?"

"I can be." She put her hands on her hips. "You're angry at me. Why?"

"Angry? Me? Don't be silly. Why would I be angry?"

"That's what I asked. Must you answer a question with a question?"

He was reminded of the last time he'd said that to her, and smiled wryly. "Retribution, I take it?"

"Something like that. Where's your splint?"

"In my tent. Ah, that has a certain cadence, doesn't it? The splint in my tent?"

Elizabeth gave him a sideways glance, and he shrugged. "All right, angel. You brought my supplies and I'm properly grateful. Don't feel you have to linger."

"Are you asking me to leave?"

"Heaven forbid I should be so rude. The ghosts of my former tutors would rise up to haunt me."

"More than tutors should haunt you, Kincade MacKay."

He leaned on a rock, more because he hadn't regained his strength than because he wanted to appear casual; he hoped she didn't know that.

"I've noticed that you usually call me by both names when you're peevish, Lizzie. Tell Uncle Kincade what's bothering you."

"I shouldn't think you'd have to ask."

She tugged at one of her gloves, rearranging the lace cuff around her wrist. It was a dainty feminine gesture, as was the way she flicked him a quick glance from beneath her long lashes. He sighed in resignation.

"Forgive me. Long periods of silence and lack of human companionship have dulled my brain. I have no idea why you're angry. Do tell me."

"I asked you first."

"Dear God. Must we flounder in banal conversation much longer? Get to the bloody point, Lizzie."

She gave her glove a sharp tug. "Elizabeth. My name is Elizabeth. You're only calling me Lizzie to irritate me, and to distract me from the real reason why you're angry. I won't be fooled again, nor will I be diverted."

"My, my—perceptive little cat, aren't you?" When she just gazed at him steadily, he shrugged again, this time with real irritation. "Why shouldn't I be angry? I'm getting rather tired of having you flit through my life like some kind of destructive moth all the time. I no sooner recover from the last time I saw you than you show up again. This time it was on the arm of another man. And you stared at me as if I didn't exist for you, as if we'd never spent six bloody weeks alone on an island."

"And after the six weeks was over," she said calmly, "you deserted me in New Orleans."

He stared at her in amazement. "What was I supposed to do?"

"I believe we've discussed that before, and neither of us could agree on the proper solution." Elizabeth moved to sit on the other side of the rock, so close he could almost touch her. A faint, sweet fragrance drifted toward him, and he inhaled deeply even while he cursed himself for being a bloody fool. "So," she was saying, "why don't we move on to another topic?"

"Such as?"

"Such as your immediate plans. Do you think there is really silver in this mine?"

"Why? Are you offering to help dig for it?"

She shot him a withering stare. "Don't be idiotic. I'm impressed that you're trying to actually work for a living."

"Delighted to have impressed you at last. Had no idea it would be so devilishly difficult, however."

A faint smile curved her mouth, and some of her tension visibly eased. "We shouldn't fuss, you know."

"Why not? It's so diverting. If we weren't fussing, we might have to discuss the sad state of the world's affairs, or some other depressing rot."

"Such as what you plan to do with your life? If nothing else, that is a depressing subject." She tugged the glove from her hand and fanned it slowly in the air as he stared at her narrowly.

"Don't repress anything you might wish to say, Lizzie my sweet. Just go for the jugular."

"Did that hit too close to the nerve? Sorry. Thought I might help you decide."

A cool wind whipped across him, but did nothing to chill the bite of hot anger he felt.

"When I need your bloody help, I'll ask for it," he said tightly. "Don't feel you have to offer."

"Kincade, try not to be so defensive. I came out here to see you for a reason."

"Pray, don't keep me in suspense much longer. Tell me the reason while I still have some sanity left."

She eyed him for a moment, and apparently decided that she'd pushed him far enough. Sliding to her feet, she came to stand in front of him.

He was still trying to decide if he could get away from her before he made a complete fool of himself by kissing her, when her soft words jerked his head up and made his heart give a crazy leap.

"I want to stay here with you."

Before he knew what he was doing, he had her in his arms. He didn't give her a chance to change her mind or take back her words. His mouth came down over her lips in a bruising kiss that felt like heaven. She quivered in his embrace like a windswept flower, and he felt that strange, almost fragile crumbling inside him that he'd felt with her before, as if glass was breaking and shattering into a thousand pieces.

"Angel," he muttered against her mouth, and felt her trembling hand caress his cheek. "You drive me to madness at times."

"Only at times?" Her laughter quivered between them in a soft whisper. "I'll have to try harder."

"Do that. Then you can visit me on the moors and listen to me bay at the moon."

"There are no moors in America."

"Hills then. I'll howl with the coyotes. God, your hair smells so sweet . . . like exotic flowers. Like those blossoms on Eden." His hand caressed her face, then slid down to rest on her hip. "Ah, angel, where are your curves?"

She pressed her forehead to his shoulder and rubbed against the rough wool of his jacket. "Under three layers of clothes. The wind gets rather sharp."

"You shouldn't want to stay with me. It's too dangerous."

He watched her, saw her head lift and her small white teeth dig into her lower lip as she studied him. A sheen of silver misted her blue eyes, and pale wisps of blond hair framed her face.

"I've missed you. I missed your courage and integrity, and even your caustic wit. Do you mind?"

"Mind?" His laugh was a painful rasp in his throat. "Mind if you missed me? What kind of question is that?"

"There you go, answering a question with a question again." Elizabeth nuzzled his chin, and he shuddered as he held her closer. "Do you not want me to stay here with you?"

"It's not that. I just wonder which of us is the crazier. This isn't exactly a garden spot, you know."

"I realize that. I'm not that delicate."

His hand tested the contour of her hip, spanned the narrow width of her waist. "You feel delicate. You feel soft and fragile, and much too vulnerable to stay out here in the rocks and rain."

"But I'm not. I'm as strong as I want to be. As I need to be. Women usually are, you know."

"So you keep telling me." His mouth pressed against her cheek. "I believe you. You're stronger than I am. Always have been. I just wish I knew why you want to stay here."

She drew back to look at him, and he saw the shadows in her eyes and the hesitancy trembling on her mouth. He put a finger over her lips.

"No. Don't tell me. It doesn't matter. Nothing matters but that you're here now. We'll worry about the reason—"

"Later," she said on wings of laughter. "I know. Your favorite time of day."

"Yes, that elusive hour when one wallows in all the undone. Fortunately it doesn't come often." He bent, lifted her in his arms despite her quick protest, and started up the hill with her.

"Kincade . . . the buggy . . . your leg . . ."

"Will all wait."

He felt stronger than he had in days. Weeks. Months. She was here, and nothing mattered but that. That and the fact that she'd managed to catch him in a weak moment. He'd worry about the consequences to both of them later. Now he just wanted to touch her and taste her and once more find that small bit of heaven he'd found on a dot of sand in the Atlantic.

Chapter 19

ELIZABETH CUDDLED closer. The winds howled, and rocks pattered against the sides of the tent like lethal rain. A fire burned in a shallow metal pot, casting leaping shadows on the canvas walls. She felt Kincade stir beside her, muscles flexing in his arm as he tugged at the blankets.

"Do you like staying out here alone?" she asked, and turned her head to look up at him.

He shrugged and pulled her closer into his side. "No. It gets bloody lonely at times. The wind sounds like a banshee out there, like the wind used to sound around the north turrets of Glencairn."

"Glencairn. Tell me about your ancestral home, Kincade. You don't seem to miss it much."

"I don't miss it at all. Just a few childhood memories were happy there. That was before my parents drowned crossing the Channel when I was seven." He stroked her arm and pulled an edge of the blanket up over her. Their shared body heat was warmer than the low fire, and they lay naked beneath the scratchy wool.

When it seemed as if he didn't intend to elaborate, Elizabeth rose to her elbow and gazed down at him. She traced the line of his mouth with her fingertips, and saw his eyes narrow slightly. They glowed green and hard, as dangerous and remote as a panther's. She smiled to ease the tension.

"They say," she murmured, "that one can exorcise their demons by talking about them. Wouldn't you like to try?"

"No. I like my demons where they are. It's easier to find 'em when I need 'em."

Elizabeth shook her head. "I don't know why you think you need them. They'll drag you down. Why won't you tell me what makes you hate your birthplace so much?"

He looked away from her, and gave a sigh of exasperation. "Why must women always pry into wha' a mon wants tae forget?"

"Excuse me—your brogue is showing. If it distresses you too badly to talk about it—"

"It's not that." His voice was cool, clipped, and she recognized his grab at self-control. "It does no good to talk about what is done. Nothing will change it."

"No, nothing can change what has been done, but how about the future? Ofttimes one can alter their future by recognizing what happened in the past and correcting it."

He laughed bitterly. "Nothing can alter my future but me, angel. And I've done a bloody poor job of planning for it, I can tell you that."

"Kincade—"

"Angel." His hand tightened around hers. "There's nothing to tell. I don't want to think about Glencairn or my uncle or my past. I want to think about you." He rose to one elbow and pulled aside the wool blanket. The fire threw him into stark relief, a shadow against the light. His palm—once so smooth, now callused and hard again—skimmed over her body in a slow motion, fingers seeking out hollows in a hot glide that took away her breath.

"See now," he murmured against her throat, his mouth a burning caress on her skin, "this is much better than light conversation."

Another time she might have offered an argument, but it was difficult thinking clearly when he was kissing her, his lips coaxing her mouth open for his tongue while his hands did delicious things to her quivering body. All reason and motivation vanished under his touch. Solving life's grim problems seemed much less important when his hand closed around her breast and his mouth kissed a path to the taut, aching nipple. She arched upward, a wordless cry on her lips as she clasped her arms around him.

After that first, almost frantic coupling earlier, the eagerness that had been over all too quickly, this was more leisurely, and not as urgent. Nothing mattered when he was holding her, when his strong arms were around her and he shared his heat and passion. Her hands spread across his bare back; the skin was taut, warm and hard beneath her palms. She felt the smooth flex of his muscles beneath her hands as he moved, and the hot possession of his mouth on her breast.

She burned wherever their bodies met, wherever his lips scorched a kiss over her skin; she was vaguely astonished that steam did not rise and fill the small tent. Pleasure blossomed inside her, focusing between her thighs at the ardent attentions of his hands there, and she moaned again.

That small sound drifted between them, and Kincade lifted his head to stare down into her face. His eyes were heated smoke, sultry, liquid emeralds. Passion gave his features a sharp edge, and she was startled at the faint look of desperation that passed briefly over his face.

"Jesus," he muttered, "I think it's too late."

She wanted to ask what he meant by that cryptic remark, but he was drawing back, his lean body solid and crowding the small tent. His hands slid under her, lifting her, and he pressed forward until she felt him begin to fill her with a heated invasion that made her gasp.

"Kincade . . ."

"What, darlin'?" He paused, panting, his shoulders and torso shining with sweat even in the chill air of the tent. She saw his tension in his braced arms and the corded muscles in his neck, and lifted her legs to curl around his waist.

"I need you. . . ."

He made a muffled, incoherent sound, and slid so deeply

she couldn't move for a moment. God, how wonderful it was to be with him like this, to have him inside her and know that she could get no closer, that this was the ultimate intimacy.

When he began to move again, his body an exquisite, tantalizing torture, she lifted to meet his thrusts. He bent to kiss her, capturing her lips with his and mimicking the sex act with his tongue jabbing into her mouth. She felt the tension rising, tightening, until she poised on the brink of release and was suspended. He seemed to be teasing her, withdrawing so that she followed him, hesitating, then thrusting inside her in a deep, satisfying move that took her ever closer.

"Tell me, lass," he said thickly when she cried out against his shoulder in a broken spate of words. "Tell me wha' ye mean. . . ."

She heard his brogue, knew that he was as affected as she was, that he'd lost control again, yet she couldn't make herself say those words again, tell him how she loved him and wanted to stay with him forever. Not until he returned the feelings.

Then it didn't matter, because he was moving against her and catapulting her over the edge into that weightless oblivion that promised blinding release. His name came out in a gasp that she felt but did not hear, and then there was only the shower of sparks that melted around her and trickled down in a warm lethargy as she held him cradled in her arms and thighs.

"Angel," he said with a groan, and rested his head against her shoulder. He held her that way for a long moment, his skin damp against hers, his body heavy yet somehow vulnerable. Then he lifted his head, and the expression in his green eyes was unreadable.

"Kincade?"

"Ah, angel," he said softly, and kissed her. "I don't know if I can lose you again."

Her arms tightened. "You don't have to."

His breath was warm, heated against her neck and shoulder. "I hope you're right. God—I hope you're right."

"When will you be back?" Kincade helped Elizabeth up into the buggy, reluctant to release her arm as she settled back against the seat. She smiled at him, and he felt that peculiar lurch of his heart again.

"As soon as possible. I can't leave Annie wondering where I am and if I'm all right."

"I wish you'd let me go with you," he began, but she reached out to put a gloved finger over his mouth.

"No. You stay here and work your claim. I can manage this myself. When I return, I'll bring more supplies with me. I have your list in my reticule."

He leaned on the buggy, and it creaked with the added weight. "'A jug of wine, a loaf of bread, and thou,' are all I need," he said softly.

"Who said that, anyway?"

"Besides me? Omar Khayyám. The entire quote is very apt to our situation, I think. 'A book of verses underneath the bough, a jug of wine, a loaf of bread—and thou, beside me singing in the wilderness. Oh, Wilderness were Paradise enow!'" When she gazed at him with a faint, trembling smile on her lips, he felt suddenly foolish and looked away. What kind of idiot was he, quoting from the *Rubáiyát* instead of saying something that would bring her back quickly?

Elizabeth bent forward suddenly and pressed her mouth to his. It was a quick, searing kiss, but he felt it all the way to his toes. "I forget," she drew back to say softly, "that you are such a complex man at times. And a romantic. I think I must be very fortunate indeed to have found you."

"Angel . . ." He paused helplessly, floundering for words to tell her what that meant to him, but none would come. She kissed him again, then straightened and took up the reins.

Whatever his sluggish brain might have produced in

response was unneeded. Elizabeth gave him a blinding smile and clucked to the horse, and the buggy started away with a jerk. He watched it out of sight, then turned and walked back to the mine with a slight limp. If he didn't keep busy until she returned, his imagination would drive him crazy.

Elizabeth stepped into the sitting room of her lodgings, peeling off her gloves. The strain of driving the buggy back to town made her shoulders and arms ache, as the horse had been frisky in the early-morning chill. Several times she'd found herself much too close to the edge of the road, with steep slopes dipping away at alarming angles. It would have been certain disaster to have a buggy wheel go off the edge, and almost impossible to right the vehicle. She'd glimpsed the bare bones of earlier mishaps below, the wires and springs and broken wheels that bespoke the fate of those who didn't pay attention to what they were doing.

Their rooms were empty, and she supposed that Annie was at one of her meetings or off drumming up support for their cause, both financial and spiritual. Money was always in short supply with their crusades, and ofttimes Annie had to depend upon the largess of supporters.

Though Elizabeth had offered to help, her cousin would not hear of it. "Not until absolutely necessary," she'd said with a twinkle in her eyes, "and we're not there yet. Keep your money for hard times, Elizabeth."

A fire burned in the grate, and she stretched out her hands to warm them. Even with the gloves and her layers of clothing, she'd gotten chilled on the ride back. It would be bitterly cold come winter. She wondered how she'd be able to stand it in a canvas tent, then followed that thought with the certainty that being with Kincade would make anything bearable.

She smiled into the flames and began to unbutton her coat. He'd been so tender and loving this time, with none of the reticence that had always tinged their relations before.

This time he'd held on to her, made love to her with a mix of driving urgency and soft words that had told her just how badly he'd missed her. Perhaps time had proven to Kincade that he needed her as much as she needed him. Annie was right—she only had to show him how to love her. The rest he seemed to be learning on his own.

"A silver mine," she murmured with a wry shake of her head. "I can't believe he's working so hard for so little."

She shrugged out of her coat and hung it on a wooden peg near the sitting-room door, then pulled out her hat pins. She placed pins and bonnet on a small table along with her reticule.

A knock on the door startled her, and when she swung it open, a young boy stood there holding a huge bouquet of fresh flowers. "For you, ma'am," he said, thrusting them at her.

"For me?" Elizabeth stared at the lace-wrapped bouquet. "But who—and where on earth did fresh flowers come from this time of year?"

"My boss has a greenhouse," the boy said impatiently. "There's a card that'll tell ya who sent 'em." He pushed the bouquet into her hand and waited expectantly, and Elizabeth retrieved her reticule and dug out several coins for him.

When he'd gone, she took a card from the fragrant midst of the bouquet and read, *To a beautiful woman with my best regards, Jeremy Lowery.*

"Well," she murmured, "this is unusual." She placed the flowers in a vase and arranged them on a low wicker table. Then she noticed the wrapped box of candy with a card placed atop them, and saw her name. The candy was from Jeremy also, and apparently Annie had left it there for her. Candy and flowers. Obviously Jeremy Lowery had decided to court her.

Another complication, and one she knew how to avoid. It wasn't as if men had not paid her court before, and usually she just ignored them until they got the message that she was not interested. A wry smile curved her mouth. What would she do if it was Kincade sending her candy and flowers? Not that he would ever think of that.

After having a maid draw a bath, she soaked in the tub until the water was cool. She'd miss the simple luxuries of life when she went to stay in Kincade's camp. But the rewards of having him to love her would more than make up for it.

She made plans while she dressed, deciding what she'd take with her and what she'd send back to Natchez until—until when? Pausing, she glanced up at her reflection in the cheval mirror, her hands still on the satin sash of her robe as she realized that nothing definite had been decided. He had not mentioned the future, except to say he wanted her. Did he mean forever? Marriage?

Marriage. Though she'd spent a year propounding the issue of marriage to women, she realized that she still hadn't settled it within herself. On one hand, she believed that women should not allow themselves to become subject to men's arbitrary wishes. Yet she knew that love made a woman want to please the man she'd chosen. She wanted to please Kincade. What if he demanded that she give up the crusade for women's rights? How did a woman settle that within herself and still remain with her husband?

Elizabeth moved to her dressing table and sank onto the cushioned chair. While she brushed her wet hair dry she mulled over every word they'd exchanged and, to her dismay, realized that Kincade had said nothing about changing his mind on the subject of women's rights. Had he? It was certainly an important issue between them, and if he hadn't—if he hadn't changed his mind, what would she do?

A noise in the sitting room and the murmur of voices provided a distraction, and Elizabeth dressed quickly when she heard her cousin ask if she could hang up their coat. It wasn't often Annie brought home guests, and she was slightly curious as to who the caller could be, as it was definitely a masculine voice she heard.

When she opened the bedroom door, she heard the last of a sentence. ". . . fortunate to have met you this evening, Miss Lee. It was most opportune." There was a faintly familiar lilt to the voice that Elizabeth couldn't quite place.

Annie was saying, "Yes, it was quite a coincidence. Do you intend to stay in Virginia City long?"

"As I told you," the man replied, "I am looking for—oh, hello."

As Elizabeth entered the sitting room the gentleman turned with a smile. He was tall and slim, with dark hair liberally sprinkled with gray. He had a commanding appearance about him, and his clothes proclaimed him comfortable if not wealthy. He inclined his head respectfully to Elizabeth as Annie began the introductions, and as he took her offered hand and she looked up to meet chilly blue eyes, she heard her cousin say, ". . . Dougal MacKay, from Scotland. He's come to find his nephew Kincade."

Chapter 20

ELIZABETH STOOD in stunned silence as MacKay bent over her hand with a gallant gesture, and when he straightened, she caught a flash of something in his eyes that made her throat tighten. MacKay smiled, but it was only a curving of his lips that somehow reminded her of Kincade's most mocking smiles.

"I understood that you've met my nephew, Miss Lee," he said in a smooth, cultured voice that held no trace of his heritage.

"Yes," she murmured as she withdrew her hand from his grasp. "Have you seen him since arriving?"

"Alas, no. I only arrived yesterday morning, and it has taken me a great deal of time to find anyone who knows him." His eyes studied her as he spoke, and she repressed a sudden shudder. "Then, while attending a meeting this afternoon, I was most surprised to meet your charming cousin. She told me she knew him, and that you were aware of his whereabouts."

Elizabeth caught her breath. How should she reply? She knew very well that Kincade was in grave danger from this man, yet she'd never mentioned it to Annie. It would have been one more reason for her cousin to warn her against Kincade, and so she'd been reluctant to confide in her. Now she wished she had.

"Yes," she said when the silence drew out noticeably, "I

know that he is in the hills above Virginia City. I was not able to find him, however."

"No?" MacKay said, arching a brow. His face was composed of sharp angles and planes, with none of Kincade's masculine beauty and humor to soften it. There was a certain family resemblance, but she found it difficult to compare him with Kincade.

"Elizabeth," Annie was saying in a puzzled tone, "I thought that you—"

"Went to the wrong mine, if you'll recall. It was not at all what we thought," she broke in quickly, and saw the flash of comprehension on her cousin's face.

"Ah, that's right. How foolish of me. I'm sorry, Mr. MacKay, to have led you astray. Perhaps if you inquire at the local saloons, you might find someone who knows him."

"No doubt. My nephew always had an affinity for those places," he said dryly. "It's a stroke of luck that I've managed to trace him this far, I suppose. I've had men working on it for some time, you know. In fact, I was given the erroneous information that Kincade was one of the kings of the Comstock, but I discovered how false that information was almost immediately upon my arrival."

His almost contemptuous tone angered Elizabeth, but she didn't dare engage him in any argument that might result in her dropping any clues as to Kincade's whereabouts. He'd find out soon enough without her help, and she needed to go out to the mine as quickly as possible and warn Kincade.

"I'm sorry you were led astray like this," she managed to murmur. "I'm certain you'll find him soon."

"Oh, so am I. After all, I've managed to come this far. A few more hours won't make much difference."

"Is he expecting you?" Annie asked, and MacKay turned toward her with a shake of his head.

"No, not at all. This was a sudden decision of mine, to visit America. There is a general assembly of Presbyterian leaders being held, and they graciously invited certain members of the Associate and Reformed synods to attend. I was elected to come to America, and as my nephew is here and I have not seen him for so long, I have made this special effort to find him. He will be most surprised to see me, I think."

"No doubt," Elizabeth murmured, and felt Dougal MacKay's quick, burning glance at her. She flushed. "After not having seen him in so many years, he will be amazed that you have come this far to visit with him, I'm sure."

"Yes. I'm just as certain of that. Well, it grows late and I've not yet eaten my evening meal. I have a room at the International, and I should return."

"The International is a fine hotel," Elizabeth said rather nervously. "Did you know it had the first elevator between Chicago and San Francisco? It is very elegant."

"Yes," MacKay said with a vaguely amused smile, "so I was made to understand. I've found it to be much more comfortable than I had thought such rugged country could manage. Virginia City was a surprise."

"There was a fire in 1875, I believe," Elizabeth said. "Many buildings burned down and were then restored even more beautifully than before."

Dougal MacKay smiled. "I'm glad to see that Americans are able to make such progress in a rustic area like this."

Elizabeth opened her mouth to say something cutting, and her cousin interrupted.

"I'll get your coat for you," Annie said, but he shook his head.

"No, no, let me. It's just on a hook by the door, and I've troubled you ladies long enough." He smiled, bowed politely, and when he had retrieved his coat and said his farewells, Elizabeth shut the door behind him.

She leaned back against the closed door and gazed at Annie. "Thank God," she said.

Annie stared back at her. "What was all that about? I think you'd better tell me why you behaved so strangely."

"It's very simple. Kincade has reason to believe that his uncle has been trying to kill him for some time now."

"Preposterous. The man's been in Scotland, hasn't he?"

"And you heard him say he'd had people looking for his nephew, didn't you?" Elizabeth countered. "There's a reason for that." She shoved away from the door. "Kincade is Lord of Glencairn and Dougal MacKay wants his lands and title."

Annie lifted a skeptical brow. "I find that rather hard to believe, though I admit that Dougal MacKay does look the part of aristocracy."

"And Kincade doesn't?"

Annie chuckled. "Don't go glaring at me as if I've said your only child was ugly, Elizabeth. That's not what I mean. Kincade would look very aristocratic if he'd take himself more seriously and not be so sardonic all the time. No, I was under the impression that trustees of the Scottish Kirk, which MacKay tells me he is, were rather upright men."

"Does he strike you that way?"

Annie hesitated, then said slowly, "No, no he doesn't."

"There's a coldness to him. It's his eyes, and the way his upper lip curls slightly when he says Kincade's name. I think he hates him, whatever else he's done or not done."

"I think you're right." Annie leaned to pick up her coat from the chair where she'd tossed it. Then she swept up Elizabeth's bonnet from where it had been accidentally knocked to the floor. "Here. You'd best put this up before I step on it."

Elizabeth moved forward. "Yes, I left my things here on the—where is my reticule?"

"Your reticule?"

"Yes, I put it here on the table with my bonnet when I came in, and now it's gone."

They looked for it behind the chair and table and under several objects, but did not find it. Elizabeth sank to an ottoman and stared at her cousin, bewildered. Who would want it?

Annie echoed that sentiment aloud. "Who would want your reticule? What did you have in it that someone might want?"

"Nothing. I know better than to carry around much money with me, and I can't imagine that anyone would want my lace handkerchief or Kincade's grocery list. . . ." She paused and looked up, her mouth still open. "Do you suppose . . . ?"

"No, it can't be. When—and why?"

"Perhaps to find out if I've seen Kincade. And it would have been simple enough for him to scoop up my reticule as he left. After all, we weren't paying attention when he retrieved his coat."

"But that's highly unlikely. Don't you think?"

Elizabeth stared at her. "I don't know quite what to think. Except that I must warn Kincade as quickly as possible that his uncle is here in Virginia City."

"You can't go out there now," Annie protested. "Why, it will be dark soon, and those roads are treacherous even in daylight."

"I know that." Elizabeth shuddered. "But he has to be warned. The disappearance of my reticule is evidence of that."

"What if you just dropped it and didn't notice?"

"I *did* notice when I put it on the table," Elizabeth said so firmly Annie didn't argue.

"All right." Annie glanced at the window, where light was slowly fading. "I'm going with you."

"You don't have to—"

"Don't be idiotic. I can't allow you to go alone. And if I stayed, I'd make myself crazy sitting here wondering if you were all right, anyway."

After a brief hesitation Elizabeth nodded. "Very well. Let me get dressed."

Kincade heard a faint clatter. He rose to one elbow and reached for the rifle that was never very far from his side.

He was a much better shot than he'd ever thought he would be, which was good, he supposed, as he'd had more occasion to prove it than he'd ever thought he would have.

Someone had once told him that the Western states and territories either changed men or killed them, and he had to agree with that statement. If a man didn't change, he died from the elements or violence. It was very simple. Life was reduced to the basics for the most part, and choices were often made for a man.

Even in Virginia City, a town of over twenty thousand that had risen from boomtown days when it was called Washoe to days of splendor and opulence, violence took many a life. Nothing was certain, and Kincade had come to trust in that simple adage.

That was why he'd taken to sleeping so lightly and waking often in the night. It was safer, and more than once he'd been glad for the precaution.

Like now, when he heard the slow tread of footsteps on gravel and the slight scrunch of sliding boots. The slopes that fell away from his campsite provided a perfect alarm against interlopers.

With the rifle gripped in one hand, Kincade slid quietly from his bedroll and crouched on his knees. Pale, rosy light glimmered in the tent, and he found his pistol and stuck it in the waistband of his pants. Then he reached out with one foot to nudge a log into place over the glowing bed of coals in the metal brazier, and it grew darker. After a moment he edged toward the back of his tent and lifted the bottom slowly and carefully. The back of the canvas tent nudged close to a high rock wall, and on one side a grove of twisted cedar trees offered some protection from the wind. The area in front fell away abruptly, and the open side dipped down toward the mine shaft.

He slipped under the lifted edge of canvas and crouched in the dark shadows, waiting. Several minutes passed without a sound, then he heard the distinct rattle of rocks sliding down the slope. He brought up his rifle and eased the bolt back, then took the pistol from his pants. Though he wore his wool pants to bed on cold nights, he usually wore only the top of his union suit, and it was much lighter than the flannel he wore in the daytime.

The wind cut through the thin undershirt and made him shiver, and he gripped his weapons convulsively as he searched the dark for whoever was stalking him. Another step crunched on gravel, and he turned slightly in that direction and peered into the thick shadows.

A silhouette appeared briefly, large and bulky, and he lifted his rifle to his shoulder and steadied it. He squinted down the rear sight and waited, and when the shadow flickered again, outlined against the lighter background of the tent, he squeezed off a warning shot.

"Hold it," he said before the echoes of the bullet slamming into rock had faded, "or you're dead."

"Don't shoot."

The voice was a hoarse croak. Kincade didn't lower his rifle, but waited. He'd glimpsed two shadows and wasn't about to take any chances.

"Step away from the tent," he ordered, and the figure moved clumsily, half stumbling into a patch of moonlight. "Now drop your weapons. Quick, before I get too nervous and this bloody thing goes off by accident."

A thud and scrape broke the silence, and then a low mutter. The figure straightened, and Kincade squinted.

"Who are you?" he asked.

There was a short pause. "Name's Hazlett."

"Well, well, Mr. Hazlett, might I inquire what you're doing prowling around my claim in the middle of the night? That could be fatal, you know."

Hazlett muttered something unintelligible, and Kincade pumped the lever on his rifle. "Excuse me? I didn't quite hear you."

"I said," the man snarled, "that nobody told me you'd probably be waitin' on me. I heard you was a tenderfoot."

"A tenderfoot. By that I assume you mean a novice at

staying alive? Sorry to disappoint you, old chap, but I'm an expert at survival. I've had to be, you understand. Now, why don't you tell that gentleman with you that it'd be to your best interest if he'd come out of the shadows into the light and dispose of his weapons.''

''Come on,'' Hazlett snapped after a moment, but no one moved, and Kincade laughed softly.

''It seems as if your friend doesn't care how many pieces he takes you back down the hill in, Mr. Hazlett. How unfortunate for you. I won't shoot to kill with the first bullet, and p'raps he'll change his mind.'' He lifted the rifle and aligned the sights, and Hazlett let out a string of curses.

''Damn you, Quincy,'' he ended in a rasping snarl, ''come out here before the bastard shoots me!''

A second man stepped into the patch of moonlight, and Kincade shifted position. ''Kick your weapons toward me, but do it very slowly or this thing might go off by accident.''

A rifle and two pistols were nudged toward him, and he sat there for a moment watching the two men. He was sweating and was vaguely surprised by that. In the icy night air, he should be shivering. He rose slowly to his feet and walked to where the weapons lay, keeping an eye on the men as he kicked them behind him.

''Now,'' he said conversationally, ''suppose you tell me why you're here.''

Sullen silence followed, and the whip of the wind cut through his clothes and chilled his damp skin. ''I'm waiting, gentlemen,'' he said, and when neither of them replied, he brought up his Winchester in a smooth motion and fired. A bullet spanged in the rock at their feet, making them jump and howl as sharp splinters sprayed them. Kincade smiled. ''This is a Winchester 44–40. Even a child could not miss at this range, and I'm long past the tenderfoot stage by now. Would you care to test the veracity of that?''

''No,'' Hazlett finally said. ''We were sent here to get you out of the way.''

"Yes, I deduced that much. Would you mind telling me who sent you?"

Another silence followed, then the man Hazlett had called Quincy said roughly, "Griffin."

"Griffin. Max Griffin?"

"Yeah."

"What have I done to him?" Kincade asked slowly. "I've never even met the man."

"You'd have to ask Griffin that."

"Perhaps I shall. In the meantime I suggest that you gentlemen resign yourselves to being my guests for the evening. Tomorrow morning we'll ride into town and talk to the sheriff. He should have some handy notions about what to do with you."

"Way I hear it, Sheriff Wallace don't particularly like you, MacKay."

"Really. I'm devastated. Sit down, both of you, very slowly. Remember, I am quite capable with this rifle, so don't do anything you might not have time to regret."

He tied them several yards apart, securing them with rope and heavy timbers he'd been using to shore up the roof of the mine. When he was satisfied they weren't going anywhere, he left them in the chill shelter under an overhang and went back into his tent. He was freezing. The sweat had long since turned to an icy mist on his skin, and it was all he could do to keep from shivering uncontrollably.

After rekindling his fire, he sat in front of it for long moments, trying to figure out why Griffin wanted to kill him. He knew who Griffin was, of course; most people did. There were wanted posters out on him all over the territory. It didn't make much sense that a man who made a tidy living robbing mine payrolls would accept a job from his uncle's henchmen. Yet it seemed that was what had happened.

He puzzled over it for a while. Max Griffin had just not seemed the type of outlaw to go in for killing unless it directly benefited him. Maybe Dougal had gotten so desperate he was willing to pay a great deal to see his nephew dead.

Kincade's mouth twisted into a bitter smile. Life was nothing if not full of surprises.

He stretched out on his blankets again, leaving his tent open so that he could keep an eye on the two men tied close by. In case someone else came skulking around, he would be ready.

"Shhh," Elizabeth said. She put a shaking finger to her lips. "We have to s-s-shout a warning first or he might s-s-shoot us."

She was shivering so hard that her words came out in a disjointed mumble that she had to repeat twice before Annie understood.

"D-d-dear G-God," Annie chattered.

Silvery moonlight flooded the area, bright and icy. It cast a hazy glow over rocks and the stunted shapes of cedar and sagebrush. Some of the shapes seemed to waver and take on humanlike qualities, and it shredded Elizabeth's nerves more than the accident that had stranded them on the rutted road. Losing a wheel seemed like a small thing compared with the long, cold trek. If the horse they'd unhitched from its traces hadn't bolted like a wild creature, they might have at least been able to ride it, but they'd been so cold and the light grown so dim by that time, the terrified animal had taken off into the shadows trailing its long reins.

Now, at last, Kincade's camp was just ahead.

"S-s-so go," Annie muttered. "I don't care if he shoots us, as long as we f-f-fall into the f-f-fire."

"We couldn't be that l-l-lucky."

Elizabeth stumbled forward on frozen feet. It was cold enough to snow. Or maybe it was too cold to snow. She'd heard of that before. The wind was bitter, and there were places that held faint, hard traces of either snow or hard frost. If it wasn't a clear night, she'd swear that there was about to be a blizzard.

When she reached the bottom of the slope that led up to Kincade's tent, she paused and gathered enough air in her lungs to shout a greeting. Before she could form the words, a shot shattered the night and the air exploded from her lungs in a wordless screech of fright.

Annie gave no cry, but made a sound something like a *whuff!* of surprise.

"Who's out there?" came the demand, and the voice was Kincade's familiar clipped tones.

Still shivering, Elizabeth managed to croak, "Me. It's m-m-me and Annie."

A brief silence followed, and she saw a dark shape loom atop the slope. "Lizzie? Is that you?"

She didn't bother correcting him, but mumbled an affirmative that had him sliding down the hill. She noticed he held a rifle in one hand and a pistol in the other.

"What the devil are you doing out here?" he snapped, peering at her in the bright press of moonlight.

"F-f-freezing," Annie said tartly. "Do you m-m-mind asking questions l-l-later?"

When they were huddled inside his tent around the fire, Elizabeth glanced back outside at the two men they'd passed. It had been quite evident they were tied and surly, and she turned back to look inquiringly at Kincade. He shrugged.

"Unwelcome visitors."

"I see," she said, warming her hands and still shivering. "You're not very friendly."

"A lamentable lapse of manners caused by an aversion to being shot, I'm afraid." His brow lifted, and he looked from one of them to the other. "May I ask again—what the deuce are you doing out here at this time of night?"

"We'd have been here earlier if that stupid nag hadn't run away," Annie remarked complacently. "Never have cared much for horses. Stupid animals. Not nearly as smart as a dog. Or a pig."

Kincade's gaze narrowed. "How enlightening. But that is not the answer I expected."

"Kincade," Elizabeth said quickly, "we came to warn you."

"Too late, angel." He gestured toward his captives. "I took care of it myself."

"No, no, not them, though I'm glad you were able to protect yourself. It's your uncle—"

"That's what I thought. Can't figure out what he offered Griffin to try and kill me, though."

"Kincade." Some of her urgency must have penetrated, because he paused and looked at her more closely. She put a hand on his arm and felt his muscles tighten. "Your uncle is here. In Virginia City, I mean. He is looking for you."

"Bloody hell," Kincade said after a moment. "Bloody *hell.*"

Chapter 21

SHERIFF WALLACE raked the two bound men with a steely glare, then glanced at Kincade. "Why were they out there at your claim, MacKay?"

"I haven't a clue. I suggest you ask them. Perhaps they will be more chatty with you than they have been with me."

Wallace, a tall, rugged-looking man, shook his head. "It beats all how you managed to take both of them. They're a pretty rough pair."

"He jumped us," Hazlett said in a growl. "We was mindin' our own bizness, and—"

"And if I believed that, I'd be a bigger fool than you think I am. Murphy," Wallace said to a tall, burly deputy standing nearby, "put 'em away while I discuss the reward money with MacKay."

"Reward?" Kincade stared at him blankly for a moment. "What reward?"

"I'm sure you didn't know," Wallace drawled sarcastically. He pointed toward the rear of his office and the door leading to a row of cells. "I've got enough posters on 'em to keep 'em for a while. Max Griffin, too. Probably you as well, if I look hard enough."

"Really, Constable," Kincade said mildly, "I resent your implying that I'm a common criminal."

"Save it, MacKay. I don't like you any better than I do

264

them. Gamblers are not high on my list of responsible citizens.''

''Too bad, as you seem to have a town full of them.''

Wallace flung him a narrowed glare and rose to his feet. ''Don't go anywhere. When we have them in a cell, I want to talk to you.''

''By all means.'' Kincade settled his shoulders against the wall and crossed his arms over his chest in a casual pose that made Wallace's mouth tighten with irritation. No matter. He wasn't in the best of moods himself.

The news that Dougal MacKay was in Virginia City—in *America,* for chrissake—had done nothing to improve his mood. Elizabeth's solution was to leave town before Dougal discovered his whereabouts, but Kincade had more than enough of running. That had begun the argument, and his roughness with the two men who'd tried to kill him had only made things worse.

After arguing with Elizabeth about the best method of getting the two men down to the sheriff, then setting about finding her blasted horse and fixing the buggy wheel, he'd not been amenable to light conversation. Her suggestion that Hazlett and Quincy be treated more gently had angered him.

What did she expect? That he sing them lullabies and politely ask them to accompany him to the sheriff's office? But Elizabeth had accused him of taking out his bad temper on them unnecessarily, and exasperation had led him to reply unwisely. Now they weren't even speaking. And just when things seemed to have gone so well between them. Ah, well, Shakespeare had warned his audiences that the course of true love never ran smooth. Kincade just hadn't expected mountains and canyons in the course; a few potholes, perhaps, but not the obstacles he'd encountered.

The metallic creak of the door pulled his attention back to the present, and Sheriff Wallace came back into the outer office and tossed a ring of keys to his desk. After a brief glance his deputy stepped outside, leaving them alone.

Wallace surveyed Kincade silently for a moment, his eyes piercing.

"Don't have much use for gamblers," Wallace began, and Kincade returned his stare coolly and silently. "I'll have your money ready for you in a few days."

"How much?"

"Five hundred for the pair of 'em. Too bad you didn't get Griffin. He'd be worth a lot more."

"I'll keep that in mind," Kincade said pleasantly.

Wallace grunted, then said, "I know you won Jim Hardy's claim. Think it's rich?"

"I've no idea. I'm not a miner, as you so politely pointed out."

"Hmmph." Wallace lowered his body into a chair and leaned back. "Why you working it if you don't think it'll pay off for you?"

"Because it seemed like the thing to do at the time. I am, however, beginning to rethink that decision. I've had nothing but a few rocks and a lot of water to show for hours of mucking out a hole full of clay and little else."

"Hardy musta thought it was worth something. Reckon that was why he shot himself over losing it."

Kincade's brow lifted in surprise. "He shot himself?"

"So we figure. Found him in his room, dead, a pistol in one hand and bullet hole in his head."

"How unfortunate."

Wallace stared at him. "Yeah. That's what I thought. My top deputy wondered if he'd really shot himself, but we can't find anybody who had a grudge against him."

"Don't look in my direction," Kincade said shortly. "I had no reason to kill him. I already have his mine. Why would I want him dead?"

"I dunno. Thought I might check around. You might want him dead if Hardy could prove you'd cheated him—"

"He couldn't, because I didn't. It was as much a shock to me as anyone else when I drew that fourth queen. And at the time I had no desire for a worthless hole in the ground. I still don't. I find it rather ludicrous that I was fool enough to think a hole was worth anything.''

"But if it's got a silver lode in it like some folks think, it ain't worthless.''

"I don't have the experience or the funds to go that far. If someone offers me a decent price for it, I'll probably take it and run.''

"Not yet you won't.''

Kincade's mouth tightened. "Is that your subtle way of telling me that you'd rather I linger in your fair city?''

"Yeah, you could say that. Something else, MacKay—I had a gent in here asking about you the other day. He said he's a relative, and seemed mighty curious about some of your . . . ah . . . activities and acquisitions, I think he said.''

"Did he now.'' Kincade pushed away from the wall, abandoning his languid pose.

"Know who he is?'' Wallace asked when Kincade remained silent.

"I've a good idea. Is that information pertinent to your investigation, Sheriff? It seems rather personal to me.''

"Reckon it is personal.'' Wallace studied him a moment longer, then shrugged. "Just don't leave the area, MacKay. I may need to ask you some more questions before long.''

"I wouldn't dream of it.''

Once outside, Kincade sucked in a deep breath of cold air and hoped it helped cool his temper. Dougal, of course. It was time to find out what he wanted. Despite Elizabeth's angry insistence, he intended to find his uncle. It was time he stopped running and met problems head-on. The only problem running had ever solved was taking care of an excess of money. He was through running. If it cost him his life, he intended to confront Dougal MacKay.

He stepped down off the boardwalk and started toward C Street.

"I don't understand it.'' Tabitha frowned.

They stood beneath an overhang of the Red Garter

Saloon. Tabitha turned from surveying the interior to look at Ian with a troubled expression. "I should have waited for Horatio instead of lingering overlong at the opera. I've a feeling that I don't know all there is to know about this."

"'Tis likely," Ian said. "There is something tha' we dinna know tha' is important. 'Tis no' just the inheritance o' lands and title, tae my way o' thinking."

"But what could it be? It's hardly likely that Kincade is his long-lost son or something. And I cannot imagine that Dougal would come this far for anything less."

"Aye, but wha' aboot *more*? Sich as his first love—money? I'm thinking tha' he wa'd come this far for sich as tha'."

Tabitha looked startled. "Perhaps. But what—besides the title and estate—could it be?"

"Tha' is wha' we must find out, madam," Ian said, "and I think it is verra important."

"You know," Tabitha said slowly, "I believe you are right, Ian. That must be what Horatio meant when he said that things are not always as they seem. He mentioned that the most trivial seeming incidents can loom large to someone else at times."

"And wha' else did Horatio tell ye?"

"Only his usual string of incomprehensible garble that he expects me to decipher."

"Sich as?"

"Such as, muddled comments like 'even gold and silver are usually found in dull lumps of rock,' and 'just because it glitters does not mean it's gold,' and ridiculous platitudes like those."

"Does he ever say directly wha' he means?"

"Not often. I think he's actually part of my penance for sins long past, but then there are times I find that he is actually quite wise in his way." Tabitha shrugged. "No matter. Now we must see if our suspicions are right about Dougal MacKay. Let's see . . . how can we go about this?"

"I've an idea, madam." Ian turned to look through the doors of the Red Garter. "Dinna ye once tell me tha' ye wore the costume o' a tavern wench?"

"Tavern wench? Oh, you mean a dance-hall girl. Yes, I did. Say, do you mean . . . ?" She clapped her hands with sudden glee. "How delightful! I do see what you mean, Ian, I truly do."

Ian blinked, and in that instant Tabitha wore a scarlet gown festooned with satin ruffles and black lace. Two crimson splotches of rouge brightened her face, and she wore lip paint as well as kohl on her lashes.

"Ye look," Ian said grimly, "like a caricature, madam. Canna ye soften the effect a bit?"

"No. I think this will do nicely. Besides, have you taken a good look at some of the women in there?"

"Nay, I canna say tha' I ha'."

"Then don't complain." Tabitha straightened a lace flounce over her ample bosom. She peered over the batwing doors in the saloon, then nodded. "I believe I see our quarry making his not very discreet inquiries. You fetch Kincade, but not too quickly. Give me a few minutes to draw Dougal out."

"Draw him out? Ye'll run him awa', is what ye'll do," Ian grumbled, but Tabitha wasn't listening. She'd pushed open the doors and entered the saloon, and the resulting swing of one door would have struck him if he hadn't stepped back. He saw a passing pedestrian pause to stare at him, and realized that Tabitha must have somehow brought him into view as well.

"Excuse me," Ian said quietly to the staring man, and turned to walk into the shadows of a nearby alley. He shook his head and glanced up at the sky. "Gi' me strength tae keep up wi' her," he muttered, and with a quick motion of one hand, was gone.

Music tinkled loudly, but was just a muted noise covered by laughter, the clink of whiskey glasses, and the rumble of conversation. Tables were scattered haphazardly about the saloon, and the long bar at one side catered to men garbed in dirty denim as well as spotless broadcloth.

Kincade paused just inside the door, blinking at the sting of smoke. The scene was comfortingly familiar and disturbing at the same time. It had been a while since he'd sat down at a poker game, but that wasn't why he was here.

The reason stood at one end of the bar, trapped, it looked like, in conversation with a pudgy saloon woman in scarlet satin and black lace. Not at all Dougal's style, he mused as he headed toward them.

The woman saw him first, and paused in midsentence to blink owlishly. "Oh," she said in a distinct English accent, "I believe we have company."

Dougal MacKay half turned, then stiffened. His eyes widened slightly, then cooled to the same cold, piercing blue, showing no emotion at all. Only the amount of gray in his hair was different from what Kincade remembered about him.

"Kincade," Dougal said smoothly. His lips curved into a smile that didn't reach his eyes. "My, but you've changed a great deal." He paused to rake Kincade with a searching glance. His eyes flicked over the pistol worn low on his hip before returning to Kincade's face. "You've matured into quite a man. How pleasant to see you again."

"Do you really think so? Why is it that I don't quite believe you feel that way, Uncle Dougal?"

His mocking reply had no outward effect on Dougal, except to provoke a rather wistful smile that didn't fool Kincade at all.

"You're angry at me," Dougal said reproachfully. "After I came all this way to see you, I expected a more enthusiastic greeting."

"No doubt." Kincade leaned against the bar and felt the saloon woman's gaze on him. Odd, but he felt as if he should know her. She was certainly gazing at him avidly, and he felt strangely compelled to speak kindly to her. "If you don't mind," he said, "this is a private conversation."

"Oh yes, quite." Her garishly painted mouth turned up in a bright smile. "Relatives always have a great deal to say to one another after a long separation, I am sure. Ofttimes the most marvelous differences are smoothed out in a unique way. As you two seem to be—"

"Excuse me," Dougal interrupted shortly, "but as I have been trying to tell you for the past half hour, I have no further desire to converse with you. Be off, or I shall alert your employer that you are making a nuisance of yourself."

"Will you now? That should be interesting."

Something in her voice made Kincade shift his attention back to her, and he found his mouth curling in amusement. The woman resembled nothing so much as a bright, frowsy bird with her wiry hair done in old-fashioned curls and her garments fluttering about her ample frame like so many gaudy feathers. But there was a keen consideration in her eyes as she studied Dougal MacKay, and apparently he began to perceive that as well.

"I hope I didn't offend you, madam," he said stiffly, "but one does not discuss private family matters in front of outsiders."

"No, no, of course not. La! I should think that you and your nephew must have a great many personal issues to talk about, what with his new discovery and all."

Kincade stared at her and heard Dougal ask, "What new discovery?"

The woman put a beringed hand over her mouth in dismay. "Oh, have I let out a secret? Dear me, I know how secretive miners can be about their claims, even when it is rumored to be richer than the Comstock Lode—but I rattle on, when this nice young man is looking at me as if he wishes to box my ears. Can't say that I blame you, sir, but pray have mercy on a woman who—"

"Listens to unfounded rumors," Kincade broke in. "I don't know what you heard, but I can assure you that my claim is worthless."

Dougal was gazing at him with interest, and with a few more apologies that made Kincade wish he really could box her ears, the woman finally sauntered away. He watched her go. She certainly didn't seem like the usual saloon whore.

"Well, it seems as if you've done better than I heard," Dougal said finally, and Kincade turned back to him.

"What do you want here?"

"My, my, ever blunt, aren't you."

"Let's not waste time. You didn't come to see me. I'm well aware of your burning desire to rid yourself of what you deem an irritating obstacle to your ends, so get on with it."

Dougal glanced about, then gestured to a corner of the room where a solitary table sat empty. "Shall we sit down and share a glass of port?" When Kincade didn't move but just stared at him, Dougal added, "I do have business that I need to discuss with you, Kincade."

Reluctantly Kincade found himself sitting at the table with his uncle. "What do you want?" he asked tersely.

"I've brought papers that you need to sign," Dougal said without preamble. "No one has been able to locate you for quite a while, and there are any number of matters pertaining to your estates that need to be settled. The crofters need guidance, and there are repairs to the buildings and lands—"

"You don't need me to sign papers. You've done it long enough without me," Kincade interrupted. "My signature was only a formality that your barrister somehow managed to remove with a legal document that I never saw but understand I requested. Of course, I can't recall requesting a form that gives him the power to make decisions on my behalf, but there are other interesting things I recall." He leaned forward, and was fiercely glad to see the flicker of unease in Dougal's eyes as he said softly, "I recall being hungry for more years that I'd like to think about, and I recall being left with little fuel for warmth and funds for proper clothes, and that was just my childhood. When I reached my majority, I began to encounter any number of obstacles in my life, some of which were engineered by you."

"Here, here," Dougal protested, "you've got matters wrong, my boy. I never tried to do anything but get you to take up the reins of responsibility. 'Twas you who preferred gaming and wenching to your obligations. If not for my steward, your crofters would have starved during the winters."

"If not for your steward, I would never have been charged with a theft I did not commit," Kincade grated. "Do not try to pretend ignorance of what happened. You're well aware that I beat it out of the man, and he confessed everything to me before I left Scotland."

Dougal shrugged, an elegant lifting of his shoulders beneath the expensive wool coat he wore. "A misunderstanding. No doubt he would have said anything to get you away from him. I can have those charges dismissed, you know."

"I imagine you can, as you were the one who placed them before the magistrate."

"Not so, dear boy. The steward filed charges upon you, and when he died—"

"Not of the beating I gave him, I assure you." Kincade couldn't keep the bitterness out of his voice. "But no one else knows that. It didn't take much to rouse the authorities against me, especially after you had brought up the old charge of heresy in the high kirk. A heretic is quite capable of murder, as far as most people are concerned."

Dougal's pleasant smile tightened, and there was a chilly glaze in his eyes, but his voice was as smooth and unruffled as before. "I daresay. Yet I have no reason to harm you. What befalls you reflects upon me. I am a MacKay also, and it pains me to hear such things about my own flesh and blood.''

"Enough." Kincade stood up, holding tightly to his temper. "I don't want to hear your sanctimonious babble that no one believes but you. If you want papers signed— sign 'em yourself like you always have. I don't think I can stomach another minute of you.''

"Wait." Dougal rose to his feet and put out a hand as if to grab his arm, but at the look in Kincade's eyes apparently decided not to and let his arm drop to his side. "I can't sign the papers. I don't know where they are.''

"That's your problem." Kincade turned away, fighting anger.

"Kincade, stop. Just tell me where they are, then.''

He turned back, realized he'd clenched his hands into fists, and took a deep breath and relaxed them. "I don't know what you're talking about.''

"The stock certificates for Consolidated Shipping. I need to account for them.''

"Consoli—I never heard of it. I don't have 'em. Talk to your Edinburgh barrister. He usually keeps the papers to all your stolen properties.''

"Not these." Dougal looked slightly desperate, but managed a smile. "Look, old boy, they're worthless, but in a silly point of law, I must account for them. If you'll just tell me where you put them, I'll retrieve them.''

"If they're worthless, why do you need them?''

Dougal spread his hands and shrugged. "I've no idea. I am not well versed in law. All I know is that Prufrock said he had to have the certificates in order to close the files. I thought he already had them, but now—''

"Now," Kincade said softly, "you've found out they're worth something, right?''

"Nonsense. They're worthless. Consolidated changed hands and went bankrupt, as I warned your father they would so long ago. Ewen didn't listen to me, and when I proved right, he was ruined.''

"Then why come all this way to have me produce them for you? I'm not stupid, Dougal. And I've learned to smell a rat at fifty yards. Right now the stink is getting stronger by the moment."

"Don't be a fool." Dougal took a step forward, his jaw clenched so hard a muscle leaped in his cheek. "You've nothing to lose and everything to gain by telling me what you've done with them."

"Why do you think I have the stocks?" Kincade smiled. "And why do you think I'd tell you if I did?"

"Because it can change your life."

"How?"

"I must account for them, you understand, because I was executive of your estate at the time the stocks were called in. If you will cooperate, I will see to it that your name is cleared of the murder charge as well as heresy."

"How bleeding kind of you." Kincade lifted a brow when Dougal muttered an oath. "Swearing, Uncle? And you a trustee in the high kirk."

"Don't be an ass, Kincade. I'm offering you a chance at a new life."

"I've done well enough without you so far."

"But you could do so much better. You could come back to Scotland where you belong. This raw, uncivilized country is no place for you. I've seen nothing but uncouth ruffians and fallen women since I've been here."

"I assume you're including Elizabeth and Annie Lee in that number. That's your second mistake."

"Second?"

"Your first was in coming here at all." Kincade took a step forward. "Stay away from me, Dougal MacKay. And stay away from Elizabeth. You contaminate everything you touch. I don't know exactly why you want those stocks, but I'm damn sure not going to tell you where they are. You've wasted your money and my time."

He wasn't unprepared for the swift strike of his uncle's arm. Light glittered briefly on the edge of Dougal's dirk, and Kincade managed to grab his wrist and hold it. Men scattered, and conversation slowed as those around stopped to watch. Dougal's face was set, intense, and the muscles in his arm quivered as Kincade slowly forced him to drop the dirk. It had grown so quiet in the saloon that the loud pop of the bones in Dougal's wrist was a sickening sound.

Kincade released his arm at once, and Dougal went to his knees, holding his injured wrist in his other hand. "I should have killed you years ago," he snarled. "You're a worthless bastard unworthy of your inheritance."

"You may be right, but I'm better qualified than you, Dougal. If you were man enough to inherit, you would have faced me years ago instead of sending your puny hirelings after me."

He kicked away the dirk with a glance of disgust and looked up to see men watching him with wary respect. It didn't make him feel any better, and he pushed through the crowd toward the doors.

It was small enough reward for the years of misery he'd suffered, but it would suffice. Thwarting Dougal like this was better than nothing.

When Kincade stepped into the swiftly fading daylight, he took a deep breath. The hammer of stamp mills and compressors thundered in a muted bellow, and the bustle of busy citizens gave the town a sense of raw energy. People came and went constantly.

In the distance he could hear the faint thread of singing, and smiled. Annie and her crusaders. He recognized the fervor. It was a wonder they hadn't been arrested yet, because many of Virginia City's more determined imbibers had threatened to run her out of town on a rail if she didn't stop her campaigning for abstinence. As of yet no violence had marked their meetings. But if he knew Annie, it would before they'd left town.

Kincade stepped down from the boardwalk and crossed the mouth of the alley. He headed toward Howell's General Store to pick up his supplies before they closed for the night.

Lost in thought, he was late seeing the shadow just behind him. By the time he turned and brought up an arm, a crashing blow sent him reeling. He had no time to go for his gun, no time for anything. Light splintered, then was swallowed by black emptiness.

Chapter 22

"Who votes for woman suffrage now
Will add new laurels to his brow;
His children's children, with holy fire,
Will chant in praise their patriot sire,
No warrior's wreath of glory shed
A brighter lustre o'er the head
Than he who battles selfish pride,
And votes with woman side by side."

As THE last notes of the song died away, Elizabeth felt a flush of pride in Annie. Her cousin had led the rousing chorus with verve and sincerity, and looked an imposing figure up on the platform. There was a large crowd this night, some important civic leaders among them.

Garbed in bloomers and short skirt, Annie took her place at the podium and waited for the murmur to subside. Elizabeth sat in the rear observing the crowd and felt a stirring at her heartstrings as Annie began her speech.

She spoke of how young girls began life with innocent hope and enthusiasm, certain that the world would embrace them with loving arms. And she spoke of how often a woman's dreams turned to bitter ashes unless she followed the narrow path laid out for her by those who did not believe each person should be allowed to have independence. With eloquence, Annie pleaded that every female be allowed a free and independent life, that she be allowed to wear decent

278

clothing that did not hamper her movements, and be given an education that could make her self-supporting in a world of equal opportunity in business and all professions. She also spoke about marriage.

"It should be," Annie declared dramatically, "an equal partnership, a combination of spiritual, mental, and physical companionship for both the husband and wife. No, there should not be the complete subjugation of body and spirit that some women are forced to endure. And it is my belief that the word *obey* should be stricken from the marriage vows, for it has no place in a mature relationship between man and woman."

A man bellowed from a chair near Elizabeth, "You're talkin' rebellion is what you're doin'! What do you want—women to run men?"

An angry buzz sounded, and Elizabeth noted that it was not only the men who protested. Several women were exchanging heated words with those who cheered Annie on.

"Listen to me," Annie was saying, holding up her hands until the audience quieted. "I see no reason why one gender should subjugate another, be it men or women. And if I'm talking rebellion, sir—why not? After all, the world speaks of women's duties as homemaker, mother, and wife, but ignores the greater fact that even if they are none of the above, they will always be women. Therefore, why should women not labor for the very essence of their existence? Should women not promote themselves as woman first, then accomplish gladly whatever task their womanhood decrees they achieve? If it is to be the greatest wife and mother—then let them do so. But if it be a writer, a clerk, a state senator—"

Here the chaos drowned out her words and she had to pause. Fixing the crowd with a smile, Annie ended softly, "Let that woman have equal rights to achieve what her intelligence and capabilities dictate. Do not hold her back from voting, from holding any job she desires, from holding a political office. Enfranchisement is an end to emotional and spiritual slavery as well as physical, I say, and women should be allowed the vote as well as making their own decisions.''

A man bounded up from his chair, shaking his fist in the air. ''Women should be at home where they belong, not out trafficking with scoundrels and loose females! Give women the vote, and before long they'll be divorcing decent husbands and leaving their children motherless just so they can follow worthless ambitions—''

''Fie on you, sir!'' a woman shouted, leaping to her feet to face the indignant man. ''Do you think women so fainthearted and foolish they would give up those they love, even for noble goals? Must men be so pigheaded and vain?''

When several other women leaped to their feet, engaging in heated debate, and the meeting hall became chaos, Elizabeth rose from her seat and made her way unhurriedly toward the double doors at the rear. A burly deputy stood in the doorway, obviously caught between duty and amusement. He glanced down at her, and she paused.

''Do your duty, Officer,'' she said, and he grinned, blue eyes crinkling at the corners.

''And that I will, ma'am, if you please. It's just that I'm not after knowin' where to start.''

Elizabeth glanced behind her at the seething mass of angry people. ''Perhaps you should start by protecting the woman speaking.''

He looked up toward the platform and nodded. ''And I'm thinkin' that you're right, miss.''

Elizabeth slipped past him with a smile and made her way into the cool night air. Annie was accustomed to such chaos and usually came back to their lodgings laughing. Unless she was arrested, of course, which had not yet happened in Virginia City. The meetings had been chaotic at times, but not violent. Sheriff Wallace had said most sternly that he would not allow such goings-on in his town. At each meeting, he posted a deputy in order to curb possible riots.

Well, as Annie observed, once people had their blood roused, they at least got the issues out into the open. From what Elizabeth could hear now, there was a lot of free discussion going on behind her.

As Elizabeth began to button her coat she heard someone behind her. She turned and lifted a brow. A stout woman dressed in peculiar fashion stood in the shadows, and she was beckoning to her.

"Psst! Come here. I need to talk to you."

Curiosity drew her nearer. "Yes?" she said slowly as the woman stepped into a pool of lamplight. Scarlet satin and black lace shimmied in the glow. Seemingly oblivious to the chill, the woman beckoned again, impatiently this time.

"Don't dawdle, child. I need to speak with you before he gets here."

"Excuse me?"

"For heaven's sake—come quickly, or all will be lost."

Elizabeth jerked to a halt. There was an urgency in the woman's tone that should have warned her, yet there was also a ring of sincerity.

"I'm afraid I don't know you," she began, and was startled when the woman gave an exasperated sound.

"Tidwell. Tabitha Tidwell. If you hesitate much longer, you will be very sorry, I assure you. Do come, child. I'm only allowed to do so much, you know. And you're not even my responsibility, yet if I don't help, Kincade may end up in the fire—"

"Kincade?" Elizabeth stepped closer. "What about him? Is he all right? What do you mean—in the fire?"

"Ah, I should have thought of this approach at once. Yes, m'dear, it's Kincade. We must help him."

"Why didn't you say so? Is he hurt?"

"Not yet . . ."

Elizabeth immediately followed the woman as she bustled down the alley between the meeting hall and a bakery. The rich aroma of hot bread filled the air, and the hard ground crunched beneath her feet as she half ran to keep up.

Kincade. Her irritation with him was forgotten. He needed
her.

Waves of pain followed the blackness. When Kincade
tried to move his hands, he couldn't, and he blinked. A
murky patch of moonlight threaded through a window high
on the opposite wall, making the interior glow with a silvery
light.

Slowly, as his eyes adjusted, he saw that he was in a
storeroom of some kind. His wrists were tied, and so were
his feet. He was lying on a burlap sack that smelled vaguely
of oats, and he gave a disgruntled oath that was quickly
swallowed up in the gloom.

Apparently he was alone.

His head hurt, and his shoulders ached from being in the
same position for too long. As he struggled to a sitting
position he saw that his gun was gone, but he'd expected
that. Whoever had hit him would have taken it, of course.
He wondered why he was still alive. After three years of
intense effort to kill him, this was certainly the perfect
opportunity. A single shot, lost in the chaos of the stamps
mills and compressors, and the assassin could make his
escape virtually undetected.

Yet he'd been tied and left, and he began to think he knew
why. Dougal wanted some papers, and he wouldn't believe
that Kincade had no idea what he was talking about. He'd
assume he was being lied to, which, if Kincade had known
what he was talking about, he would have gladly done.

He leaned back against a pile of filled grain sacks and
tried to think more clearly. There was also Max Griffin to
consider. The outlaw had tried to have him ambushed, for
some reason. Would he try again?

"Bloody bad timing," Kincade muttered aloud. He
twisted and tried to lurch to his feet, but the ropes on his legs
were too tight. He fell to his knees and then rolled to his side
again. After a moment he brought his feet up in front of him,

bent his legs, and in a quick motion that wrenched a grunt
of effort from him, rose to a standing position.

His breath was coming in harsh gusts, and it was cold in
the storeroom. Frosty clouds hung in the air in front of his
face. It took several slow minutes to work his way to the
window.

A faint shadow briefly darkened the light, and he froze
until it passed. Muffled voices sounded outside. He heard a
slight scuffling sound then the clink of metal against metal,
as of a key in a lock.

"Bloody hell," he muttered as the door swung open with
a thump and caught him broadside, knocking him down. He
sprawled back on the feed sacks, and rolled to his side,
swearing under his breath.

To his surprise the saloon whore came to peer inside,
seeming oblivious to the cold in her red satin and black lace
dress.

"God's eyes," she said loudly, "he's gone."

"Gone?" came a second voice.

Kincade straightened. Elizabeth. What the devil was she
doing here?

"Kincade?" she was whispering softly. "Where are
you?"

"Behind the bloody door," he said, and saw her jump
with fright. "I think you broke my nose when you opened
it like that. Untie me."

As Elizabeth came and knelt beside him the other woman
stood in the wide swath of moonlight. "Sorry about that,"
she said cheerfully. "Didn't know you were there. Can't see
everything, you know."

"So they tell me." He glanced back at Elizabeth. "In my
boot—remember my *sgian dhu*?"

"Oh yes. I'd forgotten you always carry a knife in your
socks," she said shakily, and with trembling fingers managed to reach inside his boot top and retrieve it.

"Dirk. Careful—it's sharp," he said as she fumbled with

the bone-handled weapon. "Cut my wrists loose first, and I'll take care of my feet."

"What are you doing in here?" she asked as she sawed at the rough ropes binding his wrists.

"I haven't the faintest notion. Someone hit me on the head, and when I woke up, here I was. I have my suspicions, however, and I'll tell you about them while we ride."

Elizabeth glanced up at him. "Ride where?"

"To my claim, of course. I've the feeling that the person responsible for my brief sojourn in this lovely garden spot is even now out there tearing my camp apart. This should be an excellent opportunity to finally pin something definite on Dougal, don't you think?"

"Kincade—"

"Not now, Lizzie." He jerked his arms apart, snapping the last frayed threads of rope, then took the dirk from her hand and sliced the ropes binding his feet. "I think you better go with me. I'd feel better if I knew where you were. And who you were with. Have you seen my charming uncle again, by any chance?"

She shook her head. "No. I attended tonight's meeting."

"Ah, the ever-popular Battle-ax Annie. She did well, I trust." He stood up and stamped his feet to get the blood flowing, then took Elizabeth by one arm. "Come on."

"Wait a moment," the other woman said, and Kincade flicked her a quick glance, his eyes narrowing. She'd been with Dougal earlier, and now she'd brought Elizabeth here. Something wasn't right. He didn't intend to take any chances that this woman might be in league with Dougal.

"You may come with us," he said pleasantly.

"Oh no, I really couldn't," she said with a shake of her head. "I'm afraid I have other business to attend, but I shall certainly—eek!"

Kincade had shifted the dirk to the center of his palm and pressed the blade against her side. "Yes," he said softly, "I think you shall be able to find the time to accompany us. I

can't have you running about like a loose cannon, now can
I?''

"How alliterative," she said, sliding a sideways glance at
him. She didn't seem afraid, merely startled, and smiled
when Elizabeth gave a shocked protest. "Never you mind,
m'dear. I'm experienced. I shall deal nicely with him.
Shan't I, sir?"

"If you say so." He pushed her slightly toward the open
door. "I don't mean to be ungentlemanly, but surely you see
the necessity for my caution."

"Of course I do. And I approve. When I feel it necessary
to be elsewhere, I won't bother you with my decision."

Kincade shot her a quick look. There was something
distinctly odd about this woman. It wasn't just her scanty
attire on an icy night, but her demeanor. It made him doubly
suspicious, but at least she'd brought Elizabeth to him.

"You have my gratitude, madam," he said, and hustled
them both out the door.

He wasn't surprised to see they were behind the livery
stable, and it fit in with his plans very well. He quickly
saddled three horses and was leading them to the open doors
when the owner barred his way.

"Here now, whar you goin' with my animals?" he
demanded in a surly tone.

"I'll return them." Kincade dug into his pocket, but it
was empty. He turned to Elizabeth. "Do you have any
money?"

"Not with me. Shall I—"

"No." He turned back to the hostler. "Look, old chap, I
only need them for a while. I'll bring you double the amount
you usually charge when I return."

"The hell you will. You pay now, or I'll fetch the sheriff
and you can talk to him about it."

Kincade's patience was running out. He was cold, sore,
and his head hurt. He moved so swiftly the burly hostler
never saw the fist that sent him stumbling back into a
hayrick. A simple whack with the wooden handle of a

pitchfork left the hostler slumbering in the hay. He bent and plucked a pistol from his holster, then turned back to the two women. They stared at him in the dim light.

"Hurry," he said between his teeth, and neither of them offered an argument.

"Someone's there," Elizabeth whispered. "Who is it?"

"How the devil should I know?" Kincade lay on his belly on the ground. He wasn't in the best condition for this sort of thing. His head throbbed, and his body was stiff.

Below, near the entrance to the mine, a fire blazed. Several men moved about in the shadows. He hadn't expected more than a few, and he revised his earlier plan.

"What are they doing?" Elizabeth whispered again. Her face was pale in the hazy moonlight. Beyond her, he could see the woman named Tabitha staring with acute interest at the scene below.

He rolled to his back and groped for the stolen pistol. After making sure it was loaded, he rose to one knee.

Elizabeth grabbed his arm, her voice tight. "Are you going to shoot that?"

"I don't intend to throw it at them."

"But they might shoot back at you." She sounded appalled, and he smiled.

"Yes, one would think that likely. Did you expect differently?"

"I don't know what I expected." She sucked in a sharp breath. "There's only one of you. There are five of them."

"If I was in a poker game, I can assure you that these would be most distressing odds. Faro offers much better odds, not to mention a civilized game of whist."

"Kincade . . ."

"Not to worry, pet. I have the advantage of surprise on my side."

"And you have us," Tabitha said cheerfully.

Kincade shot her a wry glance. "Yes, quite. It would greatly improve my chances if you two ladies would remain here in the rocks." He pressed his dirk in Elizabeth's palm and said softly, "If she attempts escape, use this."

Elizabeth stared at him in disbelief. "You must be joking."

"Not at all. I saw her in deep conversation with Dougal earlier."

"But she brought me to you," Elizabeth began doubtfully, and he shook his head.

"Maybe for this very reason. Love, do what I ask of you for once. Take my dirk."

Her fingers closed around the bone handle, and when he glanced up, he saw Tabitha's lifted brows and pursed mouth.

"I suppose it's to be expected that you're not very trusting, but I can't say that I'm pleased. Don't I look honest?" she asked tartly.

"No. But then, I'm not a trusting man, you see."

"I know. Well, all I can say is I hope Ian decides to join us soon."

"Ian?"

"Never mind." Tabitha waved at hand toward the mine. "Run along. I'll do what I can as the occasion necessitates."

"Watch her," Kincade said, and backed down the slope.

Elizabeth stared after him, then turned to look at Tabitha. "Aren't you cold?" she asked abruptly. "All you have on is that satin thing."

"I'm warm-blooded, m'dear. Don't worry about me. Worry about your young man. He's rather reckless, it seems. Or brave. Can't tell exactly which, though I'm inclined to think the latter. Quite a change since the *Tom Hopkins,* wouldn't you say?"

Startled, Elizabeth almost dropped Kincade's dirk onto the ground. "Since the—how do you know about that?"

"Doesn't everyone? You are the same two who were rescued from that island, aren't you?"

"Oh. Oh, yes. That's true. I just didn't realize that news had reached this far west."

Tabitha Tidwell waved a hand airily. "Oh, one hears things farther away than you could imagine, m'dear. But that is another story. Now, we need to concentrate on keeping him from being hurt."

"We?"

"Listen carefully. I think he means to sneak up on them and ambush them, but as he didn't see fit to share his plans with us, you have only conjecture to help you. But of course you have me, too. So you're much better off than another person would be."

"I see," Elizabeth said faintly, though she didn't see at all. Tabitha Tidwell was a puzzle, a friendly sort, but definitely a puzzle. She was so mysterious, and bossy, too, though it seemed as if she meant well. "How do you intend to help?"

"I've no idea. I'll think of something, though. I always do."

"Always do?"

"You sound like a parrot, m'dear. Do stop repeating my every syllable. It's annoying."

Elizabeth's mouth tightened irritably. "Mrs. Tidwell, though I believe that you mean well, I cannot imagine why you are here. Or how you knew where Kincade was unless—"

"Told you. I overheard the villains plotting. It's always wise to pretend ignorance when one is really paying strict attention, you know. Told Ian that, too, but he's one of those stubborn men who think they're so much smarter than women. . . ." She peered at Elizabeth in the moonlight. "I think you and your cousin are marvelous, you know. Women have been subjugated too long. I hope you enjoy your success."

"We haven't managed to succeed yet."

"No, and it will be a time before you do, no doubt, but you will. Mark my words, you will. It's inevitable. Things just never progress as quickly as you might wish, but within a hundred years—"

"A hundred years!"

"Just a blink in time, m'dear." Tabitha stared back at Elizabeth solemnly. "Trust me. You don't need the dagger he gave you. I won't attempt escape."

Elizabeth didn't know what to say. She gave a helpless shrug. "I didn't know that you heard—"

"I heard. Keen ears. Always have. I recall that one time the queen—but that's another story. Now, shall we see what can be done?"

Tabitha turned abruptly and started down the rocky slope toward the mine. Elizabeth stared after her, then sighed.

"I must be insane," she muttered as she followed.

Chapter 23

FIRELIGHT MADE eerie shadows against the hard rock wall behind the tent. Men moved casually, apparently secure in the belief that no one would challenge them. Kincade frowned from his hiding place behind a stand of stunted cedars.

What were they doing? They certainly didn't look like miners, yet they descended into his mine again and again, holding lamps high to light their way. A stack of boxes and sacks stood near the mouth of the mine, barely visible until a shaft of lamplight fell across them. As men came up carrying more boxes he was really puzzled.

Where had they come from? he wondered. He didn't recall seeing them before. Of course, there were twists and turns in the mine that he'd never explored, but he did think that he should have stumbled across that many boxes if they'd been hidden in his mine.

His perplexity grew as the men formed a human chain to hand up heavy boxes to the man behind. When he scooted closer, a wash of pebbles shifted under him and he froze. One of the men lifted his lantern, and the light played over his face. Kincade's eyes narrowed. Jeremy Lowery. What the devil was *he* doing here?

After a moment Lowery lowered the lantern and said something to a man beside him. Kincade figured it was time to change position, and began to back down the rocky slope.

"Goin' somewhere, mister?" The harsh voice was accompanied by a prod between his shoulder blades with what could only be a gun barrel. Kincade paused.

"Well," he said politely, "what's your suggestion? If you prefer that I stay, I won't disagree with your pistol."

"Rifle. And my suggestion, smart-ass, is that you keep your mouth shut and move real slowlike. Stand up and throw down your iron."

"Certainly." Kincade rose slowly to his feet, his back still turned, and carefully removed his Colt and tossed it to the ground. "Anything else? A song or two, perhaps?"

The rifle barrel clipped him behind the ear, and when he sagged to his knees, the world reeled. "I told you not to be a smart-ass, MacKay. Now get up."

"Right-ho," Kincade muttered. "I do recall your saying that. Pardon me for thinking a smart-ass was better than being a dumb-ass—hey!"

The rifle barrel caught him under the chin and sent him sprawling into the dirt, but this time he was able to see his assailant. And he was able to snatch up a fistful of dirt and pebbles and fling it into the man's eyes, taking advantage of his reaction to roll away.

While the man howled and clawed at his eyes, Kincade scrambled for hiding. Clumps of sage grew thickly here, and he was able to snake between them and over the ground in the dark, hoping he wasn't seen. Max Griffin. He recognized him from the wanted posters in the sheriff's office. What the devil was he doing at his mine?

"Damn you, you connivin' bastard," Griffin was yelling in the dark, "you better say your prayers!"

"Oh, I am," Kincade murmured softly. "Believe me."

As he crawled through the brush, it occurred to him that if Lowery and Griffin were together, there was a lot going on he should know. Lowery was supposed to be an upstanding citizen, after all.

A shot rang out, slicing into the sage over his head, and Kincade ducked and swore fervently. Bloody hell. It was getting more dangerous by the moment out here. And his pistol was lying in the dirt where he'd been surprised by Griffin.

Splashes of light flickered erratically, and he peered through prickly spines of ground plants to see men coming up the slope with lanterns. With a sheer rock wall behind him, and Griffin thrashing about in the brush below him, Kincade was caught. He waited in grim resignation for the inevitable.

"Well," Jeremy Lowery said when Kincade rose to his feet to face him, "you just don't know when to quit, do you?"

"Never have before, but one can always learn." Kincade shifted his gaze from the pistol Lowery held to the man's face. Light swayed across his features, and he saw that Lowery didn't look at all pleased to see him.

"How did you get loose?" Lowery demanded.

"Magic. I lead a charmed life at times." Kincade's evasive reply earned him a swift, hard blow to his abdomen. He doubled over with a grunt, and Lowery's knee jerked up to slam into his face, knocking him back to the ground.

"I asked you a simple question," Lowery said calmly as he knelt beside Kincade. "I expect an answer."

"*Jesus,* you don't have to get so physical." Kincade sucked in a sharp breath and felt waves of pain. His vision was blurred, and he could barely see the men behind Lowery. He blinked. There was the rusty taste of hot blood in his mouth. When he dragged a hand across his lips, it came away wet and red.

"Did someone cut you loose?" Lowery was asking. "I want to know who it was."

"No doubt," Kincade muttered thickly. He shut his eyes. He couldn't tell, of course. Then Lowery would know that Elizabeth was involved. That could endanger her. Why was it always the most upright citizens in town who were the most dangerous? he wondered wearily. One was never surprised when known rogues did something dastardly. But with men of supposedly good moral character, these kinds of surprises were doubly shocking.

He opened his eyes when Lowery stood up and ordered him dragged down to the camp. There was the distinct possibility that his life was about to become gravely painful, and he hoped like hell Elizabeth had enough sense to remain where she was. Or go for help. Or just *go*.

The short distance to his camp involved more pain than he'd guessed, but as he was dragged across sharp rocks and through clumps of sage, Kincade caught sight of something that took his mind off his discomfort. A wooden crate stood to one sight, marked *Danger—Explosives*.

He kept his eye on it when he was shoved to the ground and his hands tied behind him. He'd used explosives himself, of course, in mining, but only small charges of powder dribbled into holes in the rock to extend the tunnel a few feet. This crate held a lot more than he'd need in a small operation.

"Curious, MacKay?" Lowery paused to ask. He hunkered down beside him, amusement curling his mouth.

"Not me. It's not healthy. I heard all about that cat and curiosity."

"You're right about it not being healthy. Not that good health will matter much to you shortly."

"That sounds ominous."

"It is." Lowery's eyes were pale and cold, and Kincade shivered under the bite of the wind. Lowery saw it and smiled. "You should have stayed away, you know. But you're like Hardy, too dumb to know better."

"Hardy? The man with the straight."

"Yeah, Jim Hardy. He should have known better than to wager this mine in a poker game, especially to a cardsharp. His stupidity cost him the mine and his life."

"So I heard." Kincade eyed Lowery warily. "I don't suppose you know who killed him?"

"Don't ask dangerous questions, MacKay."

"What will it matter shortly anyway?"

Lowery shifted on the balls of his feet, frowning. "Tell me who turned you loose, and I might consider letting you go."

"Right-ho. I believe you."

"Don't be stupid, MacKay. If we can't beat it out of you, all we have to do is wait long enough anyway. Then it will be simple enough to take care of matters."

"Good. Then I shan't deprive you of that satisfaction."

Lowery rose to his feet and looked down at him in disgust. "How noble. Hope it's worth it to you."

"So do I," Kincade muttered, but couldn't help a surge of apprehension when he saw a huge man walk toward him with a grin on his face. "Ugly brute," he commented, and heard Lowery's short bark of laughter.

"That he is. His name is Quincy, by the way, and his brother is in the Virginia City jail."

Kincade closed his eyes for a moment. The inevitability of his fate seemed to swamp him, and he felt that sense of doom that he'd felt so many times before. Always before, something had happened to save him. Not now. There wouldn't be time for help to get there even if Elizabeth had done the sensible thing and gone to town for it.

Hazlett's ham-sized fist snagged in his shirtfront and hauled Kincade to his feet, and he had a brief glimpse of the other fist drawing back. Lights exploded, and pain stabbed into his middle with vicious force. The breath was driven from his lungs, and he heard, dimly, Lowery ask again who had freed him.

He opened his mouth, yet nothing came out but a breathless whimper of distress. It wouldn't help him to tell the truth, and would only endanger Elizabeth. He hoped his body realized that and didn't betray him.

Another blow sent him to his knees, yet Hazlett held him up. He was dimly aware of that, the realization coming through a white-hot haze of pain and confusion.

"Tell me who turned you loose, MacKay."

He thought it was Lowery asking, but his mind was

having trouble assimilating the noise assaulting his ears. Different sounds blended together in a confusing mix.

"Can't . . . remember," he mumbled, but knew with a sense of resignation that Lowery would not accept an answer like that.

The immediate fist in his belly proved him right. Pain shot through him in razor-sharp splinters. He thought a rib might be cracked.

"Come on, MacKay. Talk to me."

The voice sounded faraway and faint. Kincade tried to breathe, but his lungs weren't functioning properly. It hurt to drag in air, and it hurt not to inhale, and he felt as if he were going to throw up. There was the sound of rocks scrunching, then a boot caught him in the middle again and sent him sprawling. Everything went mercifully black.

It didn't last, unfortunately. He woke slowly, his entire body radiating pain. He was still sprawled on the ground with his hands tied behind him, and he could hear Lowery close by.

"MacKay? Hell, Hazlett, don't kill him yet. Find out who else knows he's here."

"Dunno why it matters. We're almost through, and then we can set the charges. MacKay will be dead and we'll be gone."

Kincade recognized Max Griffin's voice. He kept his eyes closed and tried not to groan.

"It matters," Lowery said tightly. "If they turned him loose, they must know we're here and why."

"Hell, you're too skittish. Don't look for trouble behind every rock, Lowery."

"It's a damn good thing *some*one is skittish and looking for trouble, or this whole thing could have been blown by now. If I hadn't taken care of Hardy, he would have gone to the sheriff and you'd be swinging at the end of a rope."

"So would you." Griffin laughed shortly. "Don't try to play innocent. This was all your idea."

"I didn't notice you dragging your heels at the mention of your share of the silver, Griffin."

"Why should I? It's more than I've ever gotten before in one of these jobs. With you knowin' when the silver is due to move and how much it is, it was like takin' candy from a baby."

"Until Hardy lost the damned mine in a poker game." Lowery made a sound of disgust. "I should have known better than to let you recommend a man for the job."

"Don't be so quick to jump. You liked it well enough when I first suggested it. This is the perfect place to hide the silver, out here away from everythin' else in a worthless piece of ground."

"It was perfect until Hardy got drunk and sat in on that poker game with MacKay," Lowery said sharply. "Now we have to move it, and I wasn't ready yet."

"Well, I am. The boys are getting restless and want their share."

"All in good time."

There was a moment of silence, then Griffin said softly, "You've been sayin' 'all in good time' for too long now."

"And will continue to say it until it's time. Just keep in mind who's the boss here, Griffin."

"Yeah, well, I'm thinkin' maybe it's time that changed. I don't like your attitude, Lowery."

"You liked it well enough when I gave you dates and times of the silver shipments."

"Things change."

There was a long silence. Kincade opened his eyes enough to see Lowery and Griffin facing each other, with Hazlett only a few feet away. He weighed his chances of escaping undetected. He could barely move, much less get away before one of them stopped him. His only hope was that they'd all kill each other before they did him.

That brief hope was extinguished when Lowery shrugged and said, "I concede that point. Perhaps you're right. Let's get the last of the silver aboveground and away from here, and we can divide it.''

"I say divide it here. Then we can split up.''

"It's too risky. Someone might find us before we're finished.''

"Hell, Lowery, you're as nervous as an old woman. So what if MacKay got loose and came out here? Do you see anybody tryin' to keep him from gettin' his guts tangled? If he had friends, someone would have done something by now. If you ask me, he managed to get loose and just came back to his claim to lick his wounds.''

"That's not very farsighted of you, Griffin.''

"No, but it looks much closer to the truth. I say go ahead and throw him in the mine and light the fuses. There won't be enough of him left to say anything when those charges go off, I can tell you that.''

It wasn't a pleasant thought. Kincade gave an involuntary shudder at the image and felt Hazlett nudge him with a boot.

"He's wakin' up, boss.''

Griffin turned to look, and Hazlett hauled Kincade to his feet.

"Have a nice nap?'' Griffin asked with a grin.

"Not as nice as it could have been, thank you.'' It was an effort to speak, with his head pounding and his insides raw, but he felt the desperate need to stall for time.

"Too bad.''

"Yes, my thoughts exactly.'' Kincade dragged in a painful breath. "I don't suppose you know a gentleman by the name of Dougal MacKay, do you?''

"Who?''

"Dougal—no, I suppose you don't. Just a thought.''

"He the one who turned you loose?''

Kincade considered that for a moment. It would avert suspicion from Elizabeth, and he certainly didn't care if Dougal found himself facing these ruffians. It would serve him right. He repressed a smile.

When Hazlett lifted a fist again, he said quickly, "Yes.

He is. Dougal is my uncle, by the way, so you must know that he'll be most distressed by news of my death.''

"That's too bad." Griffin eyed him for a moment, then jerked his head toward the mine shaft. "Get him down there, Hazlett. Untie him in case there's enough left of him to find. I don't want anyone to think it wasn't an accident. Just hit him in the head before you leave him there. He has a bad habit of getting away.''

"Wait," Kincade protested, but Hazlett jerked him around and sliced away the ropes on his wrists. Pain returned with the free flow of blood through his veins, and he couldn't help a grunt. He massaged his wrists, eyeing Hazlett for a moment.

"Walk," the brute ordered, but Kincade hesitated. Once belowground, he was doomed.

"I'm not too steady on my feet, you blighter. Give me a minute to—"

Hazlett slammed his hand across his face. He reeled and saw the fist coming at him again. Bloody hell. At this rate they were going to beat him to death before they blew him up. He made some sort of involuntary sound as Hazlett connected, and went to his knees.

Images floated in front of him, then behind them all a sort of loud, screaming wail cut into the air. It was an eerie sound, like the cry of a banshee over the highland moors, and he thought for an instant that a kelpie had come for his soul.

It sounded so familiar, recalling childhood memories of how ghosts came for the newly dead with a skirl of pipes to mark their passage. He focused suddenly. That was it—the pipes.

An oath curled into the air, and Hazlett dropped him. "What the hell . . . ?"

The sharp pain of being dropped jolted Kincade into the awareness that he not only wasn't dead, the pipes were very real. Gravel dug into his palms and knees, and he levered his body to a kneeling position. Panting from the pain the effort cost him, he watched as the outlaws grouped together to stare.

"Jesus Christ," one of the men growled, "shoot it!"

A figure came into view around a hum of rock, walking steadily, the pipes under one arm. He wore a bonnet with a jaunty cockade, and a kilt and sporran. Kincade's eyes widened. It was the Clan MacDonald tartan; he'd recognize it anywhere.

"I can't shoot," one of the outlaws said. "It's a woman."

"Hell, that ain't no woman," Griffin snapped. "It's a man wearin' a skirt."

Kincade couldn't help a rusty laugh. "You're both wrong, gentlemen. The English call Highlanders the ladies from hell, and this particular lady is wearing a filabeg, or kilt, not a skirt."

"I don't give a damn about none of that." Griffin drew his pistol. "Shoot the bastard."

Bullets spat dust and chunks of rock around the kilted figure, but the bagpipes didn't falter. Nor did the steady approach.

"Shoot him!" Jeremy Lowery screamed in frustration. "Can't any of you shoot better than that?"

The bagpipes shrilled more loudly, and Kincade recognized the tune. This man was no duffer; he played with the skill of one who loved the pipes. From the war song of Clan MacDonald to the "Massacre at Glencoe," the music rose above the staccato pop of bullets in a wild stirring that brought Kincade to his feet.

No one paid him any attention. They emptied pistols and rifles, and still the marching figure grew closer, until it was easy to see the emblem on his bonnet that proclaimed him a member of Clan MacDonald.

"Faith, and it's a bloody kinsman," Kincade muttered. He watched as the man finished the last of the skirl with a flourish, then lowered the pipes, his fingers still on the wooden chanter. His gaze swept the group, then came to rest on Kincade as he laid aside the instrument.

"Och, lad," he said, "ye look a wee bit fashed. Dinna fash yerself more. I've come tae help."

He reached behind his back, and when he brought his arms down, he was holding a claymore. The huge, double-bladed ax that was a favorite of Highlanders gleamed wickedly in the lantern light.

"I've need of it," Kincade said, and heard Griffin and Lowery snap out orders to the men to come back.

But the outlaws, having spent ammunition on the specter that stood before them, were having none of it. Most ran for their horses, leaving Griffin and Lowery alone with Kincade and this new intruder.

"Who are you?" Lowery blustered. His hands shook as he shoved bullets into his pistol.

Beside him, Griffin was cooler but as obviously upset. He reloaded calmly, then snapped the cylinder into place and spun it quickly. "Don't matter who he is," he said to Lowery. "At this range we can get him before he gets us with that damn ax."

"'Tis a claymore," the stranger objected. "A noble weapon for a mon tae use."

Griffin took aim before Kincade could react, and the air was sharp with the smell of gunpowder. Then he stared as the kilted figure hefted his claymore and swung it. The huge weapon whistled through the air with sickening clarity, and Max Griffin gave a yelp as his pistol was sliced from his hand with deadly force.

"Goddammit, you could have cut my hand off!" he yelled as he backed away holding his hand. As it was, the pistol lay on the ground cut cleanly in two.

"Aye, lad. Keep tha' in mind afore ye try tae shoot me ag'in."

"Who *are* you?" Griffin whispered, visibly shaken.

"One who canna abide murther," came the rich brogue.

"I think 'tis best ye gi' young MacKay here yer other weapon, dinna ye?"

"Sweet Jesus," Griffin muttered. His hands trembled as he carefully removed his other pistol from his belt and handed it butt first to Kincade.

Jeremy Lowery threw his pistol down without being asked. Kincade bent painfully to retrieve it, then glanced at the kilted figure.

"You're a MacDonald."

"Aye, lad, tha' I am. 'Tis good tae see tha' ye still know yer own kinsman."

"Where—what are you doing here?"

"As I said, I came tae help ye wi' these brigands. But 'tis up tae ye how ye go aboot the rest o' it."

"Right-ho. There's just one small detail I must see to first, I'm afraid. A young lady was with me earlier, and—"

"And she's come tae no harm, lad."

"You saw her?"

"Aye. She's wi' a friend o' mine, and is safe enow if ye dinna think aboot how much harm tha' can be caused by one woman."

"Elizabeth?"

"Nay. Tabitha."

"Ah." Kincade nodded. "If you don't mind, I think I'll find her anyway."

Chapter
24

"ANGEL." KINCADE put out a hand and Elizabeth stepped into his arms with a cry of relief.

"I thought they were going to kill you," she said into his chest, her voice muffled by wool and tears.

"So did I." His tone was dry, and she tilted her head back to stare up at him.

"Your poor face—it's all bruised and bloody."

"Yes—ouch. Don't touch me, please. There's not much of me that doesn't hurt."

Elizabeth's hand dropped, and she inhaled deeply, fighting her tears. When she'd seen him dragged and beaten, it had taken all of Tabitha's earnest talk to keep her from flying down the slope to put herself between Kincade and his burly assailant. The fact that she was his only help at the moment kept her away.

When she glanced toward where Griffin and Lowery sat by the fire, hands and feet bound securely, she shuddered. "I thought all this time that it was your uncle who was responsible for everything."

"So was I, though I'm certain he's done his share. This time it was Lowery behind all this." Kincade indicated the man in the kilt with one hand. "If not for Ian MacDonald, I would probably be dead by now. As luck would have it, he got here just in time to keep them from killing me."

"Tabitha said he's a friend of hers." Elizabeth frowned.

"Don't you find it odd that he would be wandering out here alone?"

"Angel, haven't you ever heard the adage about not looking a gift horse in the mouth? I, for one, don't intend to question either end of it. I didn't ask, nor do I care, though I admit to a certain degree of curiosity."

They both glanced toward the fire, where Ian and Tabitha sat guard on Lowery and Griffin. The two made a strange couple, Elizabeth thought, and couldn't explain why she felt so at ease with them. It was as if she'd known them a long time.

"What will happen to Lowery and Griffin?" she murmured as Kincade pulled her with him into the shelter of his tent.

"In the morning we can take them into town."

"And do you think the sheriff will believe you?"

"That's unlikely, but anything's possible, I suppose." Kincade gave her a moody smile. "It won't help that he thinks I'm one of them."

"No, it certainly won't. How can we convince him of your innocence?"

"Beats me, angel. Right now I'm just glad to be alive and not warming my toes in hell. Or blown to pieces."

"Blown?"

"I'll explain later." He slid an arm around her and pulled her closer, grunting slightly when she grazed his sore ribs. "Careful, angel. I'm not in wonderful shape."

"God, Kincade, when I think—"

"Hush." He put a finger over her mouth. "Don't think. It's much safer that way. Besides, it's behind us now."

A wave of grief washed over her. "You came so close to being killed. I don't know what I would have done if they'd shot you."

"Wept over my body, most likely."

She glared at him. "How can you tease me at a time like this?"

"It's not easy, believe me."

"Oh Kincade, I'm sorry." She stood on her toes and pressed a light kiss to his bruised, swollen mouth. She heard his quickly indrawn breath and pulled away to gaze at him through a sudden haze of tears.

She wanted to ask so many questions, wanted assurances for the future. Would she always be doomed to moments like these? Moments when uncertainty loomed as large in her mind as love? In an instant of blinding clarity, she saw her life stretching before her, a life spent wondering if Kincade would be shot in a saloon brawl over cards, or if they would have to flee from his uncle's machinations.

While she watched as he lowered himself painfully to the floor of the tent, he managed a smile that was more of a grimace. It wrenched her heart that he was trying to be so blasted noble and keep everything light, when she knew he had to be in pain and just as worried as she was about the future. Had he always done that? Why had she just now noticed that he covered his anxieties with cutting humor?

She sank to her knees beside him. "Here," she said, "let me tend your cuts for you."

"I'm not hurt so badly."

"Don't be a noble idiot. You're bruised and cut in so many places it's a wonder you've any blood left in your veins."

"Angel," he muttered with a sigh, but let her wet a cloth and bathe his cuts with water heated over the fire. There was nothing she could do for his ribs, though she couldn't help a shocked gasp when she lifted his shirt over his head and saw the mass of purple and blackish bruises.

"Dear God—"

"Ain't pretty, is it? Don't worry. I've had worse."

It was true—and would be true again. He'd had worse and would still have worse. Until one day his luck would desert him and someone would shoot him. It was a terrifying thought, and she felt a sort of rage mixed with frustration well inside.

"Is that the way you enjoy living?" she asked tartly. "On

the brink of disaster all the time? I don't think I can bear waiting for that shove over the side, and I can't imagine how you manage it."

He'd grown still, and the look on his bruised face was suddenly watchful. One eye was swollen shut, but the other held a measuring light that made her pause.

"I don't think I can endure watching, Kincade," she said around the lump in her throat.

"Maybe you shouldn't try, angel," he said softly, and she caught her breath. "It's more than I should ask of you. I think it'd be better if you stayed with your cousin. When I get things taken care of—"

"Not when. If. Don't pretend with me, Kincade." Her voice shook in spite of her best efforts, and she tied the end of the cloth she'd wound around his ribs with quick, efficient motions and sat back. The fire in the brazier made the tent warm, and beads of sweat dotted Kincade's upper lip, though she didn't know if that was from pain or heat.

"All right," he said. "You said you don't want to live like that. I'm afraid that's all I can offer you."

"I told you, I have—"

"Don't say it," he snarled with sudden fury. "Bloody hell, I won't live off a woman, d'you hear me?"

Misery clogged her throat, and she stared at him without speaking.

Kincade groaned then and put out a hand to cup her chin. "Ah, angel, I don't want to lose you. I just can't bear hurting you by staying with you."

"I see," she said stiffly, but she didn't. Her throat hurt, and it felt as if a stone was lodged in her chest.

"Christ," he muttered, then leaned forward to kiss her. When he pulled away, she saw the resignation in his gaze. "Angel, I suppose—"

A clatter outside the tent jerked his head around, and Elizabeth swallowed a cry of alarm as Kincade reached for his rifle.

"MacKay!" came a bellow outside. "It's Sheriff Wallace. I came up here to arrest you for stealing horses from the livery, but—what the hell is going on?''

A cold wind rattled wooden signs and blew traces of snow down the middle of C Street. Sunlight caught and reflected light on the metal cupola of the Fourth Ward School on the fringe of town. Shadows crept down the slopes and cuts of Sun Mountain, and the Washoe Range was bathed in contrasting shades.

Elizabeth gazed out the window of the *Territorial Enterprise* and sighed. The building hummed with printing machines and gossip.

"Never would have dreamed it was Lowery behind all those silver heists," Judge Goodwin said behind her, and she turned. Editor-in-Chief since the owner, R. M. Daggett, had been elected senator, Goodwin shrugged. "Guess I'm not a very good reporter. I should have sensed trouble when Lowery was more interested in the mine schedules than he was other news."

"He was very subtle," Elizabeth said. "I hope that I conveyed that in my article."

"Yes, you did. It was an excellent piece of writing. Of course, I have this feeling that you wrote the article more to clear MacKay than for any sense of journalistic fervor."

Elizabeth smiled. "Perhaps you're right. At any rate it turned out to be unnecessary after all. Sheriff Wallace had suspected there was someone behind all the robberies, and Lowery was one of the suspects."

"Just the same, you tied up all the loose ends for him with your article. There's not a soul in town now who doesn't consider Kincade MacKay something of a hero."

"So I hear."

"Can't figure out why he left like he did. Guess when he found out his mine was worthless, he felt there was no reason to stay." Goodwin shook his head. "If Hardy hadn't lost that mine to a fourth queen, no telling when Griffin's gang would have been caught."

"Justice would have prevailed sooner or later," she murmured, and Goodwin shrugged.

"Not always, Miss Lee."

Elizabeth thought about that when she returned to her lodging. No, justice didn't seem to have much of a chance at times. If it did, Dougal MacKay would be reaping the harvest of his evil deeds. And if it did, Kincade would have received more than a small reward from the mine owners for helping capture the outlaws.

"It seems so anticlimactic," she told Annie, and her cousin gazed at her shrewdly.

"Perhaps. What did you expect? Real life is much different than the operas down at Piper's, you know. There are no tidy solutions in the final act."

Elizabeth leaned against the chaise and smiled slightly. "Not so. Look at you."

"Ah, I suppose you mean Michael." Annie laughed. "Who would have thought I'd run into my husband in this town, of all places? And the wretch has known from the first that I was here."

"He's one of the deputies assigned to attend our meetings," Elizabeth commented wryly. "I wonder that he waited this long before letting you know."

"He claims he didn't know how." Annie ran a hand through her cropped curls. "If a brawl hadn't broken out at our last meeting, he might never have revealed himself to me. And besides—it's not a happy ending yet."

"Yet." Elizabeth laughed at the smug expression on her cousin's face. "It will be. He's stopped his drinking, hasn't he?"

"So he swears. Not a drop in over four years. And he's offered to travel with us and be our permanent guard, so to speak. I told him I'd give him my answer later."

Elizabeth thought of the burly man with the pleasant smile and striking blue eyes. "He'd do very well, I think," she said slowly, and Annie nodded.

"Yes. We'll see. I don't want to jump into anything." A

short pause followed, then Annie said softly, "I don't guess you've heard anything from Kincade."

"No. He left town right after receiving his reward money for the outlaws." Her throat tightened, and she thought of their last meeting, and how he'd promised he would be back for her as soon as he took care of a few things. She'd heard enough of his farewells to recognize another one. Why had she ever been foolish enough to think he might have changed? Once again she'd left herself open and vulnerable, and now she was paying for it.

"Elizabeth," Annie said, and she turned to look at her, "I think he may mean it this time."

"Oh yes, just like he did all the others. If we hadn't kept running into him by accident, I doubt I would have seen him after he left me in New Orleans. I should have listened to my instincts and run in the opposite direction when I found him here in Virginia City."

"Instead you listened to me."

"Oh Annie, you didn't tell me anything I didn't want to hear. I leaped quickly enough."

"But still, it was at my advice that you went back out to the mine to see him."

"I would have thought of an excuse myself sooner or later. I'm not a mindless child, though I don't always show it." Her mouth twisted in a self-deprecating laugh. "The truth of the matter is that I fell in love with a man who is afraid of commitment to anyone but himself. I've only myself to blame."

"You must admit that with his uncle loose, he does have to worry about the future," Annie persisted. "Perhaps he has realized that he must face his problems."

"Obviously he has decided to face them alone." Elizabeth rose from the chaise at a knock on the door, glad for an interruption. It hurt to dwell too long on Kincade's desertion.

When she opened the door, she was startled to see Tabitha Tidwell. "Oh, am I intruding?" the woman asked, but swept into the room without waiting for a reply. "Just came to let you know that Ian and I will be moving on now. I hope that you can manage things well enough on your own."

Elizabeth exchanged a confused glance with Annie, then said, "Well, I suppose so, Mrs. Tidwell. Er—how is Mr. MacDonald?"

"Full of himself and absolutely unbearable. Let him take a swing or two with that silly ax, and he thinks he's Robert the Bruce come back to fight the English. Or so he said smugly in an irritating moment." Tabitha paused and eyed the two women. "But I do run on when I should be telling you how much I admire you for your unselfish work on the behalf of all women. It will have grand results in the end, and I understand that you will be here to see it."

"Excuse me?"

Tabitha waved a hand. "Never mind. The wheel of destiny has been set in motion again, and you are partially responsible. Your rewards will be great and small, and carry a great deal of responsibility with them. You must not lose sight of your goals, no matter how hopeless it seems at times. Do you understand what I mean?"

"Not really," Annie said frankly, and Tabitha sighed and shook her head.

"No matter. You shall one day. Blast all this secrecy poppycock when it would be so much more edifying to just let one know it will be all right. Well, rules, I'm afraid."

Elizabeth bit her lower lip. "Would you care for some hot tea, Mrs. Tidwell?"

"No, no, can't stay. Though Ian doesn't really need me anymore, I must keep an eye on things. Men are so apt to let themselves be distracted that—well, I shan't bore you."

She turned when she reached the door and looked back at Elizabeth. "You have heard about MacKay, I suppose."

"Kincade?"

"Both of them. Dougal took off to Scotland and his

nephew is hot behind him. I've a feeling all will be settled very soon, m'dear. Have faith, Miss Lee.''

After she'd gone, Elizabeth turned to Annie. A faint smile trembled on her lips. "I wonder which Miss Lee she meant?''

"With that woman, it's a puzzle.''

"Well,'' Elizabeth said, "at least we have her assurance that everything will work out. I don't know about you, but *I'm* relieved.''

Annie smiled. "What will you do now?''

Her laughter faded, and Elizabeth moved restlessly about the small parlor before she replied. She'd finally come to a decision. Turning to look at Annie, she said, "I'm going back to Natchez. After I get the house ready, I intend to sell it, then rejoin you, if you'll have me.''

"Of course I'll have you. Why wouldn't I?''

"Well, with Michael back, I wasn't certain—''

"Don't be idiotic. We're family. Michael knows that, and we're taking it slowly now anyway. One just doesn't fall back into a relationship after so long.''

"My presence wouldn't help you now anyway.'' Elizabeth smiled at Annie's immediate protest. "By the time you two are reacquainted, I should have my business details taken care of. I need time alone, time to think and decide what my life will be in the future. It should be easier now that I don't have—now that I can focus on personal goals.''

"I wouldn't count Kincade MacKay out of your life just yet,'' Annie said dryly. "He has a habit of popping up fairly frequently.''

"Didn't you hear Mrs. Tidwell? He's gone back to Scotland.''

"Yes, and I imagine he intends to take care of his uncle while he's there. Once he has matters settled—''

"He'll take his rightful place as Lord of Glencairn. I have no place in his life.''

"Elizabeth—''

"No, it's all right. I've accepted it this time. Really I

have. Don't worry about me. Save your prayers for Kincade. He'll need them more than I.''

Glencairn rose against the gray sky like a gigantic bird of prey, forbidding stone walls just as he remembered them. Kincade paused, and felt a tightness in his chest. It had been nearly nine years since last he'd set foot inside his ancestral home, yet the memories were as sharp and painful as the reality had been.

The only difference was that now he could see it as it really was, a crumbling keep of little consequence. Once, he'd thought of his inheritance as majestic. But that had been before. The stone keep held little remnants of past glory, of the long-ago days of the Bruce, when his ancestors had fought to wrest a place for themselves in history.

The bridge across a shallow moat was rotten in places, and he rode his mount carefully, wincing at the rusty creak of the chains lifting the gate. The courtyard was overgrown with weeds, bleak indeed in the pale gray light of an overcast winter sky. It looked deserted, though he knew a few retainers had been kept for Dougal's infrequent visits.

Glencairn. Peopled with misery and ghosts from his past, and he hesitated before entering. He'd dreamed of returning one day as a conquering hero, yet now that the moment had come, it held no satisfaction. There was only a sense of depression, and the realization that nothing was as he'd envisioned it.

He was greeted by an ancient couple, the only servants left, and shown to the bedchamber that had belonged to his parents. There was nothing left to remind him of them in the room, only a vacancy that could never be filled.

His first action was to find his old room and the stock certificates he'd used to paper the walls of an alcove so long ago. They were in remarkably good condition, and enough were legible to give him a tidy income if he was frugal. Kincade's mouth twisted. Frugality had never been one of his character traits.

When he walked the dank corridors still draped with tattered, moth-eaten tapestries that depicted faded scenes of battle, he realized he'd held to a foolish dream. Despite his bitter resistance, he was a part of the land that he'd denied for so long. And yet—and yet he also knew that he could never be happy here, even with Dougal gone.

A faint smile curled his mouth. Dougal MacKay had crumbled like a slice of wet cake when the barrister had informed him of his nephew's inalienable rights to Glencairn, the few shabby clachans dotting the estates, and the stock Ewen MacKay had bought so long ago.

That stock, Kincade had learned almost immediately upon his arrival in Edinburgh, was valuable now. It had been bought by another firm, along with assets. The Donaldson Shipping Line had prospered and grown. To his surprise, he'd found himself a fairly wealthy man. To his greater surprise, he'd found that it didn't matter.

Glencairn was empty. He was empty. Even the vengeance he'd wanted had fallen flat. Somehow there was little satisfaction in watching his uncle break. It wasn't the grand dénouement he'd wanted, with Dougal being sent off to the gallows or dying at the point of his sword. Instead Dougal MacKay had been sent down from his high office in the kirk because of the scandal attending his confession, and when Kincade had declined to press charges for attempted murder that he had bloody little chance of proving, Dougal had disappeared. The unsatisfying conclusion had left him adrift and restless.

Kincade wandered the halls where he'd crept as a small boy, and knew he couldn't stay. Not here. Not ever.

"Hist, laddie," a voice said from the shadows of the corridor.

"Who is it?" he demanded sharply.

Ian MacDonald stepped into the light. "An old friend, lad."

"Ian. What are you doing here?"

"I wanted tae know if ye were happy wi' yer lot in life naow tha' Dougal MacKay ha' met justice face-tae-face."

Kincade's eyes narrowed. "I didn't know you were here. Who let you in?"

"Ha' ye no' seen the portcullis gate, lad? 'Tis but a poor excuse, and wouldna keep out a hound, much less a mon who ha' business here."

Kincade relaxed slightly. "You're right. The keep is in sad state, isn't it?"

"Verra sad. And wha' will ye be doing wi' it?"

"I don't know. Any suggestions?"

"None tha' ye canna come up wi' yerself, lad."

"Come have a drink with me," Kincade said abruptly. "If there's anything left in this pile of stones."

A low fire burned in the huge fireplace of one room, and Kincade found a bottle of scotch and poured two glasses. He gave one to Ian, then flung himself into a shabby chair near the hearth.

"Och," Ian murmured, tasting the scotch with a dreamy smile on his face, "I canna believe this. Here I am in Scotland wi' the Scotch mist outside and good scotch whisky inside. I thought tae niver ha' sich a moment ag'in."

"Did you? Can't say that I'm surprised. It gets bloody depressing when one thinks of all the sunshine in the world. I wonder that Scotland doesn't import some. It certainly has begun to make a tidy sum by importing other things."

Ian eyed him for a moment. "Ha' ye thought aboot going back for her, lad?"

"Back for who?" Kincade's narrowed stare should have warned MacDonald that he was treading on dangerous ground, but he seemed oblivious.

"Yer lass, o'course."

"I assume you mean Elizabeth Lee. No, I have not thought of going back for her."

It was a bald lie, and he saw from Ian's lifted brow that he knew it, too. Kincade swallowed an oath. Damn him for bringing her up when he'd finally managed to steer his thoughts away from her.

''Dinna think me a fool, lad. Ha' ye no' thought o' the lass more times than no'?''

Kincade turned his head to stare moodily into the fire. ''I have nothing to offer her that she doesn't already have. She doesn't need me.''

''Ye're a bloody fool if ye believe tha','' Ian said mildly, and Kincade flung him a savage glare. ''No' tha' ye ha' ever listened before, lad, but it would be tae yer best interest tae do so naow. Don't ignore wha' is in front o' ye.''

''I don't know what you're talking about.''

''Love. 'For love is of sae mickle might, tha' it all paines makis light.' 'Tis a quote from an epic by Barbour aboot the Bruce. And a more fitting quote I canna think wa'd fit ye.''

''A noble sentiment, to be sure, but hardly fitting.''

''Isn't it? Think, lad. Wha' d'ye want from life?''

''Bloody hell. How should I know? I thought I wanted this at one time.'' He waved a hand to indicate the keep. ''Now I find that what I wanted never existed.''

''Och, lad, ye're wrong. It does exist. Ye just canna see it until ye look in the right place.''

Kincade stared at him. He was right. He'd known that, somewhere in the recesses of his mind, but it had taken more courage than he had to acknowledge it. To want something he wasn't sure of was risky—did he dare commit himself to Elizabeth Lee without knowing if she'd have him? What if she said no? What if she didn't?

''Christ,'' he said tonelessly. ''It's too big a risk.''

Chapter
25

KINCADE SWORE softly as he stepped from the flatboat to the muddy shore. Muck clung to his highly polished boots.

"Aren't there any decent docks in this part of the world?" he muttered withtout expecting a reply. The boatman looked up at him and grinned.

"Downriver a bit. If you weren't in such a hurry, I'd have let you off at Natchez proper."

"Much obliged for that belated information."

The riverman laughed and stuck his pole into the muddy riverbank. He pushed back out into the brown, swirling waters. Kincade glanced downriver, then started up the steep slope. A cluster of buildings clung to the side a half mile down, seeming to hang precariously where the river had washed away the banks. Fire-charred buildings and rubble dotted the street here and there. This was a seedy area, with rough-looking rivermen and other scruffy characters lounging about. A tinny tune and laughter drifted out the open door of a saloon. No doubt a card game was going on through that portal, for he could hear the rough conversation.

Kincade resisted temptation and headed up to the town. Natchez seemed to be a sleepy little burg on the edge of a great river, dozing in the early summer sun.

Quite a contrast to Virginia City, where he'd last seen

Elizabeth. This was a more gracious town, slow and unhurried with stately homes lining tree-shaded streets.

By the time he'd found Elizabeth's house, it had begun to rain, although the sun was still shining. Huge drops weighed down the heads of heavy blossoms in flower beds bordering the street and dripped from eaves and slick tree limbs. He pushed open the wrought-iron gate and walked up the path to the house, then paused.

A sudden fear shot through him that she wouldn't be at home. Or that she would. Everything he'd rehearsed on the long voyage over vanished. He stared blankly at the freshly painted green door flanked by leaded glass.

If the door hadn't opened, he might have left without knocking, but a small women with coffee-colored skin and a pleasant smile stood in the opening.

"May I help you, suh?"

"Is Miss Lee in?" His voice sounded like a croak to him, but apparently the maid didn't notice. She held the door wide.

"Who can I tell her is callin'?"

The maid's soft drawl reminded him of Elizabeth, and he stepped inside the house and wiped his feet on the mud mat at the woman's instructions.

"Kincade MacKay."

"Wait heah in the parlor, suh, and I'll see if she's receivin'."

Kincade waited, feeling foolish and resentful at the same time. What was he doing here? He should have written first. She might not want to see him at all. He couldn't blame her, after the way he'd left her behind in Virginia City, but dammit all, what was he supposed to do? He hadn't had a nickel more than the reward money he'd been given—and what a farce *that* was—and Dougal MacKay had still been running loose. Now he had some money, and Dougal was no longer a threat, and he was as terrified of her reaction as if it was the most important thing in the world.

Would she realize how important that was to him? How important *she* was to him?

Time passed, the ticking of the ornate clock on a pristine white mantel showing that twenty minutes had passed since the maid had gone to announce his arrival. He glanced at the door with rising irritation. The least she could do was send word for him to go away, not let him twiddle his thumbs in the parlor for so bloody long.

He started for the door, and it swung open. The brass handles snapped back abruptly, and Elizabeth swayed in the open doorway. Her eyes were huge, and a blue so deep he felt as if he could drown in them as she gazed at him. Her hair was tousled, blond strands hanging in her eyes as if she'd just awakened from a nap. A gown the same shade of blue as her eyes was wrinkled, and the yellow sash was untied and hanging from her slender waist.

"Angel?" he murmured, frowning a bit at the unfocused glance she gave him. "Did I wake you?"

Her mouth curved into a trembling smile, and he saw her lower lip quiver slightly. She held out one hand in a gracious gesture, but he noticed it was off center, as if he was standing two feet to her left instead of directly in front of her.

"What . . . a . . . surprise," she said. He reached for her hand, but she turned back toward the parlor doors and shut them, then leaned there for a moment. His frown deepened.

"Are you well, angel?" He stepped toward her, but she evaded him by moving behind a horsehair sofa covered in a bright yellow fabric.

"Quite . . . *hic* . . . well, thank you," she said firmly. "What brings . . . you here?"

"You."

The one blunt reply seemed to startle her. Her eyes widened, and her mouth formed an *O*. "M-me?"

"Why else would I be in Natchez, Mississippi? It

certainly isn't because of the nightlife, though I did notice some promising entertainment down under the hill.''

"You would." Her mouth curved into a sarcastic smile. "S-so. You haven't changed at all, have ya?''

There was something distinctly odd here. Her eyes were as blue and beautiful as ever, but had a shiny—no, glassy—look to them. A fever, perhaps? Not that he'd doubt it. From what he'd noted of the insects here, they were large enough to transmit any kind of disease.

Then he stepped close and recognized the problem. His brows lifted.

"No, I can't say that I've changed," he said shortly, "but you certainly have."

"I should think so. It's not every woman who allows herself to be jilted by the same man more than once or twice." She hiccuped, and drew herself up into an indignant knot.

"This has nothing to do with that, though I admit you may have cause." He reached out and snared her arm before she could evade him, holding tight to her wrist as she tried to wriggle away. "You've been drinking, you little pest!''

"Drinking! I most certainly h-have not!" She tried to jerk away again, but he held her fast as he moved around the end of the sofa.

The odor of spirits was strong, and his nose wrinkled. "Liar. You're foxed to the gills. Inebriated. *Drunk,* my sweet.''

"D-don't try and d-distract me," she sputtered. "I have a right to be m-mad at you."

"That goes without saying. But what have you been drinking, my adorable little lush?''

"I've *not* been drinking. I do have m-medicine that my physician gave me to take upon occasion, but—''

"Ah. Medication. More than likely it should come in a brown bottle with the word *rum* written on it. Come here. No, don't be foolish. You can't get away from me, so there's no point in resistance. Sit down.''

He pushed her to the sofa and gazed down at her. Her expression was a mix between anger and confusion, and he fought a smile.

"Silly angel—what are you medicating, may I ask?"

She shot him a defiant glare. "N-none of your business."

"No doubt. Humor me."

"Go away."

"Not until you answer my questions and we sober you up a bit."

"I'm not—"

"I know. You're not drunk. You just have all the symptoms of a roaring good case of rum fever. Now sit still while I fetch your maid. What's her name?"

"Pansy," she muttered sullenly.

Kincade had Pansy brew some strong coffee, though he personally doubted it was that efficacious in curing the effects of too much alcohol.

"In my experience," he said as he applied a cool, wet cloth to Elizabeth's flushed face, "what one has after supplying coffee to an inebriated person is a wide-awake drunk. However, it may help you regain some control of your more useful skills. Such as walking."

"Devil," she mumbled through the wet cloth.

He lowered it and examined her face. Her eyes were a bit clearer, though still bloodshot. Her color was good, and her mouth—ah, he'd never been able to resist that mouth, even when it was saying vile things to him.

Without pausing to think about it, he leaned forward and kissed her gently. He felt her immediate response and heard the quick intake of her breath.

"God, angel," he drew back to say, "I've missed you."

"Yes, I noticed how quickly you found me."

"Angel—I came as quickly as I could. I never said I wasn't a fool—"

"Good thing."

"—but when I came to my senses, I came back for you."

"Is that supposed to make me feel better?"

Kincade sat back and looked down at his hands, then up at her lovely, angry face. "I want to marry you, angel."

She said nothing, just stared at him so long he had the heart-stopping thought that he'd waited too long to ask.

"So?" she finally said. "What do you want from me?"

"Well, I had hoped for a more enthusiastic response."

Her hand came up in a fist and caught him under his jaw, sending him tumbling back off the sofa. He sprawled on the floor for a moment, too startled to move. Elizabeth bent forward.

"Is that enthusiastic enough?"

Rubbing his jaw with one hand, he muttered, "Quite." He sat up, staring at her warily. She stared back at him, hot lights dancing in her blue eyes. He couldn't help a grin, then he laughed aloud. That seemed to startle her.

"You're mad," she said irritably. "Utterly mad."

He got to his feet and shifted his jaw from left to right. "Very possibly. But I intend to marry you."

"After all this time? Why now? Did you change your mind about using my money?" She shoved at a strand of hair in her eyes. "Did you stop to think that maybe I've changed my mind by now?"

"That's all I've thought about since the bloody ship left the white cliffs of Dover behind," Kincade said truthfully. He knelt at her feet, feeling as if his entire life was in her hands. "Angel, I love you. I want to spend the rest of my life with you. If you say no, nothing else will matter."

"And if I say yes? Have you stopped to consider that I may want more than you can give?"

"More times than I can count. All I can do is give you my heart and soul. It's all that I can truly call mine, and I wouldn't give you anything less."

She looked at him uncertainly, and he saw the way her lower lip quivered slightly as her eyes filled with tears. It tore at his heart, and he closed his eyes. He needed the welcoming shadows to ease his pain. What was there about this woman that left him defenseless and empty when she wasn't with him?

"You're my life," he said into the darkness, not realizing he'd spoken aloud until he heard her faint, incoherent murmur.

When he felt her mouth graze over his, he opened his eyes and saw her draw back. "And you're my life, Kincade MacKay. I love you. I'll stay with you forever, however you may want me."

His arms came around her, and he crushed her to him. "I love you, angel. Yesterday. Today. Tomorrow. For all eternity. You're all I want, all I need."

She smiled through her tears. "I may hold you to that rash promise, you know."

"I hope so. God, I hope so."

Epilogue

Florida Keys—1880

A HAMMOCK swung lazily back and forth between two sturdy palm trees. Ropes creaked a protest at each movement, and the surf pounded in the background.

Kincade shifted slightly, and curled his arm more tightly around Elizabeth. "Comfortable?"

His breath was warm against her ear, making her smile lazily. "Um-hmm. As long as you don't bounce around too much."

"You're getting lazy, sweet Liz."

"And you're getting bold." Her eyes opened, and she lifted a brow. "Must I remind you that you are to now call me Mayor Liz?"

Kincade muttered an oath under his breath. "No, you don't have to remind me. I think I can bloody well recall my moment of insanity well enough."

A smile curved her mouth, and she shifted so that she was turned into him. Draping one leg across his body, she traced an imaginary path from his bare stomach up to his chin with a fingertip.

"You should probably rethink your penchant for brandy. Apparently, it banishes your resistance more than you were aware."

"It must, for me to agree to allow a woman to be mayor of our little island paradise here."

"And have I been a bad mayor?"

"No, lass, you haven't." Kincade's mouth twisted into a faintly mocking smile. "Not that we have more than a dozen citizens on Eden, however."

"But there will be more. Once Annie informs more women about our island and how they are allowed to vote and even be a part of the government here—"

"Until the state of Florida steps in, anyway."

Elizabeth frowned at his reminder. "Eden isn't a part of Florida. Not yet, anyway. The people who have bought land from you now live in the Territory of Eden. And with all the people who have expressed interest in buying land from you to build houses down here—"

"I hear the jingle of their money already," Kincade said with a satisfied smile. "But enough of that. How are you feeling?"

"Very fat." She pushed away from him and sat up, putting out a hand to steady the swaying hammock. "If our child does not arrive soon, I'm afraid I'll burst."

"He'll be here soon enough, lass."

"*He?*"

"Or she." Kincade grinned. "It hardly matters which to me, so long as you are happy. And the midwife knows what she's doing."

"Oh, do you mean Tabitha? Somehow, I have a feeling she will be an excellent midwife. Though she does have a strange habit of going off for a time. I wonder where she goes? It's not as if there are that many places here on Eden to hide, yet she stays gone for days at a time."

"A sabbatical, she calls it. Something about concerts, though where the deuce she finds music here is beyond me. Perhaps she takes the boat to the mainland."

He laced his fingers through Elizabeth's and pulled her to him gently. Her hair hung in a bright, shining mass over one shoulder, gleaming in the sunlight. Kincade's heart contracted, and he wondered how he'd ever lived so long without Elizabeth. She was everything to him, everything he'd never dreamed he'd have. For a time, it had seemed as if he'd never find that elusive dream, but he had. And it was all wrapped up in this one complicated woman.

Sighing contentedly, Elizabeth snuggled closer. "I love you, Kincade MacKay," she said softly, and he heard himself whisper back, "I love you, too, Elizabeth. God help me."

"I think He already did."

Kincade thought about that a moment. Then he nodded. "Yes, I suppose heaven did take a bit of interest in me at last. I hope they don't regret it."

"Oh, somehow I don't think so." She turned and tilted her face up for his kiss. "I think heaven must be very proud of you now."